Jean Rikhoff's **BUTTES LANDING** . . . .

"It deserves a million readers . . . A splendid piece of work with strength in all the fictional essentials, character, action, and setting, to a degree most unusual today. It is a novel deeply rooted in this native earth . . . this is what made the America we over-30's remember and cherish."

—Hal Borland
author of **When the Legends Die**

"There is much wisdom in this book. It deserves many readers."

—**St. Louis Dispatch**

"The affinity with land and forest is translated by Miss Rikhoff into a lyrical continuity of sensuous experience. **BUTTES LANDING** is a rewarding destination."

—**The New York Times Book Review**

"A solid story, roughhewn out of a time and place which left no margin for those of physical or moral irresolution, commemorative in spirit and forward-going in interest."

—**Kirkus Reviews**

BUTTES LANDING

Jean Rikhoff

A FAWCETT CREST BOOK

Fawcett Publications, Inc., Greenwich, Conn.

BUTTES LANDING

THIS BOOK CONTAINS THE COMPLETE TEXT OF THE ORIGINAL HARDCOVER EDITION.

A Fawcett Crest Book reprinted by arrangement with The Dial Press.

Alternate Selection of the Book-of-the-Month-Club, August 1973

Printed in the United States of America
February 1974

To my daughter's "uncle,"
my son's godfather,
and to my own good friend, RICHARD TIERNAN,
this book is affectionately dedicated.

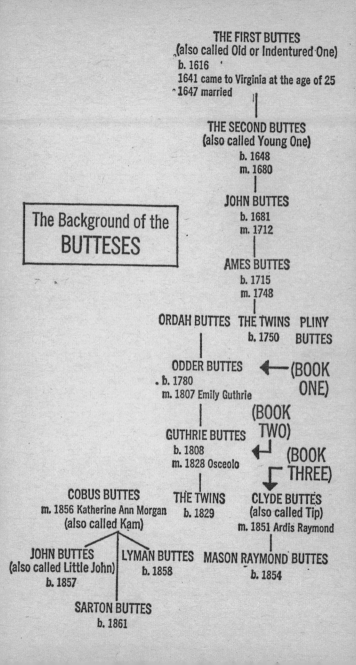

THE FIRST BUTTES
(also called Old or Indentured One)
b. 1616
1641 came to Virginia at the age of 25
1647 married

THE SECOND BUTTES
(also called Young One)
b. 1648
m. 1680

JOHN BUTTES
b. 1681
m. 1712

AMES BUTTES
b. 1715
m. 1748

The Background of the
BUTTESES

ORDAH BUTTES   **THE TWINS   PLINY**
b. 1750   **BUTTES**

ODDER BUTTES ← (BOOK
b. 1780   ONE)
m. 1807 Emily Guthrie

(BOOK
TWO)
GUTHRIE BUTTES ←
b. 1808   (BOOK
m. 1828 Osceolo   THREE)

COBUS BUTTES   **THE TWINS   CLYDE BUTTES**
m. 1856 Katherine Ann Morgan   b. 1829   (also called Tip)
(also called Kam)   m. 1851 Ardis Raymond

JOHN BUTTES   **LYMAN BUTTES**   **MASON RAYMOND BUTTES**
(also called Little John)   b. 1858
b. 1857   b. 1854

SARTON BUTTES
b. 1861

BUTTES LANDING

A Note on the Background Material
of this book

The research in this book was sometimes bewilderingly complex and often exceedingly difficult; without the help of all the members of the Crandall Library in Glen Falls, I should have put in hours and hours, days and days, in laborious looking. I should also like to take this chance to say that I am exceedingly glad to have had the aid of Marcia Smith of the Adirondack Museum Library of Blue Mountain Lake and to suggest to any reader in that area not to miss the opportunity of spending an instructive day at this unique museum.

Further thanks for help with horsemanship are due to Ann Powers and Dorothy Appling, to members of the Cambridge Saddle Club, to Charlotte Bohne and the George Warren Wood family, and of course to that gifted trainer of horses, Jim Crandall of Granville, and naturally to Harold Worthington for all his help.

I can never, of course, adequately express my gratitude to Helen Taylor for all the time and help, as well as the encouragement, she gave in the initial preparation of this manuscript.

I should also like to single out the help of Colonel Hans Handler of the Spanish Riding School in Vienna and Colonel Hans Mueller of California for allowing me to participate in the Dressage Institute course at Saratoga Springs during the summer of 1967.

Part of the makings of this book came out of the wisdom about country life of my neighbors all up and down this valley. The valley itself is a part of the novel, as are, I suppose, the confidence and love of the land the people of the Hebron Valley feel.

West Hebron, New York
October, 1971

PART ONE

Odder's Book

This is the book of the generations of Adam. In the day that God created man, in the likeness of God made He him; male and female created He them; and blessed them, and called their name Adam, in the day when they were created.

GENESIS: 5:1

I

In the beginning, when he came East over the mountains, Odder Buttes never thought of a lake. What he had in mind, coming over the Appalachians, was not water at all but mountains, a mountain farm, away from everyone, something so large that he could feel surrounded by the safety of space. What little money he had wouldn't buy much good land. Leastwise what others called good. But mountain land, land that was full of forest and scrub and rock, that was steep and hard for a man to go up and down, let alone take out trees, clear and plant, try to keep from going back to brush, that should come cheap. Nobody wanted woodland, nobody but Odder Buttes.

Valley people shunned the mountains because it was easier to till flat fields and because they believed that pine woods made for "weak soil." A man needed hard wood for "strong soil." Odder considered this a lot of nonsense; soil was soil. A man might wear it out, but trees couldn't, leaves didn't. People who liked mountains were one breed; people who liked valleys another.

A man learned to make divisions all his life—earth, air; fire, water; love, hate; endless divisions that made up the oneness of being—why shouldn't he just as naturally make that kind of distinction between men?—those who fled, and those who fought; those who had, and those that didn't; those who looked up into the unknown and those who squatted in the safe, flat places.

Odder wouldn't have wanted valley land if it had been given to him. He had been wandering over flat country for years now—horse hand, hired hand, teamster, cradler, flailer, hogger, rope winder, joiner, foot peddler, even dowser, though he had never really had the gift for finding water; still he'd given it a try. Give anything a try once—there was another dimension you could make: those who needed new scenes and experiences same as they needed water and sleep and those that were afraid of the unexpected as if it was some kind of trap made to catch the unwary. A man who went soft and safe wasn't likely to expand himself, but he wasn't likely to have got in all the trouble Odder'd made for himself neither.

Something off balance in him maybe. Any time something came easy, he got suspicious. He had learned to distrust just about everything you could think of—women of course, most men, naturally the suspicious world around him, even himself.

Out where he'd been—Indiana, Ohio, Illinois, a part of Kentucky—the seasons came at you all in a rush, ended too abruptly, or hardly came and went at all in some places, there was just a monotonous regularity, a kind of permanent wavering climate that got on your nerves, told you, don't trust 'em. You put your corn in afore the first of May, you're gonna live to regret the day. Warm as August in April, cold as Kansas in August. What he had in mind was the kind of place where the seasons were pretty well portioned out, say about three months apiece, just enough time for a man to anticipate, appreciate, and then grow tired, start looking forward to a change; and the change would come. I'm goin' upstate New York, he had thought.

It was a decision that made no sense at all. He didn't know New York. He'd been born in New Jersey and lived there the first eight years of his life. He had impressions—vivid ones—of the old farm, but he didn't know the country farther north. His father had uprooted them all from New Jersey and moved them to Ohio a year after the Ordinance of 1787 opened the frontier and settlers streamed by flatboat, barge, or overland wagon, even on foot, toward the fabled fertile lands.

New Jersey had been flat, Ohio flatter. When he got older and moved on to Indiana, he began to believe, like the people of old, the whole world was flat. You keep walking, you just drop off the end. Men tried to tell him about mountains and he listened, but it was hard to believe what you hadn't seen, didn't know first-hand. But you made pictures. He had lots of pictures up there, in his mind. Bad business, them mountains, men said, you don't want to mess around with mountains, 'less you're with a man knows his way around. You don't monkey with places like that, they said, unless you don't mind meetin' your Maker. *Bad* business, and what kind of life you goin' to have in a place like that? they would ask. No women 'less you count squaws, the men all cutthroatin' thieves, nuthin' but trouble and tribulations, more than one good man went into those woods and never come out, experienced men, too. Man, they said to one another, I'm never goin' back there no more. But as they said that, a kind of fire was kindled in their eyes, they seemed for a moment to *be* back and they were glad, it was a place they had never forgotten because there was *something* there.

What Odder wanted to find out was what that *something* was.

A man maybe could farm there? he would ask. You could maybe clear some of that land and—

Farm there? That's *woods*. People don't farm there. Even the Indians don't do more than pass through. That ain't settlin' land. It's only meant to be moved over. Hunt and fish some, all right. But farm? It's for the bear and rattlers.

But if you cleared out the trees, Odder persisted, you could farm then, couldn't you?

You clear out the trees, they'd just bolt back. That kind of place don't stay cleared. You gotta see that country to know what you're talking about.

But long years on the move had given Odder confidence. He thought he knew the worst there was to know about what could happen to a man. A lot of that knowledge came from personal experience, but he had survived, he was older and tougher, he didn't reckon there was much that could surprise him any more, or wreck him. Such things had come earlier and were over. He considered himself a man in balance now; he thought he understood the world and knew what it could do, and he figured he was big enough to whip some woods.

So he decided to go take a look for himself. It was March, springish; for Illinois and Indiana farmers the real beginning of the year, time for plowing up and getting ready for planting. He set out with enough money in his pocket to keep him going for quite a spell. When that ran out he'd find work, he always did. He had been wild in his way, yes, but he wasn't wasted; he'd saved some money, a pretty good packet of it, and that had been put away with the bankers to keep safe. He wouldn't touch that. The bank money was going to buy his land, to get him a place of his own no one could ever take away from him, some place he could say was *his* and no one else's; a man needed yardage to make himself feel needed. Odder set a lot of store on being necessary. He got nervous when he could lay up and it made no difference, always tried to keep himself in situations where he had certain obligations every open hour of the day, he was *necessary.*

But there was a difference between doing duties other people put on you and erecting obligations of your own. He hadn't found other people that accommodating to his notions, his hankerings; he was always running up against someone who was trying to make him do something he didn't want and finding he had to do it to hold onto a job or get a woman or keep a situation soft and easy to live with. He wanted some say about himself, was sick and tired of other people holding power over him.

The way he began to figure, a man had to have a plan. A man without a plan just went hither and yon; nothing kept him in pitch. He wore himself out in fretting and frittering. But a man with a plan, he had a direction he was going and it gave his life form.

He had watched most of the men he knew marry and settle into thieving work that robbed them of their vitality and gave back little 'cept debts, a parcel of children and a wife who tied more ropes around them. To Odder that wasn't a life at all, it was some kind of bondage, the kind he'd thought was over and done with when the days of indenture were finished; but there were other kinds of debts and prisons men fell into and you had to watch all the time one of them didn't reach out and nab you.

What he wanted was something just his own. A piece of earth just for him to stand on. His sky. His place. But not flat. He had been a long time figuring out everything—how much money he'd need, how he'd hike back East—a horse was too costly and most likely would be no good at all in the kind of country he had to cross—and then when he'd found what he wanted and got a deed for the place, he'd need a stake—flour and salt, seeds, a cow maybe, a man could get along on next to nothing if there was a reason for it and he knew the effort was going toward something. Being poor didn't matter so long as you knew it wasn't permanent or without cause. He was a Jefferson man in that. Every man had a right to his chance, regardless; he held with Jefferson that the country was based on the small farmer and the small farmer wanted as little of government messing around him as he could get.

A country was lucky, any time, to get men like Jefferson. Some people might make fun of Jefferson's ways and be scandalized by his clothes, but those were the people who had voted for Adams in 1800 and didn't matter anyway. Jefferson knew what he was doing all right. Take the Louisiana Purchase: whoever controlled the Mississippi controlled the country. He had been West in his wanderings and he *knew*. Jefferson had just been smart enough to guess.

It took Odder some time to get back East. Whenever he got tired of traveling, he would stop and work awhile and make a little money; then he would pick up and take off again. He met a woman on the way that took up more time than he liked, but while he was forgetting with the flesh, the mountains hadn't seemed so important, another thing was on his mind; then that other thing began to lose its interest and the vision of the mountains came back and at last the mountains were all that mattered, he was on the move again. He had been traveling over easy country, the interior plains, back through Ohio, and he didn't detour any out of his way to go back to the family farm, he just kept going East. There wasn't anyone there he really wanted to see and going home would have only meant counting up the dead, reckoning at last with what had happened since he'd left. The way he figured, he didn't have any family any more; he hadn't since the day he walked off the place.

He crossed the Alleghenies and went up through the Finger Lakes and into the Mohawk Valley. That valley made a sick emptiness inside as he looked at the neat farms, thinking back to all the skirmishes and scalpings, the endless raids that had destroyed place after place, the people stubbornly hanging on, even though all they could do was watch helplessly from the forts as their houses and barns were burned, their livestock butchered, their crops put to the torch. A lot of those early settlers had been caught and tomahawked before the fort gun boomed the alarm that Indians were on the warpath again, and they had been cut down wherever they were—out haying, berrying, just walking up a road to their homes. He went quickly across the Mohawk Valley; it had been bought with blood and the stain, the smell, were still there for him, a place of bitterness for all its lush greenness, the fertility of those fields that had been bought in lives— in butchery. Land was maybe the final thing a man would lay down his life for, Odder thought, more even than his religion or his family—because, Odder supposed, it endured.

Then he hit the mountains, the real mountains. The first day wasn't bad, not too much snow. At the beginning, going in, he was contemptuous, remembering all the stories he'd heard about how wild the country was. Hell, he'd been through a lot worse in the West. Then he got in, really in, and his sense of superiority disappeared. He knew what all of them had been trying to tell him: this was the kind of wilderness that set itself against a man, a vast, dark world where the trees shut out the sun and the lakes lay like great smooth sucked stones, and the snow was five feet deep in places even though it was the end of May.

The forest was a wall of trees, most of them over a hundred and fifty feet high, with huge trunks ten, twelve, fifteen feet around, so high that Odder, looking up, could not see their tops. The sun was shut from sight. He went mile after mile dwarfed by those monolithic trunks, making his way over thick fallen hemlock and pine, fighting for a path through thickets that choked back any other growth save the massive forest of trees, the whole earth twisted with vines intertangled like writhing snakes, a wild dark place of roots and the rubbish of trees. Evil.

He got lost he didn't know how many times, and he was winded all the time, big and strong and tough as he was. It took courage just to keep going—hacking away, inch by inch through creepers, vines, shrubs, bush, bracken, thick spongy cushions of moss, swamps stinking of fetid water and rotting leaves with broken, black tree stumps sticking up in the air.

He felt the enmity all around him. Up and down, hacking his way bit by bit: he never seemed to get anywhere and yet he kept going. Sooner or later, he kept telling himself, he was bound to come out somewhere where there were people.

Nights he would stop and sink down in a stupor, hunch in, every muscle stiffening, his body a senseless quiver of aches, his head dizzy with the day he had put in and the dark night closing around him with its furry night sounds and its feeling that the trees had eyes to look down and laugh at him.

After a time he would rouse himself to take out the flint and start a fire; sometimes he just rolled himself in his blanket and slept, not even bothering to chew on anything before he fell into an exhausted sleep, lying under those almighty menacing pines, sunk in an unconsciousness through which, in flashes, the pain of his body nudged him and he rolled over with a groan and felt the whole dead weight of the forest and his fatigue bearing down on him.

Dawn in these woods didn't come the way it did anywhere else. In open land light came with a jolt and a stab; in forests, most forests, it dripped in slowly, probing at the undercover

19

world uncertainly; here the darkness grew gray, but there was never really light. Some places Odder doubted had *ever* been touched by the sun in so long that it no longer mattered. The woods crowded together to keep out light, moved its branches this way and that to prevent the sun from getting through. But at least with dawn the sense of foreboding lifted a little, not much; enough, however, to shift shadows, the great bulk of the woods rousing themselves to press up to what they needed for still more growth, the unseen sun.

Odder would shift and press his eyes closed, trying to shut out the knowledge that it was time to get up, eat (if he could get his stomach to accept something), press on. He lay cold, aching, unable to make his will work, until a massive assault of pain made it easier to shift and rise than lie still. He stood, blinking, under the great trees, hating.

He had forgotten how strong an emotion hate was, hadn't really felt this intensely about anything since the year he'd left home. Love he knew, a little, leastwise, he told himself. But hate was something strong and sure, something he didn't mistake. It could keep a man going day after day, he was learning, without any hope at all (hope was what love was, wasn't it, leastwise the way he understood it). Maybe there was an element of hope in hate, too, because a man knew he was going to get his own back on the thing that was eating away at him. Like these woods. Because there was one growing certainty in Odder and it was this: he wasn't going to go through an ordeal like this without paying something back, and if the woods put him through it, then it was the woods he would pay back.

A man with an axe could see to that.

He had been moving five, maybe six miles a day (time had become a strange insubstance under these trees, a dream he could only partially keep track of) when he came out on top of one of the endless mountains he had been moving up, down, up, down, up again, and there was the lake below him—long and slender and silver, like a great fish that dipped and disappeared into the tangle of trees, the darkness of ridges beyond.

The sight took his breath away. He didn't know what to do with beauty—he never had—it always made him feel a little ashamed, as if he had been given something he didn't deserve. He stood staring, looking at the great slash of silver in front of him, not even thinking, just looking, unable even to compose a phrase about it in his mind, just standing there breathless and moved. Then after a time he started down, thinking, There's where I'll have my place, not this side, *people* on this side, but over there, on the other side, where there's nothing, just this silver water and those brown mountains. The house'll be on the water and the farm in back cut right out of that mountain, take down those trees and make me my farm there, looking right out on the water. There won't be any place you plow you won't be able to look out and see that silver water.

Odder went into the little cluster of loggers' and trappers' shacks, a place they called Algonquintown, though strictly speaking it was in old Iroquois territory. Some trapper from up north, not knowing or caring the difference in Indians, had named it. It wasn't much to dispute over anyway, just a clearing in the wilderness where men who scraped a living from the elements hung together. It didn't stay Algonquintown long anyway. After Odder started coming across the lake for supplies, the trappers, hunters, and halfbreeds stopped calling it Algonquintown and started referring to it as Odder's Landing. First it was Odder's Landing, then Odder Buttes's, then at last, permanently, Buttes Landing. Which was right: Odder was the only one in the area who took root; the rest were just sort of passing through.

He spent two weeks walking the east side of the lake, figuring out just where he wanted his farm. When he had the markers clear in his mind—Indian River, past the big rocks and the slide on one side and the long natural boundary of shale on the other—he figured he'd given himself more than enough to keep him busy a lifetime.

He saw just the spot for his house, at the end of a cove, a natural little inlet where he'd be protected from the open lake but where he had the great expanse of water in front of him. A man looking out on that, he figured, would be all right.

Having worked it out in his mind, he set about getting it put down on paper, where it would all be legal. It took him two days to walk back to Burroughs' general store. The land was for sale all right, Burroughs said, spitting, if anyone was fool enough to want it. It's no more than rock and scrub, what you seen for yourself from the look of you, and then big unbudgeable trees. You figurin' on buyin' *that?*

Burroughs was a spiderlike rusty-looking man with red hair and close-set eyes; now in those squinting eyes there was a thin red little speculative flame.

I'm figurin' on buyin' if it's the right price, Odder said. He waited a moment before he set himself up as a real fool. To farm, he said, setting the words between his teeth.

That ain't plantin' land.

I'm aimin' to farm.

Go down valley—

You know who owns that land or not?

I own it, Burroughs said, I'm the land agent man here leastwise.

You got the papers?

I got the papers.

Then how come you're runnin' down your own land?

Burroughs laughed. Now if a man's got money—

I got money.

He shrugged. A speculator, heh? he said.

No, I told you, I'm fixin' to farm.

Burroughs shrugged again. It's beyond me, he said.

I 'spect so, Odder said. You want to talk price or not. Talk never hurt no one.

You spent too long in the woods if you believe that, Odder said, and they went in to look at the township charts.

People came from miles around to see what the damned fool was up to, even though the trip back and forth took, by boat, the better part of a day. Burroughs came with a jug, told him (again) he was crazy, he didn't know winters up here, he didn't know the lake. Move back, he said when he saw the patch at the end of Blue Cove that Odder was clearing, that's no place to put a house. The lake'll git it.

The valley farmers came, shook their heads. You don't know nuthin' 'bout this lake or this land. You can't put your house there. You put your house there, the lake'll get it. Go back down to the valley, they said, that's where you farm. This here is woods land—

Odder worked on, clearing the patch where he would put his house, worked harder now, angered, the heavy heat all about him, the lake perspiring, midges and mosquitoes graying the air. July came upon him unexpected; with all the traveling, he had lost track of time. It seemed to him he ought to be rounding into June and here it was midsummer. He had a lot of work to do before winter; he began to get up earlier and earlier, push himself harder and harder. He wanted his site cleared by mid-autumn, stumps and all (he had decided not to waste time waiting for a winter to rot them out), and that was going to take some doing.

He pushed himself, eating in snatches, never stopping for

a proper meal, finding that eating oftener in smaller amounts gave him more energy. In the morning and at night he set a small fire and boiled up tea. He had no sorghum or hard maple sugar to break off, which would have given him the pleasure of something sweet, but he drank the boiled tea as hot as his mouth could stand it and it kept him going knowing that there was the fire and the hot tea waiting for him twice a day, something of civilization and the outside world, a little symbol of the things other people took for granted. He found the hotter it was the more he appreciated it.

During the day he wrestled with trees—axing, sawing, dragging, piling, pulling. An ox or a horse was going to be essential when he got to the work up in the big woods but here, near shore, a man could clear by himself. The onlookers when they came were full of advice, but Odder soon found you couldn't count on them for much work.

What you want to come up here for, a hard place like this, on this side of the lake, away from everyone? they asked, looking up at the gaunt, grim mountains, the thick forest running down nearly to the water. You can't farm *this*, they said. How come you come up here?

All they had to do was look around, but what could *they* see, a parcel of damn valley-lovers? Flat land, soft land, he thought contemptuously, that's all they want. Let them have it. How could you explain anything at all about mountains to people who hunched down and were content to live in the midst of mud flats when they had hills all around them where they could climb up and look out?

The valley people were afraid of the lake. The bones of a lot of men lay at the bottom of that water—men who had fought grim brutal wars to determine who would hold this land, the French and Indians, the British, Ethan Allen's boys, Roger's Rangers.

The farmers were afraid of the dead; they were more afraid of the floods. They had been told that in some storms the lake would rise over its rim, creeping up until only the hills held it in. All nonsense of course, as any one of them could have verified during one of those storms just by climbing to the top of the hill to look. It was easier, safer, to stay in the valleys and live by valley-knowledge.

Where he came from, back in Ohio, though you could walk for miles, you'd feel nothing but the imprisonment of the place; it was sun and sky that fell in on you and held you down, pinned against that flat earth. Odder's father had had a fine big farm back there in Ohio, and Odder didn't care whether or not he ever saw his father or the farm again.

Years of wandering on the road, keeping close to himself, giving little, getting little, expecting nothing. Use people, yes, and let them use you a little when it suits you, when you get something out of it, but don't never give.

It was a philosophy that took him through barren, lonely times without scarring him. A man who is not willing to give much to life can't blame it if it withholds a good deal from him. A bargain, that's the way Odder thought, a bargain I make; not to want to feel much. I done my feelin' back there in Ohio with *him* (*him* for Odder always meant his father), now I'm finished with feeling. I just want to be left alone. Not get involved. You don't get involved, you don't extend yourself, you got nuthin' to fear, a philosophy that had worked out well, all things considered. And might have gone on interminably working out well except—

—Except he needed a horse to get the logs down off his hills. He had selected, after days of scouting the woods, the biggest best trees for logging off; he had logged the first of these himself up at the north part of the property after first clearing out a path down to the lake from the underbrush, the smaller growth and trees, the rocks and bad inclines, so that after his trees were cut he could get a driver in to bring them down. He figured on working as long as he had to, even into winter; he could put water on the path to make a smooth frozen slipway. He rose with the first light (often sleeping right out in the woods to save time) and methodically worked his way through the road; then he began axing at the thick trunks of the trees he had selected, working hard, losing count of time, July swallowed up before he knew it, determined to get the north grove out before the really bad summer sweating days, the dog days, set in.

When he had felled all the trees he needed, he went out and contracted to have them slipped down; but when the logger came with his big oxen and began to take out the lumber, Odder was enraged at the haphazard way he worked, his slowness, the oxen's awkwardness and limitations. Finally he drove the man off. There was no other way to describe it; his face was red with rage, he was shaking his fist and shouting, trembling with fury—like my father, just like my father, he thought, shaken. It's in the blood.

I got to do something, he thought, I can't let something get through to me like this. It's because I'm pushing so hard, he thought. No one else will work that hard, and it makes me tighten up to see them takin' their time. I have to think of a way to get them logs out myself.

A good logging horse was hard to come by, but he would have to have a horse. He could see that.

Oxen were of course the common way to clear the land down in the valley. Those sluggish bovines were just the sort of animals people who lived in the hollowed-out parts of the earth would own. But oxen were useless on land such as his. He needed the intelligence and mobility of a horse. Absurd, everyone said. Burroughs over at the Landing of course thought he was crazier than ever. "Take a horse over there?" he asked, incredulous. Then, "Where you gonna git one?"

It was a good question. No one except the rich and an odd crank here and there had a horse, let alone a logging one. Horses cost a lot of money and they couldn't take the punishment oxen could; they injured themselves easily, needed more care than steers, were likely to die of unexpected ailments and leave a man in the lurch. But the very precariousness of having one was in some ways what appealed to Odder. He asked around and all he heard was that the mill man, Guy Guthrie, had a horse, but he wouldn't *never* let it out. Anyway, you don't want *that* horse, everyone said. There might be some down near to the Falls, it was finally conceded, so he went there.

He wanted an animal that had training, one he could depend on, one that would keep on the slipway, that was capable of maneuvering the bad places and of learning the route and following it, then forgetting that one and learning a new one. Logging horses had to be big and powerful, reliable and, above all, calm.

His was a fool's errand. He lost valuable time looking, and he fretted and raged around the countryside, stamping up and down the valley searching, aware that in his stubbornness and anger he was just like *him*, unable, even as he recognized the similarity and absurdity of his behavior, of changing it—maybe families were doomed to repeat generation after generation the badnesses in their blood because if you knew you were acting atrociously, why couldn't you stop? He knew all right, but he went right on ranting and raging. Like father, like son: the idea made him even madder.

Well, he didn't care. He *would* git himself a horse. But where? Where?

Those who had good horses of course didn't want to sell. He saw worn-out animals for sale, animals disabled by accidents whose owners still insisted they were sound; he saw horses with the heaves, blind in an eye or lame in a leg, horses whose smooth mouths showed their advanced ages, upper jaws protruding grotesquely, and yet their owners hopefully brought them out for barter, "they were jest a little gimpy or jest gettin' on a little or jest a little off their feed"; he saw animals mistreated to the point where they shied when a man came near and others that had so little discipline they reared and plunged when a man went to examine their teeth. He saw animals undernourished and overworked, ones with sway backs, splints, spavins, their wind given out, their forelegs gone or their spirits broken; he was taken to view animals whose owners advised him any child could ride them but whose nicknames in private must have been Killer or Outlaw; he came across one liar and swindler after another trying to masquerade as a kindly old horse trader, men who claimed they were only in the game because they couldn't stay away from a horse, but whose real larcenous hearts thrived on cheating, misrepresentation, deception, defrauding, plain old hoodwinking.

Yet he kept on. He did not let himself worry about how to pay for a horse once he found it. Nor did he let himself worry about how impractical a one-man operation would be, with no one to help. He would cut, load, go down and unload, and still save time. If you wanted something done, do it yourself; then it was done the way you wanted or if it wasn't, you had no one to blame but yourself.

So Odder Buttes plunged on from one farm to the next, doggedly determined to find a horse, resolutely setting aside the constant nagging notion he could no more do it all on his own than he could do anything worthwhile. Like having a son: which brought up the question of a wife. He would have to have a wife to have a son, and to have a wife he would have to have a house and to have a house he would have to have a horse . . . so in the end in order to have anything he wanted, he had to have a horse, and it just didn't stand to reason with the money he had he would get that horse. So. . . .

So he went to see Burroughs again. Burroughs did him the favor of keeping his satisfaction to himself and of assuming an interested, worried expression, as if he gave a damn whether or not Odder got his horse or his house. "Well," he said at last, "Guthrie won't sell no ways, but you might try borrowin'."

Odder shook his head.

"You got somethin' else to turn to?"

Odder shook his head again.

"Then what you got to lose? Guthrie's an odd one, he jest might. Mind the bull though. Don't go cuttin' across his place, you never know where that damn bull may be."

Guthrie ran a small mill and was thought odd. For one thing, he had "family," a daughter—his woman had died years before. But even one member of a family made it family; there were few men for hundreds of miles around who could claim that. The daughter had a reputation for being wild and Guthrie for running young men off before they even got near his filly. Emily, she was called, the redoubtable Emily.

There is always for every man a woman somewhere he hadn't counted on, one who will look him over (much as he would look over a horse) and size him up and set her sights on remaking him and that was as good as the end of him. A woman with an image inside her head was a powerful force to reckon against: she could outwit, outwait, and outflank any man who tried to harden his heart against her—that is, if she was halfway good looking, well enough built, and overwhelmingly single-minded. Also Emily Guthrie had one thing working for her most of the women Odder had known didn't. She knew more, it turned out, about what he was trying to do than he did. That was a hard thing for a man like Odder to hold out against. She would be a help—God preserve him, a help . . . and. And so . . .

The horse and the woman were both, he saw in an instant, prime stock, and by any conceivable stretch of the imagination he couldn't afford either. Anyway the moment he and Guthrie went out to see the horse, things got off to the wrong start. Guthrie certainly didn't want to sell the horse—he made that plain enough from the first—but he was so damned proud of his horse, he couldn't resist bragging about it, urging Odder to see it. Showing off, Odder thought disgustedly. These horse people are all alike, got no sense whatsoever. One man buys a blind horse and makes excuses for it, another rides around on a lame old nag and tries to say it's only a passing stiffness, and the next babbles on about his animal as if it were some kind of blamed miracle. To hell with him. He don't want to sell nor loan, that's his business.

Odder started down the road, the miller walking along bragging about what his horse could do, mares were sent from all around for servicing, wasn't a horse anywhere in the whole state could touch him. Odder stopped and said to him, "Maybe so, but kin he log?"

"Kin he log? Course he kin log. Ain't nuthin' any horse kin do, this horse can't do better."

The damned fool deserved to have his bluff called. "Kin he go on command, jest your talkin' to him?"

"Course he kin. Any halfway decent horse can do that."

Odder trotted alongside Guthrie, the pleasure of seeing this vainglorious son-of-a-bitch taken down a peg or two already filling him up. Jest like his Pa again, like to see men put down a peg or two. Ain't nuthin' his Pa liked more than see another man made a fool of, especially if that other man was his own son.

A heavy sun was hanging over the hills; not a breath of air was moving from field to field. Odder walked happily, chewing silently, remorselessly on the cud of Guthrie's coming comeuppance.

A man got what was comin' to him. Might have to wait a spell, but the wheel turned. Nothing had been said of the girl. At the last moment she just materialized. From where, Odder never knew. One minute she hadn't been there, just Guthrie and he walking under that merciless baking sun; the next she was standing by the barn, a tall scornful thing with thick black hair and big black knowing eyes. She had on men's clothes, rough men's clothes; they was hauled across her like they had shrunk on her, so tight you would have to cut them off, Odder figured, to get her out of them with the skin unscraped. Her thick black hair was tumbled up on her head and anchored there with a big bone pin. She had on gloves and she aimed, Odder saw, to his and Guthrie's surprise, to put the horse through its paces herself.

"I seen you come up the road," she said to Odder (which, to a more thinking man, would have been warning enough). "I knowed what you come about," she went on without waiting for a reply. "You're the man's been all over asking about horses." She said horses hor-says, as if he didn't know a damn thing about hor-says, and all up and down the county they had been laughing their fool heads off at his backassed ignorance. "There are hor-says and hor-says," Emily Guthrie said, hitching up her pants, "and I aim to show you what a real hor-se is like."

Then she was gone, vanished God knew where; in a moment she had materialized again in front of them, a big bay in back of her.

28

The stallion was enormous, seventeen hands at least—fourteen, fifteen hundred pounds—and had the look of the outlaw. How that girl had the nerve to turn her back on him was a question so frightening to contemplate, Odder immediately cast it out of his mind. If Guy Guthrie's girl wanted to let that creature kill her, it was up to her father to holler. Odder just wished he'd gone on his way and left the Guthries to kill themselves with their own conceit. It had suddenly come to him that that raw-boned stubbornness of theirs might end up crippling or killing him.

The bay was moving back and forth behind the girl, nervously shifting from one foot to the other, its wild eyes never still. When the stallion's flaming pupils weren't focused for a brief, feverish instant on one of them, they rolled back deliriously in a kind of spasm of power, as if the animal were anticipating the instant when he would rear and plunge forward on top of all of them.

Odder tensed, ready. He felt there would be a second of warning when those eyes finally stopped for the briefest instant and focused, just before the attack. Oblivious of Guthrie or the girl, his whole body concentrated on intercepting that warning. He did not think through what he would do. There was no need to: his body was already alerted, instinctively ready to direct action.

The girl was laughing. It took Odder a moment to realize that she was laughing at him. From the tone of the heavy, insulting sounds, he was sure her head was thrown back (he did not take his eyes off the horse); he felt a quiver go through him, a kind of reflex contempt of his own for his fear (but he still did not take his eyes off the horse).

Then she was touching him lightly on the arm.

There was no hope now and he knew it. He had to look at her. He couldn't call himself anything but *coward* if he didn't match her disdain of danger. In that instant he gave up —at the time he thought he was simply relinquishing any control he might have over the horse, but later he saw he had given up something he could never get back, the sense of being able to survive solitary, the pride of being sufficient unto himself.

When she touched him on the hand and he felt he had to look at her, she had won the game right there from the start; but at that moment it was impossible to draw any such rational conclusion, to see any long-term implications, he was acting solely on the message of the moment. It was a long,

long time before he began to understand and when he did, he was already glad of the changes she had made, he thought himself a better man for them, so that he rejoiced in that mastery and said to himself, When she touched me on the hand . . . meaning many things, not the least of which was, That was the beginning . . . and then—

He looked at her. Her hair had partially blown free; there were black wings in the wind at either side of her head. Her white teeth were large and glittering in laughter, her eyes big and bright—but she was laughing real laughter; it amazed him to find she was not laughing at him, but simply and naturally, *happily*, aglow with her pleasure in the moment. She was not making fun of him. There was a joke, yes, but it was not necessarily turned against him, but against all of them, all men.

"Watch," Guy Guthrie said with a chuckle, proud of his daughter for having played an old trick on a new man. (Later Odder learned how many other men in that valley at one time or another had been the victims of the Guthries' perverted sense of humor, heard with some kind of curious pride that he had stood his ground when most of them had turned tail and run.)

The girl stopped laughing. She was watching Odder calmly, scrutinizing him with clear eyes of appraisal, and he looked back at her with the same quick sense of knowledge. It was as if they were saying with their eyes something their tongues would never be able to put into words. A strong, beautiful, frightening girl. And that laugh, *that laugh*—when you held her in your arms, he was sure, she would give that same sure laugh just before you put your mouth down on hers and stopped it—for a time. But you would never stop it forever.

Then he was ashamed. Guthrie was standing beside him and must have recognized what was in his eyes. When a man got that look on his face, other men usually understood. He turned for an instant to face out Guthrie and was caught instead by the quiet gentle stand of the horse. The big stallion was standing quiescently, enormous, but tranquil, a big, gentle obedient beast that was amiable to any command.

There were all three silent, noting the change, a thing to be marveled at. Emily went up and put her hand to the horse's head, gently running her fingers over the muzzle; the stallion did not move. Its great strong legs seemed set in the earth, its eyes were still now but filled with what seemed to Odder a certain sadness.

30

Guthrie was speaking. ". . . always had a way with animals. Once there was this bull, out in that pasture there," Guthrie gave a vague, indicative nod of his head toward a small cleared sun-blistered field. "No man could come near him. You could take and tie him down so you'd swear he'd never get away and some man would go in that field and start walking toward him and that critter would catch sight of the man and commence rearing and rearing and pulling and throwing his head around and pretty soon he'd pull free, tear big chains right outen a log and scramble away, pulling the chain right after him, and he'd head straight for that man and never stop, no matter what he was pulling or dragging, just keep his eye on that man and keep coming and if that man didn't have the sense to turn tail and *run,* he was a goner.

"Nuthin' stopped him, nuthin', he'd keep on a man once he got him 'til he'd near kilt him. You could take and harass him with sticks and spikes and whips, it didn't come to nuthin'; he didn't even take no notice of you, all he cared about was that man down on the ground, just keep at him and at him—"

Guthrie paused. "Emily, she pestered me and pestered me about that bull. 'Don't let no one go out there and *bother* him,' she kept saying to me, 'jest let him out so he can be free and nobody at him. It's chaining him and worrying him with sticks that way that riles him.' And finally I got so sick of her nagging I said, 'All right, all right, I'll leave him free, but I'm not comin' in to get you if—'

" 'I'm not goin' in,' she says quick as a wink. 'Jest let him out so he can get by the fence and leave him be.'

"So I let him out—if her mother were alive, I'd probably never have got myself in such a fix, women got more control over things like that, but her Ma died gettin' her, and I raised her myself, this girl, right from the time she was a year old, had an Indian woman who helped me, but it ain't the same as blood, and this girl, she knows me inside and out, but the trouble is, I don't know her, women always have the upper hand in knowing things like that, seems. Somethin' born in them. Me and Emily been close, there bein' jest the two of us left like that, but she knowed me better'n I knowed her, and she got the best of me on this bull the way she got the best of me on most everything.

"Every day she'd go down, two, three times a day, and stand there by the fence and talk to that bull, take him some corn. She never made him do nuthin' for the corn, she jest put it out to come and git, stood there talkin' to him while he

31

et it. Day after day, week in and out, it begin to git on my nerves, that big brute gettin' bigger and bigger, I figured we'd never git him out of that field and into the barn come winter, so I says to her, 'Cut it out, don't give him no more, you're only makin' him worse, grainin' him up like that. All that corn's gonna mean the death of some man, come fall.'

" 'No,' she says, 'I'm goin' in and bring him out.'

" 'You're what?' I says. '*You're* goin' in and bring him out?'

" 'That's right, Pa. When the time comes, I'm goin' in and bring him out.'

"Well, that's when I put my foot down. 'Don't you go near that animal, *not one more time,* you hear? You go near that animal one more time, you take him any more corn, you don't come to *my* table and eat, you understand?'

"She never answered me yes nor no," Guy Guthrie said. "And to tell the truth, I never looked too close to see whether she done what I asked or not. So long as I didn't see—so long as I didn't look too close, we didn't have to make no issue out of it.

"Well, that tenth of November come, the time we all take the livestock in, give the grass a little time to git a new start before the big snows set in, and there was the bull to git barned. We both knowed it and seeing as how, as I said, I didn't want to make it no test of wills, I sent her off for the day. Some errand, I forgit jest what now. It don't matter, we both knew. She *seems* to be gone and I tell the men who's come up to help, we got to go in and git the bull. There's not one of them will go in and I can't blame them. They figure the same as I do, the man who goes in there's dead, it's as clean cut as that. So finally I says, 'I'll go in and git him.' No one says nuthin'. They jest stand there and wait, wait for me to go and git kilt; then I guess they figure they can shoot the damn thing and be done with it for good.

"He's out in the middle of the field and he don't come near when he sees us, just stands there with them wicked eyes watchin'. Watchin' and waitin'. That's what they were doing, all of them, those men and that bull, watchin' and waitin'.

"I opened the gate and went in. I had this long pole with a big hook on the end. As soon as he got anywhere near me, I was goin' to give it to him good, and I started, slowlike, across the field. I figured if I could git up to near where he was and badger him with the pole I could run him up toward the men. They had ropes and we was goin' to lasso him and tie him down and drag him up to the barn. It was a darn fool plan but the best we could think of.

"I didn't have much faith, but it was either git him in the barn one way or the other or have him die on me out there when the real cold hit. A bull like that, it would stay out," Guthrie said matter-of-factly, acknowledging hardiness and tenacity when he saw it, "but if we got a real dip in the temperature, its parts—well, they git froze in the real bad weather and then there's nuthin' you can do but shoot it. So I had to git him in. I had a lot of money in him, mean as he was.

"He seen me comin'. Christ, I could see him watchin' my every move as I come acrosst the field slow as a man can go and still keep movin'. It was like walkin' to certain death, knowin' you're goin' to die, there's no way out of it, you gotta go, but not wantin' to, goin' slow and reluctant, but goin'. That's the way I went.

"And then all of a sudden he springs out and he's comin', he's comin' at a full run and *nuthin's* gonna stop him. I put out that big pole with this big hook on the end and he jest come straight on it, snapped it right in two, we had to let that hook work out of his neck, it was buried in there so deep we couldn't git it out, he had to let his system work it out; and the first thing I knew I was on the ground and he was atop a me. I got marks on my chest to this day to prove it. And then he stops. He's jest standin' there, on top of me, all this slop from his mouth drippin' down on me, and I don't move a muscle, I'm lyin' there not movin', jest looking up. I tell you, I *never* git over that moment. And there's this voice sayin' real quietlike, 'Paul, come on, Paul.' That was the damn fool name she give it—Paul—can you beat it, a critter like that with a good Christian name? This voice callin' over and over, real calm, 'Paul, you come over here, I'm over here, Paul, come on,' and after a moment he goes. He walked straight over, jest like he was in a trance and he goes, straight away from me, right acrosst the field, and there's Emily standin' with a pail in her hand, and talkin' real quiet and calm to him, and he come up to her and starts eatin' from that pail she's got in her hands, and she says to me, quiet and calm, 'Go let loose of the gate,' and do you believe it, I got up and done it, I was so stunned, and then she leads that ragin' bull as quiet as a lamb right out the gate—the men all jumps back over the fence—and she goes down the road and into the barn and puts him up. Ain't nobody else's ever touched him since and we got him still, down over there to the back field. You want to see?" Guy Guthrie asked, "Or you satisfied lookin' what she ken do with the horse?"

II

The next morning, early, Guthrie and the girl brought the horse, whose name was Arthur—all the Guthrie animals seemed to have names like that, Mary, Paul, Arthur, Felicity —and the three of them began working. At first Odder said he'd take the horse up into the woods and do the logging, and Guthrie and the girl could stay back where he wanted the house and unload.

"Won't be no use," Guthrie said in the same laconic way he had said a moment before (and left it at that), "No place to put a house, the lake'll git it."

Odder argued with him, just as he tried to argue about the house, and with the same results. Guthrie didn't argue back; he just stood his ground, repeating his original unshakable judgment. Finally he said, "Try and see. He won't work for nobody but her'n me." Guthrie seldom called the horse, as he had not called the bull, by name. They were simply "he."

Arthur was standing docilely beside the girl and Odder went up to him confidently and grasped the halter to turn him around. The instant his fingers grazed the leather, the animal plunged away from him, striking out. The next instant Odder lay on the ground, the breath out of him and a rib, he thought, cracked or broken. There was a terrible searing sensation in his side. The girl was bent over him, her face expressionless, even the eyes unmoving. She seemed to Odder some kind of witch, the animal standing patiently behind her, looking over her shoulder at him, gently, reprovingly. If she asked him if he was hurt, he would kill her. No matter what the horse did to protect her. But she had the sense, for once, to stay still.

He struggled, panting, to his feet. There was a hot stinging all up and down his side and he had a moment of blackness when he put his weight down on his legs and stood, a moment where he began cursing inwardly at the knowledge that he was sure to pass out; but miraculously he remained on his feet, gasping for air, his side burning so badly that he couldn't speak. Guthrie had turned his back and seemed to be gazing out on the lake in contemplation of the early morning beauty. The girl said nothing; she took hold of the horse and started leading him up the small trail. "You comin', Pa?" she asked over her shoulder and plunged into the thick foliage, the horse at her side.

"How far up you want us to go?" Guthrie asked, his back still to Odder.

It took Odder several seconds to get enough breath to answer. Finally he said, between gasps, "Almost—to the—top. You'll see."

Guthrie turned and went past him without a glance. At the edge of the brush, he said over his shoulder, "I know jest how you feel. She done it on me with the bull." Then he was gone. He stayed up there all day, sending Emily and Arthur down with load after load. They didn't even stop for lunch. Emily gave him some thick bread spread with lard and an apple somewhere around the middle of the day. They ate while they were unloading. In the middle of the afternoon, she gave him some maple sugar, "to keep you going," she said. He was tired and hot, his rib hurt and he was stung, the flies were terrible. There were red welts on her face, her neck and the back of her hands, the rest of her covered by the tight rough men's clothes and so (he hoped) protected; and she was working just as hard, maybe harder, than he. When he tried to remonstrate with her to stop and take a rest, she only gave him one of her black-eyed looks and went on working. It was beyond him. No price had been agreed on—"We'll git what's right out of it, we're not worried," Guthrie had said, and refused to discuss the matter after that. Odder couldn't figure out what drove them. They didn't seem to be looking after themselves at all. All his life he had been protecting his own interests and watching other people jealously guard theirs; but these people seemed to be worrying about *his* interests. It didn't make sense. Why should they drive themselves for *his* house? (He thought of his bull-headed, hard-hearted father saying, It takes most men a lifetime to get a good-sized farm going . . . I got mine in ten years. And I built me *this* house and I made me *this* farm. And this is the biggest house in the valley, and the best built, and the best land . . .) But what did they want?

He paused. My God, what a pain there was in his side. He

36

heard the grumbles of an empty, protesting stomach, felt the nerves in his shoulder, that shoulder that had never been right since the summer he was fourteen and had had it out with his Pa, and the muscles in his arms, strained to the point where he had little control over his hands, his badly swollen, bitten mouth so sore and dry that he could hardly speak. Still he made himself keep going when he knew he couldn't go on another moment. But what kept them at this terrible punishing pace? It was his land, his logs, his house. Why should *they* care?

He had lost all track of time. The horse and the girl would come down with the logs, he and the girl would unload, not speaking, she and the horse would go back up, he would start squaring the timber. He was a little unsure of himself as he began to chip away at the logs to make them square. He had cut the timber, as he ought, on a waning moon, but the best building timber should be cut in February on the "old moon," and he had not been willing to wait six or seven more months to fell his logs. He had deliberately cut at the wrong time, and that made him wonder how good the wood was going to be. Fence rails would have been all right to cut during the second running of sap in August, but good building wood you weren't supposed to cut in the hot months. Still, as he examined them, the logs seemed all right. He rolled them up onto the two big logs lying perpendicular, with spikes stuck in both logs to hold them so that they wouldn't roll while he worked. He found the rolling and lifting hard work, probably as hard as anything he'd done in a long time; but he liked working the sharp shot-handled wide-bladed broad axe and he was fairly proficient with it. He could square all four sides of a good-sized log in a little over two hours. It wasn't hard work, but after a time it became monotonous; all he did was make a series of back-cuts along the grain, split out the chips, and make a new series of cuts until the side of the log he was working on was finished off the way he wanted it. Then he turned the log, started in on the second side, finished that, and went on to the third and fourth. The only variation in the process was in the last cutting; here the chips were hewn away with the edge to give a better finish although the marks of his work were still plainly visible. To give logs a smoother finish, an adze was needed, but an adze was tricky business and only employed on beams that were to show. Since Odder planned to plaster his house, he did not trouble with the adze.

After a time, immersed in work, he would suddenly be

conscious of an intruding sound over the endless short chopping sound of his broad axe; he would look up and there would be the horse dragging the new logs out into the clearing and a moment later the girl behind him.

Odder had no idea how many times this happened when suddenly his arms gave way on him, his fingers opened of their own accord, the axe slipped from between them and fell to the ground. For a moment he stood in the midst of that humming, crying wilderness—insects and birds, small animals shrieking, buzzing all about his head—and then he dropped to the ground, bent over on his knees, his side swallowing him up in one great white grinding clutch of pain. He fell forward and wept. She had beat him again. And on his own terms this time.

The second day she stayed down at the clearing with him. "Arthur ken find his own way now," she said stiffly before the protest came out of his mouth. And she gave him one of her looks. There was no way to fight her. He watched Guthrie and the horse go off into the woods; then he picked up his axe and went over toward the pile of logs. She stood quite still, very straight. He was thinking she would probably come and take the axe away from him and do twice the job he could, and he was seared by a shame worse than the pain in his side, a murderous kind of helplessness he could do nothing about.

"That side, I want to see it."

He stopped and turned, staring at her.

"That side, *I want to see it,*" she repeated and he could hear her saying a long time ago, Jest let the bull out so he ken git free and leave him be, and Odder knew why her father hadn't argued with her or tried to discipline her and why when she said something, people listened to her very careful and did as she directed, even though one of those had been her father who ought, long ago, to have beat that willfulness out of her. Women like her shouldn't be allowed around. A man was just no match for them once they had found out what it was like to get their own way. It was all her father's fault, he had let her have the chance to tame the bull, and she *had* tamed it and now she knew. Odder just shook his head stubbornly. Words wouldn't be any good against her.

She stepped forward and said so quietly that he had to strain his ears to hear, "Please, I want to see your side. I just want to help."

For something so untameable, so wild, so damned perverse, and *always* right, she was a beautiful thing. He thought about

38

what her strong fingers would feel like on his flesh. He closed his eyes and put temptation away.

She took another step forward and gazed at him. She was so tall that her black eyes were almost on a level with his. Buttes let himself do what had to be done. There was no use trying to fight back. He didn't want to anyway. He took her into his arms and listened as he brought his mouth down on hers. He was expecting laughter. But there was no sound save that of the summer moths and the swarm of cicadas in the trees, the incessant whine of flies and the scandal-mongering shrieks of the busy birds.

The third day Guthrie didn't come back. Buttes supposed that the girl in her inimitable way had let him know there was no need. The house was to be theirs and she didn't want outsiders involved, not even her own father.

When she came into the clearing she had the horse and his tackle, a sleeping sack of sorts fastened to his sack and some pots and pans. She was carrying a bundle which later he saw contained flour and maple sugar, some honey and salt, a kind of coffee made from ground dandelion roots.

She had come to set up housekeeping and like a good wife she began nagging him right away. The lake was no place to put a house. They had lost most of the summer, but with two of them they could get something going farther back up in the woods where—

He cut her short. "The house is going to be here," he said. She could have her way in everything else, she could do with him what she wanted in every other thing, but on this he had made up his mind, the house was going to be here. He prepared himself for the worst struggle of his life. She could leave, she could take the horse with her, she could do anything she wanted, *but the house was going to be here.*

"You made up your mind, ain't you?"

He looked at her.

"All right," she said. "The house will go here. But the lake's goin' to get it."

They had worked so hard the last weeks of that hot insect-ridden summer and into the cooler, rainier days of September that they were too worn out to care about anything—eating, sleeping, even touching one another. At the end of one of those back-breaking days, they would lie down on their pallets and stare up at the rough roof of the darkening sky. He didn't know how he could get through another day. And in every task he set for himself, he found she set a harder one for herself, keeping up with him from dawn till dusk and still going on after he had finished. She was up before he was, fixing food; long after he quit, she bustled about getting them something to eat. When he was too tired to make an effort to chew, she cajoled him and comforted him, told him the beans were nearly done, he had to eat to keep up his strength. He wanted to finish, didn't he? So he ate. And watched, disbelieving, while she got up and tidied the fire, worked sand over the pans to scrape them out, then went to the spring and fetched water to wash up, and finally sat down, feeding the fire, dreaming a moment into the rosy flames before she let down her long black hair and began to brush. Night after night he fell into a deep impenetrable sleep to the steady sound of the strokes of the brush going through her long black hair. An Indian woman had taught her that one inflexible rule of living: always brush your hair before you go to bed.

In the morning the fire was always going; that meant she must have been up in the night feeding it. Once or twice a week Guthrie came up in the late afternoon and brought them a slab of meat or part of a deer. He brought tea, too, real tea, and Emily would drop whatever she was doing and go to the fire to boil up water and fix them a pot of good hot strong tea. She had been very good at finding substitutes for real tea, which was far too expensive for them. She had little packets of birch bark, tanzy, camomile, and sassafras that she used. He liked these better than the dandelion drink or the coffee made from chickory root or ground locust seeds. She said they tasted almost the same as the real thing, but he was not convinced. They drank Guthrie's tea gratefully, sitting in the late afternoon light looking out over the lake. It was full fall and the first flights of Canadian geese flew overhead mornings, sometimes settled in on the far side of the lake at night. Odder heard them coming long before he saw the queer thick V-formations overhead. The birds migrating meant he and Emily had three, maybe four more weeks left to work if the weather held, but he felt they were going to make it; and as they sat by the fire, with the mugs of hot tea steaming in their hands, they would take time out to talk a little, he and Emily, of what they—and Arthur—had done. For without the horse, without the girl, Odder realized he could never have come halfway near finishing. He tried to put in words what he felt, but it wasn't much use. He wasn't any good with words. In any case, it would have been impossible to describe his tumultuous feelings. All his life he had worked toward *not* feeling; now suddenly he was nothing but feeling. His bitterness against others, his belief that standing alone was the only way to remain safe, all his defenses were breaking down. He was unlearning many things, lessons from the merciless brutality and lovelessness of his childhood that had shaped his whole life. It seemed to him he had to be reborn, to be what he had never been before, another kind of man entirely so that he might equal her vision of him, to be even fractionally worthy of her. Impossible to *say* any of this —he would have to show her, and the horse—how grateful he was and do it the only way he knew, with his hands. He puzzled it over the long days working, thinking about how he had come to love a girl and a horse—a horse!—and that in some mysterious way they loved him back, too, even that ornery old animal whose first instinct, Odder was sure, was to stomp him to death. Now the horse came and laid his head against Odder's back, scratching, nearly knocking Odder over; but it wasn't meanness, it was affection. Affection in a horse. Crazy, crazy.

What could he make for them, or give them, to show how much he cared? He would have to find something special, but what? He wanted to give her something no other had—and Arthur, Christ, what could you give a horse to show you cared?

That in itself proved how far he'd come since the beginning of the summer, that he could even think like that. But sometimes it seemed to him he was too tired to know what was really happening to him. He got up, he worked, he ate, he slept, he worked in his dreams and arose tireder than before, and always he went back to work again. They had got all the timber they would need squared; they had cut the lumber that would be driven across the lake after the ice formed and left to season over at Guthrie's, to be cut into clapboards in the spring. Odder had figured at first he would cut the clapboards himself, but this was precise and tedious work because the boards had to be placed on the house in graduated widths to preserve the proper proportions, the upper boards narrower than the lower ones, and he wasn't sure he could do the job anyway. It seemed an insult not to give Guthrie the work, the girl working so hard putting up the house. So the clapboards would be mill cut. Still there was an enormous amount of work left. There were three mammoth piles of logs stacked on shore ready for the January freeze. He and Arthur would transport them across the ice on a log sled. He had dug most of the foundation of the cellar that would serve for winter storage of their root vegetables, but there was still the final work to be done, no real problem—the cellar floor they had decided to leave dirt, but Odder wanted the walls stoned in. The shore was lined with every conceivable size and shape of stone; it was just a question of gathering them, back-breaking work, yet some of the best days they had were when he and Emily and Arthur went along the shore collecting rocks.

The weather was warm during the day, but the nights were crisper now, and the bugs (thank God) gone; they were able to let up a little on themselves. He even remembered the first time he laughed. It struck him then how long it had been since he had been able to do that. The house was always with him, an obsession, she said, frowning, then brightening, smiling, as if, after all, obsessions were the rule, not the exception of life.

She was right: he was obsessed. Nothing else mattered, not even the girl herself sometimes. He had forgotten any other call on him, and then one day, down by the water, when she suddenly rebelled against something he wanted to do and stuck out her tongue, he laughed, and saw how out of proportion his life had become. He couldn't understand why the girl had stayed with him, lopsided as he was, a kind of fanatic, but then he didn't really understand Emily at all, he knew, any more than he understood any of the things that kept him going—his heart or lungs, even this senseless obsession—she was just a part of him, of what made his life go on, he accepted her the way he accepted his lungs breathing for him, his heart pumping his blood; but when he laughed, he also knew for the first time what would happen to him if she ever took it into her head to leave him. It would be the same as if he quit breathing; he stopped laughing, suddenly afraid.

"You don't have to do it," he said. "None of it. I don't know why you do it."

"Everything interestin's a challenge."

"You figure you're gonna tame me, have me eatin' out of your hand, come to your callin', gentled, like that bull, like this here horse?"

No answer: she had turned her head, he saw only the blowing strands of black hair. She was right to brush it that way, it was beautiful. He was still filled with his fear, he wished she'd say something. Maybe he ought to try to tell her what having her with him working that way had meant to him, but he didn't have the words, he wasn't even sure there were words for that kind of feeling in a man. Still he didn't like this small, humble, frightened feeling inside him; he had to do something to make it go away.

He just stood, a damn frightened fool. Finally he said, "You figured yet on when we're supposed to—you know, make it *permanent*," he said with difficulty.

When she turned her head, her eyes, big and black, looked right into him. "I guess I figure *a man* should do that kind of decidin'."

The horse was getting agitated, he wasn't used to all that standing around and talking.

"I never figured a man ought to ask a woman 'til he's got a house he can take her to," he said stubbornly. "But then if you—"

"Then you done the decidin'." She went up to Arthur and began to scratch his withers, moving her hand slowly and methodically toward the root of his mane; Arthur laid off twitching his tail and moving his feet about, quieted. The horse and girl stood there, watching him.

"But you got your rights, too."

"I know my rights well enough. You heard me complainin'?"

It was beyond Odder, he gave up. But he was suddenly tired and sat down.

"Let's go in the water," she said.

"*What?*"

"Let's me and you go in the water. It looks nice and cool and it's so hot and anyway we could do with a good wash."

Here he was talking about marrying and she wanted to go bathing. She was already taking off her boots. "You gonna go on in now? I mean, jest as you are?"

"How else you want me to go?"

"But it's plain daylight and—"

"Nobody around, maybe an Indian or two, it's nothing to them," she said matter-of-factly. "It's good and warm, no better time."

"Emily," he said, choked.

"I wondered when you was gonna notice."

"But how come you never said? How come you—"

"You had the house on your mind," she said. "I didn't want to worry you with nuthin' else. And I thought you'd find out for yourself soon enough. You don't hide nuthin' like this long."

There was no preacher in the area and if they wanted to go

43

to the Falls, there was something about posting banns, take a long time and cost a lot of money—Guthrie and the girl decided to bring one of those circuit-riding fellows back and have the wedding over at the mill. Odder was a little upset because all this meant more delay on the house and because he had finally come to the only conclusion he could: he would have to put up a log house for the winter. He couldn't camp out in the cold with a wife and baby—no, there was nothing to do but put up something temporary for the winter. She and Guthrie would get a preacher while he stayed behind and worked. Before he'd seen how she was, he'd never really thought much about winter. He'd had the vague notion she'd go back with her father and he'd get some winter work and then in the spring they'd come back together and begin putting up the house. Now he had to make a considerable revision of plans.

He decided first off to get a place up for them and quick; they could let the beams stand down on the house site by the lake and season over the winter there. In the spring with all the wood dry, they could get the house up fast with a little help. The cellar was in, it was just a question of getting the boards for the frames ready and raised. But being a Buttes the unexpected upset him. He hadn't figured on having a wife and baby before he had a house, and with Emily nursing and a baby to look after, he couldn't expect much help out of her. Come March she'd hardly be up and around; the baby was due in February, the worst part of the winter, he thought with foreboding. If he'd planned it—well, he hadn't. That was that. The week before she went off with her father to arrange the marrying, she kept putting his hand on her abdomen. *Don't you feel him?* she'd ask, impatient. Odder felt nothing but the deep rhythmical give and take of her breath, but to make her feel better he said he did. He could tell he had done the right thing, lying; she was happier than he'd ever seen her those three days before she went off with Guthrie.

The first day she was gone Odder felt a strange sense of relief. She had made him nervous putting his hand on her all the time that way and asking, *You feel him? He's kicking hard,* and his lying and saying, Yes, he sure was strong, wasn't he? He had begun to get jumpy, so he was glad to see her go, though he felt ungrateful and disloyal at his relief. He realized now how many months it had been since he'd had no one to answer to but himself. (They'd taken the horse, which was just as well, all things considered; Arthur liked him well enough with Emily around, but there was no counting on his reaction if she went off and left him alone with Odder.) The opportunity of not having to consider another human being (or animal) was a pleasure he could not deny. He felt suddenly, extraordinarily happy, as if some insoluble problem had been settled or some great grief lifted from him. When he arose that first morning, the woods were unfamiliar to him, as if he were seeing them for the first time; he marveled at them, glad to be in them all by himself, nothing to spoil his sense of satisfaction that first day, and everything went unaccountably well as he went about the first morning chores. Things that usually annoyed him, he paid no attention to; decisions he had put off suddenly and easily presented solutions almost by themselves; he felt none of the pressures and tensions he normally experienced on waking when it seemed to him there were more things to be done in the day ahead than he could accomplish. Instead of hurrying, hastening through breakfast, rushing himself into the day ahead, showing off, he supposed, before Emily, he took his time, nor did he feel guilty, recognizing only now that he had felt guilt about the way she was up before he was getting the fire going or the way, after he quit at night, there still seemed so much for her to do. He didn't worry about her at all. That was the best part, no one to worry about, just himself to pleasure.

He got up and built a small fire, made himself some strong birch tea, spooned honey into it, sat down on a log looking up the hill to "her tree," the big larch—the tammyrack, she called it. Perversely, or characteristically, she liked it because it was the only one of the pines that shed its needles. Why should she like that? It looked so bare while the other pines near it were still green and full. Still, he had to admit it did have a grace the others lacked, something to do, he thought, with the daintiness—if you could use that word about a tree—of its branches. He himself preferred the big maples. Their huge-fisted boles were like dissected hands from unknown giants.

He drank his tea, munched bits of hardened corn cake. Emily had made them for him before she left. Corn meal was the staple of their diet. She cooked the cakes before the open fire, the corn meal simply mixed with water, patted into cakes, and baked on a board before the live coals.

He dipped one of the hard crusty cakes into the birch tea to soften it, taking his time, relishing the clear early morning air, the busy morning noises of all the birds and animals while he himself luxuriated in silence, in idleness, in the sense of

45

peacefully evading responsibility. Yet he was not unbusy; his mind if anything was overactive. Ideas, plans, schemes teemed in his brain as he sat sucking his tea through the lump of cornmeal cake he had anchored between his teeth.

He savored the full measure of his liberty, putting down his empty cup and deciding once and for all the kind of water they would have in the house, a decision he had been putting off for months. The lake water of course was readily available, but there were problems about getting it up to the house and in winter—

A well was a lot of work and not to be counted on even if you put off digging it until August, the driest month of the year. If you found water then, you were likely to have it all year around, but a real long dry spell—two, three years of drought—could run any well dry, and then where were you? Of course he had the lake water he could always fall back on, but a man didn't like to put in the work of digging a well and shoring it up if he wasn't sure it would hold water all the time. No, gravity feed was the only answer. Find a good spring up in the hills and run it downhill by trough to the cabin.

He would give part of this clear bright morning to finding a suitable water for their cabin. A spring, yes, that was the answer. He would put a giant hogshead in the kitchen, in the barn, with wooden drains for the overflows; there would maybe be a breezeway out from the kitchen or a summer kitchen off the wellway. He would see what Emily wanted.

Sham summer. Beautiful, though in the old days he supposed the settlers didn't think so. Indians didn't like the cold, they wouldn't go on the warpath when the weather was bad; but when it warmed up briefly late in October, then they roused themselves for a last skirmish before winter thrust them back into their long houses for the long dark months. Warring parties were usually in a bad mood in October after being closed in with the first cold. They could be counted on to commit worse atrocities than usual. Probably why this weather was called Indian summer, because the Indians were out and up to no good. He remembered coming across the Mohawk Valley, that sense of blood being ground up in the very earth.

Funny how Emily's attitude and his were so different on the question of Indians. He wanted no truck with them, but she had a whole part of her life bound up with them because of that Indian woman Guthrie had got down from the reservation to help raise her. Come with a girl near her own age,

46

Emily had said, the two of them had growed up like they was the same blood. It made Odder cringe to think of her feeling that way. In some way that he didn't like to admit, she was almost Indian herself. All those barks and roots and herbs that she used were secrets handed down by Indians. Half the things she told him about the woods were Indian things. So much of her Indian-made. She loved the grouse but thought them too beautiful, for instance, to be wild, surely an Indian idea. To her wild things had to be tough and toughness meant ugliness. She could never understand how the partridge and deer had endured. She was afraid for them all the time. Her concern over animals, her way with them, something in her hands, only a few people had it. Mostly Indians. Not white people, though, not any he'd ever met, leastwise. Except Emily.

She was a whisperer, too, the way the Indians were, standing next to a horse making those strange windy Indian sounds into its ear, witching it. The animals understood. He wondered whether the animals knew other things about her he didn't, if there were ways of expressing emotions less limited in animals than in man. A man's vocabulary for his feelings was so small.

A brilliant sun raked the water below; yet a deceptive softness lay over the landscape as if it were spring. The beauty of the weather, the sun shining on the leaves so that they seemed glazed with gold, shadows hanging in the pines, the whole atmosphere made him ache as he gazed now at the renewed green of the grass under his feet and at the small open knoll at the top of the hill, the green leaves sprouting from a dead branch near his feet.

There came the insistent sound of moving wings, grouse— Emily's bird, he thought of it, just as the larch was Emily's tree. He saw the male first, fan-shaped tail, ruffed neck. It was gone, trailed by a pair of hens, before he could see whether or not the feet had begun to change. In winter the birds put on "snowshoes"—horny combs that made their toes grow in order to help them over the snow. *Mitchiwess*, Emily said the Indians called them, the canoe builders, because the sound of the male drumming in spring sounded like an Indian building a birch-bark canoe.

Wherever she was at this moment he knew she was sorry to be parted from him, pressing to get the business about the wedding arranged so that she could get back without wasting any time, her energy concentrated on helping him get what *he* wanted. Emily was willing to sacrifice any pleasure the trip might give her if she felt she should be doing something for him, and the worst part was that she did this willingly, happily, without thought, none of it out of duty. She was unselfish and self-sacrificing, uncomplaining and more energetic than he; it was a woman's nature to submerge herself in a man, find her life through his, lots of men would have said, but they wouldn't have been talking about Emily.

She gave, it came to him, because she was completely without self-interest in getting any return on her investment of giving; she was absolutely, completely sure of herself. Nothing frightened her or made her feel insecure (look at the way she had handled that business about having a baby) because she had a total reliance on her own ability to manage her life. She relied on her courage and common sense; troubles would come, disaster; there would be deep deep times of despair, but she would get through them all because if for thousands of years other people had, why shouldn't she?

He stood under Emily's larch recognizing for the first time how much of his view of the world in the last few months was altered because he saw it now in relation to her —*her* tree, *her* bird, in a way *her* house more than his.

Yet she would never have looked at these as hers. She would never have seen the world selfishly, as he did—another trait inherited no doubt from his father, his father who could never break out of the prison of himself, who, in direct contrast to Emily, could see the world in nobody's eyes but his own.

His father loathed the world while Emily loved it. To Odder it seemed as simple a distinction as that. His father had seen the world as an instrument of punishment, one which daily reached out to destroy him. Life was harsh payments for things you did not really want.

He understood, Odder thought, at last the reason for his father's unaccountable rages. His father was rebelling against having grown up. Being an adult meant having to assume unending responsibilities, reconciling yourself to the sacrifices you made for others, often without their even realizing it; Ordah Buttes had felt betrayed every day of his life by the chores ahead, by the unfairness of all the work he had to do, all the mouths he had to feed, all that flesh he had brought into the world and must now be accountable for. There was nothing in his father's life to make the endless chores, the constant worry, the unrelenting pressure of responsibility, worthwhile: nothing that might be called love

48

illuminated the dark moments and set them in perspective.

Nothing eats up energy like rage; nothing so lays down the spirit as hate. Ordah Buttes's life had been one long tense holding in of hate. He had been like a great explosive force held in by very fragile fastenings.

How had his father stuck it out? What had kept him simply from fleeing, leaving them all in the lurch? An age of doing right, of dedicating yourself to duty, possibly that was it, but more: where was his father going to flee? A valley-dweller, Odder thought, and for the first time he was able to think, untroubled, about his relationship with his father, accepting the fact now that he did not love his father; possibly once he had, possibly not, it was hard to say; but at any rate the important thing was he hadn't at the end, didn't now, and his conscience had finally let him off: *there was no reason why he had to love him any more, not even his own feelings of guilt.*

The Butteses were a family of individualists and when they tangled, as it was inevitable they would, it took more than the claims of blood to sort them out. Perhaps there was something about the blood though: a male family. There hadn't been a girl born into the Buttes family for more than a hundred and fifty years. *Never on this side of the Atlantic,* Odder's father always said proudly. The Butteses were special, singled out, he was saying. Look at what they had done, all on their own, with their own determination: The First Buttes had come to Virginia from England in 1641, indentured for five years on a tobacco farm. It was said of him that he had always been proud of the fact he'd given a good day's labor for each and every one of the days of those five years he was in service. A man put his word to something, it was his duty to live up to it.

Odder did not even know that ancestor's name; he was always simply called The First or The Indentured One, his son The Second or Young Buttes.

The First Buttes received with his release five acres. He sold this, moved North and wedged his way in between the Dutch settlers in the Raritan Valley. (It bothered Odder that The First Buttes had been a valley man.) His original plot of six acres in New Jersey grew to six and "sixty-five across the two-mile brook," then forty more "the other side of Styles's grove," and finally one hundred and sixty pasture acres "over the brook and across the next hill." The Inden-

tured One was gifted at the American game of amassing.
Work was hard, with wooden plows and slow-moving oxen, and at harvest the two-wheeled cart, but The Second Buttes in America, The Young One, was his father's son. He worked hard, increased his lands, married late but fathered soon, and made the Commons Farms, as his place was known, almost equal to his father's.

Young Buttes's son, John, stayed on the Commons, as did his son, Ames, Odder's grandfather. There were always enough sons to manage the work, and though some of them left home to make it on their own, others stayed to help and set up homesteads in the far corners of the fields and raised families of their own. Their farms prospered, their wives produced, their families flourished.

The family prospered too well, the women were too fruitful; the parcels of land began to diminish in division so that by the time Odder's father reached marrying time, there were squabbles and hard feelings about those who stayed behind and asked an equal share. Ordah Buttes had struck out on his own, taking a wagon and two oxen, seeds and supplies, a wife with a strong back and good working hands, and a bit of money the others had guiltily given him as his "fair share." "When times are thin," his father would say acrimoniously, "there's no such thing as a 'fair share.' "

Ordah Buttes's first house was a crude building at best, but he was proud of it. I put up the house first on my own land, he had told Odder, so we wouldn't be living in covered holes or shanties the way some folks did, and then I got the land going. A good workman can clear four or five acres the first year if he works at it. I did *nine*. It takes most men a lifetime to get a good-size farm going, four horses and some oxen, ten cows, sheep and swine. I got mine in ten years. He looked out on his plains. And I built me *this* house and I made me *this* farm, the biggest house in the valley, and the best. I got the best land and the most cows for fifty miles around.

He would say, "Before I built me this house" or "In my first house . . ." The first house was down at the far end of the pasture, deserted and ramshackled, but still standing. It was as if Ordah Buttes had given his buildings life, as if buildings were for him an act of perpetuity. His buildings would emit, almost audibly, his name long after he was gone.

He was a strange man, hard to understand, perhaps never understood, at least by Odder. There was something secret and silent and hidden in him that shut him off from others.

There was also something violent and uncontrollable that made him dangerous. People who could stand his silence could not bear his rages. Almost everyone in the Ohio settlement avoided him. His family lived trying to fathom his unfathomable moods. The only clues he ever gave were desultory and moot. "There was two of us," he would say sometimes, "and Pa preferred the other. My brother got the farm and I got some silver. And it was him, my Pa, they called the most honest man in that valley. But he weren't fair to me, his own son. I jest wish he could see what I done here."

Then he would retreat out of his rage into silence, a stonish figure in the midst of his fields, planted like a pillar against the earth, hands on hips, an air of expectation about his whole body, as if he were waiting for something or somebody. But for whom? For what? Judgment? Retribution? An unsolicited redress of those wrongs he felt his father had done him? If you asked him what he was thinking, he only said quietly, "He give Pliny the farm." Sometimes he added, "Of course he tried to be fair, he give me money to git my own land—" Then his voice trailed off, silenced by some grief so old and deep that it was impossible for him to express. "Don't matter now," he would say at last. "Look what I done *here*."

His outbursts were terrible because they were completely unexpected. He would be working placidly beside one of his sons or with his animals or eating at the table across from his wife when from out of nowhere, he would be seized with a violent outburst of temper and he would begin to rage against an ineffectual animal, the ineptitude of his sons, the oversights and omissions of his wife. That none of these had done anything to bring on his anger made absolutely no difference. He would begin to flail the animal or the person nearest him, usually Odder who, as the eldest, worked most closely with him. He struck with big, powerful hands, kicked with nailed boots, beat and kicked and pummeled without restraint like an enormous obsessed animal who had no control over himself.

Odder was a slow grower but what he lacked in height, he made up in bulk. By the time he was fifteen, he was a formidable opponent, but though he might thrash boys and men up and down the valley, he never won with his father. Ordah Buttes had the advantage of muscles heavily settled in, of an experienced body, of tallness, which seemed to make every outcome inevitable; yet to each Odder went with a stubborn fixity to win.

51

It was hard training for a boy; it made Odder brutal against opponents in other fights and contemptuous of the weak, for he was used to the brutality and contempt of his father. The first opposition against one of his father's brutal rages found Odder broken and bleeding. He had a smashed rib, his face was swollen out of shape, something had happened to one of his shoulders so that his arm flopped as if it were broken. The bone protruded up through the skin at the elbow, a knob of throbbing pain that moved this way and that at crazy angles.

He lay on the ground, half covered with mud, sick with pain. He was cursing his father in the same way he had occasionally heard his father curse his father, and there was the same breathless, gasping hatred in his voice, so similar in fact that he recognized it immediately and stopped—one thing he had determined was not to be like his father and if he cursed like this and blasphemed his father, he was becoming his father, he would carry on in himself all the bad things he hated in his father.

He couldn't have moved had he wanted to. He was waiting, he supposed, tracing the series of events later in his mind, for his mother or one of his brothers to come and help him. He lay a long time before he understood that no one, not one single member of his family, was going to come; he could count on no help when he was weak and hurt and alone, he saw, and he said to himself, Well, it looks like it's me and me alone I gotta count on, can't expect nuthin' from no one else, and that's *that*.

He raised himself a little and took note of his torn and bloody clothes, the shoulder wrenched out of joint, the flopping arm hanging at his side. He wasn't, he saw, going to get very far on his own, but all he had to do was work his way up to the house and maybe he could get someone to help him upstairs to his room.

A strange burning orangeness lay over everything; the landscape beat down upon him with a flickering flamelike pulse that he finally identified as a combination of the throbbing pain inside his head and the flashing fire of the noon sun on the fields.

He must have been lying in the barnyard for nearly two hours. The fight had begun around ten because his father had found something wrong with one of the plows, a broken plane left unrepaired. Odder had not broken the plane, but he had not done most of the things for which at one time or another he had been blamed and beaten.

He brought his body slowly across the back barnyard until he made the fence; there he rested, his weight propped against a thick post, void of emotion, experiencing neither hate nor sorrow nor disappointment, only the emptiness of acceptance. He would have to go on with these brutal encounters until he won or his father killed him. It was as simple as that. So long as you understand, he told himself, and don't expect mercy nor compassion nor love, you got a chance. But if you once, just once, let down and expect him to show any feelings for you at all, you're goin' to be beat until you never git up again.

He faltered opening the gate, as if he felt that he had left part of his trust, the inherent boyhood belief in the goodness and greatness of his father, somewhere back there in the blows and the mud, that from now on he would have to stand all alone with no expectations of quarter from anyone, a man who had at last learned the prime lesson, he told himself, of life, that he who fights only for himself and stays pure and simply alone is the only one who is safe. People used me up to now, he thought bitterly, but it's gonna be me who uses them from now on.

For three more years these terrible battles took place in the back barnyard, and every one of these battles for Odder ended in defeat. He lay in mud, in rain, in snow, in the green grass of spring behind the barn month in and month out; the years passed, the silent deadly seriousness of the encounters increased, for Odder was beginning to get his own height, he was almost at eye level with his father, but the added inches had eaten up his flesh; he was thin and rangy, ill-equipped to pit himself against the hard, disciplined body of the older man. He knew now, too, the first lesson of defense, to force out of himself the courage to be ugly and, when necessary, absolutely and completely merciless.

One day his father broke his hold for a moment, his face blue with effort, his whole huge frame rattling with its endeavor to suck in air. Odder struck him with both fists in the stomach. His father gave a great grunt and fell to the ground. Odder sprang on him, hands circling his throat. He began to squeeze. The cords in his father's throat were thick and hard as hemp; his father's face was grotesque with distortion of pain and the effort to get air into his lungs; he lay beneath Odder stiff and unyielding as rock. And Odder was swept with exaltation; he was going to win. He would squeeze and squeeze until—and then he found himself in midair. His father had somehow forced out strength enough to bring his great knees up; they had lifted Odder off his chest as easily as if he were some small helpless infant clinging to an irritated adult's breast.

Odder saw the stone but there was nothing he could do. He was going to be hit, that was all there was to it; there was no time to put out his arms and soften the blow or shift slightly the arched angle of his body to miss the rock.

It struck full force. The only thing he remembered later was that moment of knowledge that he was going to be hit. He did not feel the impact of the blow; all that came was a swift and immediate cessation of senses, darkness, but a darkness with substance; he lay under it as if he were being pressed into the earth itself.

He should have broken his back or shattered his skull. He came out with a cracked collarbone. Not bad enough for even the cow doctor to come, but bad enough to keep him half-crippled all the rest of that winter. His bones had perhaps suffered so many blows and bruises that they were beginning to rebel; they refused to heal the way they should. At night Odder would sit up in bed using his good arm to force the stiff joint at the shoulder back and forth. It was a strange time of the year, early winter; the skies were sharply outlined against the waxy light of the moon. The clarity, the coldness, cast midnight shadows on the newly fallen snow. He would sit looking out at the eerie yellow light, the black shadows on the snow, grinding his arm back and forth, saying to himself, Don't feel bad, don't feel nothing. The trick is to learn not to feel at all. If you don't let yourself feel, you can't be done no hurt. No feelings at all, that's what you gotta work for.

He did what chores he could with one arm; he brought his battered body to the table and made it go through the motions of eating. His stiffness, his aloofness, precluded all offers of help; when there was meat that needed to be cut, he went without. He was lonely, but his badly injured pride had need of this loneliness, too.

His mother sat with her thin mouth and strange bright eyes; she had these bright eyes, bright, bright, like glass beads, bright and expressionless as glass beads, and this thin little mouth as if someone had drawn one straight line across her face. Her sons looked nothing like her. They all resembled the big thick cut of the father, sinewy, full-lipped, fat-faced, all except Odder who had her mouth. He hated it when he looked in the mirror and saw that one straight line drawn across his face just the way it was drawn across hers. They all ate alike though, big slurping movements that conveyed the food from the plate to their mouths; different though the mouths were, the eating was the same, fulsome bites with the food escaping now and then and sticking to their chins or edging out the corners of their mouths. Odder was fastidious in his eating; he had a horror of being like them. And yet he wanted them to love him, he wanted to love them —but the gulf between was too big. They were like some strangers from another county that he could not feel any affinity with, nor could he in any way identify his flesh with theirs; they were thick and bulky, with big clumsy bones and large heavy heads hanging on short necks, while he was tall and thin and rangy, long-necked, long-armed, almost delicate in build next to their sluggishness. The dual emotions of wanting on the one hand to belong to them and on the other being repelled by their awkward, massive movements to the point where he despised them, wished them all to hell and gone, himself free forever from that intolerable bond of flesh, kept him at the table breaking the same bread with them at the same time that he found it impossible to talk with them.

They shoveled their food back and forth, back and forth; they spewed, they sucked noisily; they made gurgling sounds in their throats over the liquids and rasping grunts on the solids. It seemed to him there was an animal strain in all of them, even his mother, thick and aproned, soaking her bread in her gravy, wiping up the plate with its end, sucking tea between her bad teeth, smiling or talking with her thin mouth full. That brutishness had come, he believed or tried to make himself believe, from his father; and he wanted none of it, kept close watch over himself to cut out any trace of their mannerisms.

Yet there was no denying he was a Buttes—"looks *jest* like my father," Ordah Buttes would say, looking at him with narrowed eyes. "The spittin' image of him." Was this why his father hated him? Would he hate a son of his own if he looked like his own father? Instincts ran deep; sharing blood didn't mean you necessarily felt for one another.

Love was still in some ways inside, but it could not operate at the level that things now stood; he had for a time the hope that things might change, the belief that in their hearts shame was working away at their hardness, and that they would come to feel they had done him harm. Then, gradually, he came to accept what was at first unacceptable to him: his father hated him and he had transferred that hate to them. They stood with his father. He was the outsider.

Yet he was the eldest son. To him belonged the right to inherit these fields.

Why didn't his father love him?

My brother got the farm and I got some silver. And they called my father the fairest man in the valley. One of these days he was going, walk right off the place, the whole lot of them be damned, but not 'til he licked his father and evened the score. If he pulled out before that, he would look like a quitter.

It took all that winter to mend Odder's shoulder, spring and the early part of the summer to loosen the joint and get it moving so that he could get some real use out of it. By haying he wanted to be able to take his place and hold his own as if nothing had happened.

The younger boys were not anywhere near skilled enough to have mastered the cradle scythe—Odder himself still had trouble with it—so they would all use the simple hand and blade with fork. Even using that took skill. A man could only learn after long experience how low to hold the snath-heel, how far up to tilt the blade, so that his scythe would cut the windrows easily, evenly, neatly, rhythmically. Ordah Buttes had a passion for uniformity. He wanted them all to move at the same rate of speed, cutting on the same stroke.

Odder was proud of his scythe. He had searched the woods several seasons before he had found the willow limb curved in just the right way for the snath. This he had shaped to perfection by constant application of warm oil; for the nib and the finger he had used hickory, which now had what looked like a polish but which was really the stain from the sweat of his hands.

At first the scythe had been too heavy, but he had taken that into account when he was making it. He wanted to grow into it; if he had chosen wood light enough to handle at the beginning, he would have soon outgrown the tool. Now he was man enough to handle his scythe without trouble, and any other year he would have eagerly awaited haying so that he might show off his new prowess, but with his bad shoulder, he was afraid he wouldn't be able to manage.

He often went to the barn and took the scythe down from

56

the wall, running his fingers over the carefully carved initial O, the name Buttes, the date, 1795. It had taken hours and hours to carve that into the handle, but he had done a good job. The time had been well spent.

He carried the scythe down into the far pasture where no one could see him and tried to swing it. Every time he began the first circular movement, the pain in his shoulder was so intense that he came to a standstill. Even when he forced himself, he could never follow through with one complete swing. His shoulder locked shut.

He hung his scythe up in the barn with his name to the wall. When he was in the barn, he tried not to look at it. Finally one afternoon he took it down with the resolution he would keep working until he made himself swing freely, following a natural uninterrupted motion of shoulders, arms, waist, hips, knees, all of them flowing freely, so that he could cut evenly hour after hour without interrupting his pattern. Pain was a part of most things, he was learning; inevitably it had to become a part of the beauty of the scythe, too.

He swung and a shock went all the way through him. He brought the scythe back into position, planted his feet firmly on the warm earth, swung again with all his might. For a moment—but only a moment—the shoulder seemed to shut; then it opened and he made an arc as far as his arm could bend. If he could force and force and force, it would have to give a little more each time until—

He brought the scythe back, took his stance, and swung again and again and again.

The first hay was always cut in the field closest to the house, the next in a field a little farther away, the men moving farther and farther from the house until they came to the last and most distant pasture. In that way the women gradually accustomed themselves to the greater distances they had to carry lunch each day.

For the haying Ordah Buttes got one of the young girls from the neighborhood to come in and help in the kitchen and in the years before his own sons were big enough to help, he had hired a boy or two to aid with the cutting. Generally people in the neighborhood pitched in and helped one another, but Ordah did not go along with this. He had more sons than the others and would, hence, have to supply more help than his neighbors if he started this sort of reciprocation. He paid for whatever help he got and thus incurred no obligations.

The hay had to be cut and put under the ricks in good weather. It could not lie out in the fields for fear of rain. Wet hay became moldy and would sicken an animal. Because time was of the essence, the men followed the custom of "nooning," or having their midday meal in the fields. This dinner was usually substantial, suitable for men expending their every effort for several hours in a punishing sun; and as the men moved farther and farther away from the house, the problem of carrying vast amounts of food out to them became very difficult. Toward the end, when the distance was formidable, Odder's mother used an ox and cart to carry everything out.

During the nooning, Odder's father would stretch out on the earth and rest; he might even tell stories, reaching out in remembrances of the past that he still held an important part of himself, and then he sometimes spoke calmly, affectionately of his father. He would tell his sons about the summer fair when his father did most of his trading, and the boys ran foot races, wrestled, competed to catch a greased pig. Odder's father had once won a silver buckle in a bout of cudgels. There were singing contests, Ordah Buttes said, which were a fine thing because the singers were given rum to limber up their vocal cords. He had been, he said, something of a tenor. He sang sometimes, lying on the newly mown field, his voice sweet and sad.

Now in the big magnificent meadow that ran down from the back of the house the five Buttes boys took their places; in a moment Ordah Buttes would give the signal and they would take, all together, the first round clean swing that cut the grass.

Odder felt a strange deadness in his mouth. He had seen the look on his father's face as they all lined up, a look compounded of expectation, irony, and satisfaction. He was waiting for Odder to make one false movement, to throw off the rhythm of the mowers even ever so imperceptibly.

Odder waiting, watching his father out of the corners of his eyes, felt the tenseness of his brother; in silence, under the first almost cool rays of the sun, the five stood, motionless. Then the cry came. Odder swung and the blade moved swiftly through the air; the first swatch of grass lay at his feet. He did not look up. The trick was to keep with an inner beat, looking neither to right nor left, feeling the timing inside, letting your body move with it. In the split second that a glance around took, a man lost looseness of motion.

58

Swinging, cutting, sweating, they went up the rows of the first field.

He tired, but he was pleased to see that his shoulder was holding up. At ten they rested, a five-minute break, leaning on the handles of their scythes, the sweat running from their faces, looking out blankly on the vast fields ahead that still had to be done. At the beginning like this, it always seemed impossible they would ever finish, there was just too much work; when it was all done and they looked from bared field to bared field, it seemed impossible to them that they *had* done it. Only in the middle, looking at half their work done, half ahead, did there seem any real chance they could finish.

The thing to do was to take a short break at noon, eat, get right back to work, even if he had to mow awhile by himself just to keep in action. He was pretty sure by now he had a chance of lasting; after the lunch break he would know for sure. It was at that moment that his father called Sedder. "Go up and tell your Ma not to bring no food out here. I want you to tell her we don't stop for lunch until we're finished with this field." The others stared at him. "I want you to push," his father said, *"hard. Now,"* he said, and the scythes rose in an arc and beat the air, the hay fell before them like the fluttering of birds' wings.

The tempo picked up, each one increasing his speed, making the necessary adjustments to get in pace. Their movements were ragged at first, trying to synchronize, but this was to be expected, or always had been, when a change of timing took place.

Odder tried to get the feel of the movements on both sides of him, to absorb the motions of his brothers' scythes through his pores so that he would not have to look up, but the only feeling he had was of all of them out of kilter.

A blow struck his bad shoulder and he pitched forward. "Pick it up, pick it up, I said," his father raged at him. "You're out of step. You're the one who's holding us up."

He was not any more out of step than any of the others; they were all awkward until they picked up the beat. His father knew that and yet—

Odder straightened, gripped his scythe and swung fiercely at the grass in front of him. The blow had put him behind; he could see his brothers now because they were ahead of him a little. He was pushing his pained shoulder beyond what he should, wanting to catch up, knowing that if he could

59

just keep up his accelerated pace five minutes more, he would be in line again and have regained the beat.

He panted on, a thick lace of hay in front of him, his brothers swinging, their hay falling, their scythes singing as they cut a heavy embroidery of musty gold on top of the hard earth. The newly cut hay gave off a cloying sweetish scent; as it lay under the sun an unexpected freshness rose in the air.

He kept his arm swinging, calculating closely; in three more cuttings he was again moving in line with his brothers.

The sun had now swung midheavens; it was past noon. They would not eat until nearly two unless they picked up speed, and they had had breakfast before six. The youngest of his brothers, Sedder, who had rejoined the line at the end, was working way beyond capacity already. Sedder's hungry, Odder thought, he needs his lunch, he needs a rest, but he's too proud to call it quits before we finish this field because he wants to hold his own.

It was stupid nevertheless. They would not finish the field in even an hour at this rate; the boy would fall out before then, spent, and they would lose him for the rest of the afternoon, probably tomorrow as well, simply because his father had arbitrarily decided they would finish this field before he let any food out to the field. What could be done? Nothing, nothing, Odder thought, swinging in anger and rebellion. Sedder will be sick. We won't finish this field till near three, the rest of us like as not sick on empty stomachs too, and all of it because of *his* stubbornness.

He was swinging faster and faster, his rage a force he could no longer control. He was ahead of the line now, chopping with furious, awkward strokes, the hay only half severed, his scythe swinging wildly. He recognized from the sick sensation in his stomach that his father must be moving toward him; he did not know how he knew, he just knew, the way he knew when they were all together in their motions as they cut or when they were off.

You can't have everything right, he told himself. You have to make the best of things as they are. He's tired, too. He's been out here all morning the same as you. He's hungry the same as you. Get it over with, here and now. Leastwise it won't be in that muck behind the barn, it'll be out in the open. Now, he told himself. He gripped his scythe and spun around.

The sky was a crust of hard cruel blue, the prairie pastures might have been hollowed out of gold; everything glittered at him through the veil of his anger.

I'm goin' to kill him, Odder thought, right now, he thought, raising his scythe, with this.

He heard his mother, her voice coming high on the still air. She must have come down to see why his father didn't want the food. "No, no," she was screaming, "not with the scythes. *Not with the scythes.*" They held their scythes up, confronting one another across ten feet of fallen hay.

"Not with the scythes, not with the scythes . . . Graham—Sedder, Noah, stop them . . . not with the scythes—"

It was Graham who pinned his arms, Noah his father's. Sedder stood. *Too tuckered out to do anythin'*, Odder thought, hearing Graham's voice, "You hear Ma, not with your scythes. Drop your scythe, Pa," he shouted, "and Noah'll let go of you. Drop it, Pa, Noah'll let you go. Drop it, Pa—"

He dropped first, Odder thought.

He let his own weapon fall. His arms free, he ran at his father, head lowered, legs pumping to gain momentum to make the collision count. He hit his father's chest; his father tottered back, brought up one knee and caught Odder in the chin. Odder's teeth slammed together with such force that he felt the two front ones shatter. He took time only to spit the fragments out; an instant later he was on top of his father, ramming with his head, using his fists, trying to bring one leg up to knee his father in the groin. His father's fists were everywhere, smashing into his face, pounding his chest, balled into the hollow of his stomach, but his father could not use his legs, Odder's body had fallen across them, pinning his father to the ground.

I've got him, he can't use his legs, I've got him. Just one blow in the right place and—

He brought his fist down with all his might on his father's neck. There was a strange rattle in his father's throat, then silence. His father lay stretched out motionless on the ground.

I broke his neck, Odder thought. It's over and done for good now, he thought.

No one touched the fallen figure, no one spoke. His mother and brothers stood gazing down, as Odder gazed, on the still figure lying on the freshly mown hay. There was blood running from the corner of his father's mouth, blood running from his own; his hands twitched and, as he looked down, he saw one of his father's make a slight, convulsive movement. His father was not dead, just defeated. If he bent forward and offered his father help—he faced the possibility for only the briefest moment. What were such fathers for, if not to be overthrown?

Closed inside himself he had been incapable of really living—like his father, niggardly of himself, a denier of life, contemptuous of others, jealously guarding his small ways, never never extending himself, a spoiler, one whose touch made base the bright metals of existence. A tarnisher, Odder thought.

He did not deserve Emily, he was not nearly as decent and loyal and self-sacrificing as she, but by God he did love her, and he would make her a fine house even if for this winter—all right, she would have to do with a cabin this first year, but there would be something in that cabin, he determined, and every time she looked at it it would tell her how he felt. Something alive, he thought. She is so alive. Nothing dead, static, something warm and touchable, something that returns love, something that would be company in the long months ahead while she was waiting for the child.

A dog would be best, of course, but the only decent dogs around were hunting hounds, hard to come by and a good price on one if you could find it, and what with the money he'd paid for the land, more than he should have laid out, but the temptation had overcome him and he had bought more than he originally planned, money was more than scarce, it was just nonexistent. And in the spring they would need to put in seeds, they ought to get a cow, there were tools necessary, the house would have to have things they couldn't make—

Money, there it was, always intruding, spoiling everything. The meanest and most persistent worry was money. It never went away, it could ruin most of the good and decent things in life, even things that did not cost, like the magnificence of this day, his pleasure at the thought of a pet for Emily, even the whole concept of the life he and Emily had ahead.

Get the cabin finished, he thought, then figure me a way to make money. There's always trapping, he thought. The woods would provide. Deer, bear, beaver, raccoon, otter, marten, mink, fox, even wolves—meat and skins; grease for frying, for soap and light bait, barter, and covering for the beds. The air provided grouse, turkey, geese, pigeons, ducks; the lake and rivers were filled with fish—trout, eels, bass, mussels.

I should be able to get us enough skins this winter to—and he felt better, a man with a plan always felt he had the future under some kind of control.

III

He trudged the spiny ridge of the mountain, barely conscious now of the loveliness of the lake, the gathering of the morning below; yet it was impossible to ignore for long. From where he stood he looked all the way across the point, over which an early morning blue haze now hung, across the two large islands at the end of the cove, all the way over to Algonquintown and the settlement of shacks, Burroughs' store, that meant "civilization." Let others have it, all of it: hypocrisy, betrayal, lies, cheating, deceits, the whole corrupt corner staked out as theirs. This was his.

Salt, milled grain and tools, stock—*that* was also civilization, he reminded himself, and he would never be able, no matter how hard he tried to be self-sufficient, to do without those, and because he would have to deal with men to get these, he would be tainted. He knew from the long years of knocking about what money could do to a man's morality. He had had one good friend in all his life and that friend and he had been at each other's throats over five dollars. At the time Odder had told himself it was not the five dollars, but the principle involved; but the fact was it *was* the five dollars; otherwise he wouldn't have cared that his friend had taken it. It cost money just to breathe: all the accoutrements and supports you needed to be allowed just to arise and walk about were exhaustingly expensive. Needs never ended and needs meant money to satisfy them.

They would have to have a cow, for instance. He could hardly invent that. Or make it. Or wish it out of thin air. Couldn't trap it. Might steal it, but that begged the point. To be owner of a cow meant that he had to have a certain amount of money to purchase it, to keep it alive. It ate, it got sick, it needed halters, harnesses. Why did he have to have a cow? Well, on his own he could have got along perfectly well without one. But the point—the *very* point—was that he was no longer on his own; in the course of the way events in a man's life moved, he had been moved: he was about to become a family man. A family man had to extend himself. Emily would need milk. Hence, the cow. And he ought to think about sheep, for wool; pigs for the larder; oxen, for farming. His life began to grow complicated, and more expensive. Making money—the need for making money —piled up. He was getting "caughter" and "caughter." All because a girl had looked at him in a certain way and laughed. Instinct had, maybe, had the last laugh.

If he was going to farm, no way out of buying oxen anyway. They were easy keepers, they were easy to yoke for heavy work, and in an emergency (God knew, he foresaw enough of these to make a few practical plans), an ox made better eating than a horse. The hide could also be salvaged and used. Yet for all their practicality, they would never, to Odder's mind, come anywhere near being a pleasure the way a horse was. Oxen were like valley people, something fundamental missing in them, something admirable and exciting and unpredictable. A dimension a man couldn't quite put his hands on. Horses had *character*.

Just as the men who lived in the mountains were a different breed from those who squatted in the valley—perhaps there was something about the mountains that forced the men who lived with them to form stronger characters and superior strength. At least Odder chose to believe so. The effort required to deal with hostile land was herculean, but the broader outlook on the world which the mountains gave back more than compensated for the strength expended to subdue them. Odder even believed mountain water was purer, the food grown in its soil stronger, and a man was as much what he ate and drank as anything else.

The house, he told himself, has to wait, you know that, stop wool-gathering and get to work on plans for the cabin.

He had been turning over various designs in his mind and, now, pausing briefly, scuffing the autumn-hardening earth with his foot, he let his mind drift toward a decision; he didn't make a decision, it just more or less came. He would model his cabin on those Swedish ones that had been built along the Delaware, the ones so popular later with the Germans in Pennsylvania and the Scotch-Irish pioneers on the frontier. He had always admired the cabins those people put up: rough though they were, they were extremely durable, far superior to the bark-roofed dugouts and wattle-and-daub buildings supported by crotchets so many settlers threw together, to say nothing of the primitive bark and woven-matting wigwams of the trappers and hunters. Emily certainly wasn't going to live in something thrown together, no matter how hard pressed they were.

Like his father again, wanting his building to be permanent, to say something about the kind of man he was.

Well, why not? With just an axe a man could erect a very substantial dwelling. The axe was more important than a gun, a hoe, a spade, or even that scythe that Odder had left behind and still thought of with pain. You didn't carry bulky scythes when you went alone on the road. He wondered if anyone back there in Ohio ever used it and, using it, paused and read *O Buttes, 1795,* and remembered for a moment who he was.

He had taken very little with him when he left his family, but he had carried an axe. An axe felled trees to clear land for planting; it could build a log house. With a good axe a man could go right into the midst of the wilderness and begin clearing and building. With that one single tool he could begin to master the environment around him. He could make traps and snares with which to catch game; he could cut down trees, he could construct a shelter; he could cut and clear fields; and he could, if he was careful, hold the bright blade in his palm and use his axe like a knife to whittle nice things to comfort himself with, for a man needed those "extras," things some people said you didn't need, but which you did, things that filled the imagination and gave the mind's eye something to feed on.

He would use an axe now to fit together the cabin—cut the logs the right size, fit them together in a uniform stack, the ends notched to interlock, and the logs slightly flattened so they would fit together snugly. He would use hemlock bark for the roof. The axe would make a fence, too, to keep the cow close to home. Fences would keep his own animals in and wolves and bobcats out, would prevent the deer from coming into his garden to forage. Later when the land was cleared of stones, the stones would make property boundaries and eventually replace crude stumps pulled together for fences, but in the meantime, he could hold Arthur and the cow in with a big stump fence with railing in between.

He began the morning working hard, with purpose, and by the end of the fifth such Indian autumn morning, he had the chimney for his cabin up, the sides more than half raised. He imagined Emily opening the door to the cabin and stepping onto the clay floor, the smell of newly cut pine welcoming her. She would smile when she saw the deacon seat he was working on nights and hoped to have finished right along with the cabin. He hoped he could get a table made by that time, too. He wanted everything to be ready, to be right. He was just sorry that they had to make do with a clay floor, but there was no point in setting in logs or getting boards from Guthrie for just one season. He was dissatisfied, too, with the greased paper windows, but glass was out of the question. He would put a small borning room off the kitchen before hard winter hit to make up to her these primitive aspects of her life and if there was time—but time was getting awfully short, he realized.

He found himself now pausing, looking, listening, waiting for her. He was pretty sure she'd come by lake if she and Guthrie had found a preacher. It was much faster than trying to go around the lake overland on Arthur. So, if he saw a canoe headed toward Blue Point, that would mean the trip had been a success. Very few trappers and hunters pulled in on this side of the lake. And not this time of the year, they'd be up north already laying out camps and getting their traps ready. People had quit coming, too, to look at his fool scheme to put a house up at the edge of the lake and to lay out a farm. Heard about Emily, he supposed. News always travels fast, news like that anyway. You take a lone girl out in the wilderness and you let her find a man, that kind of thing travels like forest fire.

On the other hand, if he heard the sound of breaking brush in the woods, that would mean she'd come by horse and they were in trouble. He kept scanning the radiant ribbon of lake, but the only activity came from a couple of boats moving north early in the morning, trappers getting a late start.

Be good to hear, too, what was happening outside. He'd been so bound up in his work he'd forgotten the world outside. On second thought, maybe that was better. Only news that sifted through was usually bad news, the kind that unsettled a man because it had to do with things he couldn't control but which were apt to influence his way of living. Let the world stay away. He wanted to feel he could control his own life and when the news from outside came in, he was robbed of that illusion. So long as he and Emily were here by themselves, with an occasional visit from Guthrie, they got along all right. He wanted to hold onto that.

She had been gone little more than a week; yet the loneliness inside him was terrible, that first euphoric feeling of freedom had died out, to be replaced with a sense of loss and deprivation. The effort of boiling water, eating the hard cornmeal cakes, of lying down alone and looking up through the tall fringed pine treetops toward the dancing stars, stars making a sudden demand on him to understand the universe, the vast incomprehensible earth and sky, the firmaments around him, to understand himself, and Emily, her place in his life—it all seemed too complex. He was afraid in his smallness and lay alone on the hard earth and wished for his woman to press close to. In her warmth his fears and anxieties faded; it was an unmanning feeling to acknowledge how much he had become dependent upon her; his insignificance in the face of the multiplicity of the world around him intensified the knowledge that it was she in the end who upheld him, that only with her did he feel stronger than that vast world that he lay looking up at, stronger and superior— a little strutter under the stars, he thought amusedly, because a woman kept me warm and unafraid.

A man was so afraid to die and yet so often glad to shut the world out with sleep.

He wondered what kind of preacher she would get. He and Emily had never talked about religion. Too busy. He didn't even know what she was. Papist? Irish mostly were. He wasn't quite sure what he himself might have been called. The Butteses were never what you'd call a formal religious family. His father saw to it they did their duty (his father always saw to that, Odder thought) as far as the church was concerned, they went to the Sunday doings and picked up the Bible learning that was necessary; but about real religion, there was little concern in his father's house. About the only time Odder could remember hearing the name of God mentioned was in connection with an ornery cow being cussed out or an unruly boy whose behavior was held up to the Almighty as an example of ingratitude; deep thinking, Odder supposed, wasn't a Buttes attribute. Deep believing— he wondered about that. *How deep did thoughts go?* In the end maybe that was what counted, to see into yourself, then maybe you could see into others, understand a little the whole make-up of the world around you.

Sleep would never come this way, and he needed sleep if he was to work well. He was all twisted up. A moment before he had been saying that "seeing inside" was what a man ought to put in prime importance. Now he wanted to push down that seeing because it was becoming too troubling.

He sat up. The fire had died down, a few sparks glowed, orange in the darkness. He felt, looking at them, less alone, and he roused himself and went to the fire, stirring it up, adding twigs and some small branches. There were just too many demands made on a man, that was the sum of it. A man couldn't fix his attention on all of them at the same time and the ones he neglected made him feel uncomfortable.

He stood under the stars trying to understand, and not understanding, a man who could not decide what orders of importance the demands inside himself had.

Emily had tamed two or three chipmunks. They would scamper from log to log, nervous and alert, full of high, querulous advice, while Emily prepared a meal. As soon as she sat down, they would run all over her, pestering her for something to eat. Emily always broke off bits of cornmeal and threw the crumbs out, laughed as they fought for their share, shoving crumbs into the pouches of their cheeks, squabbling, scrapping shamelessly. She would lean forward and cluck to them, her voice low-pitched in contrast to their high scolding, but remarkably like theirs in intonation and inflection. When Emily began to chuckle at them, they stopped whatever they were doing and sat up on their hind legs, their bright knowing eyes fixed on her. They came close to Odder, but they never let him touch them. Yet they ran all over Emily. She had broken up almost all her cornbread for them her last night. "They have to fatten," she said, "for when they go underground." She had smiled, but he could tell she would be sad when they went. They were companions for her. What puzzled him though was the way she talked to them. Why didn't she whisper, the way she did with Arthur?

He asked her about it. "Only to the big animals, the horses, the cows, the bull," she said. "Only big animals understand. Arthur understands, Paul understands, but these little ones, no, they can't understand."

It bothered him she could get so close to animals, tame them so easily, and he couldn't. But of course she never demanded anything of them, never seemed actually to make her wants a contest of will against theirs; what she entered into was some kind of reciprocal arrangement he did not even begin to understand, where no actual demands were made, but certain things were expected as a matter of course, were taken for granted. It never seemed to occur to her, for example, that Arthur might kick. She admitted the possibility, but the actuality was beyond her. "I know when he has

69

his bad days," she said. "I know when you have yours, so why wouldn't I know when he has his? I stay out of this way on his bad days just the way I stay out of yours on yours."

He gave it up. Apparently she made no distinction between the behavior of Arthur and himself, and perhaps there was none. But still—*still* . . .

It bothered him more and more that she should have this secret world of understanding with animals. He didn't exactly resent her knowledge, but he wasn't exactly happy about it either. If she had wanted to give him an animal, for instance, she would have simply tamed one, with no trouble at all. One of those "monkeys" of hers, probably; he understood why she called the 'coons that: he had begun to look forward nights to the dusk and the coming of the ring of eyes, the raccoons. They came every night, hoping for scraps, curious, wondering what went on. They had amused Emily. She called them "little monkeys," and told him the Indian word was *arathcone*, "he who scratches with his hands." An Algonquin word, she said, but all the Indians she had known used it.

He thought now that it was odd that she had never tried to tame one. Though she laughed at them, she remained fundamentally indifferent to their mischievousness—their getting into the food, for all the effort she took to secure the pipkins against them, the way they crept up and peered into the fire, then retreated, hissing, and fell to fighting with one another, their tiny hands so like a man's with the apposable thumb that could dig and creep and sneak, showing an intelligence and cunning that fascinated Odder. Why shouldn't she have a raccoon with its quick, almost human hands, to go through the winter with? True, they hibernated as a general rule, but in the warmth of the cabin there would be no necessity, though the animal's activities would probably be slowed down—a Godsend, when Odder thought of it, imagining what troubles one could instigate—and by spring, when the blood was up again and the animal began to get rambunctious, out it could go.

That night Odder looked at the ring of eyes with new interest. A plan was forming in his head. He could now distinguish the two ages of the raccoons, the older, parent ones and their half-grown offspring. The older ones were bigger, more combative; they had acquired a craftiness that was not altogether admirable, as if time had taught them to be mean as well as mischievous. What he was looking for was a young animal, one that had been born the previous spring, but was still with its mother. A litter usually stayed under family protection almost a year, from the spring of their birth until the coming of the next litter the following spring.

He threw some acorns and broken bits of cornbread and the usual jostling, spitting, scuffling took place. While the older ones contended between themselves over these crumbs, Odder threw some more among the younger ones. He wanted them to get a taste—and an appetite—for what came from a man's hands. Emily had told him two things about raccoons that he was banking on working in his favor: they had long memories and they formed strong attachments.

He was surprised to see how large some of them were. Those would bear watching. If they took it into their heads, they could be formidable adversaries, and he needed no warning about what damage those talons might do or how fast; even with winter fat slowing them down, they could move with lightning speed.

He respected intelligence. And was familiar with the countless stories of the raccoon's reputation for using his teeth and hands to drag a dog to water and drown it by holding its head under.

Odder threw them some broken pieces of maple sugar and almost instantly was rewarded with excited cries of "churrr! churrr!"

He tossed the big animals a new helping of acorns, and as they scraped and quarreled, the young ones moved closer to him, taking the places their parents had vacated. Odder took a step closer, dropped to a half kneel, and threw cornbread and crumbled maple sugar just in front of him. To keep the oldsters occupied, he threw them some more food; then he put a line of maple sugar bits directly in front of him. He wanted to see if he could tempt one or two to come close.

The young ones regarded him with greedy but guarded eyes. The bigger ones crouched low, warnings issuing from a deep growling in their throats, the fur of their bodies upped in danger so that they looked even larger than usual. There were eight or ten of these animals and Odder was suddenly struck by the notion that if they decided to rush him, he wouldn't have much of a chance; overpowered, he could be emptied of his food without delay.

His supply was almost gone now, and he was just as glad. He scattered the remainder to the young and retreated to his log and pipe. The job was going to be harder, he thought, than he had anticipated.

But the next day a new idea offered itself and that night he put some maple sugar bits in a pan near him and waited. The raccoons were there all right; it seemed to him they had sent word to their friends. They began their wait patiently, but soon he heard mutters and hisses. He was beginning to recognize what extensive sounds these animals had to show their feelings—screams, snarls, growls, purrs, hisses, grunts, and that odd churring sound used to keep a family in contact with one another.

He picked up his pan and rattled it, then sat, without moving, for what seemed to him an eternity. At last he saw a shadow come around the far side of the fire, approach, stop, pause, contemplate, retreat. Though he waited and waited, the animal did not come closer.

He threw no food out that night.

The next night he broke cornbread and maple sugar again into the pan, rattled it, put it down a little distance away from him, sat down on the log to wait. This time he did not have so long. The animal came directly to the box and with swift hands grabbed, then scurried back, eating; Odder could hear smacking sounds from behind the fire.

The following night Odder put the pan close to his foot. He had a long wait, but the raccoon came. He was being pressed from in back; several other animals had overcome their timidity and were approaching him.

The next night was the crucial one. Odder had constructed a large slatted cage big enough, he thought, not to look like a trap. He carried this to the fire during daylight so that it would seem a part of the surroundings, and he put it down where he always sat. That night he put the pan in front of the cage, but not in it. His raccoon was uneasy, but he finally came and ate. This time when he finished, however, he stood on his back feet and looked Odder over. He was large for a youngster, with a look that said he would be one of the last to bed down for winter and that he would be making the woods aware of his existence right up to the very end. A fellow who knew his own mind and abided by it, independent, no matter what everyone else thought and said, sassy—Jefferson, Odder thought. "Thomas Jefferson," he said aloud.

The raccoon had a name now, he had become individualized. Before, Odder had only thought about raccoons in general; now that he had a specific one in mind, his feelings deepened. He was not just trapping a raccoon, he was catching Jefferson.

Jefferson seemed to have some stake in the affair, too. He came lumbering out of the woods just as the last light of day was fading; Odder called him by name—he hoped it *was* Jefferson—and went over to the pipkin and took out some hard cornbread, a wedge of the dark brown sugar. Jefferson was peering from behind the bole of an enormous pine near the fire taking everything in.

When Odder put the pan down in front of the cage, he kept one finger on the edge, but Jefferson wasn't troubled. He came running, gobbled up the cornbread and then gave Odder an irritated look. His expressive face seemed to be saying, "What you done with the sugar?"

That was inside Odder's other hand and he bent down and put it inside the cage. Jefferson looked at him. Right up until that look, Odder's plan had been perfectly clear. At the moment he got Jefferson inside the cage, he was going to clamp down the overhead shoot. Now he wasn't sure he could do it. There was something cowardly about catching an animal like that. He left the sugar but he did not shut the door. Instead he went and filled the pan with water, gathered some old boughs and came back, finding the raccoon sitting on top of his log, washing and grooming himself. He was crooning a little tune, licking and singing and cleaning. He looked up as Odder crossed the clearing and passed in front of the fire. Then he began pacing back and forth on top of the log, looking first at the ring of eyes in back of the fire, then at Odder bending down putting bedding and water, more food, inside the cage.

When Odder stood up, Jefferson was already going inside the cage. Giving himself only a moment to reflect on how unfair he was being, Odder brought the shoot down and locked Jefferson in. The namesake of the great democrat never even looked up. He was too busy sucking sweets.

She came by boat, Guthrie paddling. Odder was up on the hill when he spied a thin dark sliver on the water, identified it as a canoe and at the moment of identification knew it was *their* boat. He went down to the lake, took off his clothes and beat the dirt out of them as best he could with a stick, hoping they would look better; then he washed, the water so cold that he was gasping when he got out. He ran around to dry himself, put the clothes back on, and set out for the inlet where Guthrie would put in. Then it occurred to him they would probably want him to go back with him and he walked the few steps back to the campsite for his pipe. He looked at the raccoon in the cage and tried to decide what to do. He couldn't go off and leave him there, it wouldn't be safe; besides he didn't know how long they'd be gone and Jefferson would have to have food and water and company: even wild things needed sociability, companionship. Left alone too long an animal turned sullen, stubborn, mean.

Odder picked up the cage and carried it down to where the boat would dock. He had decided this was as good a time as any to give her her present, maybe the best since it would show her how glad he was to have her back. He sat on a rock and smoked, Jefferson in the cage putting out his small claw-like hands trying to clutch his pants. He supposed he looked a damn fool, sitting on a rock smoking, with a 'coon pestering the life out of him, but that, too, seemed the way things were destined to be. Part, he supposed, of the whole business of having a woman of your own was to look a damn fool in her eyes most of the time.

IV

Odder had been waiting impatiently to get the logs across the ice ever since the first of December. Guthrie had told him the lake would freeze sometime in January, early or middle-ish, depending on the temperature. They'd had three sizable snowfalls in four weeks, two of them blizzards, and Odder kept hoping some miracle would make the lake freeze by Christmas this year, but this was childish and he knew it. There was nothing to do but wait, and any sensible man would have done it graciously, but Odder couldn't help chafing. He was furious to be held up. He could not even get around to check his traps, the snares and the log deadfalls in the heavy snows.

Guthrie, arriving for the Christmas holidays, told him to relax and enjoy the season, he wasn't going to get anything done anyway.

Emily was pleased at the Christmas things her father had brought, real store-bought things that meant they'd have a feast. She had worked two full days and half those nights getting things ready and all three agreed it was worth the effort. When Emily would admit her cooking was any good, it was; and Guthrie's pork was a real pleasant change from the game and cornmeal mush they'd been eating steadily all fall.

But Guthrie seemed not much interested in food. For one thing, he was obsessed with the idea that having once won its independence, the country was now going to lose it back to the British because of a lot of silly sailors. He could not seem to grasp the moral issue of impressment at all, possibly because as a land man the life of men at sea was improbable and, in the end, not very interesting to him. He was like a man who would say, If God wanted a man to move on water, he would have given him fins and webbed feet.

Odder tried to explain to him it was wrong for the British to stop American ships, forcibly remove Americans and press them into service aboard British ships, but Guthrie did not follow the line of argument. "We could settle the whole thing easy enough," he insisted. "Just git *their* ships out of *our* waters."

It was absolutely impossible to shake the old man's conviction such a proposal was feasible. Sailors and their ships were too small an issue, Guthrie said, to turn a nation upside down over. The President will do something, he said. He was an ardent admirer of Jefferson's and Odder could not convince him Jefferson was hardly likely to get Congress to pass a silly act like excluding British vessels from American waters. (When this did come to pass, Odder could still not see it as anything but wishful thinking, but by that time he had far more pressing matters on his mind and was apt to let the country go about its own business the way it wanted without getting too excited so long as it let him alone to go about his.)

Guthrie had taken to dressing sloppily, drinking heavily; he was no longer the sharp, intuitive sizer-upper of situations and men Odder had first known. Liberty had corrupted him. Emily's leaving him seemed to have cut something free inside him—or set him adrift, it was hard to tell which—all that could be said for sure was that he was a changed man. In the Village one old trapper put it best. "Lately," he had said, looking uncomfortable, "he's been sadly embarrassed by intoxicating beverages." An understatement, if ever Odder had heard one.

Emily did not like the change, though she did not say so directly. But Odder did notice that she was very pointed when she removed her father's tankard from the table immediately after he had finished eating; she did not want him to sit and linger and drink. If Guthrie noticed, he paid no attention and he certainly wasn't annoyed. When she took the tankard away, he shuffled after her and retrieved it, but Odder also noted that after a few of these withdrawals and retrievals he never took his hands off it long enough for her to get hers on it.

She was always reminding him as well about something he'd forgotten or pointing out in a voice unlike her own, edgy and irritated, that he had left his pipe smoking on the table or forgotten to close the door tightly, the wind was whistling in, and she'd be obliged if he'd *try* to remember in the future to leave Jefferson alone, he was confused enough

76

as it was, doing without his winter sleep, spending his wakeful hours more and more half-asleep in his nest, getting up to eat, to drink great quantities of water, relieving himself once a day in the dirt box in the corner, then going back to his bed and sleeping again. Jefferson, she said, did not want some blamed man poking and prodding him. If Jefferson bit, she wouldn't blame him. It was his *right*, Emily said indignantly, and what's more she didn't want to freeze to death if there was no need, letting the door stand open whenever he went in or out.

Her father remained untroubled. Odder came on his smoldering pipe half a dozen times a day, closed the door behind him every time he came in or went out, and noted with concern that Guthrie never passed Jefferson's spot by the fire, where the raccoon was usually curled up on a bed of wood shavings, without pausing to bend down and prod him with one gnarled finger, until Jefferson finally raised his head and peered up with bright, angry eyes. Then the old man chuckled. "Git up," he would admonish the animal. "Git yourself goin'. You can't sleep all day."

"Let him be, Pa."

"His fur's goin' to dry out, lyin' near the fire like that all the time."

"There's nuthin' wrong with his fur, leave him be."

"Git up. Move. Exercise yourself," Guthrie insisted, and the raccoon, resigned, would get up and lumber about a few minutes, his soft-palmed hands with the sharp prying claws exploring the cracks along the table for crumbs. As soon as the old man turned his back or lost interest, Jefferson would swing round and make for his bed, nestle down, and sleep once more, a brown and black circle of contentment in front of the fire. The only times he roused himself on his own he went in search of the bright objects he loved so much—buttons, kitchen tinnery, colored thread, an immense collection that Jefferson cached under the rope mattress of the bed. At night, instead of sleeping in his box as he had done before Guthrie came, Jefferson curled up on the end of their bed.

Odder had been looking forward to male companionship, but a quarter of an hour after Guthrie arrived, he could see that was a faded dream. He was a man waiting to be given to, not thinking about giving.

"He's gettin' old," Emily said. "He don't really care no more, he jest wants to be comfortable." She was still and sad looking out on the thin winter light. "It makes me feel old—

77

old, Odd—as if," she said, "it's like I have to look after him now, 'stead of his lookin' after me."

He saw what she meant. Well, I got a long ways to go before I end up there, he thought, and the idea comforted him. He went over to her and stood next to her, and she did an unexpected thing. She put her head down on his shoulder. It's the child, he thought, it makes all of them feel different. *It's my child she's got inside.* He took hold of her. He could feel the infant against him; nowadays the movements were easy to follow. The child was between them, but they were close, closer, it seemed to Odder, than he could ever remember, even on the day they were made man and wife.

He thought of the simple ceremony, the joining of their hands as they made their affirmations. Now she needed him: for the first time he could ever remember she seemed weaker than he. Afraid, he thought. Parents, the protectors, he thought. And hers had just fallen. "It's the way it is," he said.

Against his shoulder she nodded, silent.

He held her against him. It would have been so easy never to have found her at all. Luck had brought him to this place —and her. There wouldn't be any point without her, he thought. His arms tightened. Take me first, he thought. Or—better—let us go together. "Emily," he said in a hoarse anguished voice, "you know I don't always know how to— you know—to say things. But I couldn't do without you, you know that, don't you? I couldn't go on without you and that's the God's honest truth."

"I ought to get back," Guthrie said. "It's an unpredictable time of the year." He was right. The night after he left, a bad wind began to rise. It came up somewhere around midnight, strong enough to waken Odder, but not strong enough to alarm him. Still he made himself get up to check the fire. When the wind came from a certain direction, it backed down the chimney and sent sparks into the room. What worried Odder was the possibility of one of those igniting Jefferson's bed of shavings—and Jefferson.

January thaw, indeed—it must be twenty, thirty below, the cabin wracked by wind and cold, though the fire was up and the chimney had held better than he expected. Well, next year they would be in their house, they'd have stoves. In spring when he took the skins down, he expected to net himself quite a tidy sum. And then after the planting—he figured

78

to get four or five acres in at least this year—they would be pretty self-sufficient. Game and fish, a good supply of corn, a cow for milk (essential, most of the money from the furs would go for the cow, he reckoned, but still they'd get enough for a big kitchen stove and maybe one more, although if worse came to worst they could hole up bad weather in the kitchen), he had sugaring trees all over the upper part of the property—no, they wouldn't be too bad off.

The wind had heightened just in the few minutes he had been up. He moved Jefferson back out of danger from any flying sparks and Jefferson, ungrateful, grumbled and hissed.

He went to the door and opened it a crack. Branches were beating against the side of the cabin, battering by like huge birds on the wind. Trees were bent almost flat; it seemed to Odder far too cold to snow, but flakes were whirling, sound-less, all about: he could not see the sky overhead, closed off as it was by great gusts of snow funneled against the house. He felt as if the cabin were going to be uprooted by that wind. The paths and land around the house were hidden in white.

He remembered how the lake had looked earlier in the day —a blackish slick with balls of fog tumbling over it; some-thing strange and dramatic was going to happen, and the lake knew it, even if he hadn't. It would freeze this night; when the storm cleared, he could start hauling his logs over to Guthrie's mill. Once they were there, he'd feel better. If an early spring gave them a break, the house would be up in time for the best part of the summer. They had been happy here in the cabin of course, but he wanted a proper house for his wife—and child.

He closed the door against the wind and turned, silent on socked feet, to creep back to bed. She was sitting up, sweat-ered, pulling on her boots. "The logs," she said, tugging. "We have to get down to the logs, Odd."

She stood, forcing her foot down into the boot, a big un-wieldy woman, hair streaming, bulky clothes and big belly obliterating her beauty; but the mouth was the same, deter-mined; there would be no arguing with her. He cursed silently that relentless determination, at the same time ad-miring it.

"We should've moved them back," she said. "I thought about it, but I was sure the lake'd freeze afore we got a storm like this. I counted on January weather," she said, forcing the other foot down. "Hurry, Odd," she said. "If

79

we don't get down there, the lake's goin' to get the logs."

"You're talkin' like all the others now—"

She pulled herself up and looked at him. "You know this country better 'n me?"

So he shut up and went for his boots. He was slow by Emily's standards, she who was quick at everything, and he was conscious of her waiting impatiently at the door while he fumbled over the thick laces. But just *what* did she aim to do down there? "What do you mean 'move them back'? *You* can't go movin' anythin'."

She didn't mean to answer, she was opening the door. "Here, you wait up, I'm comin'—" The wind was in the room, a force to itself. Jefferson started up, his eyes frightened in their thief's mask.

Odder pulled on a thick coat and stumbled out into the wild, roaring darkness. Things were flying up all around, but she strode downhill as if she didn't notice or care. The path was hidden somewhere under an ugly lip of ice; two days before a wet, sullen snow had fallen; now this was frozen through. Odder found staying on his feet a trial in itself; yet up ahead his wife was speeding along unattentive to danger. He tried to call to her—there was a shelf of rock off the path with a sudden drop and if mistakenly she went over that— "Emily . . . Emily . . ."

Stumbling, cursing, he tried to catch her, but she was skimming across that glaze of ice as if it didn't exist. He had no bearings; the world was simply wind and white, all unknown around him; his brain warned him how necessary caution was and yet, up ahead, she recklessly ran on. A tree crashed somewhere near. Odder did not see it come down; he only heard the piercing sound of splintering, the explosion as it hit the ground.

The tree's falling had brought her to a halt. He grabbed her arm, turned her around and shouted into her face, anger as well as concern motivating him—and cold.

This whole damn expedition was useless, useless as tits on a boar hog—and yet she insisted, and when she insisted—he sometimes wondered if danger had any meaning for her at all.

"I'm not goin' back," she shouted, stubborn, yanking to pull loose from his grip. "We'll lose it all—" she screamed at him.

It was absurd, their standing in the midst of that howling wind screaming at one another. Snow was blowing against them, twigs blew up and smacked against their bared faces.

He was afraid a tree might come down right on top of them, yet she went on struggling. He shook her, much as one might seize a misbehaving child and shake it; she was heavy in his hands, and suddenly limp: her strength was only surface deep. "Odd," she said in a terrible stricken voice, "the lake will come up in this wind—"

For the first time he understood—wind whipping up waves and the waves getting higher and higher as the wind drove against them harder and harder, and finally the lake rising over the rocks, reaching out over the land, sucking up their logs, the great pile dispersing in an instant, all the neatly stacked timber swallowed up, the dark waters dispersing them in a tumble of foam, splintered wood, bark and debris; he would never recover them. As everyone had predicted, *The lake would get them.*

"Why didn't you warn me?" he screamed at her.

She shook her head, impatient. "It's never been like this," she said. "Not this time of year."

He could believe her. He had never seen a storm like it himself. Great craters, wind-excavated, yawned on either side of him; it occurred to him that if he could see these, the sky must be lightening. Dawn was driving through, not much, but enough to lay a hand on the darkness; what he could make out looked utterly alien, a landscape he would have sworn he had never seen before, a broken world. Most of the tops of the big pines had been snapped off, all the birch broken right in two, the heavier limbs of the maples disjointed, amputations so severe on the elms and oaks that they were unalterably doomed to come down, perhaps now in one of those wrenching gales that suddenly smashed over everything, perhaps later when the pull of their multiple maimings weakened them and they fell, slow, silent, still.

He felt the air grow colder and colder, heard the trees groan and crack in the cold, a sound like a man cracking his frozen knuckles, only intensified a hundred times over; and from below, coming through the cove, he thought, a rumble, gathering in intensity until it became a roar, the water rising and driving toward the land, the lake coming to claim his wood.

He let go of her and ran, falling, down the steep side of the hill, but missing, thank God, the cliffside, falling in holes that had never been there before, rising, swearing, stumbling on, Emily behind him, falling where he had fallen, picking herself up, screaming at him to wait, sobbing as she tried to catch up, and Odder plowing on, arms waving as if he were going to part the snow, voice screeching against the wind, legs giving way so that he was sent sprawling, then legs working under him so that he got himself upright again, hands clawing, voice still screaming imprecations, Emily sobbing and shouting behind him——

Until they came out on the point and saw it was all gone, each and every log. The lake had taken them just as everyone had said it would.

He sat at the table and tried to chew, and gave it up. He tried—once or twice in a voice he didn't even recognize as his own—to speak, and gave it up. He even tried to do some things, the simplest chores, and got as far as putting on his coat and boots, opening the door on a calm white world with sun pouring over it, and gave up.

He reviewed all the labor that had been washed away by the lake in one great grasping wave; remembering Burroughs and the others coming up and standing, shaking their heads, saying, You can't put a house *there*. Crazy, crazy, you don't know nuthin' about this lake or this land.

They were right, he was crazy, and now it was all gone, the big hewn timbers for the frame, the fine logs he was seasoning to split at the mill for the sides; the wood he had set aside for the floors, which he had planned to finish off himself. There was nothing left except the site, washed clean, just an expanse of earth down by the rock, raw where the logs had been sucked out over it, nothing left but that, and all the work they had done, oh God, the work they had done, day after day, all for nothing, because he had been so Buttes stubborn, he had wanted his house down there by the water; they had tried to tell him, all the hunters and fishermen and trappers, the people who knew; she had tried to tell him; Burroughs and Guthrie had tried to tell him; but he wouldn't listen. He was going to have his house on the lake and now the lake got it, and nothing was left, *nothing*.

He sat in his boots and stared at the table letting his mind fill up with logs, then washing them away. He turned, he had to say something to her. Something, some small thing.

She was lying on the bunk, her back to him, Jefferson curled up in the crook of her knees. Crazy 'coon, get in bed like that. He saw she had left food out for him on the sideboard, thick slices of the Christmas pork, some Johnny cake, a tankard of cider. He wondered how long the food had been there; he hadn't heard her—hadn't heard anything —in so long. Funny, too, the raccoon not getting it.

Odder knew he ought to eat, if only to please her, but the thought of chewing and swallowing was beyond him. He supposed the proper thing would have been to get good and drunk; that's what most men would have done. There was probably the better part of a couple of bottles around that Guthrie had left. But getting drunk seemed as futile as anything else. "Some winters here," she said, her face to the wall, "they go meek and mild. You usually get them in runs, two or three in a row; and then the rough ones come and you get those two, three years in a row. Supposin' this winter'd been mild and we'd gone ahead and put the house up, and then next year we'd had a wind like that, the lake'd come up, we might have lost everything."

"A house would have stood. A good, big house wouldda stood," he insisted, Buttes-stubborn still.

She didn't argue. She sat up on the side of the bunk, her hands resting on her stomach. "Well, it's no use worryin' now," she said. "What's done is done, can't bring it back wishin'."

"If a man eats, he's bound to go," he said. He ought not to talk like that, but he couldn't help it; the sourness was inside, spoiling everything. He could not think of one solitary thing in the whole world that he could look on with good will at this moment.

When she stood up, a startled look came over her face.

He could only remember that expression in her eyes once before—when he'd handed her Jefferson in the cage and said, "Here, he's yours. I trapped 'm for you."

"Oh," she said, her hand going to her mouth. "Oh." Then she straightened up. "The storm and all the agitation." She looked puzzled. "Don't look so scared. I don't even have a pain—well, not much of one. The thing to do is get the fire stoked up and water on and the clean things out—and a knife," she said. "For the cord," she said, making a face. "It's going to be all right, I'm the kind that has an easy time, you'll see."

Matter-of-factly she was taking things off the bunk, laying them aside, getting ready to make up a clean bed for the birth of the child. She folded each blanket carefully, then knelt down and dragged out the big oak box under the bed. She had what she called her "lyin'-in linen" in there, the special covers she had washed and aired weeks before. Once she stopped and caught her breath and said, "It's havin'"—then she went on sorting and hanging up the fresh bedclothes, putting the others away, very painstakingly. He was heaping

83

wood on the fire, keeping an eye on her, but she seemed fine, maybe a little slow and too fussy about making the bed, but after all she was the one having the baby, she had a right to have it on the kind of bed she wanted.

She stood up and he caught sight of her face for the first time. It was gray, the mouth drawn back in as thin a line as his mother's mouth had always been, but she didn't look like she was in any pain; she just had that funny gray color. She looked at him and started to say something, caught her breath, gripped for the bed; then she relaxed and smiled—*smiled*—and said, "It's not bad, just for a moment, and—you put that wood on good, Odder, we're going to need a big fire." Then she commenced making up the bed again.

He fed the fire until he was afraid of it. Sparks were flying every which way, the flames roared up the chimney, the logs as they were consumed gasped and choked; the heat was terrible, he was sweating something fierce—then he remembered, he still had his coat and boots on. He pulled the coat off and went to work on the boots, thinking it was just something he'd set up: to bring a kid into the world isolated in a cabin out this way in the woods, away from everyone, on the other side of the lake from civilization.

She gave an awful cry. "It's all right," she said as if she were angry with him, and he supposed she was; God knew she had every right, a man pumped up and down for a few minutes' pleasure and a woman went all those months cornered under the weight of that brief pleasuring, then had to go through something like this. Deform and destroy, he thought. "We got plenty of time, they're nowhere near close together. You want *to worry*," she said, "when you hear me call out like that *close together*." Then, suddenly, unexpectedly, she sat down, caved in. Finally she said, "Where's Jefferson?"

"With his things, under the bed—way in back. He ran under when you commenced changin' the bed."

"I gotta change these things," she said, as if he were going to argue with her, and pushed herself up, determined, with that determination more set than he had known in anyone else, and stood by the bunk. She looked down. The floor looked like something had been spilled on it. "It's the water," she said. "It's broke. Give me one of them flannel things I washed for the young 'un."

He handed her a strip of soft worn material, wool and cotton she'd used for a shirt in the past and saved when it wore through and had cut in lengths to wrap around the baby and help it stay dry. "Look away," she said.

He had heard women going through childbirth before, he knew it was no easy job; but he had never really paid attention because it wasn't his woman. "You got any idea how long this is goin' to take?"

"Don't have nuthin' to do with me. It's how long *he* wants to make of it. Some of 'em are in a hurry and some of 'em takes their time, and that's about all you can say. Odd, could you find me that long wool wrapper I laid up. I think I'd feel better maybe if I was to lie flat."

He hunted, but he was never much good at finding things. She was neat and they didn't have a lot of stuff, but in the past couple of months she'd taken to moving things all around, arranging and changing, shuffling and rearranging. Nesting. "You remember where you put it?"

"What?" Her breathing was irregular; her chest went up and down jerkily, as if she were having a seizure. Then she commenced moving her head back and forth; he saw the edge of her mouth pulled back, her teeth bearing down. She let out a cry and her whole body went into a convulsion, her hands flying up toward her face as if she could not stand the thing breaking inside her.

She seemed to sink for a moment into the bunk. Her breathing relaxed, her body unstiffened, the hands sank like stones on either side of her; she was breathing easily, regularly. "What? What did you say?"

"I said, do you remember where you put it?"

"Put what, Odder?"

"That nightgown thing you wanted."

Her body began to gather itself together again, tense, in expectation, the long rolling pain was beginning. Her hands clutched the sides of the bunk, her mouth was bared again, with the teeth working at her lower lip; her head was rolling back and forth, her eyes were closed, and from her throat a low, rising moan broke. "Oh God—God—oh my God," she cried, thrashing back and forth. "Oh my God—oh God." She half rose in the bed, her words lost in a shriek, hands beating at the air. Then she sank back; he heard her take a deep draught of air, her body began its regular, rhythmical breathing, her hands lay quiet on top of the big belly. "I think it's probably in that pile of baby things over there."

"I looked."

"Well, then, it must be under here—in that other box, the one I—oh, oh God—oh God, God, God—"

She was trying to get up. He ran to the bed and pushed her back. She struck at him, strong powerful blows; she scratched, she tried to bite; then she suddenly clutched his arm. "Oh God—God—*God*," she screamed. He felt as if she would snap the bone in his arm between those strong, insistent fingers. "Oh, Odd, oh, Odd—Odd—"

She was wet all over, the birth water, her sweat, saliva dripping; a strange smell, something acrid and not quite right rose from her. She lay against him, done in. "I feel so sticky," she said. "I want to change." She tried to get up. "No," she said, falling back, "you'll have to do it. Look under the bed," she said, beginning to cry. It was the first time he had ever seen her weep, and it was one of the worst shocks of his life. "Oh, it's so awful. I told myself I *wouldn't* carry on, no matter what, and I can't help it, I just can't help it—and look," she cried desperately, her hands pressed on her big stomach. *"It hasn't even moved yet."*

He sat down beside her in an effort to comfort her, but she turned her face away. The body under his hands shook with sobs. "I'm so sorry, Emily," he said. "If I'd had knowed it was goin' to be anything like this—"

"It's not your fault," she said. "I can't stand myself like this—screaming and carrying on. I told myself—oh God, here it comes again. Oh, Odd, here it comes again," and she grabbed his hand this time and began to grind it in hers. His fingers felt crushed in that rigid, unrelenting rotation. "Oh God—God—*God*," she screamed. "Oh, my God in heaven, *help!"*

She had pulled herself up, his mangled hand a lever; her eyes were almost white and she was screaming with all her might—one long drawn out rising shriek that echoed in every corner of the cabin.

Odder felt the whole world shimmer in that scream; it would never end; she broke off for an instant to catch her breath, and then, louder, more pleading, the sound rose from her throat so that he found himself crying out with her, "Don't, Emily, oh please don't," trying to take her in his arms while she fought free; the pain was so terrible, so intense, that she could not stay still; the only way she could begin to bear it was to move and thrash and grab and scream.

Jefferson, under the bed, ran back and forth; then he began to peer out, duck back, run, peer out again, duck back in. Finally he came out altogether and began to pad back and forth, anxious, not making a sound but not taking his worried eyes off the bed where she twisted, damp and moaning.

Odder knew no way to console him. He knew no way to console himself. The twisting, moaning woman turning back and forth on the bed was beyond their help. Jefferson paced faster and faster, back and forth; once he came to the bed, stood up, his hands clutching the sides of the bunk, and poked his head next to hers, still for a moment, watching her. Then he dropped, ran into the corner and turned his back, his head hidden under the lump of fur of his stomach. That day, for the first time, he would not go near her; he stayed in the corner, unmoving, as if he were dead.

Odder fumbled with the strings at her neck, wet with sweat; she lay under his hands now, quiet, nothing alive in her it seemed to him but those big black eyes, and they were burning up at him. When his hands came in contact with her skin, he felt as if his own flesh had been seared; she was on fire with fever, she was rank with it—that was the smell he had not been able to recognize. About childbirth, he knew nothing, but he knew enough about sickness in general to know she was going to die if he couldn't get that temperature down. He took out his knife and cut the clothes away from her body. She did not even object; another of those long, rolling, all-embracing pains had begun, and she was hanging onto the sides of the bunk, bracing, as if in this way she might hold it back. Her eyes were growing bigger and bigger; he did not understand why they were not expelled from her head; but the mouth drawn together in a razorlike, bloodless line refused to emit sound.

He tore away the soaked undervest, the stained rough pants; her body was moving now, back and forth, set in uncontrollable motion by the demands of the pain inside. He saw in a blur the dark streak, never there before, running up from the hair at her crotch over the hump the child made, stopping at the brown curled flower where her own umblical cord had been cut. The freckles on her stomach were enlarged, the skin had been stretched; there were stretch marks along the veined bluish flesh where the foetus pressed; she looked damp and bloated and sick, terribly sick, and she had started at last to scream; the sound came like something sucked out of the center of her, something mortal and irrevocable that she could do nothing about.

Odder ran to the door, snatched up a bucket, unbolted the latch with a blow and bent over, scooping up snow against the sharp wooden staves. Then he kicked the door shut, seeing the wind funnel a hurricane of ashes in the room, heard the big pot in which the water ran down now on one side, sizzling, and sputtered against the ashes; he let it go, he could always boil more water, rebuild the fire; but he hadn't much time to bring that fever down.

He knelt beside her, grasped a fistful of snow and began to run it up and down her body, grabbing up handful after handful of cold snow and applying it to the hot skin, while she tried, turning, to escape those cold relentless hands. Then as the snow began to do its work and the fever went down a little, she lay still—for as long as the pain would let her. Then the pain would pick her up again, lift her, drop her, smash her, recede, leaving her quiet until the next onslaught sucked her up, tumbled and threw her from force to force, then dropped her, broken, on the bed.

He kept rubbing; when the snow ran out, he replenished it. He also began to take heart. It seemed to him her face had lost its gray tinge, that the pains were not quite so intense. The worst, he told himself, was over.

He didn't know how she could stand it. It seemed to him something ought to break, either she or the pain, but nothing changed; the horror went on and on. What kept her going? He supposed at first it was the stubborn will to go on, no matter what, but later he didn't know. Perhaps there was nothing she could do to give up, she just had to lie there and be broken again and again, that was all.

He tried to get her to take a little nourishment, then compromised on just water; she only shook her head, closed her eyes; even swallowing, she seemed to be saying, was beyond her; then she would start up and begin to scream again, and he would bathe her, if the fever was up, with snow, or if she were cooler, with warm water. She seemed oblivious of anything he tried to do to help, far away wrestling all by herself with this thing inside, trying with all her strength to expel it and not succeeding; the dumb, disbelieving look that now occupied her glazed eyes he took to be the inability to understand how little control she had over what was happening to her. It seemed to Odder that she, who had had that mysterious and magic power over animals, must be wondering what had failed her now that she could not even coerce her own child to come into the world. Hour after hour her belief in herself—that wonderful just esteem she held, without pride, in her own ability—had been ebbing away; now it was all gone, and never again, he felt, would she walk with her head held quite so high nor give that quick, low laugh like nobody else's. Sooner or later the world makes us all come to terms, he thought. But, oh, it was a terrible thing to see, especially in someone you loved. He turned away, stumbling toward the door and a little deliverance from that destruction.

Night had come, with a full moon; under its light the snow gleamed like tin across the ridges and spines of the mountains. Below near the lake, a milky light lay on everything, even the water; high overhead planets and stars blazed down on him; the world looked clean and good and fair here; inside it was sick and ugly and evil. Nothing separated the two views—only the enclosure of the cabin and the encumbrance of a child refusing to free itself from inside the woman, both of his own making. He would never understand, never, and this was a hurt from which he would never recover, that passion and love should come to sweat and stink and screams; how could anyone understand why such pain and squalor were a necessary part of the coming of life?

He sat down under the stars, hostile to himself, an enemy. Her pain seemed to sentence him to some irretrievable loss. He considered briefly—and put the reflection away quickly—how he had come East thinking he pretty much knew all there was to know, that he had been to the bottom and had nothing more to fear; now he knew there is always something more to fear, the bottom is always farther down than a man thinks. We let others suffer, he thought bitterly, and we congratulate ourselves on how well *we* endure. It was she, he thought, who was holding things together, not he. But he was so tired and had been through so much these past hours that he was almost past being able to bring any further judgment against himself. All his emotions were upside down—he felt as if love and hate had been waging some sort of war and had ended in canceling each other out. His head hung low, his senses were so blunted that he felt everything he had that equipped him for life—thought and feeling, heart and the heaviness of his mind, the blind dumb animal instinct to survive—were of no use to him any more. There were moments when nothing a man possessed could turn the tide of what was happening around him, when he understood that any number of things outside his power to control could reach out and touch those he loved and doom them without his being able to do one single thing to save them.

Two men stood in the moonlit clearing in front of him,

dark clouds passing over the tops of the trees against the milky sky, the forest filled with a kind of singing, and he realized a wind had come up again, there were swirls of snow snarled in their clothes. "Guthrie?" It was a question. Then he saw the horse, and on the horse a figure, a woman, dressed like an Indian. It surprised him. There were no Indian women around here, scarcely more than a couple of halfbreed trappers who were left over from the exodus to Canada under Brant. "Burroughs?"

"Aye, it's us, lad," the red-haired man said.

Guthrie and Burroughs and an Indian woman up here, it was beyond him. "She's bad, real bad, has been all day. It just don't seem to come. The lake got the house," he said, "jest like you said it would."

Guthrie stamped his feet, warming them. "I brang her," he said, nodding toward the woman on the horse. "I reckoned you'd need some help. But not so soon. We come the long way round. The lake's not froze solid yet or we'd a got here sooner. The lake git it, did it? During that big wind," Guthrie said, nodding. "I feel kind of responsible," he said, not looking at Odder. "You know—" he was taking a bag from the side of the horse. "I come up to help, you know, cut wood and all, if I could." Burroughs said nothing, fussing with Arthur, not looking at him. His face was hard to discern, hidden under a fur hat, but the locks of flame-red hair that escaped made him unmistakable.

The Indian woman got down from Arthur and shook some snow from her clothes. Odder couldn't see her face. She had a blanket thrown over her head and as she went past him and up to the door, she opened it and stood for a moment calling out, Odder not able to identify what she said. Then she went in. "I sent word up to the reservation for her to come down," Guthrie said. "I figured she'd be the only person Emily'd want to help. They was brung up together, you know, her and Emily—her Ma was that Indian woman I had. I sent word awhile back, but she only jest got in. You got anything to warm a man up? Me and Burroughs is near froze. We walked and let her have the horse." He sounded apologetic. "I raised that one," he said, gesturing toward the house, explaining, "like she was my own. I cain't git it clear in my head sometimes she ain't no more than an Indian. Clyde," he said to Burroughs, "you know anythin' more useless than two old men at a bornin'?"

Guthrie turned around in his chair and stared, then turned

away, almost angrily, as if all that pain exasperated him, and commenced drinking again, sneaking looks furtively at Burroughs to see how he was taking it. Burroughs was sunk into himself, his red head hanging down. He was staring at the floor and he had his shoulders hunched as if to say, What right *I* got to be here? From time to time Guthrie raised his head over the mug and looked helplessly at him, but Burroughs wouldn't look at him, he wouldn't look at Odder, because to look at either, to meet eye with eye, would be to admit there was a bond. Burroughs was trying to deny that bond. He was wishing, Odder understood, with all his heart that he hadn't come; but now that he was here he was going to stay as far away from the hurricane of pain as possible, and that meant *everyone's* pain, not just Emily's; for if it was clear that Guthrie was suffering, it must be just as clear that Odder was—but Burroughs was not going to admit any of that suffering if he could help it; he sat hunched over, his agony so obvious even Odder, with all his other preoccupations, noticed it. Burroughs wasn't drinking any more either. He had given up, Odder presumed, under the same despair that Odder had. Guthrie was drinking, but wasn't getting drunk. Who could with Emily moaning, calling out for help, screaming, the quick break of silence, and then the gasps while she tried to get her breath; the Indian girl making funny throat noises, meant to comfort, Odder supposed, but they set his teeth on edge—yes, it was a fine picture they must have made, there in the cabin.

Once the Indian girl got up and said something to Guthrie, Guthrie shook his head. Finally he turned to Odder and said, "There any *runnin'* water near here?"

"There's the spring," Odder said. "But even it's froze over now. We melt snow—"

The Indian woman shook her head, no, at Guthrie. She needed running water, she said, from a stream. It didn't matter how far away it was, someone had to go get it. Odder commenced putting on his outdoor clothes. The Indian opened one of her packs; she gave Odder a wooden cup. "In this," she said, using her head as a bobbing pointer to the cup.

"This is all you want? You don't want no more 'n this?"

"Just this. But water must come from runnin' stream."

No use arguing with any woman, even an Indian. Part of the creek up near the little waterfall might still be running. Odder figured it could still be moving fast enough not to freeze.

It was a terrible cold, colder than it had been all year. Full moon cold. He could feel his breath freezing at the base of his throat as he gasped along, climbing. He had been all right on level land, but the ascent, though small, was steep; he was getting into the foothills, following as best he could the frozen route of the stream. Occasionally he was cut off by a tangle of growth too difficult to get through, but for the most part he kept to the creek. It would lead him direct to the falls.

Halfway to the top he stopped, catching his breath. He was nearly midway, his face bared to the wind now as he strained to see ahead. Waterfall was perhaps a grandiose name for it. It was nothing but a rush and tumble of white water over the rocks and built-up branches of an incline. He remembered the tree ferns, the little green mosses, the pebbled bed where the water quieted.

He heard the running water before he actually saw it. It was a cold aching sound here in the silence of the snow, the soft shaking of the trees which sent new but short snowfalls on the air. The cold, the quiet, made him feel vulnerable, as if his strength were being sapped by the snow. He was anxious to get back to the cabin, to the others. Out here he was too alone. He filled the cup and scooted over the snow. It would be quicker going down than climbing up.

The Indian woman took some dried leaves and put them down by the cup, mumbling something in her own language, then throwing the dried leaves on the fire. Tobacco: it smelled strongly in the small, closed-in room. After a time she went to the pack and took out a small piece of flat skin and some small round skin bags. She laid one flat skin by the fire; from one of the packets she poured herbs in neat, well-defined piles on each corner of the skin. Then she took up a wooden spoon, dipped it in each of the little piles of dried compounds and touched the water three times, as if she were touching the three ends of a triangle. She watched the cup carefully. Finally she got up.

"Did it stay on top?" Guthrie asked.

She shook her head no.

The old man began to cry. "Throw it away," he said.

Now the woman turned and Odder saw her face clearly for the first time. She was not a woman at all, just a girl, no older than Emily, or not much, he judged, and when she spoke her voice was clear and clipped, a white woman's voice, the f's, b's, l's, v's, m's and p's precise, with none of the windy, singsongy quality of an Indian. "It's not the only thing, O-ma," she said.

"Pa," Emily said in a small voice. "I'm all right—I'm gonna be all right. Don't you worry none, you nor Odder—oh God, oh God, oh *God*—"

Odder rose. Then, sat down again. He looked at the floor and tried to put down the rebellion rising inside. Why should she have to suffer so? There were some women, as Guthrie said, who just popped 'em out like peas. Why couldn't she be one of those? Why did she have to go through something as meaningless as this? Because Odder couldn't for the life of him see what good all this suffering was. It certainly wasn't going to make her want the baby more. It didn't him. He was at the point where he had begun to hate that thing inside her that would not come out.

A numb kind of despair filled his heart. He could see no way to stop the increase of her misery, let alone diminish it. It seemed impossible, absolutely impossible, that he should have to endure any more. He set his teeth and said to himself, Stay calm. Act confident. The worst thing to do with a man going to pieces like Guthrie and a woman scared to death like Emily is to lose your own control.

"Jest like her Ma," Guthrie said savagely. "Jest like her Ma—*it's the same story all over again.*"

He's got to keep control, Odder thought. He took hold of Guthrie and spun him around. "You got to stop that," he said. He took up the jug of whiskey and shoved it at Guthrie.

Guthrie took it like a sleepwalker and held it up. He held it a long time before he put the spout to his mouth. Then he drank, wiped his hand across his mouth, and cleared his throat. His eyes seemed to be focusing. Odder took the jug and handed it to Burroughs. Burroughs shook his head; then it lay inert upon his neck like a big red apple ready to be peeled and sliced.

Odder went across to the bunk. Emily's face was gray again, like a strange parasite he sometimes came upon in the rotting interior of an old log, one of those misshapen mushrooms or toadstools that thrived on dark and dampness and felt spongy and sick inside a man's hands. Her eyes, open, dark, with dilated pupils, stared up at him without comprehension. He bent and kissed her quickly.

The Indian girl took up a cup, put a finger in it, testing, withdrew it hastily, blowing on it, blew on the cup and then began to feed it to Emily drop by drop with her finger. It came to Odder that his wife was too weak to drink. And yet nothing had changed; the big mound was where it had always been. The baby hadn't budged.

"Where's that 'coon?" Guthrie demanded. He rose, tottering, bald-eyed drunk. "I ain't seen that damn 'coon since I come. Where's he hidin' hisself?"

Odder shoved the jug toward him, hoping to distract him.

"You ain't drinkin'," he said accusingly. "Where's that 'coon I asked you."

Odder rose and turned toward the bunk. The Indian girl was standing. "We must—walk—her," she said, her eyes never leaving Odder's face. "You, me—we must walk her."

"Ain't nobody opened the door," Guthrie was saying in back of him, "that coon couldn't've got out—it was Clyde done it," he said suddenly. "When he opened that door, he let that 'coon out. You did it, Clyde, you hear? Clyde—"

"I need bag on the saddle, O-ma."

Guthrie stopped raving and looked at her.

"The bag on saddle so—we left it so it would keep frozen, O-ma. The other bag. Must get her on her feet, and the bag, O-ma, the bag on the saddle, I—must—have—that."

Odder saw that Jefferson had curled up at Emily's side, his eyes big and wide and terrified. Every once in a while Emily would lift her hand a little to touch him; then the hand would jerk out and grab at the cover, clutch it while her mouth moved and her eyes enlarged, but no sound came from her chest. It was as if all sound had been extinguished in her.

"Wash your hands," the Indian girl said to him.

He washed and waited for Guthrie. He could hear him stamping and cursing about outside. Burroughs was crying with a soft, blurry sound. Sun poured in through the oil paper; outside it must be beautiful, clear, cold, *clean*. The whole cabin was thick with the smell of sweat, stale liquor, body fluids, the grease of the Indian girl, all the men's musty animal skin clothes.

"I can't find no bag," Guthrie said, shaking himself like a bear in the doorway. "You sure you brung it with you? That horse is near froze. He needs grain and water and maybe cover of some kind. I'll do it," he said after a moment. "I ain't as drunk as I seem," he said. "And I hope I never am."

The Indian girl waited, her eyes expressionless. "We must have the bag," she said, not insistently but stating a fact that he had to accept.

94

"All right, all right," Guthrie said impatiently, slamming the door.

The air from the opened door came in an onrush, clearing the cabin. Odder felt as if he had been lifted back to life; he realized that he had been weighed down partially by the oppressive atmosphere of sickness that had grown heavier and heavier these past two days.

Guthrie banged the door closed and the Indian girl looked at him. Her eyes were clear and translucent; he seemed to be looking into the depths of deep water; the lake, he thought, out in the center where no one knows how deep it is, you drop a plumb line, it runs out and you ain't touched bottom. Bottomless eyes like that. With a tiny censorious center. She despised these poor country types scratching between girdled trees to get a little corn to grow, a technique her ancestors had had to teach, corn also a gift from her forebears. The Iroquois had controlled thousands and thousands of miles of land, including this tract Odder was now settling on, more white men's cheating and conniving. Such people, such a cabin, the way such land had been sneaked away, she was right to despise him. Yet at the same time the smell of the bear lard on her was strong and repellent to him.

Guthrie came in and, grumbling, handed her the pack. It had dropped in the snow, he said, and that's how he had missed it. "Had to dig around some to find it," he said as if he were waiting for praise.

The girl took the pack wordlessly, impersonally, almost as if she were administering a rebuke. That condescension, carefully masked, but not so carefully that it didn't come through as a penetrating look, the hasty withdrawal of a hand, there was no question about it—she held herself better than them.

She began to lay objects on a skin that she had spread on the floor, a piece of darkened wood, a strangely-shaped stone, a bowl in which she lay some deers' hooves that had been made into rattles, a shell from a snapping turtle. The rattles made little stony sounds as she lifted them. She opened the big pack further and extracted small packets of dried leaves, herbs and roots, powdered bark, dried blossoms, some withered berries. The odor of sassafras spread over the room.

He wished for a good doctor with strong practical knowledge, but Guthrie had brought him instead an Indian girl with her belief in dreams and wood gods, animal spirits, charms and talismen.

He bent over the bunk and looked again into Emily's face. The only things alive in it were the two big brilliant black eyes; her hair was a tangled mass, her skin a dull pearly gray; but the look in her eyes, he saw, was still capable of pain—he was looking at a trapped, helpless, maimed animal. In the midst of the promise of so much to come, she lay dying.

Yet it was absolutely necessary to hide what he could of the truth; miracles still did happen, perhaps if she could only hang on, keep going, she might—

He looked down from her face into the raccoon's eyes and he thought he found there the same expression of bafflement that he was sure his own eyes revealed. Jefferson was looking at him as if he should do something, as if he were the last hope the raccoon had; then, gradually, Odder fancied he saw a dawning on the animal's face. Jefferson looked at him; he looked a long time; then he rose and sat a moment, his bright eyes on Odder, as if for the last time he was making sure.

He looked down at the floor and sat a moment, as if in reflection. Then he got up and began to pace back and forth nervously. He had given up hope, just as a moment before Odder had abandoned it.

When Guthrie opened the door to throw out the accumulations of his pipe, Jefferson bounded out, too fast for the old man to catch. It was the last Odder ever saw of him, a quick blind blur of brown and black. He wondered how Jefferson would make out in all that cold; then he thought the raccoon would be all right. He would find a hole in some tree and curl up and sleep until spring and warm weather and he would come back to life. His sleep would only be a small, temporary death.

They tried to get Emily walking, but she was too drained. She leaned against them and pleaded to be let alone, and when they dragged her along, ignoring her pleas, she wept in a low helpless way, Odder and the Indian girl pulling her between them, her dead weight wearing them down so that every few minutes they were forced to haul up and rest. Odder wanted to get Burroughs, who was stronger than the girl, to help, but the girl wouldn't hear of it.

Finally they gave up and got her back to bed where she lay inert, a shudder passing over her now and again, her hands twisting and turning convulsively on the bed. Her face had shrunk back against its bones; she was all eyes and teeth, her mouth drawn back against its bones, so filled with pain and despair that she seemed to have lost her lips. When Odder remembered her later, he only saw her in his mind's eye as teeth, huge eyes, grinding hands.

The Indian girl asked for some water, she would sponge Emily off. He could tell she had given up, too; all she could do now was to try to make Emily as comfortable as possible. When he went for the water, Guthrie and Burroughs were sitting side by side in the corner, the jug between them. "It's empty," Burroughs said. If they had to get through this, the least he could do was help them stay drunk. He brought the water first and then took out a fresh jug. He was sure that would last, but he was wrong; though it took the two men all the rest of that day and part of the night to empty it, the child was still not born nor was Emily dead.

In the morning after the liquor ran out Guthrie and Burroughs began making preparations to go. Nothing was said among any of the three men, they all understood leaving was all that could be done. Maybe, too, if they left, it would be a kind of signal for the child to emerge into its rightful place in the world. The woods made people curious in their instincts: having come to help, maybe the two men had had the opposite influence. Since they had not helped, perhaps their going might.

Odder saw them to the door. Burroughs was still somewhat drunk, but the harsh air would sober him up sharp enough; Guthrie maybe had never been really drunk, drunk enough so that he was no longer aware of what was going on, and for this Odder felt sorry, but there was nothing to be said or if there was, Guthrie had said it the first hour he had come. Some women popped them out like peas, and some didn't.

"I never thought she took after her Ma none," Guthrie said as he went to get Arthur ready. "I always thought she was like me, but it don't look as if that was so." He shook his head.

Odder helped him get Arthur hitched up. Guthrie would ride a spell until he felt Arthur was tiring; he would dismount, tie Arthur up and go on foot. When Burroughs came to where Arthur was waiting, rested, he would untie him, get on, and ride past Guthrie for a distance, then dismount and tie Arthur up for Guthrie to come on. They would spell each other (and the horse, Arthur resting while he waited for the second rider) until they got back to Algonquintown.

"Soon as we start," Guthrie said disgustedly, "it'll start to spit snow."

Burroughs looked up at the sky, shrugged, stayed silent. If it snowed, it snowed.

Nothing was said about a doctor. The nearest man with any book knowledge at all was about fifty miles away; to get there and back in any reasonable length of time, granting the man would come, was out of the question in this snow. Guthrie got on the horse, silent; Burroughs had already started off, the walker always beginning at a disadvantage; Guthrie looked down unspeaking; finally he started off without anything having been said at all. As Odder watched him go, he wondered how long it would be before he had to start out on snowshoes to fetch him back. If he would come back —the old, those from the woods, were as superstitious, more superstitious, about the dead than anything else.

The pines shook snow as Guthrie passed under them; for a time after he was out of sight the echo of Arthur's hooves, hushed from the snow, came back toward the cabin; then even the faint sound was swallowed by the forest. Odder went back to wait.

Emily was fighting off the restraining hands of the Indian girl, suddenly come by strength Odder would never have believed still existed inside her. The white face was flushed, the hands were like twin assailants against all the unreasoning forces against her in this world; she was using her whole body once more as if it had purpose.

"It's comin'," the Indian girl said. "Help hold her down. You have to hold her. Not let her touch herself. Hold her arms down and I'll tend down here."

Odder was too gentle at first. Emily's nails made long red trails up and down his wrists, scraped the flesh from the back of his hands, drove deeply into the softer flesh of his arms. Finally he pinned her down as if she were a man, using all his strength and for a moment he thought it wasn't going to be enough; she was thrashing underneath him, twisting back and forth, trying to break away. He was having a hard time, but the Indian girl had the worst of it with her legs. "Hit her," she said. "Hard. Do you hear. HIT. *HARD!*"

Odder hit her. Her body flopped still.

There was blood all over the bed, bright red, fresh, wet— and a head, held on the girl's hand—sticking out. The shoulders were just beginning to come through. In the moment he looked, fascinated, horrified, there was a bearing down and the shoulders pushed though.

"The cord, it is around the neck. Must get it clear. The

baby suffocates if not. I don't want to let go. You unwind it. *Wipe your hands first,"* she said sharply and Odder looked at her in surprise. There were beads of perspiration all over her face, but she seemed calm. She would stand supporting the baby's head forever if it were necessary.

"Don't pull," she said. "Must not rip." She paused, fathering words as well as life. "Have to wait for what comes after. Can't cut cord until then." She held the child up, taking care that the cord was slack. Odder cautiously unwound the cord from around its neck. The baby's body was covered with a thin, white waxy substance. The hands and feet looked blue. The girl took her free hand and put it under the baby's forehead, bending its head back. Mucus ran from its mouth.

"It's a boy," Odder said.

The child began to cry. It at least was alive. The girl laid the child down beside Emily, the cord still attached. It was pulsing. "Is there something to cover it with?"

"She had the things all ready."

"I need something good and heavy."

Odder found the things where Emily had left them. He remembered back three days before when she had been making up the bed and the pains first started. When he brought the blanket to put over the baby, he saw that Emily was bleeding badly. The Indian girl was busy kneading her stomach with an intensity that showed how serious the situation was. The covers had been pulled back and his wife lay almost completely naked, her nightdress pulled up over her breasts, blood pooling between her legs, the Indian girl's hands knotted into fists bearing down harder and harder on the now-slack stomach.

Odder covered the baby as best he could and waited for some instructions, but the girl kept grinding, the blood kept coming. Finally she said, "We've got to put something else under her."

Odder took one of the clean squares that were supposed to be used for the baby, folded it and laid it carefully under his wife's legs. "Don't touch her," the girl warned. The blood began soaking into the blanket from underneath and above.

The Indian girl stopped kneading and pulled up the nightgown further, exposing her breasts. She lifted the baby carefully, keeping the cord slack, and laid it up against one of the nipples. The child began to root for the breast. "Maybe that will stop the flux," the girl said, and began to massage Emily's stomach again, harder. The baby had the nipple, then lost it; Odder pushed its mouth up against it. There was nothing he could do and he wanted to do everything. His wife's eyes remained closed; it was difficult to tell whether she was still breathing or not, but the blood kept flowing. Odder wondered if that meant she was still alive. Did the dead bleed?

Odder and the girl stood side by side, he routing the baby's mouth back to the breast when it lost it, she grinding her hands into Emily's abdomen. It seemed to Odder the bleeding had slowed down, but he couldn't be sure. Maybe he only wanted it to stop so much that he thought it had. Nothing was sure for him any more; everything was filtered through the fever of his brain. He was afraid even of speech, that if he spoke it might in some way shut off Emily's breathing. He was afraid of the baby nursing; that might suck out the last of Emily's strength. He could not look at the girl's balled hands burrowing into his wife's flesh; their strength might extinguish what little of Emily's was left. He was all blind hope and bottomless despair. If the world had suddenly stopped turning, he would not have been surprised.

They worked on, blindly doing what they could against the inevitable. It was wrong to stop, ridiculous to go on. Yet they kept at what they felt they could do, Odder guiding the baby's mouth, the girl digging into Emily's flesh with her fists.

A strange smell came from the child. Odder was afraid to ask. He was afraid of everything. Only the flow of blood mattered to him; life was flowing away with that. And then, looking down, he felt sick. A red pulpy mess lay between his wife's legs. The girl's hands were still; a small sigh stopped the silence. She was standing taking a deep breath; she even made a tentative movement to push away sweat. Unbelievingly, looking at Odder, she almost smiled, as if they had accomplished a great, momentous deed. "It's the baby smells," she said. "It's the wax. But it's best leave it. Keep it warm. Is there anything left in that jug?"

Odder looked at her.

"For when we cut the cord," she said. "We still have to cut the cord and wash her off."

"Is she going to live?" Odder asked.

She shook her head. She didn't know either.

Her eyes were open, but her breathing was shallow, rapid and irregular; it frightened Odder to hear the quick painful gasps; it frightened him to see the dull drained eyes with their enlarged pupils; when he put his hand out to touch hers, the translucent skin was cold and clammy. She simply lay, past caring it seemed to him, motionless, pale, fighting for breath. After a while her eyes closed, and he thought she was asleep, but when he leaned over her, he realized she was unconscious; her breathing was almost impossible to detect; as he leaned over, his ear near her breast, her heartbeat was very faint and irregular. He grabbed hold of her hands and put them between his, chafing them; he cried out for the girl and found she was already beside him, looking down, resigned, seeing the gray woman, with rattling breath, as outside their ministrations.

Odder leaned over and called Emily's name, once, twice, a third time; the frantic fight for breath slowed, a kind of resignation seemed to flow through her; her eyes opened for a moment, vacant, sightless, staring; then, for one moment, they focused, she was looking at him, *seeing* him, and she struggled not for breath, but for words, while he bent closer, trying to shush her, willing part of his own vitality into her. Her mouth moved, trembled, and found a sound, the shape of a word. "Tree," she said. "By the tree, Odd," she said. "I want to be under my tamarack tree."

PART TWO

Guthrie's Book

_____

Alack so sweet a tree as love
Such bitter fruit should bear,
Alas that ever a merry part
Should draw so many a tear.
                    —"WHO WILL MOW
                        ME NOW"

I

The summer of 1816 no crops matured in the valley, but Odder Buttes had a harvest. The warm lake air kept his fields growing while the rest of the world around him frosted over, corn drooped and died, the wheat and rye lay frozen to the earth. In the fall all the valley people for miles around came to beg seed corn for their spring planting; they had gone through the worst summer anyone had ever known: that year there had been snow and frost every single month of the year. On the fourth of July the streams had been frozen over, and almost all summer the men had gone to their chores bundled in winter coats while the clothes the women hung out to dry froze solid to the lines. When the rains fell, they were the cold destructive drizzle that laid crops to waste and rotted the potatoes in the ground. Odder's getting in his crops was his vindication, his triumph over the valley-dwellers, and in some ways that victory raised his spirits as nothing had since the death of Emily.

He had a sizable amount of girdled, cleared land now. Since there was no demand for timber in the area, the trees he cut were burned, and a continual bank of smoke hung over the land; the smell of burnt wood was something Guthrie, Odder's son, always associated with the house, with growing up, with the silent, uncommunicative man who was his father.

There were cows now, and hogs fattening in a pen, his father's big mean horse Cobbie, and in the spring Odder Buttes was finally, he said, going to get his house up. It was all he thought about, the reason he went to the Landing so frequently; he was seeing about supplies. It was going to be the best house around, just as he had the best farm. There was going to be a big stove in the kitchen for Kateri to cook on. Kateri would have a room of her own; Guthrie would have one all to himself; his father would have a great big room just to sleep in. There would be a room for people to visit in (his father was very emphatic about this although Guthrie wondered what company his father counted on coming, his father wouldn't have Kateri entertain her Indian relations there and the only white visitors were Burroughs and a few trappers and some valley people his father despised and would never invite into his house).

There would be real glass windows and real plank floors and a full cellar a man could stand up and walk about in where during winter they would store their potatoes and onions and root vegetables. The windows were what was holding them up. They cost dear and his father was paying for them one at a time. Although all the lumber was sawed and seasoned, Guthrie's father wouldn't go ahead until he had everything ready; but in late summer, if all went as Guthrie's father planned, the raising of the house would commence, and they would be in by the first full snow.

Though most of the time his father was busy with chores or away at the Landing negotiating about his furs, occasionally he took time out to eat with them and during these times he talked about the house; otherwise he went his way, silent and preoccupied, almost as if Kateri and Guthrie didn't exist. He treated Guthrie—whom he never called by his name, just The Boy—as if he were some puzzling part of his life who had turned up and would not go away; Kateri he took for granted, just as he accepted noncommittally the Indians who drifted down from the reservation and who sometimes stayed for weeks, temporary foster-fathers who filled Guthrie's loneliness.

Most of the time he and Kateri ate early, his father coming up for supper after dark when the last of the chores were done. At dark, or a little after if his father ate late, they all went right to bed. Guthrie and Kateri slept on pallets in a little boxlike addition to the cabin, what others farmers would have called the borning room, but there was no birth going to take place on the Buttes place now and the room hadn't been added until after Guthrie's third or fourth year, it was put on for Kateri really, because his father slept in the cabin proper and he was going, he said, to keep things the way they should be.

In the Landing there was always talk. Ain't right to bring a boy up with Indians around all the time . . . What's up with that Indian woman, you figure? Nuthin', she come when his wife was ailin' and she been there ever since. Raisin' the boy, nuthin' more. Old Odder Buttes ain't that kind, too proud. Well, she ain't no regular ordinary Indian woman, she was white raised. And Odder Buttes ain't no ordinary white man. He wanted her, he'd make it right by her. Don't no one dare say anythin' agin her when he's around, agin her or other Injuns. Funny man. A little unbalanced since his woman went.

Kateri did the cooking and cleaning, she did the squaw work in the garden. She never complained, she never said if she was glad or sorry to be with them. Indians wouldn't. What was, was.

She had been named for a famous Indian saint, Kateri-Teg-a-quith-a, She-Who-Moves-All-Things-Before-Her. That Kateri's father had been a Mohawk and her mother a captured and adopted Algonquin who had been taken into the Mohawk tribe. Both of Kateri-Teg-a-quith-a's parents had died in a smallpox epidemic when the little girl was four. She had been brought up by a foster mother who resented and hated her, just as Kateri-Teg-a-quith-a's stepfather hated her, but his hatred was for the missionaries that he said had killed the girl's mother. He blamed her death on their wicked ways and the fact his sister had been "contaminated" as a child when she was with the Jesuits at Trois Rivières.

Kateri-Teg-a-quith-a's childhood had been miserable, and when she was twelve she ran away. She had become, like her mother, a convert. She was baptized and given a new Christian name, Catherine, which the Indians translated Kateri and added to her own name, Teg-a-quith-a. Here, at the "Praying Castle," as Kateri called it, she became known for her holiness, for the tests of endurance she set herself —holding (Indianlike) live coals between her toes, sleeping on blackberry briars, walking bare-legged kneedeep in snow, retreating more and more from the world around her into a world of isolation that seemed to the Jesuit fathers a direct communication with God.

For two years the girl fasted, prayed, and tried to bring herself into what she thought was a state of grace. She was dying—of the great Indian killer, tuberculosis—and yet she seemed somehow to have transcended her suffering. All that winter before she died, Indians began to pour into the mission begging for conversion, frightened by the fierceness of the winter, the great comet that seemed to them an augury of Kateri's coming death, and drawn to the dying girl by the report of miracles she was said to have performed.

In April Kateri-Teg-a-quith-a died, but her power continued to be felt by both the Indians and the Jesuit fathers. Among the Indians she was believed to be one of the sacred ones. And there were countless "visitations" by the girl to the Jesuit fathers; she was said to come to them in a blinding intensity of holy light, showing them the essence of God's love.

He had never needed to ask his Kateri why she had stayed. The answer was clear: because his father had asked her. That asking had been a great honor. White men did not ask Indian women, they demanded. She was a different person in turn, one with more privileges. All these distinctions were very important.

He thought of his mother dying, his body being torn out of her; she was in him, Kateri said.

Guthrie wondered what kind of life he would have had if his mother had brought him up instead of Kateri. It was impossible to imagine. In the scheme of things he was more Indian than white, really.

He thought Indian. He ate Indian: meat fried in raccoon fat, beans and squash cooked in the same pot and flavored by what Kateri called her "cooking bone." This was a bone used as often as it held up. Bones from the hominy were best; they had the flavor of wood ash and lye from the boiling of the corn. What he liked most, though, were the things she did with maple sugar, especially "wax on snow," when she poured the thickening syrup from the sap pan over snow and it hardened. If the weather was warm, he had to go a long way into the woods to get good clean snow, but he didn't mind. Half of the delights of his life, he was beginning to see, came from the anticipation of a thing, not the thing itself. When he tried once to explain this to Kateri, she saw at once through the thick, awkward speech to what he was really trying to say. She said she had never thought of that herself, but it was something to be turned over and considered. There was real respect in her eyes when she examined an idea and found it worthwhile. He wished he could come up with ideas like that all the time, but he was handicapped, he felt, by the fact his mind didn't really run to thought, it dealt more with pictures—like the horse. He would see the horse in his mind, he would see him and the horse going out together and running over the hills, lazying alongside the lake. He had tried to explain that to his father, but his father hadn't seen it the way it was in Guthrie's mind, he had only seen it in his own mind. "No, no horse you can get attached to. You git attached to somethin',

107

git close to it, and then somethin' happens to it, you're worse off than you was before. What you don't have, you cain't miss. Maybe," he said, thinking a moment, "maybe when you're older and can take loss better, but not now."

He wanted to tell his father that the Indians had taught him how to hold his emotions in, but he didn't have the words to explain how the Indians drained themselves of all thought, all feeling, and then when they were completely blank, they could harden and stay rigid forever without any thought or feeling creeping in.

Guthrie had tried to copy them. He had practiced suppressing his emotions and, like them, he too believed that bad feelings, strong feelings, were weaknesses. A man who let his emotions rule him was womanish. A warrior *never* let his emotions show, especially fear and pain. Kateri had told him stories of brave warriors who under the worst kinds of torture managed to keep themselves completely under control. They *sang* as strips of their flesh were peeled away; they *chanted* at the moment the hot coals were thrust into their eyes. In the old days Kateri said young boys toughened themselves by pouring boiling water over each other and putting live coals between their toes to teach themselves the unimportance of pain, the necessity of never showing how they felt. Nothing could have hold over a man's spirit, the Indians believed, if a man could master the power of pain.

He loved Kateri, but he liked being with her cousins best. As long as he could remember they had been coming, singly or in twos and threes. He liked it better when they came alone because they stayed longer then. When they came in a group, one of them would get restless and that restlessness would infect the others and they would all move on. Ohguesse was the one who came oftenest and stayed longest. He was a big tall man with a brown square face and very bright expressive unIndian eyes. Kateri told him Ohguesse's eyes had earned him his name, "Partridge." Like most Mohawks, he had been given one name at birth and earned another as he grew up.

Another of Guthrie's favorites, Odianne, had the name of a great ancient orator because his tongue was said to move even Sa-go-na-qua-do, "He Who Makes Everyone Angry." Guthrie was fond, too, of Cayenguirago, Swift Arrow, but Swift Arrow, true to his name, came and went like lightning; it was Swift Arrow who was the first to talk to Kateri about Guthrie's growing up. Characteristically, Swift Arrow himself wasn't interested in helping educate the child, only in stirring up controversy; as soon as the notion that Guthrie's father wasn't doing all he could to teach the boy the way of the woods had been implanted—"He has his split heart," Cayenguirago said, "and when it is sewn back into one piece, then he will forget his pain inside and look out into the world and see you, his son, and take care. But now it is we who must look to your teachings"—then Swift Arrow lost interest in the controversy and went off somewhere else to foment trouble, leaving Kateri with the worry of how to finish what he had started. "He comes, he says, he makes me see," she said angrily, "and then he goes away." After a moment the anger washed away from her voice. "But he's right. Your father don't do what's right while he is still with his sorrow, and so that leaves us to see you grow straight and right." She paused, looking at Guthrie, whom she did not call Guthrie, but Ro-de, an Indian name that made him uncomfortable sometimes when white people were around. "There is much that he denies his heart to feel or say—just as there are many things he has put away from himself, buried them when he buried your Mama—your Mama's Pa, O-ma, and your Mama's horse, which he sent away so that he would not have to see him—" When she broke off, Guthrie thought it was because she knew and was afraid he recognized that if he could have done so, his father would have sent him away, too, far, far away where his presence could no longer recall to Odder Buttes that terrible winter night when Guthrie's coming into the world here at his father's farm had killed the one person his father had ever loved.

"We must straighten you," she said, "and prune you right." She went to the fire and threw some tobacco leaves on it. The tobacco was not an offering to the spirits; it was to clear her head and calm her passions so that she might better see the path where true wisdom lay.

The sizzle, the scent, the smoke brought a look of satisfaction to her face. "Ohguesse will come. Cayenguirago has gone, as always at the moment he comes he is preparing to go, but when Ohguesse comes, he comes for a reason, and he stays until his reason is finished."

She had great faith in Ohguesse. She said men with such eyes saw more than other men, that Ohguesse was wise beyond simple sight; he could see, she said, into the heart of a thing and understand what others didn't even know existed.

In time Guthrie agreed with her. It seemed to him that Ohguesse was able to make more of things than anyone he had ever known. Take the bow, for instance. Anyone else would have thought learning how to use the bow was enough in itself. Not Ohguesse. "It will teach you patience and cunning," he said. "It will let you learn how far you can take yourself, how much you can rely on your body. Skills come from training the body to do what the mind wants. Some men's minds are lazy and will not carry them very far, and some men feel safe when they come up to the company of most of their fellow-men, but a few men cannot rest until they have pushed themselves to a place where no one else has been. The bow will show you which kind of man you are."

Ohguesse made a fine bow for Guthrie. About three feet long, it made an arch, then bent in, then came out in another arc that repeated the pattern of the first. The arrows had been beautifully feathered.

The feathering was spiral to give balance during flight, but Ohguesse typically had cared for more than the feather's principal purpose; he liked things to be beautiful as well as useful. He gave the boy the unstrung bow to hold. When Guthrie tried to bend the bow, he found it so heavy that he could not move it. He was ashamed for Ohguesse to see how weak he was, but when he looked up he saw the Indian was not looking at him. He was laying out arrows. "The bow is reserved for hunting," he said. "The bow does not go to war. Some," he said contemptuously, "like our enemies of old, the Algonquins, used it for war, but never the Iroquois. The Iroquois has *orgajewa*, his club, and *ganerrgoodusha*, the weapon of deerhorn which, when you understand the bow, you will then come to know.

"The good hunter has love for the bow and love for the animals he has made the bow for. The good hunter does not kill animals without first making an offering to the fire nor without giving the animal spirits warning. The good hunter does not kill the deer who swims nor the doe with fawn; and when he does kill, the good hunter does not forget to thank the spirit of the animal for the meat he eats."

The arrows lay in a neat row, side by side, barely touching. "Now," Ohguesse said, "I am going to help you string the bow. Today we shall shoot together, and tomorrow, and the day after. Many days we will shoot together, will hold the bow together until the time comes you do not realize my hands are no longer on the wood guiding you, that you are now shooting alone without knowing it."

Ohguesse stayed a long time that spring teaching Guthrie

how to use the bow, camped up near the tamarack, Guthrie's mother's tree; when the wind was right, the sooty smell of his early morning fire drifted down toward the cabin; otherwise they would not have known he was about. Ohguesse fished and hunted, left most of his catch for them, but he never came in the house. Often Kateri went up to his camp to smoke and talk. Sometimes she took Guthrie, and the three of them squatted Indian-fashion around the hollow where Ohguesse made his fire in the morning and talked about the Iroquois. When it rained, they did not see Ohguesse at all.

Only on the days that it rained did Guthrie realize how the lessons with the bow had become the focus of his life, how he was beginning to uncover inside himself strange secrets he did not know lay waiting to be claimed. He was standing in the presence of another person's way of looking at life, a person whose view was totally different from his father's or even Kateri's, one who was perhaps more a person than anyone Guthrie had ever known, but a strange and disturbing one, for Ohguesse's view of the world was totally that of the Indian. His people might be dispersed and subjugated, sickening, dying, fallen into depravities, but he held himself responsible for what *he* was; and what Ohguesse was in his own eyes was the carrier of a great tradition; so long as he lived by that belief, it endured. And he, Guthrie Buttes, who was white, was going to be privileged to be a bearer, too, of the code of the brave Iroquois because Ohguesse had singled him out to teach him. "You are special to me," Ohguesse said. "I have no son and you are like a son to me."

He was no longer a boy. But of course he was not a man either. Somewhere in between he hung suspended in the mysterious process of becoming. And the man who led him toward the knowledge he needed to grow up was Ohguesse.

Ohguesse told of things as if they had happened yesterday or last week, perhaps a month before, not as if they were events that had gone on fifty, a hundred years before; time for Ohguesse belonged to the house of greatness, he carried it inside him, there it existed. The Federation was still living and vital to Ohguesse, the warriors of the Long House, fierce, implacable fighters to be feared; he never touched on the present, the disfranchised, landless penitents who had gone to Canada with Brant, the diseased and despairing ones on reservations, rum-ruined, cheated out of their lands by unfair treaties. Ohguesse had a world of the past, the one in which his people had been great hunters, warriors so mighty

111

that they were feared by all other tribes; men who walked with pride in long silent strides through the great forests; and in this world Ohguesse lived, alone, far away from reservations or the white man's towns. He lived alone, in the woods, up near Cold River, hunting, trapping, seeing himself the sole survivor of a great race. He could not fight in the old way but he could resist change, assimilation, conversion. The symbol of all that he held honorable was in the war club which he always carried with him; it had belonged to his father and his father's father before him. Ohguesse's grandfather had served with the British with Brant and had been given medals, which had also been passed on from father to son; Ohguesse wore these on his belt, looped with leather into the skin so that they could not be lost. The club was of hickory and about two feet long with a heavy stone ball on its end. When Ohguesse swung it, Guthrie felt a prickle of fear run all over him. It was dark—stained with blood and sweat and fear and courage and all the things that went into war, things he did not understand save that they belonged to the rite of manhood that all young men in Ohguesse's tribe went through in order to take their places as warriors.

The rites which made an Indian boy into a man were carefully prescribed. There were no similar laws laid down for a white boy, but there were nevertheless, Guthrie was sure, rules which he had to obey and tests which he had to pass to earn the respect of the white world, ordeals he had to endure in order to see himself in his own eyes as strong and responsible. In many ways an Indian boy was better off than a white for he knew what was expected of him. And the Indian boy had symbols to show that he had passed his initiation into manhood, that he could endure pain without calling out, that he could suppress any trace of emotion no matter what he felt inside. The club was one. Ohguesse's father had given him the club on the day that he had taken the tests for the warrior. He carried it proudly and sometimes with a certain sadness, as if he were aware he would never have a son of his own to pass the club to.

Ohguesse had wonderful stories about the club. He told, for instance, of the two white prisoners who had been made to run the gauntlet and how one had been awarded a club because of his cunning and courage. The Indians were all armed with clubs and spikes and they formed two lines through which the two white captives had to run. The prisoners were only allowed a long pole with which to defend themselves. They were to run as fast as they could and they could fend off the clubs and spikes with the pole, but if one was hit and fell, the two sides closed in on him and beat him to death. The first white man to run the gauntlet was dreadfully mauled, but the second, beginning his run, had struck out with his pole, upset an Indian, grabbed his war club and begun to swing. He had run the whole line smashing from left to right. The Indians had great respect for that man; they had given him a club. Somewhere in the special place in his mind where he enlarged his image of himself, Guthrie imagined he would one day own Ohguesse's club and wear Ohguesse's grandfather's British medals around his waist.

He knew that Ohguesse would never marry. He understood it in his heart a long time before his mind was able to give reasons. Finally one day Ohguesse himself had given the reason. "No boy of mine for the white world," he said. "You my boy." He put his dark hand on Guthrie's shoulder. "Women unclean. Weak. Dangerous. No man pure with women, no way with women. Women make black medicine, make men weak, make sons who do bad things.

"Be strong, Ro-de. Stay away from people. Stay to yourself. That is the only way to stay strong, to be alone. Out there" —and he looked across to the Landing—"that's where all the bad things come from, when men live together and make evil on one another. Keep away from evil and it will not touch you. Your father know that. That is why he come here."

He took his hand from Guthrie's shoulder. His bright partridge eyes glowed. "Over there, all they know is to break. Break people, break worlds, all bad, but the worst is break a boy. All boys must be broke, they say. Like a good horse you ruin when you swim him out instead of teaching him by hand."

Many of the Indians mastered their horses by jumping on their backs and driving them into a deep stream, making the animal exhaust himself fighting the water, the man on his back, trying to keep afloat. When the horse finally gave up, he was allowed to come ashore, and he was obedient to the rider, but Ohguesse did not believe in breaking a horse this way. He said something in its spirit was broken fighting unfairly that way. The horse would never again hold its head with the same untamed look it had had in its eyes before it was driven into depths over its head.

There were very few men you could trust, Ohguesse told him, Indian or white, but sometimes a man came along and you made a bond with him and that bond went beyond death. For Ohguesse loyalty was the supreme virtue. White men couldn't feel about loyalty the way Indians did. Money had spoiled the white man's way of working with the world. The Indians didn't *own* things the way the white men did. They didn't own land, and that was the most important difference. The land belonged to everyone, the Indians believed. Men were just allowed to borrow it and use it while they were here. But to the white man land was something to be owned and guarded. And money was what made you able to hold land and keep another man from going across what was held in your name. If you owned a stream on the land, other men could not take the fish that swam into your part of the stream; they could not hunt the animals that happened to run on your land. Why was it that you owned the animals that just happened to be running across your land, the fish that were passing through your waters? But you did, because you had given paper for other paper and one piece of paper said you had more right to own more than other men.

Yet all white men were not under obligation to the service of green paper. Some white men, like Guthrie's father, understood the deep virtues of the earth. They knew about mountains and water and about how small the human heart was in proportion to how many things there were that could destroy it. Guthrie's father was honorable and it was a thing you could say about very few men who walked on this earth.

Sometimes when Ohguesse and Kateri had not seen one another in a long time and Ohguesse came, Kateri would stand straight and expressionless as a piece of stone even though Guthrie knew she was bursting with happiness to see Ohguesse. "You have come," she would say, expressionless, and Ohguesse would answer, "I have come," as if they had no interest in one another.

This feigned indifference seemed impolite to Guthrie, but when he argued with them, they told him a lot of things he couldn't understand came from his white way of seeing; it wasn't natural to his blood to see. They said if he wanted to come to the reservation for the great feast he would have to act in an Indian way.

The reservation was a two-day trip north and Guthrie didn't think his father would see his way clear to letting him go. He didn't ask himself. He could see right off that would be a mistake. If another adult asked, his father would have to give the proposition consideration; but if he asked, his father would turn down the request as nothing more than a child's whim. Still, for all Kateri's graveness, his father was

114

not convinced. He said the trip was too far, Kateri could go, they would get along without her all right, and probably The Boy could go next year, he would think about it, but this year was out of the question.

Guthrie tried to erase everything from his mind, the way an Indian boy would have done, emptying his heart, his head, of both feelings and longings. If he remained calm and drained a long time, the poison of disappointment could not spread; finally he would be able to expel it. Disappointment was not wrong, but when it became self-pity, then it was not good. A good Indian kept his heart hidden.

He sat across from Kateri and his father eating slowly, not speaking. She did not look at him and he recognized that she was trying to help him do the right thing, to be manlike. In order to show her he had control he asked her when they would bring the corn in.

Soon, she said, and the pumpkins and squash. The signs were for a long and hard winter; the birds were early going south and she had missed signs of many other animals around. Some, she said, were hidden, waiting for winter already.

They ate. She asked him if he meant to begin laying the leaves along the side of the house soon. This was Guthrie's particular fall job. If the leaves were laid heavily against the house they would help keep the cold out. He nodded without answering. His father got up and went outside to put the cows up. His father was talking to them, grumbling as he led them down the path. In the barn they would have their grain, his father would milk. His father took very good care of his animals; Guthrie tried to tell himself that his not being allowed to go to the reservation was his father's way of trying to take very good care of him. He ate some more samp and listened to the cows and his father going to the barn; he did not understand why, but in some strange way he wished he were one of the cows.

Kateri let him leave the table without protesting the small amount he had eaten; she understood him better than anyone in the world, he thought, and in a way that was odd, her being a woman and an Indian, he cared for her more than anyone.

Nights were cold now, faint signals of coming snow in the air, heavy frost falling; the chill that was penetrating would get much worse in another week, the turning point of the year; soon winter would really be here. He knew part of the reason his father didn't want him to make the trip was that he was afraid of the weather, afraid of an early storm farther north. It was difficult for Guthrie to imagine his father truly involved in what happened to him. He was just The Boy—The Boy whose coming into the world had changed his father's life.

The trip to the reservation would be long and hard this time of year, Kateri had explained to him. A woman and boy could not do what a trained man could, no matter how strong and willing. It might take three days with the necessary frequent stops for rest. They had told his father two—still, his father was no fool, he probably knew.

Making camp at night was what Guthrie had looked forward to, but mostly he wanted to see the feast, the commemoration of the gift of the medicine that gave life. Well, there was no point in thinking about it. He was not going and that was that. Next year . . .

"Ro-de . . . Ro-de . . ."

She was calling him to bed. He whistled in reply, came slowly through the click of wood on the back porch, trying to hold his face expressionless. It was very important, too, that when he passed his father he showed no sign of resentment or disappointment.

His father had come up from the barn and stood with the hot barn air steaming off him on the cold back porch. Kateri was standing outside too, a shawl thrown around her head and shoulders. She was waiting for him, going, he thought, to help him guard himself in that quick but dangerous journey across the porch past his father. She had an investment in him, too, and it was necessary to be proud of those for whom you cared. Nothing, she had said, destroyed love so much as lack of respect.

He said good night to his father quietly. They never demonstrated in any way affection for one another. His father looked at him briefly, nodded absently, immediately returned his attention to getting out of his muddy barn boots.

Guthrie went into the small stuffy slanting shed, closing the door behind him, and began to pull off his shirt. A moment later he heard the outer door open and the big noisy footfalls of his father. Kateri moved so silently he could not distinguish her steps. The firm-footed sound of his father going back and forth across the room was easy to chart; he heard his father's cough as something lodged in his throat. Outside the peepers made an incessant cry, though in another week they would be gone. Guthrie tensed his ears for the

116

call of the whippoorwill. It usually began at this time every night.

His father's voice was gruff and thick with protest, Kateri's low and musical answering back. They sounded like two white people talking. Anyone who heard Kateri without seeing her would never have guessed she was an Indian. He heard her quite audibly. She said it was not up to her to give an opinion. Her father persisted in defending himself. Was The Boy *very much* disappointed?

Guthrie waited—as his father must have been waiting—for the reply, but none came. Suddenly Guthrie pictured her, standing quietly, her great dark eyes turned on his father in answer. It was a way she had of subduing Guthrie when he got out of hand, giving him that look, that deep penetrating look; Guthrie wondered how it would affect his father. He heard the sound of his father's footsteps crossing the floor, then a long, long silence in which no sounds came from the other room. Clearly the whippoorwill called, the peepers chanted. He heard sounds, but he could not understand what they were or why. Then all was quiet.

In the morning he was told he could go.

Ohguesse had told him he was to pace the first part of the trip. Not too fast, not too slow—he must make sure always he had enough energy to last through the day, that was important, yes, but what was even more important was having enough extra strength to meet an emergency. A bear, for instance, though this time of year bears were sluggish, sleepy; snakes, bobcats, an enemy—these were all unexpected occurrences a man ought to keep his mind on as he went along. The pack which was strapped to Guthrie's back did not seem heavy now, but he would feel it picking up weight all day. Eventually it would slow him down. Nevertheless, he needed the blankets; Ohguesse would carry the supplies; Kateri, he thought, could manage her own blankets.

Guthrie put his hand into the top pocket of his shirt and touched the silver coin his father had given him; then he set off at a measured pace down the narrow old trail that had been used for hunting and for war parties as long as the Indians could remember. It was a good well-beaten path, narrow here, but in some places wide enough for four or five to go abreast. At other times of the year they would have been certain to meet other Iroquois going south, but now they would encounter no one, Ohguesse thought, unless they overtook or were overtaken by others on their way to the feast.

They were lucky to have clear weather; when it rained, the ruts were slippery and the trail was muddy. If the weather held and if they kept going without too many stops, they might make it in two days at that.

They went well the first part of the morning, making one stop when the dew began to dry off and the sun burn through. It was a good time of the year to travel, not too hot; the weather was turning out to be a help to them, clear and invigorating. At the stop Kateri gave them each a broken bit of maple sugar. His was the biggest. He was ashamed she felt he needed more than she and Ohguesse, and while it was true he was terribly fond of sweets, he was fonder of his self-esteem. He put a chunk aside with his coin and conspicuously ate a piece smaller than either of theirs.

Ohguesse had said that normally on the trail he followed the Indian custom of eating only once a day, at night, but for this trip they would stop at noon, too. Guthrie felt they were babying him again, but later in the morning he developed a stitch in his side, his breath came in short gasps and with difficulty, the pack was unbearably heavy, just as Ohguesse had predicted, and he began counting on that rest. He was stumbling often, pitching forward on ruts, losing his balance on loose stones; but he kept on going using a trick his father had taught him, counting one . . . two . . . three, four . . . five . . . until he reached a hundred, then going back to the beginning and starting all over, one . . two . . . three, four . . five . . . until he reached two hundred, then going back to the beginning, until he reached eight or nine hundred and lost track, putting one foot in front of another, stumbling, half-falling, but going on until, miraculously, he came out into a small clearing beside a swift bright stream. Ohguesse called a halt. Guthrie sat down on the ground too numb to look about. His chest was heaving and he thought he might perhaps have burst his lungs like the horses he had heard about who had been pushed and pushed until the breath was completely gone out of them and they finally, straining for air, ruptured themselves. He lay down and closed his eyes and was almost immediately alseep, but not before he saw, in amazement, Kateri and Ohguesse calmly washing themselves down with water from the stream, preparing for their food. How could they even think of eating after a march like that?

He awoke to someone shaking him. He was stiff, sore, unable, he was sure, ever to rise; he felt nailed to the ground. But Ohguesse was pulling him up. When he was on his feet, Ohguesse began rubbing him with hard, balled fists. Gradually Guthrie could feel his knotted muscles loosening, a little of the stiffness lifted.

They started out, side by side, the path was wider now, following the stream until it narrowed and they could cross by jumping from rock to rock. The brush was denser, the trees thicker, more pine and hemlock, less birch and poplar; they were farther north than Guthrie had realized, they must have covered quite a distance. He was reassured, too, by the fact that while his body ached, it still obeyed his commands. The first few steps he had been afraid he would have no control at all. He even felt a little pride just in the fact he could keep going. He set his head low the way Ohguesse had his and told himself the whole secret was in not letting yourself think. The Indians were right: the white man ruined a lot of his natural power just by questioning it. By his side, her head up, Kateri walked with a small smile. She was proud of him. He had never before seen her look that way, and he put the image of her proud smile inside where, among his treasures, he gave it first place.

The sun was beginning to lose power by early afternoon and Ohguesse explained only very poor woodsmen tried to make camp in the dark. They would have a good night's rest and leave early with the dawn. If all went well, they would be on the reservation late the next day. He, Ohguesse, did not feel snow in the air.

Kateri made the fire. She piled it high and built up a good supply of wood to keep it going. As darkness came on, so too did the cold, the sense of isolation. Guthrie was grateful for the fire and for the blankets he had carried all day, for the cold cornmeal cakes and the hot tea, for his share of the jerked meat. He was dead tired, but the fire was bright, his blankets good and warm, and overhead the stars burned in the blackness like a thousand approving eyes. He went to sleep slowly sucking on the leftover hard stone of maple sugar.

Just as Ohguesse had predicted, they made the reservation late the next afternoon; Kateri and Ohguesse began an endless exhaustion of visits, introductions, indoctrination; the feast began the next day.

Only the medicine men would take an actual part in the ceremony, though all the chiefs were present. Ohguesse had claimed the right for Guthrie to be at his side because he did not have a son of his own. The Iroquois believed that when there was a place in a clan, someone—even an outsider—could be adopted to replace the lost member. In Kateri and Ohguesse's clan, the Bear Clan, there had been a place for a long time that had gone unclaimed.

Guthrie was proud to be with Ohguesse. His strong eyes went darting from face to face, missing nothing. Everyone deferred to him; to sit next to such a man was a distinction in itself. To be white and chosen to be at the side of a man like Ohguesse seemed to Guthrie so remarkable that he could not associate it with himself.

No one spoke, a pipe was passed, occasionally the rustle of wind sounded outside. Guthrie felt cramped and uncomfortable, but he forced himself to sit still; if the others did not need to move, neither would he. Without warning, an old man stood up. He bent forward and took the head of a deer from a pair of outstretched hands. First he bit into it, then cradled it in his arms; then he began a strange cry. He was imitating the call of a crow. No one moved. Inside this lodge it seemed as if a bird were caught and crying for help.

The old man bent over and passed the head of the deer to the medicine man next to him. He, too, bit the deer's head and commenced to cry out. But this time, instead of the crow, it was the bob-o-link he imitated. As the head went around the circle, each man brought forth the new call of a bird or an animal. But, slowly, as light began to creep into the lodge, the cries died out.

The old man who had first lifted the deer's head and who had sung as the crow now lifted up a duck's bill. He held it high so that all could see; then he bent forward and dipped the bill into a large vat of herbs and roots, filled the bill, raised it to his lips and sipped. The most important moment of the ceremony had arrived, the distribution and wrapping of the magic medicine. Everyone would receive a small portion. Kateri had carefully explained this part to Guthrie so that he would know what he was supposed to do. When the duck bill was passed to him and it was his turn to scoop up his share of the magic herbs and roots, he must put his medicine upon a piece of skin and wrap it several times to protect it. Ohguesse had given him a piece of panther skin for wrapping.

Singing began. While Guthrie feasted on meats and dried blackberries soaked in honey and water, and while the orators narrated and even while the jubilant dances were going on, the singing never stopped. It got into Guthrie's head and became a part of him, as if he would always carry, like the soft buzzing of some strange insect, the echo of that sound inside. Late that night when he lay down exhausted and thought nothing could keep him from sleep, the singing kept him awake. For the first time, too, he wondered why if the medicine was so full of the miraculous power of restoring life, as it had returned life, the old legend said, to the great hunter of the forest, why had not Kateri given it to his mother and kept her alive?

In the night it snowed. When they awoke in the morning ten or twelve inches covered the earth. It was soft, wet snow. It hung in the trees, weighing them down; it gave the world around them a gentle touch, as if soothing hands had covered it; when the bright sun began to melt away the white blanket and the hard crust of the earth showed through, the ground gleamed and glistened as if it had been rubbed with oil.

Ohguesse was anxious to start back for Buttes Landing. He had hoped to get back before such a storm; now his prowess as a trail-breaker and leader would be tested, especially if another storm began.

They did not move nearly as rapidly as when they had come up. The snow was deep and the going rough; they walked slowly, took frequent rests, and there was an air of dread about the march. The sky turned gray and menacing in the late morning and the feel of snow was in the air, that soft wet dampness that clung to clothes and made their skin feel sticky.

Guthrie was traveling well, he knew, using his strength fully like an Indian, but conserving, too, in case of an emergency. The wind was high in the trees, but it was dropping, a bad sign; when it stopped and the hush fell, the snow would begin to fall. Then they would have to have a good place to shelter; there was no knowing how long they might have to wait out the storm. The open places where, in good weather, a traveler simply blanketed down were of no use at all. If they could find a place with good thick brush, they might be able to hatchet out cover inside.

He went on, his eyes sharply spying out the growth on both sides of the path. They were in a large pine woods, the big trees shading the earth so that under them there was no chance for any growth to get a hold on life. The ground was half an inch thick with brown needles; the branches kept out light, but not rain or snow. Though the stand was beautiful, it was useless as cover. They went on.

Inexperienced as he was, he saw they were in trouble. To be caught out in the open in a bad storm was unnecessary—and dangerous. If they were able to keep moving until they found something suitable before the storm struck, they would be all right; but it was obvious that that was asking a lot of luck.

He tried not to panic. The first snowflakes were falling and instead of being sparse and scattered, they were thick and determined: the sky had broken apart and was coming down on them in pieces. It was going to be one of those big, long blizzards.

He thought about all kinds of things that went wrong—the weather, the land not being right for shelter, the fact that Ohguesse and Kateri had him on their hands; he thought of his father not letting him come and then, for some reason, changing his mind, maybe understanding how important the trip was to Guthrie; now his father would never change his mind again, never go against his better judgment because of sentiment. It seemed wrong for things to turn out this way. It puzzled Guthrie to see that there were so many different levels on which life should be disrupted or spoiled.

The path covered rapidly, then accumulated an inch of snow. They could not see ahead, the downfall was so dense; but the clearing was wide enough for them to find their way. When they started to go wrong, they would run into a wall of trees. That was what saved them, being in a part of the forest where the path was so clearly marked. Had they been out in the open, they would have foundered and lost their way, but the pines trapped them right to the trail.

Guthrie and Kateri paused at the stream, shivering, while Ohguesse searched out shelter—if he could find one, he said in a dead voice, they would be all right. There was nothing about his manner to show he was alarmed, but there was a certain hollowness in the center of his words that had not been there before. Guthrie, used to being with Indians and detecting the smallest sign of something not normal because they had taught him to do so, knew he was worried but trying not to show it.

He was gone a long time, too long. The storm was getting worse and he and Kateri were cold. She had spasms occasionally when her body got away from her and she started trembling from the cold. He was shaking, too, but he didn't know whether from cold or fright. Something inside him had started to panic and he was trying desperately to control it, but he wasn't sure if he was going to succeed. He knew that if he started to act scared, like some small boy, he would lose respect in their eyes, but this thing inside him which was all fear was something he wasn't sure he could keep quiet. It had a life of its own. Maybe, no matter how hard he tried, that thing, which was growing and fighting to get out, would leap out on its own and shame him.

All his training was deserting him. He thought that if Ohguesse didn't come back in a minute and tell them everything was going to be all right, he might start shouting or something worse. That something worse—undefined—was what alarmed him most. He felt that he couldn't hold himself together much longer, and he knew that when that panic inside him got away from him, he would never again feel the same about himself. He would have to remember the shame and disgrace of being a white boy who couldn't hold his feelings in.

He remembered that Kateri and Ohguesse had told him that the great warriors sang when their flesh was pulled away in strips; they chanted when the hot coals were thrust in their eyes. He began to hum, softly, to himself, so that she wouldn't hear. If she heard she would guess. She knew everything about him. Sometimes it seemed to him she knew everything about everyone.

He looked at her. Except for those brief bouts of trembling, she was standing as quiet and serene as if she were back home in the bright, warm kitchen. Her face was calm. She had her arms folded across the front of her and when she caught his eyes, she gave him a small, small smile. It reminded him of the smile she had on her face when they had started the trip and she had been proud of him, and he felt better, encouraged, as if she knew he would hold together. How could she know a thing like that when he wasn't sure himself? Still, he felt better. He stood, the snow bleaching him into the landscape, standing and counting one . . . two . . . three, four . . . five . . .

He was almost to four hundred when Ohguesse came back, shaking the snow off his shoulders He had found a small hard knotted table of brush that would do, he said.

They beat on against the blizzard and staggered down the rocky river bed. None of them spoke. They were getting themselves still in the heart inside, where control lived. When you were in one world, you acted by its rules, and when you were in another, you observed those. And if you had to make a choice? He didn't know. He just didn't know. But he was awfully glad that out here in the woods in the midst of this terrible storm he was in the Indian world.

The blazing white world flickered around Guthrie as if he were in the process of being cut off from Kateri and Ohguesse; he hastened to keep up, but even so the snow and wind contrived to drive him back so that, plunging through that explosive whirl of white and wind he feared suddenly finding himself alone and abandoned. For a moment he almost cried out to them to wait, he was falling behind. Then he struggled against the fear and bit his lip and told, silently, his raging heart to still its terror, everything would be all right so long as Ohguesse was there. A man was not a boy, did not lose his nerve because he knew the odds were against him; a man calmly took inventory of all that was working against him and said, Well that's how it is, but I'll get through anyway. Nothing without hope.

They plunged into a deep bank of snow. Kateri went down to her knees, snow blowing up all around her. Guthrie waited for Ohguesse to stop and help her but, though he had certainly seen the fall, he took no notice of it; some code of the Indian world Guthrie only had sensed seemed to be at work: that you and you alone were responsible for yourself. He must remember that.

Farther up the trail Ohguesse was standing beside a thick outgrowth of brush, hacking at the tangle of central roots and dead splintered stalks. Kateri, still rocky, stumbled toward him, stood a minute motionless, then leaned over and clawed at the bushes. Guthrie saw what they were doing—clearing out a space inside where they could nest down in relative protection. He began to claw, too.

In an hour they had hollowed a small opening and were inside pulling at the heart of the brush, piling up dead branches for a fire. He was cold and miserable, but the hysteria of an hour before had passed, in its place a chilly acceptance that probably things were going to work out all right—so long of course as Ohguesse was with them. He worked stiffly, his fingers frostbitten and his body weary, but with the heat of proving himself. To be a boy, a white boy, who caved in was a worse future almost than death; yet when the fire smoked and caught and he and Kateri sat huddled under the canopy of brush, he watched almost without feeling as Ohguesse unfolded a birch bucket, caught up snow, and laid it on the smoldering coals to make hot water. They drank that and ate some stiff, half-frozen meat; then Guthrie just gave up and lay down and died, or so it seemed to him; for one moment he was bitterly uncomfortable on the stumps of roots and in the cold blight of the wind, and the next he was swallowed into a gullet of darkness from which he assumed he would never return. Memory and action of mind deserted him. He felt nothing, he knew nothing, he lay on the bottom of darkness and sank.

Then he sat up, some primitive instinct scourging him back to consciousness. He knew again the long strands of fear that were wound round his heart and the pain of uncertainty. Squatting in sweat and panic, he looked out.

Ohguesse sat, gazing out over the fire. Guthrie felt his heart subside. It was Ohguesse's voice that had put his fears to rest. "Ro-de," he had said very quietly.

Snow flew about; darkness fell down from above. The white and black collided, Ohguesse sitting with high bright black eyes staring at him, his dark hand feeding wood to the hot light. The fire leapt up, reddening his skin. His hand looked bloody. Guthrie saw inside his own skull the crushed and scalped skulls of small children and young girls. Survival meant also the club, the knife, the victim's frightened cry under the hatchet. Love was not the only law; yet at this moment love beat against his chest like a trapped animal frantically tapping its way out.

As if Ohguesse were repeating the words Guthrie heard inside his own head, Ohguesse said slowly, ". . . pride . . . and strength . . . and being always brave."

It was the sum of his code. "I'll try."

"Yes," he said, a command, Guthrie saw, that he had been given to carry all his life.

Yet when he lay down, he was comforted and strong. Someone had handed him rules he felt he could trust, that would make a path through the dark forest of his own ignorance. Guthrie slept, stirred, slept again, finally woke with the first light, the sharp pains in his stomach of hunger. It was almost twenty-four hours since he had eaten.

Then he noticed that Ohguesse was missing. He moved carefully—by his side Kateri slept, rolled in a ball, her face blank; outside the tunnel of bushes he found Ohguesse clearing the snow, using a long branch to scrape it back. He looked up, nodded—formally—when he saw Guthrie. The snow was still falling, but much slower now; the force of the storm was spent. Guthrie shivered, shook himself, began moving toward Ohguesse. He did not know what Ohguesse had in mind, but he wanted to help. He felt keenly his inadequacies.

Ohguesse had piled small branches and was clearing away the snow for a cooking fire. The boy took an axe and began chopping the larger of the limbs into small, easily ignitable pieces. He wondered if anyone had brought along tea. The notion of tea seemed to him the most wonderful in the world.

But what they ate was boiled pemmican and then drank the water. By late in the afternoon the blizzard was over; a hot brilliant sun burst out, the tops of the trees dripped, the air was clear and sharp, everything glittered out at them like a declaration.

Walking was difficult because of the depth of the snow and because they had no snowshoes; it did not take long for Guthrie's feet to become soaked through; soon he was wet to the thighs. The sun began to dart in and out, and under the bigger pines it could not get through at all. He felt chilled and miserable, but he kept on, silent.

That day they went only as far as the end of the big pine forest. Since the snow had stopped, they cleared an area and camped in the open. Ohguesse built a big fire and soon most of their clothes were spread out to dry; they sat on their blankets and watched the drying. Guthrie's bare feet were actually hot, he sat so close to the flames. Later he and Kateri curled up and slept, but Ohguesse did not lie down, squatting guarding the fire. Once Guthrie awoke and Kateri was gone, squatted by the fire talking, both smoking and talking, their backs close together, as if they had moved together to close out everything around them, even him, as if they had a world all their own he would never penetrate, even though he was adopted into a vacant place in their tribe.

The last day they traveled fast; they were home by late noon. His father came out to see them and stood, stern, ready to lecture, a big solemn block of a man who had been proven right in all his dire predictions and now wanted to reap his righteous reward. Ohguesse went up and raised his hand. "He complained not once, not one time, He-Who-Owns-The-Mountain, not once did he say he was wet nor hungry nor tired nor afraid."

To bear suffering without crying out, to "sing" in the midst of pain, to face death so that one proved the spirit endured: he knew he had not been brave, but neither had he whined, neither had he once said he was afraid. That in itself was a beginning.

Ohguesse did not come near them all that winter. Christmas came and passed without any word from him; the new year—1818—opened and there were stories of a new family coming in in the spring, but no one knew if the stories were true or who the family was—Burroughs did not get up from the Landing and though Guthrie's father went to the Landing several times using the flat stone boat as a sled on the ice, he brought little news that was of interest to Guthrie. Adults were interested in who had deserted his farm and family, who had become diseased and died, who was beating a bad bargain out of his neighbor, who had it unfairly good, who reckoned on going West; they talked a lot about inches of snow and rainfall, velocity of wind, abundance of crop yield, depth of frosts, probable dates for the ice going out on the lake, mud week, safe planting time. They had opinions about the Governor in Albany, the President down there in Washington, D.C., foreign heads of state in strange faraway places, even God up there in Heaven with His Mysterious Unworkable Ways. *They* knew how things ought to go with Him—and never did. The things Guthrie was interested in—an eclipse, the school catching fire, a bear treeing some man in his own orchard—they gave little thought to. Try as he might, he couldn't settle down and be sensible; his father was always having to speak to him. "You got to look sharp, Boy, your mind's wandering again."

His father *always* looked sharp. He made one thing do the work of two and most last a lifetime. Wear it, work it, patch it, make it do: that was the creed his father followed, and there was another commandment, too, that was just as important—suffer to pay your way as you go. A man who got off too easy was running up a powerful bill to pay later. But a man who had his hard luck parceled out bit by bit could rest easy, knowing that he hadn't used up all his good luck before he had replaced it by some bad. His father had a strange idea that the universe ran on a big accounting book with two pages facing one another: ADVERSITY and FLOURISHING. You had to balance these two columns out. If the sheet got lopsided, then you were in for trouble. It was all right though, as far as his father was concerned, to build up an excess of adversity because that meant that the future owed you a lot of flourishing. But if you reversed the accounts and overbalanced the sheet on the side of good fortune, then you were in for an awful run of bad luck. On the whole, Guthrie thought, his father only felt safe when the two went along nicely balancing each other out.

Ohguesse came the end of June. He brought a friend—it took Guthrie a moment to recognize Swift Arrow—and he arrived in the evening. Kateri heard him in the forest before he was anywhere in sight. She was out with water for the squash and beans. They had had a dry spring and she used washing-up water. Guthrie was by her side, but he heard nothing; he only noticed that suddenly she straightened, stiffened, which was for her an act of listening. "Someone is crossing the hills," she said in her precise, accented voice.

They knew it could not be his father who was over at the Landing getting salt and tea and, perhaps, if he got a good trade on the last of his skins, ordering more panes of glass. Gradually his father was accumulating the windows for the new house. Most of the fixtures for the doors he had. His father was not going to build until he had everything ready, he kept saying that over and over. Guthrie had begun to wonder if that day would ever come.

The two Indians came soundlessly into the clearing. Ohguesse wore deer leggings that went to the waist, with a seam running up the front covered with embroidery and quill work, loose but notched at the bottoms, front and back, so that they opened over his mocassins. His medals jangled at his waist.

The weather was warm and his hide shirt had been left behind, but he had on the diagonal shoulder belt that carried his tobacco pouch and he wore on his head the feathered skull cap with its single spinning feather in the middle. His chest, beaded with sweat and grease, caught the sun and made a dark wet shine. His quiver holder with its arrows was against his back; he carried in his hand a present, a fan of dead birds which Kateri would put on the spit, roast for supper. Because there were guests she would bring up to his camp maple sugar; one gift deserved another; she would be sure Ohguesse got the biggest piece she had.

The two Indians took their time crossing the clearing. They would push themselves at an incredible speed through the forests, but once they had arrived where they were going, they would seem slow and lazy; it was their way of doing things, to show contempt for the long hard trip they had made. An over-anxious Indian, Guthrie's father said, was a contradiction in terms. But in battle, he had said, things were different. During the wars they had shown fight enough. Too much. A ruined race now, he said recently, looking around to be sure Kateri was not within earshot. And Guthrie knew that in a way his father was apologizing, was remembering how good Ohguesse had been to Guthrie. Just try to remember that they were once a great people and when you're older and do understand, you'll know maybe a little more than most men who only look at what is and never think of what was and how what is came to be. Think of how good Kateri's been to you. Kateri and Ohguesse.

As the two Indians came closer, Guthrie saw that Swift Arrow was dressed much like Ohguesse, but his buckskins were dirtier and he had on his head a big, limp, battered hat. He was also, Guthrie perceived immediately and disbelievingly, quite drunk.

Ohguesse raised his eyes and looked squarely into Guthrie's. The impassive face remained expressionless, but it seemed to Guthrie that those eyes were fiercer and more glittering than he remembered; and there was a strange, unnatural little point of fire in the depth of each. He is proud, Guthrie thought, very very proud, and he is doing this deliberately.

He caught his breath and prayed to whatever spirit reigned to make Swift Arrow go away before his father came back.

Ohguesse asked Guthrie about his bow. The bow was an excuse. So long as he had been coming, he had been coming with a purpose; now Ohguesse had come back to take his old place, and that made it doubly hard for Guthrie to understand why Ohguesse should have come with one who was drunk.

Ohguesse's Indian voice—low, strange, but insistent—drummed against the silence. His words were so slow and precise that Guthrie could follow almost all of them. He was no longer speaking of the bow. The word *land* leapt from sentence to sentence . . . "our own houses pulled down," he was saying, his bright unIndianlike eyes ablaze, ". . . our hunting grounds worn down by white feet . . . our men are not men any more . . . We are like a people," he said very slowly and darkly, and Guthrie realized, drunkenly, "from whom the breath of life wishes to escape. Because we were too few," he said, his eyes on fire, "and did not understand the greed of *one* man wanting to own the land. No one among us owned land. It belonged to all of us, the land, but these," he said, gesturing over the Buttes land, across the lake toward the Landing where the shacks clustered, "took and took and took and left us nothing. Paper," he said. "We shall go from 'your' land, we *Genherontatie*," he said bitterly, and Guthrie remembered a story Ohguesse had told him of Brand's march north when he had used the word *Genherontatie*, "the dying who march."

Guthrie understood that what had given Ohguesse's eyes

their unnatural partridge brilliance was bitterness, and he thought perhaps now he understood a little what had made Ohguesse come with his anger and his liquor and the other sad, drunken Indian by his side and defy Guthrie's father's hospitality on the one hand and put himself in a place of shame on the other. It was a gesture that meant, This land is mine, this is rightly my people's land, and you, you Butteses, all of you whites, are trespassers, and drunk or sober I have as much right here as the thieves who have taken this away from me with their pieces of paper.

And Guthrie agreed with him. It seemed to him that neither his own father nor he who had been a foster father to him had greater claim of loyalty. His father held power over him, yes, but Ohguesse held power, too; it was the love and loyalty Guthrie gave to him for all those months and years when Ohguesse had taken time with him when his own father might just as well not have been alive, and justice told Guthrie that if Ohguesse said at this moment, "Come, Ro-de, you belong with us," Guthrie would have had to follow.

But the Indian did not even glance his way. His contempt was centered—Guthrie suddenly perceived—solely on himself; he had no time for the plight of small boys. Ohguesse and Kateri faced one another, the one angry and unrepentant, the other still and past the necessities of redress; yet both straight, sure, and now in their sudden stillness as remote from Guthrie as they had been that night he had awakened in the woods to find them huddled together in front of the fire. He saw that Ohguesse had come to say good-bye permanently—but it was not the usual impassive Indian farewell, it was an angry unIndian parting, one that said, We have come to this breaking of our friendship because the time has come for you, one of my own blood, to remember you live in the white world now and because you, who are like one of my own blood, must remember you are white. You will never be a member of the Bear Clan, not even an honorary one, because I have at last seen I can never be friends with those who are white, no matter what my heart says. Here is where you belong, on your stolen land, and no sacrifice you can ever make will undo the wrongs your people have done to mine. You don't know anything at all about our world, you who came to see a feast, and went through the woods for a day or two: a day or two is not a life. How could you with your white skin and your pieces of green and white paper know what goes on in the world *we* live in?

"I am going North," he said to Kateri. "With the others."

130

For a moment he stood looking at her. Then he turned and looked at Guthrie. "Good-bye, Ro-de," he said. "Good-bye, white boy."

II

"He's an ornery son of a bitch," Clyde Burroughs said, shaking his red head disgustedly. "It beats the shit out of me why you'd want him back." He had the big stallion on a short lead. The animal was throwing his head; one foot kept pawing the ground. Guthrie recognized the horse immediately; it was his mother's old bay, Arthur.

"I thought maybe he'd see something in him," Guthrie's father said, jerking his head toward Guthrie. "You know—of her." It was the first time his father had ever referred to his mother directly. It gave Guthrie a queer feeling, as if many birthdays had passed in such a rush that he did not realize he was suddenly older, people had begun to take him seriously.

"Well, they're look-alikes, and that's a fact," Burroughs said. "Same build, same shape of the head, same eyes. Your nose, though." He swiveled his head around. "Katy gone up to the reservation on a visit?" he asked.

"No, she's gone up there to stay—for good." Guthrie's father looked Burroughs straight in the face daring him to ask for an explanation. After a moment Burroughs said in an unnatural voice, "Well, I reckon you'll make out all right."

"I reckon," Odder said.

Burroughs turned his attention to the horse. "Where you want this critter? You'd think at his age he'd settle down, but this is one hoss ain't *never* gonna settle down. Tell you the truth, I'm glad to git him off my hands. He never done me no favors. Didn't even earn his keep. You cain't catch him and if you somehow does, it ain't worth the fuss and fuel. He'd give it to you any chance he gits. I jest left him loose over to the back pasture and let him forage on his own. He's one of them hosses with a headful of ideas, all of them bad.

Still," he paused, considering, "you see him, it makes you think—well—back."

"Twelve years," Guthrie's father said. "Well, let's take him out to the field and see how he settles in."

Burroughs snorted. "*Settles in.* That's a good one. You know what they say—a leopard don't change his spots."

"You got your animals mixed," Guthrie's father said with a dry little smile.

"You git the meat of the meaning though," Burroughs said with one of his characteristic shrugs.

The horse had been standing immobile and without interest, but when Odder took the lead rope from Burroughs, Arthur jerked his head up, and his eyes began to roll. Guthrie's father gave him a smart crack on the neck with the whole of his hand. "Sassy," he said, jerking on the rope. "Always was. Git along," he commanded in a strong voice. "And no nonsense." The horse planted his legs apart, his whole body set in a stubborn, balky stance; he had decided *not* to move. "In a contest like this," Guthrie's father said resignedly, "a man cain't never expect to win unless he's willin' to outwait. It's no matter of strength, *that's* for sure. What got into my head, having him back, a natural born troublemaker like he is? Sentiment," he said. "It creeps up on you and sucks your strength. He was meant for you," he said to Guthrie, holding out the lead rope. "You see if you can do anythin' with him. He's your horse," his father repeated. "See if you can make him move."

Guthrie walked up to the animal. He was big, really big, a hand and a half over most good-sized horses, and there was a small swatch of white over his nose, not a star—though some people probably would have called it that—not big enough for a blaze, just a scrap of white that was noticeable when you were up close, that was all, but it looked significant to Guthrie somehow, maybe because the animal's whole head seemed to be twitching; only the eyes were quiet, alert and calculating.

Guthrie had watched his father work with Cobbie, his own horse, mean and cranky and given to kicking, not an animal he had felt any affection for, but one that had interested him simply because it was a horse and in his heart for years he had wanted a horse of his own. Now here it was.

He knew, he thought, what the steps were that you went through to gain an animal's confidence, but this was only theoretical knowledge, nothing that had ever been put to any practical test. He stood in front of the big bay, feeling totally inadequate, totally foolish.

One thing he had heard his father and his father's friends say time and again: Never hurry with a horse. He stood in front of the animal and, with his back to his father, his eyes on the horse, he said in a low voice, "Arthur." The horse did not move, but its eyes were sizing him up. Guthrie raised his free hand slowly and let it fall gently on the horse's neck. The flesh there ran nervously under his fingers; the horse had also laid back its ears until they were almost flat against its head. Guthrie took his hand away. Gradually the ears began to stand back up. He was certain there must be a way to get through to the animal, to establish a rudiment of communication, but did not believe touch was it. Perhaps talk would help. He knew that the Indians believed that a man's voice, if it were pitched right, could do more to break and train an animal than all the punishment in the world. He began to speak very quietly, very slowly, the horse nervously listening, its ears moving back and forth as Guthrie's voice changed tone. "You a bad horse?" Guthrie asked. "Is that it, you're bad, and won't do what anybody wants . . . is that what's the matter, you one of those natural-born badders? I don't believe it," he said softly, firmly. "I don't believe it at all. I think you're a real nice horse, that's what I think." The horse shifted, fidgeting—possibly embarrassed—from foot to foot. Guthrie took the hand that held the lead rope and very slowly lifted it in front of the horse's face. "You see this?" he asked. "This is a rope, for leading, for going down to the field. It's a good field. You'll like it. Let's go down and see the field." He leaned forward and, holding his breath, tapped the leg nearest him under the fetlock. He expected Arthur to kick out at him, but the horse lifted his leg, as Guthrie had hoped, and Guthrie seized it and hauled it forward.

"Look at that." Behind him, Burroughs laughed. Guthrie tried to pay him no mind. If he listened to the two men's reactions his attention would not be solely on the horse, he would start hurrying. Concentrate, he told himself, remember how Ohguesse showed you to put everything out of your mind but the one thing that mattered. Think of how it was with the bow. He thrust all the force of his will against external distractions, focusing his thoughts on the one necessary central idea: dealing with the horse.

Arthur was now off balance, one leg thrust quite far forward; he had two choices. He could either come forward or

134

he could pull back, settle on his haunches and refuse to budge. Guthrie coaxed, and while he was coaxing, bent over and tapped the other leg; it moved forward, but the back legs had remained in place, the horse was now "stretched out." He looked extraordinarily handsome but he was certainly not on his way to the field.

I mustn't yank on the rope, Guthrie told himself.

He shifted position so that he was beside the horse instead of in front of him; without looking, he put his hand back on the haunch and pushed down, not insistently, but firmly; he felt Arthur move his back feet a small step forward. Guthrie used his foot to tap the foot in front of him; as the horse brought his foot up, he tightened his hold on the lead rope and started to walk, encouraging the animal with what he hoped were the kind of verbal inducements a horse would like. They started quite briskly down the road. Once Arthur had made up his mind, apparently he wanted to get on with the matter at hand with alacrity. At the fence he crowded Guthrie while the boy worked with the gate. When the gate was opened, he jerked up and suddenly pulled free; he went into the field at a nice loping canter, the lead line flapping beside him. There was a chance that the line, even though it was short, might tangle him up and trip him. A horse caught in a line was a horse in trouble: more animals had broken their legs like that than Guthrie cared to remember. He ran after Arthur crying out to him to stop.

The horse turned, looked, then ran, the line whipping his side. But it was not, Guthrie thought, premeditated ornery flight; it was just natural exuberance, delight in being free. Guthrie went forward and waited, the horse running around the field; when Arthur came near, he whistled, and the horse jammed to a halt, ears quivering. Guthrie whistled again. The horse slammed down on him at a full run. He stood for a moment torn between the thought he'd better turn tail and run if he didn't want to be crushed and the feeling that if he lit out, he would have lost face with the horse forever. In the second of hesitation the horse ground to a halt, snorting. "Good boy," Guthrie said, trembling, "good boy." He hadn't really made a decision; events had made one for him, but he felt the same sense of triumph as if he had. He reached up and undid the rope. "Now, run," he said. "Run—"

He heard his father's voice in back of him. "You done that real good, Boy. I'm right proud of you." His father was talking to him just as he, Guthrie, had talked to the horse, with the same singsongy inflection. For a moment Guthrie was flooded with resentment, then a great lightness flowed through him; he thought he understood—this was the voice of connection a man used on the things he cared for. For him it had been an animal, for his father it was his son. But he hadn't *said* "son."

"He's got his head down, he's got his head down. You're goin' to come off, you're goin' to come off—" I know I'm goin' to come off, goddam it, Guthrie thought, just at the moment he did.

There had been two moments of recognition just before the darkness: the first had been when Arthur stopped dead and he tried frantically to grip mane and hang on; the second had been when he flew through the air and saw he was going to come down, face first, on the stone. Then darkness.

But it was odd—he was still conscious of sounds, of his father saying very close, "He's all right, I think, jest the wind knocked out of him," and Burroughs chanting, "That son-of-a-bitch, that no good bucking son-of-a-bitch. You'll never break that son-of-a-bitch of his bucking."

When Guthrie opened his eyes, they were leaning over him. They usually were. It was a familiar pattern. Ever since the first of the week when Burroughs had brought the animal over and Guthrie had somehow managed to wheedle him down to the pasture, the same scene had taken place time and again.

He went out and got Arthur—or tried to. For when Arthur saw him coming, he lay back his ears, turned and ran. A twelve-year-old boy, even if he was a good runner, as Guthrie was, was no match for a determined horse. And determined was the least that might be said about Arthur—he was piss-iron stubborn with a mind that would erode by the natural processes of attrition before anyone made a dent in it. Guthrie had come to the conclusion that he was just about the most ornery animal he had ever known. But that made it more of a test for him as far as his father was concerned.

Guthrie thought it rather peculiar his father would *want* to test him like this, but he bowed to the exigencies of his father's inner images. People made these absurd pictures in their mind and, absurd as they were, they were more real than what was. Arthur had been his mother's horse and that for his father had decided the fact that the horse should be Guthrie's. What his father saw was an idealized picture of Guthrie being close to that horse the way his mother had been

136

close to it, and no amount of practical evidence to the contrary could alter his father's pretty picture.

He had tried his best to live up to the ideal, but it was damn little so far as his father was concerned.

He would go out, an apple concealed in his pocket—his father had a mania against bribing animals, insisting anyone ought to be able to catch and halter a horse without any difficulty whatsoever; it was one of the things he prided himself on with Cobbie, he went to the fence and called his horse in—but short of some unforeseen miracle, Guthrie could not figure out any other way to get *his* horse to settle down long enough for him to get near it so that he could catch it except bribery. Greed was the only thing that undid Arthur.

Sugar would have been easier to conceal and he could have carried more of it in case of emergencies, but his father kept a careful count of that. The apples were easier to snitch; he felt no guilt at all about taking them and for the first time began to see the sense of some of Ohguesse and Kateri's attitudes about being light-fingered. He hoped some of their talent for lifting things undetected had been unnoticedly absorbed during his long years with them. He needed all the cunning he could muster.

Guthrie approached Arthur cautiously, not wanting to alarm him into instant flight, walking and talking so that the horse knew he was coming, pausing seemingly unconcerned, but he knew he had not fooled Arthur. Whenever Arthur saw him coming, he would look up and watch. He might be difficult but he was certainly not dumb. He stood watching, his big eyes gauging just the moment when Guthrie was close enough to catch hold of his halter; at that instant he whirled and ran. Guthrie would start off after him. If he were patient enough and kept holding the apple so that Arthur could see it (but not, he hoped, his father) eventually lust overcame the horse. But it was a long and wearing war and by the time Guthrie did catch him, the thought of riding him and being thrown again, getting up and having to get back on, riding and riding until at last Arthur was somewhat compliant, was so distasteful that he could have plunked down in the pasture himself and refused to budge, no matter how mad his father got.

But Guthrie kept at the task. When he did manage to get the horse on a rope and get him to the fence and tied, he then had to try to bridle him. He was a caution, even tied, to

137

do anything with—weaving about, kicking out if you didn't watch, deliberately stepping on your foot, throwing his head up so that it butted so hard that his teeth shook in his jaws.

And of course there was the problem of mounting. If Guthrie untied Arthur, the horse danced about so that it was impossible for Guthrie to hoist himself up. But if he mounted with him tied (and even then he had trouble with Arthur crowfooting about), he had no way to get the lead rope loose from the fence, and he couldn't ask his father or Burroughs because the point was that he was supposed to manage the horse himself. So he had worked out a system whereby he took the reins firmly in his right hand, quickly unfastened the lead hook with his left, grabbed hold of the mane and tried to haul himself up before Arthur took off. Often he would be dragged halfway down the field before he got on or Arthur finally spilled him off. On this—and this alone—they about broke even.

If Arthur ran off, he would yank the reins loose from Guthrie and run with one wound round one of his legs and Guthrie would close his eyes and pray that he wouldn't break a leg. Sometimes he even prayed he would. Even if Guthrie did manage to get on and stay on, Arthur knew the moment would come when Guthrie would let him out a little to run. Arthur would run about a hundred feet, get his head down, stop dead, and Guthrie would sail through the air and—usually—land on his head.

This was what had happened an instant before. Guthrie felt the weakness all over him as he tried to open his eyes. Then he managed to push himself up onto his feet, shaky, but in one piece, no bones broken apparently. He would have to get back on and try again.

Arthur was perhaps a hundred, a hundred and fifty yards down the field, grazing. The reins lay loose on either side of him while he ate unconcernedly. Guthrie was so weak that he wondered how he could even cover that short distance, but there was no question of not getting back on. Then, suddenly, his legs gave way and he fell back to the ground, sick. His head hurt terribly, worse now than ever before, and something funny was going on inside his brain. It seemed all mixed up, he wasn't quite sure exactly where he was or what he was supposed to be doing. Something about a horse—

When he awoke, he was in the cabin, in his bed. He had

a splitting headache, his eyelids burned terribly; his throat was dry, but when he tried to turn over to ask for water a terrible nausea washed over him. He began to retch.

"Well, at least he's conscious," he heard his father say.

"That was a real bad knock he got that time. He's goin' to be laid up quite a spell."

"I guess I can look after him between chores."

"I reckon you can," Burroughs agreed, "But not like—you know—a woman could."

"I told you, Clyde, she's gone. Up north, to Canada. She's got the right to go if she wants."

"It ain't none of my business—"

"No, it ain't none of your business, Clyde, and I wish you didn't make me say so."

There was a silence. Guthrie went on retching in the basin his father held up. Then he leaned back and closed his eyes and lay surrounded and engulfed in pain. Someone was driving a very sharp nail into the middle of his head and turning it slowly round and round. Someone else must be heating it up because it was also burning its way into his brain at the same time that it was being smote into it. He thought that if he could just blank out he could at least escape the pain, but for a long time the pain kept him in its grip, jealously guarding him from escape.

He remembered little of that day or the next except the spike working round and round, his waking, vomiting with either Burroughs or his father holding the basin, one of them was always at his side; then, drained of strength, lying back, feeling the spike go into the frame inside his head, and finally darkness closing over him again so that he forgot everything. When he awoke once more, the whole painful process began again—opening his eyes, conscious of the boring going on, being sick, darkness finally, blessedly, descending.

On the second day he knew an answer to his problems was somewhere in the pain and confusion of his brain, but he could not find it because the pain blocked it off or made it back away. Finally, late on the second night, he awoke and for a moment the sickness did not break in on him; he had a respite of a second when he was able to think clearly,

You have to know more than the horse,

and he said to himself, So *that's* it, and closed his eyes, feeling relieved. There were principles that would work with a horse, even a bad horse, just as there were rules that worked with everything else. The real problem was not the horse, or the other difficult, seemingly insoluble things in his life, but it was to find the rules that made him able to deal with them so that he could change the relationship of things from im- to possible. It was odd, he thought, how he'd never seen this before. He wondered if somewhere there was a giant set of master principles to which everything might be referred. He hoped there was: it was a comforting thought.

He felt stronger the third morning—dizzy, disoriented, but not so sick in the pit of his stomach and with some of the tension inside of his head relieved. The spike was still there, but it seemed to have grown smaller and it was not rotating and no one was heating it up. He was able to open his eyes and keep them open, though often his vision blurred, but the most powerful urge was still to sleep. He would watch Burroughs or his father for a moment, focusing carefully on the face, then relax and let his eyes blur, clear, blur again, while he tried to talk or take a little nourishment. He did not feel like eating, but his father seemed to set such store by food that he made the effort. He liked the tea—to have real tea for a change he took as an indication of how bad a crack his head must have taken—and he could get a little broth down, but the samp stuck to the roof of his mouth and he had to give that up. Mostly he slept. He dreamed of another Arthur, one who came and carried him mile after mile into the woods, along the lake shore, an animal who had found the meaning of *loyalty,* an Arthur who *cared*.

He awoke. His father was kneeling by the side of the bed straightening the handle of an axe. Even though forced to stay in one place, his father had found work for his hands. Idle hands lose the land, he said over and over.

He was getting the axe ready for the new house. It was strange, he hadn't heard his father talk once about the house lately, not since—Guthrie figured back—not since Kateri had left.

"You feelin' better?" his father asked stiffly. His father put down the axe, laid aside the leveler, and rocked back on his heels. He looked at Guthrie, inspecting his face for something, Guthrie had no idea what, then looked away and said in a low voice. "Clyde—he thinks you got hurt maybe pretty —you know—hard. He thinks maybe you should have—you know—someone around. Someone who knows more'n us," his father explained.

Guthrie struggled to understand. The way his father was speaking, hesitant, almost embarrassed, told him his father

140

was having a hard time finding the right words. "Clyde—he thinks maybe, you know, I should git Kateri on back. For a while," he finished after a pause. "What do you think?"

"It's up to you, Pa. Do what you want, but I'm all right, jest a little—"

"That's what I told Clyde, that we could git along on our own, but he thought, you know, *you* might want her, bein' hurt and all."

"I'm all right. I can make it all right—"

"That's what I told Clyde—well," his father said, "I guess you oughta eat, keep your strength up."

"I don't feel like it jest now—"

"A little somethin'—"

Guthrie shook his head.

"Maybe some tea?"

"Maybe a little tea."

His father moved awkwardly as he rose, standing over the bunk for a moment wanting to say something but unable, apparently, to get the words organized. "If you do want her," he said at last, "all you got to do is say the word. I'd ask her to come back, you know that, I'd ask her for you. It's jest that I don't like to ask for myself. Can't blame her if she wants to be with her own, only for you—"

Guthrie's head had commenced to throb again; he did not even want tea. He just wanted to close his eyes and retreat in sleep. "Of course . . ." his father was saying—

I went too fast with him, Guthrie thought. Never hurry a horse . . . never hurry a horse . . . never hurry . . . if I was to go slow, real slow . . .

"You asleep, son?"

Outside a green drowsiness hung over everything. Bugs hummed in the heat, birds disputed in the brush, animals made faint rustlings in the low scrub—a hot day, a hot green day bursting with the confusion of growth. His father had allowed him outdoors for the first time provided he kept to the blanket spread out under the great sugar maple. There was to be *no* running about, his father's exact words.

He lay stretched out, a canopy of leaves protecting him from the deep molten sky. There were darning needles darting in and out among the dusty, drooping bushes; overhead the deeply blue sky breathed down upon an earth that smelt of dried grasses and crushed leaves; he was dizzy with scent and heavy heat and the brilliant color of butterflies swirling in green dregs.

If he raised himself on one arm, he wondered if he could look down to the pasture and see the horse. The horse was just about the only thing on his mind now. He was twelve, old enough to make plans and carry them out on his own. In some ways it seemed to him his father didn't understand the change that was coming over him at all—for instance, his father still thought he needed babying by some woman; all his father talked about was should he get Kateri back or should they try to make do on their own. She was gone; all right, let her go, but any hour of the day found his father wondering if he shouldn't go up to the reservation after her.

"If you want her, Boy," he would begin and Guthrie would answer for what seemed to him the thousandth time, "I'm all right, I'm gettin' along jest fine, but if you want her back—"

"No, no," his father would insist. "I was jest thinkin' of *you*."

There the conversation would die—for a time. But his father was unable to leave it alone. "You sure now you don't think maybe you'd be better off with Kateri here lookin' after you"—his father's face puckered with worry, his father fretting, fretting. What a blessing it was to be away from that awhile.

The sun, seeping through the sieve of leaves overhead, was wonderfully warm on his face, not so hot it flushed him, just as if a kind of softness were dropping down. He leaned up and looked down toward the meadow, but he could not see the horse. Go slow, he told himself, just kind of hang around until we git used to each other. Once he's used to me—

Guthrie closed his eyes and let his ears listen to the pleasant sounds of summer—insects and birds, a little broken breeze in the trees. He drowsed, dreamed, saw himself riding Arthur wildly, recklessly, without fear, up and down the hills near the lake, felt his father's and Burroughs' admiration; he was referred to as "the boy who could really ride."

The pleasant sensation of his dream was still with him when he awoke; for the first time it seemed to him such a scene might eventually be real instead of a dream, and he felt better than he had in a long time, not just physically better, though this was true too, the sun and air and outside had made his body better, but in his mind there was the urge to begin, not to count himself out because of his failures in the past, but to use those mistakes against the future, to change its course, to try another way, to know Arthur as well as he knew himself, what Arthur liked and what he didn't, Arthur's fears and the things that gave *him* confidence. They would be friends instead of adversaries. You were not afraid of friends.

All his life he had heard Kateri and his father complaining because there was never enough time to do everything they wanted, and he had thought how ridiculous they were, he had scads and scads of time, too much of it. Often it preyed on him and made him lonely and miserable because there were great swatches of days with nothing really to do, he seemed somehow to be waiting for something, but of what he was never quite sure; and now, here under the big maple, he was suddenly seized with the sensation his waiting was over, he had to do important things, first and foremost of which was breaking the horse, but this was only, he saw, part of it. He was really beginning to break himself in, teaching himself patience and perseverance, a core of the crafts and skills a man needed to be sufficient on an isolated farm like this. And he was twelve—*twelve*—and he did not have a lot of time to learn all that was needed. There were hundreds and hundreds of things to do, that he should have done already, and he hadn't even given them a thought, he had wasted all that time and there was no way ever to get it back.

He had not heard his father and the horse until they were quite near. His father never took Cobbie around the lake in summer, that kind of trip took too long; his father could cross the lake by boat in a fourth the time. Then Guthrie understood. His father was going over to the Landing for things for the new house too big and too awkward to bring back by boat; his father would ride the horse over and use him to haul coming back.

"Clyde," his father said, reining up, "he said he didn't mind stayin' and watchin' after you. I'm goin' North," his father said. "To bring Kateri back."

Clyde Burroughs was the only man with red hair that Guthrie had ever seen. His being out of the ordinary that way made Burroughs seem somehow more important than most people. If you had hair like that, people called you crazy names like carrot-top and crocodile bait (whatever that was), and you had to grow up to be different inside, too. You'd feel more. So when Guthrie turned it over in his mind he decided he could take a chance on trusting Burroughs. He wasn't like other adults.

He was more like those other loners, the trappers, even the halfbreeds, than like the white Landing men with their soft mouths and fluttering eyes, their deceptive speech and

Landing ways. He belonged to the world of the flat-bottomed boat covered with thick bundles of furs, the bleached head of something, a bear or an owl, on the prow, a skull that twitched in the wind while the woodman paddled, his back always toward the town, his eyes gazing out over the lake toward the hills and beyond; small men but lean and hard, with leatherlike skin, wind and sun and straining to see had shrunk the flesh back on the bones and tanned it ochre in color.

Maybe his being drawn into himself had to do with his woman running off. "She was the kind didn't know how to settle down and stick with one man," people over at the Landing said. Some were kinder. "Him and his woman don't live together no more," that was their way of not putting the blame some place. They had too much respect for Burroughs to say his wife had preferred another man.

Guthrie's father and Burroughs were close, closer, Guthrie guessed, to one another than any two men he knew. No man, Guthrie's father had said once, knows who he is until he has to fight it out against odds against him. Some men just ain't fighters by nature, so they never find out. Some men fight and take fright and run away. Maybe they knew a little about themselves, but not really much, not really who they are. But a man who gits on to bein' near a man and has the guts to stand and see a bad time through finds out what he's got inside. And don't think it don't take courage to go down inside and find out what you really got in there—he tapped Guthrie sharply against the place where his heart lay beating up against the question, What would I be like when things went wrong? Not what I wished I would do but what I really would do.

You take Clyde Burroughs, his father said. He knows how to stand up, no matter how hard hit he is. He don't say nuthin' about his standin', he jest does it.

Even his father recognized Burroughs was different from other men.

If he got Burroughs' help, he could begin right away on his project, he couldn't fail. He was still a little shaky, but he wasn't planning anything strenuous, just kind of moseying around Arthur and trying to move him away from his snarky ways. Make him more agreeable, more *manageable*. Get that damn horse so that he would go along with at least some of the things a horse was supposed to do. So far as Guthrie was concerned, jumping on his back and hanging on as long as he could, which was never very long, was pointless. They—

144

provided of course Burroughs would give him a hand—would have to start right back at the beginning, cut out all this chasing around the field. The very first thing Guthrie was determined the horse was going to learn was to come when he was called.

He tackled Burroughs on the subject as soon as his father had a good start. The red-headed man never sat in the sun, his skin burned too badly, but he did like to take his food out in the open when the weather was good. He carried out two plates at noon—one with samp and another with some kind of cooked beans he had made—and he sat under the maple where Guthrie was sitting, propped up, gazing out over the lake. He handed one plate to Guthrie, sat down with the other in a patch of gloom and began to wolf down his food. He was not the kind of man who was sociable while he stoked up. He chewed, and swallowed with intent, absorbed. Guthrie ate politely; the dish needed salt. He said nothing, however; there were larger things on his mind than Burroughs' flat cooking.

Finally Burroughs put his finished plate aside and got ready to smoke. He had a strong taste for tobacco. He said it warmed his blood. Guthrie cleared his throat and Burroughs looked up attentively, but went on rolling tobacco between his fingers; he had the paper between his teeth. In a moment one hand would grasp the end of the paper, he would fill it with tobacco, lick down the outside edge and seal it. It was a series of actions that, with years of practice, Burroughs and his father could execute in a matter of seconds, an accomplishment Guthrie much admired. He longed for the day he would be rolling and smoking tobacco. He sighed and began. "The thing is—well, you see, it's about Arthur."

"An ornery son of a bitch," Burroughs said, as he always did, and held up the rolled cigarette to see if it was satisfactory. "No animal for anyone, not even an adult to mess with, much less a twelve-year-old boy. Told your father so, but he had his mind made up. No use arguing against him when he sets a matter inside him. You lucky you wasn't hurt worse." After a pause, he added strongly, "And that's a fact."

"I don't think we went about it right. I mean, he could be all right—my mother, she used to handle him—"

"Your mother could even manage that crazy bull you heard us talk about, the one your grandpa had to shoot after she—you know the one I mean."

"Well, Arthur, he isn't a bull—I mean, bulls are just natural born mean, but Arthur isn't really mean," Guthrie hastened to explain when he saw Burroughs' red eyebrows rise in disbelief. "I mean, it's more like he jest don't want to do what we want him to, but he's got a—a reason."

"What reason?"

"Well, I don't rightly know. I mean, maybe that's jest the point. If we was to find out the reason and change his mind about it, he might change the way he acts. Not be so, you know, ornery."

"I doubt it," Burroughs said with absolute finality. "He's a mean son of a bitch and that's all there is to it. All your cozyin' up to him and tryin' to git him to do what you want won't come to no more than another toss on the head. That's the way he is, that's the way he's gonna stay. It's a losin' battle."

"But suppose—jest suppose—you, say, didn't think he was all that hopeless, and you decided to see what you could do to, you know, break him of his bad habits. How would you go about doin' it?"

"First place, he's too old to break of bad habits." Burroughs stopped. He looked at Guthrie. "You aimin' to git back on that critter after all that's happened?"

Nothing was to be gained rushing him; Guthrie was willing to let him take all the time in the world so long as he finally saw it the way Guthrie did. Because he was sure that if Burroughs understood, he would help. He sat for a moment smoking and looking out at the lake. "Well, it's an old horse," he said slowly, "but you *might* wear him down." He looked at Guthrie. "But is it worth it?" Then, as if answering himself, not looking at Guthrie, he said, "I suppose that depends on what you want out of it." He examined the boy once more. "What you want out of it?"

"I want to see if I can do it."

He smoked, he turned the matter over in his mind. Finally he conceded. "Well, I suppose that's as good a reason as any. Let's jackass ourselfs down to the pasture and see what that ornery son-of-a-bitch is up to." He rose, creaky, flame-headed, stretching. "I'm glad to give advice now and then, but don't expect me to git on."

But the first piece of advice he gave boded well for the whole adventure; it showed a perception of First things First. "You gotta git up and put your *left* shoe on first thing you git dressed; otherwise you're gonna have bad luck the rest of the day." He said this walking down to the pasture, smoking, thinking things over. They paused at the gate, looking down the field. Arthur looked quiet and calm and—Burroughs' word—wise. "That's one wise horse. Don't you let him git away with nuthin'. That's the secret of dealin' with a horse, *you* gotta be boss. So long as he kin throw you, hump you off agin a fence or tree, crow hop or buck, jump around and run for the barn, you got no control. A horse has *got* to know who's boss. It's the one absolute essential.

"So, if you want *my* advice," he said, "don't go near him. I don't care if you got to wait a year, don't you go out to him. Make him come to you—if he don't come, he don't git no grain. Don't you go out there and give it to him. You make him come down and git it from you."

He and Burroughs went down every day with a bucket and leaned against the fence. Arthur, grazing, lifted his head, looked at them, then went back to grazing. They were of absolutely no interest to him.

"Greed'll git him," Guthrie said hopefully.

"Don't count on it—oh, don't think I didn't see you and your apple. But you was runnin' after him then and he knowed he had you where he wanted. Now you're aimin' to make him come to you and do your beckonin' and biddin' and it's a different story and he knows it, too. He won't come—not for that reason."

"Did Pa know—about the apple?"

"I couldn't rightly answer that. He was always lookin' off lakeways when you showed it too prominent in front of us. I reckon he felt sorry, too. It was mighty hot some of them days you was racing back and forth after that damned horse." He leaned over the fence and shouted downfield, "You hear me, you no good son-of-a-bitch?"

Arthur raised, slightly, his head.

"Impossible," Burroughs pronounced. "Absolutely impossible."

Guthrie's father came back with Kateri and Burroughs went back to the Landing. Guthrie was still going down to the pasture every day, unsuccessfully, though he could not go down until late in the day. His head was healed and he had to do chores. His father had begun the real work on the house and expected him to pitch in there and do his part, too, which became day by day almost the work of a full-grown man. His father had begun laying out the frame; when it was finished and ready to go up, the men would all come over from the Landing and help raise it, but first Odder would have to have everything set to go.

They ate hastily in the early morning light, then went right to work. These early mornings were cool and pleasant, but by noon the sun had burned all the coolness out of the air, they were hot and sticky, with the flies bothering them something awful. Kateri usually brought the food out at midday: the cabin was too hot and stuffy to eat in. They ate inside only when it rained or a couple of days when cold spells came on and it was a relief to feel warm. Guthrie was undecided which he thought worse, working in a blinding, blistering sun or in a wet-cold rain. But no matter what the weather, they worked; his father was pushing to get the house up.

Guthrie thought his father's haste must have something to do with Kateri's coming back. She was different now; he couldn't put his finger on just what it was, but the change was there. For one thing, she who had never seemed in a hurry, who had always taken her time, going slowly but surely from chore to chore, now seemed perpetually busy, too busy. Guthrie felt she was playing some kind of role, as if she were showing his father and him how much her industry meant to the welfare of their lives. It made him nervous, all that empty bustling. And then, too, along with her busyness there were the constant outbursts. Before she would never have dared carry on like that, but now his father stopped whatever he was doing when she got mad and listened. He went further; he paid attention. She got her way with whatever she wanted. His father was straining, it seemed, to do exactly what she wanted, and that seemed odd to Guthrie. It was more than just seeing she got her way once in a while or that things went as well as they practically could, it was more as if his father was organizing his very existence around getting the world exactly the way *she* wanted it, as if the sole mission in his father's life was keeping Kateri happy.

There were other changes. She didn't sleep back in the shed with Guthrie any more. She said he was getting too big for that, she'd put her pallet outside or, if the weather went bad, by the kitchen part of the cabin. She said this quite firmly so there'd be no mistaking the fact that she would be glad when the house was finished and she had a room of her own; so that was one of the reasons, Guthrie was sure, that his father was hurrying.

All day long—long days with the light lasting and lasting—he and his father prepared for the house-raising. At night, so tired he felt sick, Guthrie sat on the porch steps, eyes closed, resting outwardly but inwardly urging himself to get up and go down to the field, to the horse. The way he saw it, the only way for his efforts to have any effect was to make

148

them absolutely dependable and trustworthy; to come every day at the same time so that Arthur began to understand that, no matter what, he could count on Guthrie. Guthrie had this theory that the person you could trust completely was the one you loved most.

Finally he would get up from the porch steps and go down through the thickening twilight, listening for the first calls of the whippoorwills. Their clear, bright calls went from tree to tree, circling, sending up songs from first one part of the woods and then another, as if they had to make the great wide circle of the earth with song.

At the edge of the lake tall pines of seventy, eighty feet ridged the water; midges and chimney-sweeps were darting back and forth in chase, in flight from one another; the water was dark, shining under the last sun, its surface scarcely rippled by the slight breeze blowing from in back of them; the meadow ran to one side, sloping gently down to the water; under an old oak Arthur dusted the flies from his back with his long coarse black tail.

Guthrie went to the fence and leaned over, head resting on his crossed arms. He had set the pail of grain at his feet. He was tired to the bone; all he could think was that that goldarn horse had been resting all day. "Burroughs is right," he said to the twilight and the horse, "you *are* one ornery son-of-a-bitch."

Arthur raised his head and flicked his ears, but he didn't move. He's never going to come, Guthrie thought. I'm doing nothing but making a fool of myself in front of a no-good ornery son-of-a-bitch of a horse.

He sat down, angrily broke off a long blade of grass, split it, held it to his lips, pulled it across and blew. A shrill whistle came from the green blade. He blew again. Two, three times, that was all one of them usually lasted. He threw the broken blade away and picked a broader, better one, carefully made a split in the center, put it to his lips and blew. A sweet sound filled the air. A feeling of contentment came over him; he felt more a boy again—no responsibilities to a horse or house, all he had to do was pleasure himself. He put his head down, cupped his hands, and blew.

The horse was coming at a jog, a look almost of joy on his face. Guthrie jumped up and looked at him. He held the pail up and rattled the grain against its sides. The horse stopped, looking almost angry, but also expectant. Guthrie rattled the grain again. The horse tossed his head from side to side, as if he were saying, No . . . no . . . *no* . . .

149

It was not the grain that had moved him. What was it? What was I doing, Guthrie asked himself, what was I doing tonight that I—I was whistling, he thought. I did it that first day, too, when Burroughs brought him over. I whistled him to obedience.

He picked up a blade of grass, slit it, and began to whistle with all his might. The horse raised his head and held it up; then he began to trot down the field. He came right up to the fence and nuzzled his head down against Guthrie's shoulder. Guthrie went right on whistling his heart out as he scratched the back of Arthur's head. Not one of them had thought to whistle him in; stupidly they had gone on calling and calling when all he wanted was a whistle.

The next day Guthrie could hardly wait until the work on the house was done and he could get down to the horse. He ate supper hurriedly, but not so fast anyone asked what the rush was. Then he went down the hill at a race; the last hundred yards he began whistling. By the time he reached the gate, the horse was there; they met with a great rush of delight, Arthur whinnying, Guthrie crying out with pride and happiness and holding up the pail of grain. He scratched and rubbed the horse's rough hair while Arthur ate. He dug out the dirt and fly eggs from the cleft under Arthur's chin when he was finished and then, smiling, produced the brush he had wedged inside his belt. He showed it to Arthur, he ran it roughly over Arthur's neck so that the horse would get the idea; then he climbed up on the fence and leaning over ran the brush up and down his neck, Arthur pulling over so that Guthrie could get farther along his spine.

Guthrie slipped off the fence. He was standing next to the horse and he kept up the friction of the brush against his back. He was a great roller, Arthur was; there was earth packed all over him. Guthrie took a long time, ran the brush under the neck and as far beneath the sides of the belly as he dared. He was getting along fine, but there was no point in pushing his luck. He wondered what he would do when the time came for the legs; the feet were big and powerful. It was no difficult matter for a horse to kick a man's head in. Still there was no getting around it, the legs would have to be done. And then the feet.

Burroughs had explained to him he would have to clean the feet, check that no stones were lodged in the upper part of the hooves. Stones in the hooves were a prime cause of lameness. Burroughs had explained how Guthrie should run his hand down the horse's leg to give him confidence, then firmly grasp the foot, lift it up and hold it by wedging the bent leg in the crook of his arm. "Stand close," he had been warned, "right up against him so that you can feel if he's gonna do somethin' strange. Stand real close or real far away. The worst mistake you can make is to stand a little way out where he can really catch you. If you're in close you can feel what's coming and git aside, and if you're way away, it don't make no difference; but if you're in between he can catch you by surprise and *really* git you."

Guthrie ran the brush down Arthur's back once more, pressing hard so that the horse got the sensation of being scratched. There was no use putting off what had to be done; he patted Arthur nervously on the neck, ran his right hand tentatively down the horse's right leg to the foot and waited. A fly was droning over Arthur's left ear and he twitched it, but that was all. Guthrie kept running his hand slowly up and down the leg. Finally he bent down, his heart beating very fast, his stomach somersaulting, and tried to raise the big hoof. Arthur's whole weight seemed concentrated in keeping it firmly planted where it was.

"Give it to me," Guthrie said softly, trying to lift the leg up. "Come on, Arthur, let me see your foot." Guthrie tapped the back of the horse's leg. "Up," he said at the same time, "pick it up. Let me see your foot." The horse raised his foot and Guthrie seized it, clamping it between his arm and thigh. He looked for stones. "Good boy," he kept saying, trying to encourage Arthur's cooperation. "Good boy."

The horse paid no attention. Arthur's eyes were half-closed, he seemed to be dreaming. Guthrie released the right leg, ducked under Arthur's neck, and ran his hand down the left leg with a good deal more confidence and Arthur, surprisingly, raised the foot at once, as if he understood what Guthrie wanted. Guthrie cleaned the foot, extracting with some difficulty a small pebble under the frog. He worked slowly, talking continuously to the horse. He even showed Arthur the stone after he had gotten it out.

The back legs remained.

It was a cool evening, but Guthrie found he was sticky with sweat. The horse seemed enormously large in its rear quarters. The hip bones were wide, the haunches and hocks thick almost as a workhorse's; the back feet seemed to Guthrie twice as big as the front ones. He knew he had been in little real danger working on the front feet. There was always the chance of course that the horse might rear, the remote possibility he would let fly with one of those front legs; but rearing was no true danger so long as he was standing near and could grab the halter and bring Arthur down, and the likelihood of being kicked while he was within easy sight of the horse was not great. But working with the rear legs was another matter altogether. Horses were nervous about anything in back of them. Their eyes were so constructed that it was almost impossible, without completely swiveling their heads about, to see what was happening directly behind them. Guthrie had no stomach for the job ahead, but there was nothing he could do.

He said a sort of prayer, more a silent supplication than any formal prayer, and went back to the right side, the better side to work with, to start anything on, and began patting Arthur's flank, moving his hand gingerly along the withers, sliding it down across the belly and up the hip, pausing there, then slowly slipping over the thigh down the path of the hamstring, resting again on the enormous hock, seeing the patches of scaly callous where Arthur had rubbed himself so many times, then with a final burst of fatalism dropping his hand down the lower leg onto the fetlock, over the pastern onto the crown of the hoof—he was bent over now and if the horse decided to kick him the blow could conceivably kill him—talking, all the time talking, trying to give the animal confidence, trying to reassure both the horse and himself, at last taking the hoof in hand and trying to haul it up. The leg gave, came halfway up, then dropped again with a loud thick clunk. Arthur seemed grown into the ground.

Guthrie let that much effort suffice for the time. After all, there was no point in overdoing and anyway the left rear foot remained. It seemed to him he had been most of his lifetime bent down trying to get the horse to raise his legs.

He could easily move back up and slip under Arthur's neck, but that was the coward's way out and he knew it; courage, all that unaccountable conscience that shamed him into recognizing his faults, called for him to walk around the rear; he did not give himself the time for imagination to begin working; one hand near the root of the tail, he walked, talking a mile a minute, around the hindquarters (in something, he supposed, like record time) and faced the left back leg. It was raised, flicking at flies. Arthur's tail was also swinging back and forth, back and forth; suddenly it went a little further out than usual and struck Guthrie across the face.

He staggered back, more in surprise than pain. His face

stung, but not badly; what was worse was the feeling that Arthur had done it on purpose. Blinking, for his eyes still smarted, Guthrie looked at the horse. Burroughs had said one very last thing to him before he had left to go back to the Landing, something Guthrie had deliberately tried to put out of his mind, he wanted no part of that particular piece of advice, and yet as he stood regarding the big bay, he knew that of everything Burroughs had told him, this was the most important. What Burroughs had said was simple but essential: "That horse minded your mother. If you knew what *she* was like and were—well—like that," he had paused. There seemed no way for him to finish. "You see what I mean?" he asked.

Guthrie had seen. But Guthrie didn't want that kind of knowledge because it would mean he would have a tie. What was the good of being bound to someone who was dead? Now she was just "up there," but if he began to go back and try to track down what she was really like, she wouldn't be just up under the larch, she'd be here, inside, he would be carrying her around; in some way he couldn't identify but which was nevertheless true she would take on shape—shape, substance: life. He didn't want her to seem real, to have that false kind of reality. She *was* dead.

"She's dead," he said to the horse. "And it's me you're gonna have to deal with."

The horse turned and gazed at him uninterestedly.

"It is." He saw some glimpse of comprehension, he thought, in Arthur's face. "And don't you go and hit me with your tail nor your foot. Give me your foot and let's git this over with. Give it to me. Stop this nonsense." He gave the foot a smart tap and Arthur raised it—slowly, tentatively—but he raised it.

"That's more like it," Guthrie said. "That's the way to do it, you old bastard, you."

The next day Arthur was waiting at the fence, almost as if he knew that Guthrie had special plans. He whinnied when he caught sight of Guthrie, a long low plaintive greeting, as if he were asking impatiently, *Where you been?* It was the first time the horse had been at the fence; usually he waited for Guthrie to whistle him over to the grain pail, but then a lot of things were changing between them.

He opened the gate and Arthur jogged over. "You want somethin' to eat? Is that it, you greedy old bastard, you want somethin' to eat?"

The horse put his head against Guthrie's shoulder and nuzzled; he nearly knocked Guthrie over rubbing against him that hard. He had the saddle astride the fence. Arthur turned and looked at it as if he understood. The bridle hung over Guthrie's shoulder, the reins hanging free. He put the halter rope on Arthur and tied him to one of the fence posts. It didn't exactly look reliable—the posts along here were wobbly, rotted under the ground probably. That was what came of using oak. Should have put in cedar, but it was way up back, too hard to get to, and Cobbie, his father's horse, was a problem to fences, always breaking out. His father had decided that since the posts had to be replaced so often they might as well use oak. The posts along here seemed sound, but Guthrie knew the ground got at them and they rotted below the grass line. If Arthur were to take it into his head to pull back, settle his weight on his hind legs and bring all his strength against one of those posts, Guthrie knew it would give. But he reckoned that with normal stress he would be all right. Just so the horse didn't take it into his head to be ornery.

It's an ornery horse, he told himself. But he's changed, he argued back.

He brushed the horse slowly, stopping every once in a while to say something to him. He stroked behind the ears and cleaned the cleft under the chin, examined all four hooves for stones, brushed thoroughly under the belly, then took the saddle and held it up, letting Arthur see. Cautiously he brought it down on the horse's back. The stirrups were up and the cinch lay over the back of the saddle. Guthrie put the saddle on Arthur's back, letting it rest there freely, letting Arthur get used to it. He could toss it off if he wanted, but Guthrie began talking again to keep him quiet and cooperative. After a while he let the cinch down, leaned under and pulled it up, tightening it, but not too hard. Arthur had blown up; the thing to do was lead him around, let him relax, then tighten the belly band.

He gave the animal plenty of time to get used to everything. He was surprised how easily the horse went along with the whole thing; even when Guthrie went to slip the bridle over his head, he had no trouble. Arthur gave him a little fight about opening his mouth for the bit, but what horse wouldn't? When Guthrie had the bridle fastened, he checked the cinch again, gave Arthur several reassuring pats, put his leg in the stirrup, his right hand on the top of the saddle, and before the horse had a chance to think things through, he swung himself up and into the saddle.

He walked the horse down to the fallen apple tree, clucked and let him trot on to the pines downhill. He was careful the whole time to keep his finger flexed, ready to draw in every inch of rein if the horse started to get his head down, but Arthur made the turn at the pines agreeably enough, he didn't even try to gather himself in for a run. They trotted back toward the fence at a brisk but relaxed pace.

Dusk was rising all about them, like smudges of smoke. Guthrie leaned over Arthur's head and patted him, telling him what a great horse he was.

He looked at the gently bobbing head. The present bridle was not right. Now there were just straps running up either side of the horse's head from the bit and a strap that fastened under the chin. The reins ran to loops at either side of the bit. When Guthrie drew back, the bit brought pressure on the horse's mouth and drew back a narrow leather strap under the chin which exerted a pull on the horse's underchin. Any animal with an ounce of determination could get a bit like that between his teeth, all the pulling back in the world wouldn't help; and against the thick steel-like force of the muscles in Arthur's neck, Guthrie's hold on the reins and bit were weak. Once the horse got his head down the bit was useless. He would plant his feet, lower that strong powerful neck and buck.

Guthrie slipped down and stood next to the horse, still stroking him, but his mind was on the problem at hand. If there was some way to run the reins up the sides of his head and along the strap, attach them—right behind his head, Guthrie thought, loose but not too loose, so that when he starts to put his head down, he feels a tug, there's some restraint, and if that doesn't stop him, then I could really draw them up, *that* would stop him dead; he'd have to bring his head up because the bit—

Would it work? If it worked, if Arthur couldn't get his head down, he couldn't buck; and if he couldn't buck, he, Guthrie Buttes, couldn't be thrown off; and if he wasn't thrown off, his father would let him keep the horse.

He was excited now. He unlatched the chin strap, slipped the bridle over the horse's head, and told himself there was nothing to worry about.

He had it all worked out, step by step.

The next day he let Arthur out in a run. When the horse

155

tried to get his head down, the shortened extra reins Guthrie
had improvised pulled him up short. He stopped abruptly, but
Guthrie held on, gripping with his thighs; then he urged
the horse on, drumming against both sides with his heels.

The horse sprang forward, his sides heaving with excitement; he was in a full gallop now, his feet pounding harder
and harder for a hold so that every time he came down with
that fixing force he pushed himself ahead faster and faster;
they were racing downfield full force, everything flying by,
Guthrie gripping with his thighs, the inside of his legs, his
back rammed down for further support, one hand on the
main reins, the other up on the side ones, ready. Arthur was
going to stop dead and—

He saw the head start to go down and Guthrie yanked with
all his might, kicked at the same time with his heels, using
his back as a driving force to thrust the animal on, bearing
down as if he were making a swing soar up toward the sky.
There was only the slightest hesitation; then they flew on,
faster and faster, down to the bottom of the meadow, wheel-
ing near the fence into a sharp turn, flying back again, faster
and faster, Guthrie's hand on those extra reins ready, ready;
the sound of the hooves like a wild tattoo and the sound of
Guthrie's heart answering, saying over and over, We've won
. . . we've won . . . we've won. For it seemed to him as much
the horse's victory as his own.

He brought his father down the next night, trying to seem
nonchalant. "I've got somethin' I'd sort of like you to see,
somethin' I been workin' on."

The horse was at the fence; he started to whinny, saw
Guthrie's father, and stopped. Guthrie had the brush, the
saddle and reins, waiting by the fence. He took the brush
first, opened the gate without saying anything, closed it, and
went up to Arthur.

"You been messin' around with that horse?" his father
asked sharply. "After what happened and I told you—"

"It's all right, Pa, jest watch."

He put out his hand and stroked the horse behind the ears.
After a moment, when he felt Arthur was quiet, he put the
lead line on the halter and led him over closer to the fence,
tied him, then began to curry him down. He went slowly,
taking his time, not hurrying or bypassing anything, neither
the underpart of the belly nor the back parts of the legs, his
father just standing there watching, not saying anything, but
watching closely.

Arthur was quiet under the brush, under the smoothing of his hands. Guthrie kept talking to him reassuringly, but he was elated, it was hard to keep from hurrying, he was so impatient to have his father see all he had accomplished. He had to keep checking his impatience, cautioning himself to take it slowly, not to get Arthur excited or let himself get that way either. Yet the excitement was there. It was as if he had brought his father to some kind of initiation and when it was over his father would look at him with new eyes, see he wasn't just a boy any more, he was growing up. Like a man, he could master a difficult horse, make it do what he wanted, because he had taken his task step by step, instead of rushing it, forcing what had to be won with time and care.

There was a split second of warning, like that warning Guthrie always had when Arthur put his head down just before he bucked Guthrie off—only this time the head went up. Guthrie felt the horse's haunches settle back, pulling. Frantic, he tried to reach up and grab the halter and get hold of the horse's head, force it down; but the animal had pulled sideways and back, he was out of reach; there was a wracking, splintering sound, an old post broken off in the ground gave way, and the next instant, Arthur, seizing with all his strength the opportunity to break free, settled all the way back down to the ground on his haunches; there was a terrible shattering sound and the upper cross boards of the fence gave way, splintering, tearing, flying. The horse was almost free now, rearing, plunging, dragging the post he had pulled from the ground. Then the whole contraption—post, broken boards, fence—came away, an end of a board tearing across Guthrie's back as the horse—wild-eyed, terrified—panicked and lunged, stumbled, fell, legs kicking, the post flailing against one side, the splintered board banging the other, then on his feet again, pulling everything free with him, racing downfield, post and boards dragging, the boards coming free as they caught on tree stumps, banged against rocks, while Guthrie stared disbelievingly, hearing his father shouting, and saying to himself, *But I had planned everything so well and worked so hard, I—*

The horse gave a final high scream as the post smacked against his back leg. "He's broke that leg for sure," his father said in the brief silence that followed. "We'll have to go up to the house for the gun."

But slowly, from the ground where he had rolled over, Arthur rose, and, limping, came back up the field toward them. The leg was badly torn, there was blood running all down one side, but it did not crumple under him.

Guthrie went toward the horse, numb, unable to speak. Arthur came right up to him, the post dragging at his side; he was trembling all over, but he stood quite still while Guthrie unfastened the halter and freed him from the line dragging the post and the two remaining splintered boards of the fence.

"He has to go."

"He doesn't *have* to go," Guthrie said, but he knew that of course there was no other reasonable course of action. He had tried everything and he had almost been killed for his efforts. If that flying post had been an inch or two lower, it would have made full contact with his head and crushed it in. He had done all he could and he had failed and the animal was finished here on the farm. An animal like that you could *never* trust. Why had he suddenly spooked like that and pulled back? No way of knowing, no way ever of predicting when he might do it again. And although new posts might hold, there would always be some time, some place, in some other way, that the horse would do something totally unexpected and someone would eventually be hurt. An unpredictable animal was one that could kill you. It had to go. Guthrie knew that as well as he knew anything in the whole world. He knew he himself would never be able to trust Arthur again. He had tried, as Burroughs had counseled him, to use patience and resourcefulness. He had asked of himself a residue of perseverance he didn't think he had—that he hadn't had before he had begun—and because he had insisted on these things in himself, he had brought them into being. And yet he had failed. Wanting and working with all your heart for a thing—neither one was enough; both weren't enough. You had to choose the right thing to spend your efforts on.

"You know he has to go," his father said. "He's unreliable —you can't trust him, not for one minute."

Guthrie did know, but he couldn't accept. It was too hard to accept. He tried to keep his face expressionless, the way a well-trained Indian would; he asked only that he be like a stone or a tree, to be empty of all feelings, to put himself, stationary, like an inanimate object in the universe; if an Indian could do it, he could.

Why had the horse turned and come back to him? It was like Arthur knew Guthrie would help him. It was like there was something in Arthur that wanted Guthrie to be master, but there was something, too, that wouldn't permit that, something that maybe was stronger, a wild instinct the horse couldn't master. It would be best to think of it like that—as something they couldn't help, he or Arthur, no matter how hard they both tried. They had both of them failed, for reasons they would neither of them ever understand.

"You grow up," his father said, "and you learn to have to give up the things you care about. It's a sorry thing to learn—and it's bad when it comes so young. I had to wait a lot longer than you to learn it. But maybe that wasn't good either. Maybe you should learn young or maybe you shouldn't have to learn at all. Every man has a part of him that wants to keep the thing he cares about forever, as long as he lives; and every man learns he has someday, one day before he wants, to give it up, Guthrie . . . son," his father said, calling him "son" for the first time, while Guthrie saw Arthur coming down the field on a late summer afternoon when the twilight had just begun to gather in the ridges of the hills and when, hot and tired, suddenly he felt his spirits lift and he ran forward to meet the horse. Only that would never happen anymore except inside his mind.

His father had been talking about his mother. He must have loved her a great deal, Guthrie thought, and putting that thought into words gave it substance and power, as if for the first time he could reach out and touch that love. The abstractness of the concept was removed in the concreteness of words; a whole questionable part of his life was suddenly cleared up and something fundamental absolved about his birth; it was a matter of great import to have been born because of love, not merely chance or expedience or blind desire, but out of the controlled circle of love, that circle which, it seemed to him, *was* the symbol of life—the earth, the sky, the universe itself, were they not sound and symbol of the endless completion of all else? Where could you say a circle started or stopped?

Yet he felt the pain of disappointment, the pain of loss in the center of that circle, as if someone said to him, at the center of the mystery is the knife, that which can cut through the circle and make it have parts—a place where there it now began, there it ends. How else account for the idea of his mother's death, of his failure with her horse?

He thought about her, he thought about her horse. He stood amid the wild larkspur, the heavy scent of honeysuckle. There were swallows and goldfinches darting over the high grass, plucking at the buds of flowers, dots of yellow and orange between the long stalks of wild grass.

It was impossible to imagine, as his father must all the time, that terrible week when the storm had raged over these trees, down on this lake, drawing it up and claiming all the lumber for his father's house, bringing on the difficult birth which had killed his mother.

She was in him, Kateri said. The Indians were in him, too. Ohguesse. He went downhill toward the pasture. Others had done things to strengthen themselves. Kateri-Teg-a-quith-a had mortified her flesh to purify it. Kateri, his own Kateri, had worked, wordless, all these years among strange people, people of a different blood. Ohguesse had raised him as if he were the same as the redbloods, Ohguesse who had gone back to the "dying who march." Good-bye, white boy.

The horse browsed at the far end of the field. This was his last day. Burroughs was going to take him back and put him out to pasture for good.

Guthrie began to gather up dead leaves, a few twigs that lay like brown fingers in the green grass. He would need knots of wood as big as his fists to make coals.

He spent half an hour selecting, discarding, his pile of leaves and twigs, little boles of wood grew. Different spirits stalked the darkness than the light. After supper when he had done his chores he would—

In the heavily descending darkness he held the flame to the dry brush at the bottom of the pile. A few leaves caught. In a moment the flames reached out hundreds of little hands to catch at things dead and dry. He saw the mutilated fists of old trees reach back and redden and glow; his bare feet looked translucent in the crimson light. He was sure he saw bone and vein, and bending over, with the pincers he had brought with him, he caught a live coal and thrust it between his bare toes, biting his lips until the blood ran red down his chin, but not a sound came from his throat.

Ohguesse had taught the principle of the bow. "It will teach you patience and cunning," he had said. "It will let you learn how far you can take yourself, how much you can rely on your body."

He emptied his mind of all thought, his body of all feeling as he had been Indian-taught to do, letting his blood run at one with the darkening night, the bright instantaneous light of whirling insects, a flash of pointed star far overhead.

Red father, he said to the black and red night, I do this in honor of what you taught me and in penance for what was

160

done to you and your people. White mother, I do this in remembrance of you, you who could whisper to horses and make them understand things I cannot.

He bent and took another coal for the other foot. Half obeisance was worthy only of the weak.

He began to chant.

III

In the five years since Burroughs had come and taken the horse away, very little had been said about Arthur. For a fact, Guthrie thought, everyone went out of his way to avoid the subject. Tact, it would have been called by valley people; common sense, his father would have said. His father knew a lot about both, though from the rough way he spoke and the seemingly obtuse silences into which he often subsided, an outsider would have remarked probably that he was a blunt, tactless man.

But though Odder Buttes did not talk much about things, he was a doer. He had gone and got Guthrie a horse he could manage, an old pinto, with a pretty reliable disposition (no horse, Guthrie had concluded, was really reliable), not too pluggy, but not given to running away with you either. A horse cost twice as much as a cow; a horse was maybe a necessity for a man, but for a boy it was a luxury, and Guthrie knew how his father felt about luxuries, but his father had gone and bought that mare without a word about waste not, want not, or how a penny spent was a penny lost. Usually his father squeezed the joy out of life and held up the bitter rind, but for some utterly inexplicable reason he had bought the mare and brought her back and *happily* (that in itself still astonished Guthrie) given her over, without any rancor about the money he had spent.

Narko was a good horse, worked well, had few bad habits —she was a cribber and had to be kept away from the barn where she was likely to gnaw quite large holes quickly in the boards—but there was never the sense of challenge there had been with Arthur nor, on the other hand, was there ever the knowledge of defeat. Slowly the sense of failure and the guilt that was unaccountable but nevertheless acutely present had waned; Guthrie never, in all this time, felt anything for

Narko like what he had felt for Arthur, but he respected her for what she was, and he had a good time on her riding through the woods, over the hills, even finally, last year, at seventeen being allowed to go alone around to the Landing while they were getting the house up.

Now, at the dock, helping his father and Burroughs unload the boat in which Burroughs had come across—Burroughs and his father were going off on their own for a week trapping uplake; they would go not in the big heavy boat but in a lighter canoe—Guthrie had stopped quite still, watching Burroughs handle the canvas provisions, unloading them, his back turned, but the words quite clear. Burroughs was telling him the horse would have to be put down. He was old and heave-y, his teeth were gone and grain wouldn't stay with him. If Arthur were dead, Guthrie thought, maybe the whole thing would finally be finished. He didn't think, though, that for him it would ever be finished. There were the scars on his feet to make him remember.

"You *fell* in a fire—barefooted? You might have crippled yourself for life—answer me, Boy, tell the truth. What happened. Oh my God, you're worse than an Indian with your ways. Do something with his feet, Kateri. I've had a bellyful of this business."

He heard Burroughs say, ". . . your new neighbors."

Guthrie's father stopped, a pack hanging loosely from his hands. "What did you say, Clyde?" His tone was sharp and angry.

"Ain't you heard? You're gonna have next-door neighbors." Burroughs was grinning; there was nothing he liked better than being one up on Odder Buttes.

"The hell we are. You storyin' agin, Clyde. Jest to git my goat."

"Suit yourself."

Guthrie's father considered that the land on this side of the lake was *all* his even though he didn't own it outright; he was the only one with a house on this side of the water, wasn't he, and that meant it was his side of the lake, didn't it?

"People name of Raymond, down south, Albany-way." Burroughs pronounced it Al-*ban*-ee. "They don't aim to farm it, Odd," Burroughs said in a conciliatory voice.

"What they aim to do with it, then?"

"Beats me. Funny, ain't it, being standin' there so long freelike no one ever thought of someone buyin' it. I don't reckon I'd worry none if I was you. You reckon this weather'll hold until tomorry?"

"I reckon." Guthrie's father picked up the pack and swung it up on his shoulder. He was going to take it up to the house to redo. "What you heard reliable or jest hearsay?"

"Pretty reliable, Odd. Raymond hisself was up a week or so back to look his place over. Rickety lookin' little fellow with skinny legs and a big pocketbook. Got hisself a big fancy watch. I heared it myself, right inside his pocket, ping-ping-ping every quarter hour. He takes it out, it's gotta big silver face that opens up, and some thingamabob inside rings off the hour bong-bong-bong. Takes a man with a big purse to own a watch like that. He ain't gonna git around much in these woods with them rickety little legs of his though, I kin tell you." Burroughs threw two or three small packets from the boat onto the dock. "That's canoe stuff, no reason it can't go right in if you think the weather'll hold. Don't want it rained on, but don't want to carry it up and back down neither if'n I don't have to." Guthrie's father made no comment. Burroughs knew more about the weather in these parts than he did. What Burroughs wanted was to share the responsibility of leaving the equipment in the canoe so that in case it rained, he could say, "But I asked you and you yourself said it wouldn't rain."

Guthrie picked up the canoe packs and started down the dock to where the birch-bark canoe had been hauled up on shore; that morning his father had been putting things in it, too. Almost all the loading would be finished today so that the two men could get away at dawn. Guthrie wished he were going along; he was old enough to go, but he understood that Burroughs and his father were getting away to pretend they were back ten, fifteen years before, in a different time. The Landing was opening up now; more and more people were coming in, outsiders buying large tracts of land were not unusual. Always before it had been on the other shore; now their own part of the lake had been touched. The tracts that had been bought were vast, but no one knew what was to be done with them. All that could be said in any surety was that thousands of acres had recently been sold, not just encompassing the lake but running far, far back into the woods. It was a puzzle and it made people nervous because it was obvious no one would pay good money for these vast parcels of land unless something was going to be done with them, and yet no one came to open them up; they lay, lonely and untouched, under the vast blue sky, just as they had always been, uninhabited and undisturbed.

Burroughs was with the boat at the water, his father going

up the hill toward the New House, he himself at the canoe. The climb was steep, but his father made it effortlessly, his head turned up, admiring again, as he always did, the big white clapboard house at the lip of the hill, the house he had said he was going to build and finally had.

It would have been a handsome building anywhere; in this area it was outstanding, with its covered crossbeams and its flat oak flooring, its plastered ceiling and real sloping staircase instead of the usual notched log stairs. It had a shingled roof whose wood had been dried a year before the shingles were rived; its big iron stoves, Albany-bought, were the talk of the countryside—the mean asked where Odder Buttes got the money to buy them and the mischievous wondered if, in his grand house, he would take a serving girl and put his Indian woman in the parlor. The money had come from hard work and scrupulous saving; Kateri stayed in the kitchen or out in the garden as she always had; nobody used the good parlor, it was waiting for a wedding or for a death, as it properly ought. New house or no new house, they lived almost the same, only they had privacy; Guthrie never got over marveling at what a wonder that was. His own room seemed to him the most wonderful place on earth.

He might wish for company once in a while, for almost no one came except Burroughs and a passing trapper—the Indians never came down from the reservation to see Kateri any more, though Guthrie's father had said she could send word up for any of her family who wanted to come visit; apparently none so desired, nor had Kateri gone back North on a visit. It was as if the Indian part of her life were closed.

The three of them made their lives here on the farm, closed in, a circle unto themselves; his father trying in winter to get a little learning into him, his letters and numbers and enough reading to get most of what he wanted and needed farmwise out of the Almanac; the Bible was reckoned for later on, if later on ever came. Guthrie worked with a crow quill for a pen. His father spent a lot of time sharpening these for him; there was an art in getting the points right and though Guthrie practiced he could never get the quills sharp enough. He had a little stone well for his ink, ink made for him by Kateri from the boiled bark of the swamp maple. School at the Landing had been briefly considered and promptly discarded; although the term was not overly long, finding a place for him to stay would mean asking a favor; the Butteses did not ask favors, and since Guthrie himself had no great hunger for learning, the matter was dropped. The Boy, as his father said, was getting the kind of education he needed: reckoning the seasons for plowing, planting, and reaping, learning tool-making and tempering, trying his hand at carpentry, building, mending, and repairing, mastering the care of the cows and the butchering of the beef and hogs. Sugaring he knew, and shooting and trapping. But his father was never satisfied until he had got the final knack of a thing. "Industry is a man's best habit," he said time and again. He said a man had to work *hard* to make his way. To his father work was something you set to with grim determination, but Guthrie found genuine pleasure in many of the tasks his father seemed to feel were irksome and onerous. For a time, while the house was going up, his father had been different; now it was up he had reverted to his old ways.

The house-raising had been done in the old way. The major part of the frame, the key posts and stringer beams and compression braces, were put together on the ground; a group of men had been invited over to help hoist. Afterwards there was a feast that Kateri had spent a week getting ready. There was dancing; a fiddler played, people sang, and everyone kept gesturing to the tree on the roof and laughing. The tree had been put atop the house when the last rafter was in place; it was a symbol of good luck, and after it was in place one of the men took off his hat and soon all the men were swinging theirs and giving a great hurrah. Guthrie's father kept going from group to group repeating his wonder. "My house is finally up," he said over and over. Late in the evening the drinking—the serious drinking—had started, and his father had been with the rest of the loud-mouthed, loud-laughing, running and stumbling and wrestling men.

Guthrie wanted his father to be special, stronger in every way than other men; but his father, he was learning, might be stronger in some ways, but he was also weaker in a lot of others. He wondered if the changes he was noticing were weaknesses that had been there all the time and he had never observed them or if they were part of the process of growing old and less sure. Kateri had changed, too, ever since she had come back. There was something bitter in her, something close to hate. It had changed the expression in her eyes so that they seemed blurred by a continual look of resentment. She hated him, Guthrie felt, and his father. But if she did, why did she go on endlessly, painstakingly cleaning up after them, preparing food for them, waiting on them, working for them day in and out in that awful rustle of over-anxious activity, all the time making that elaborate show of busyness. Perhaps it was for all the work they made that she hated them. But women had to do these things, just the way men had to do the things they did. Work, it seemed to Guthrie, ground everyone down. He didn't want her, or his father, made old and bitter by it, but there seemed no way to stop the pace they had initiated: now there seemed never a time to stand and just look at the hills and dream a moment or two.

Sometimes when the atmosphere was particularly tense with the recognition of chores still waiting to be done and time running out, when Kateri and his father were angry with themselves and everything around them because they were so harried by uncompleted schedules, he wished he could just say something, point out to them that they were skimping on everything, even their own regard for the farm, which, instead of being a place they loved, had become a cruel task-master who whipped them on and on, until they sank exhausted into their chairs at evening and stared with dull eyes at the tasteless food that was all Kateri had had time to put before them. He ate with his head down, attention fervent to the food in front of him, chewing and swallowing as rapidly as possible so that he might get out into the clean air or, if the weather was sour, up to his room where, on the natural wood bench he had found in the woods, a piece perfectly shaped with four legs—all he had had to do was split it across the middle to make the seat—he would huddle up to the window looking out up to the hill where the larch stood and his mother's gravestone pointed to the sky, a great granite piece on which, after much coaxing, his father had got the stoneworker from the Landing to carve initials only, a full name being too expensive. Then he would go over in his mind for the thousandth time, rooting for an answer, the buried truths that he knew, or what he could apprehend of them, the focus of which was he knew in that sound he some-times heard, muffled (deliberately, of course) of steps cross-ing the hall from one room to another. He was sure he did understand, but the tree—the grave—did not somehow permit such an admission. It would have been disloyal to his father, and to Kateri, for whom he had love, too, not the flesh-and-blood sort he felt for his father and mother, but one that was deep and profound nevertheless and full of his own obliga-tions.

His father was standing midhill gazing at his house; he said something over his shoulder and Burroughs shouted up *What?*

Guthrie's father put his pack down and turned. "I said, 'Whadda you say the name of them people was?'"

"Raymond," Burroughs shouted up. "From Al-*ban*-ee way."

"You know the lines where they bought?" Guthrie's father had started back downhill. His face was set. "I reckon I best go over and see for myself," he said in a voice to match his face.

"But, Odd, what about our trip?"

"You figure you'd be put out to postpone it a day or two, Clyde, while we went round the lines?"

Burroughs spit. "I knowed you was gonna wanta go the minute I brung the subject up. Why can't I jest keep my big mouth shut, jest *shut* till we're uplake and it don't make no sense to backtrack?"

"I want The Boy to go with us. It's near as much his business as mine."

They left no more than an hour later, on foot, carrying back packs with dried meat, hard corn cakes, some sugar and apples, a couple of onions. Each pack, smallish, was fastened to a roll, the lone blanket they would wrap over and under them. The packs were so light that after a time a man could walk without realizing he had much on his back at all. Burroughs would walk them over the lines in a day and a half, possibly two, the lay of the land was rough; they could see Raymond had bought himself quite a piece but—Burroughs shrugged, characteristically—he'd be damned if he knew what the old goat wanted to do with it.

They commenced at the lake following the line of their own property, east, near the shale, moving upmountain along the common line between the two pieces of property. When they reached the end of this boundary, they would head south along the top line of Raymond's property, then finally return to the lake. If they made good time, Burroughs thought, they might end up near the Landing by late the next night, hitch a ride crosslake the following day and be off on their trip north by late that afternoon. He was willing to walk the boundary line with Odder, but he'd much rather have been off hunting and trapping.

The first few minutes of the journey were easy; down by the shore the trees were formidable, but growth was down; as they advanced up into the foothills, passage became more difficult; it was uphill on uneven ground, around big boulders, over loose shale and through burry brush. The shale broke

168

underfoot and made their movements awkward; they climbed clumsily, stumbling, sliding, often finding it difficult to keep a toehold. It was a cool, pleasant day, but they were soon sweating, and the constant chipping and flaking stone underfoot bruised their feet; their hands were cut from trying to break falls.

Two hours later they were into the foothills. It was a relief to be rid of the shale, but here the ground growth was at its worst, tangled, thorned, prickly, thickly nettled; they had to cut their way a good deal of the time, often were blocked by huge granite boulders, bare, awesome, unclimbable. Guthrie looked on them with wonder; they seemed to him symbols of some force in nature larger, more powerful and enduring than anything he himself, or any man, any group of men, knew. But men, he thought, did move mountains. And he climbed, panting, behind his father and the carrot-headed man ahead, hearing the raucous cry of the pileated woodpecker, then a moment later seeing the huge flapping red-crested bird rising and falling close to the top of the tall pines.

The three men scrambled on, not saying much to one another. Because they had got a late start, they were pushing to make as much time as possible. Already the sun was losing power, shutting down as it set. The air was cold in the deeper shadowed woods where, after the heat and sweating of the more open slopes, Guthrie felt a distinct chill settle over his flesh.

The great pines and spruce, the hemlock, larch and balsams, secreted the sun. The ground was knee-high with browning ferns, bracken, brush; occasionally a stand of hardwood, mostly yellow birch and shag hickory, broke the columns of conifers, but the woods were almost entirely gymnospermous. He was looking forward to a fire, rest, food, but he saw his father and Burroughs were going to push until the last light faded.

It was never a good idea on the trail to travel right up into darkness, Ohguesse had taught him that, but apparently his father and Burroughs felt confident enough of their knowledge of the terrain to take the chance. Guthrie resigned himself to a long wait for a night's rest. But he was uneasy. It seemed to him no matter how well they knew the area it was a bad idea to push on this way. In any woods there were always too many unknowns. But it was no good his saying anything; they were the men and made the decisions.

He padded alongside them, rebellious with the remembrance of a saying his father had told him over and over,

"They ain't no accidents in the woods, they is only errors—bad judgments, bad decisions, bad equipment."

Guthrie's father was still troubled, still grousing. "I don't know," he was saying, "a man might be fool enough like me to farm for himself, but he couldn't talk a lot of other fellers into being such fools, so it's not likely all them fellers that bought land around here aim to break the woods up and sell off parcels fer farms, not 'less they cleared first and they ain't likely to—" Suddenly he stopped. "They must want the wood. They aimin' on loggin' it out, you figure, Clyde?"

Burroughs was disgusted. "Odd, there ain't no way to mill it for miles, you'd have to get it all the way to Wings' Falls, nobody's gonna go to that kind of trouble. The old mill Guy Guthrie had ain't nowhere near big enough to begin to do the job. And nobody'd be fool enough to drag all them logs down to—you hear that?" he demanded, stopping suddenly. Burroughs raised his gun. Guthrie's father, at his side, followed suit. The two men stood side by side, their rifles raised. The noise closed toward them, then suddenly stopped: the animal had caught wind of them.

Burroughs moved forward a few steps. "I aimed to make it to the spring," he said. He was pointing out what they already knew, that something large lay between them and water and that with the light almost gone they could not attempt the longer, safer way around. Nor, Guthrie knew, could they move ahead in such deceptive light; a man groping his way through such brush could not distinguish a waiting animal until it was too late. Beast and brush blended in the twilight. A deer would have run. A bear—a bear *ought* to run, too, unless she was with cubs. A she with cubs wouldn't run.

But it was fall, the cubs of the spring brood would almost be ready to fend for themselves, though the mother would find a place for them all to hibernate together over the winter. There, huddled up to one another, under a fallen log or in a rocky ledge, they would wait out the winter. In the spring the cubs would go their separate ways. Some shes were fiercely protective of their young right up until the very last, but others seemed to relinquish that wildly irrational protectiveness little by little.

"Can't camp without water," Burroughs said slowly. "Leastwise, not comfortably." He considered. "Can't go on neither, not in this light. So it looks like—"

There were sounds starting up again, this time violent and purposeful: a large animal was crashing through brush at a run toward them. Guthrie lifted his own gun.

It was a bear all right, the biggest bear Guthrie had ever seen, and it ran straight at them, he and Burroughs firing at almost the same time, his father holding back, waiting for the perhaps necessary last shot.

The bear was hit, but it kept coming on, a desperate, dying charge, all the more fatally effective for that. There was not time for Guthrie or Burroughs to reload. Guthrie threw himself to the ground at the same time that he heard his father's gun go off over his head. The bear had been advancing straight toward him. There was a split second between his father's firing and a crash to the left; he had been waiting for the bear to begin mauling him, but the moment he heard that crash he knew that the aim his father had taken had forced the bear toward Burroughs. Between son and friend, the friend had had to give way.

His father had made a shoulder shot which had thrown the animal violently off balance. It was the only aim that could divert the charge, though it might not kill the animal instantly.

Guthrie scrambled to his feet, then stopped in paralyzed disbelief. The bear had fallen on Burroughs. Frantic, dying, enraged, the bear was raking Burroughs again and again with its claws. Burroughs screamed—Guthrie thought that was the sound, though it was like nothing he had ever heard before, it was a cry heard perhaps once in a lifetime, and then only by very few men.

Guthrie threw himself on top of the bear, groping blindly for its neck. It was absolutely impossible that he could snap the neck of a thrashing animal whose weight was seven or eight times his own and whose fury was the fear-force of the wounded, but it was, his father testified later, an absolute, utter and complete physical impossibility which Guthrie had nevertheless accomplished.

The red-haired man lay almost completely scalped, the top of his head ripped open. His eyes were glassy, enormous, hysterical with pain and shock. His torn face, ripped apart all the way down one cheek, hung loose, a rattling breath rose and fell, bubbling in the blood. One of Burroughs' ears was ripped off; his nose hung loose. His chest lay exposed under the torn buckskin shirt; he was lying on his back staring up at Guthrie with terrible eyes, eyes trying desperately to say something. The blood kept bubbling up from the hole of his mouth, gurgles from the deep well inside.

Guthrie knelt, sweat streaming down over his eyes, his legs loose and trembling. He vomited, vomited again, then tried, with only a dry heave shaking him, to get himself in hand. They had to help Burroughs. It seemed impossible they could do anything to help him, but there was no choice; life rested solely in their efforts, in their unshakable belief he would survive. "Clyde," Guthrie said, using that name for the first time in his life.

The bubbling gurgled faster.

"Don't try to talk," Guthrie said. He took a breath. He was glad at least Burroughs couldn't see what had happened to his head, the way the whole top of his scalp was ripped away. On any man such a wound would have been horrible, but for a red-headed one— "Pa," he called over his shoulder.

"Guthrie," he heard his father say in a hoarse voice after a moment. "Guthrie?" It was a question. "You hurt?"

"No," he said, "Jest—spent. You all right?" He looked over and saw that his father was lying a little way off, crumpled up. Overhead he saw first one star, then another. The trees were black-branched giants; they seemed to Guthrie to be reaching for those shining points in the sky.

"Something pulled," his father said. "I can't hardly walk. But I'll be all right as soon as I catch my breath."

He sounded terrible; pain was part of his voice, every word a wound. "Can you git together a fire?" If they were going to get Burroughs back to the Landing, he would have to be washed and bound before they started.

"I guess so. Only—well, it'll take a minute."

Guthrie ripped away Burroughs' buckskin shirt. He had to close up the chest wound right away. He recognized the significance of the sucking sounds that came from it. It was a bad wound and if it weren't taken care of immediately it would kill Burroughs very shortly.

He had to close up the chest so that Burroughs could still breathe but also so that the lungs were sealed off from outside air. How? Common sense, he said to himself, just use your common sense, it's all you got. You can't do nuthin' and some things might be worse than nuthin' but if you think it through—

Guthrie put his hands on either side of that big gap in the chest. He needed something fairly clean to cover the hole, but there was nothing at hand. The best substitute would come from the forest, but it was too dark to search; even in daylight he supposed he could not take the time to leave Burroughs and hunt.

He waited until Burroughs' breathing bubbled out; then he pushed the sides of that mangled chest together, tore a
172

strip from Burroughs' leather jerkin and bound it around the body, using another strip as a direct compress over the wound before he tightened the binding. Not clean, but at least it closed the hole. He remembered that his father and Burroughs never set off on a trip without a jug. "Get me the whiskey, Pa," he called to his father.

He put the cork between his teeth and pulled, poured a good dollop over the buckskin compress, resealed the cleanser.

I ought to git his head up, Guthrie thought. With his chest that way, it might help him breathe. Have to patch the scalp, the mouth, the nose, but first the top of the head. He needed water for that. Behind him he heard the rustling noises of the woods. They ought not, he reasoned, move Burroughs, at least not yet; with that bad chest, probably not at all, but he had to be kept warm. "Build that fire up good," he told his father.

Burroughs lay with his eyes closed, his body twitching now and then, but mainly still. Guthrie hoped he was unconscious. He had never worked on a man hurt bad like this before. Come to think of it, he'd never sewn skin at all. All he knew was what he could remember from seeing Kateri work.

Sewing? And with *what?*

He could not stitch together the torn flesh, he had neither needle nor thread. Burroughs was going to die unless he did something. But what? *What?*

He had no sharp bone needle, no dried animal tendons; all he had was this torn dirty shirt. And his hands.

He looked down on the red-haired man. Burroughs had cared for him, had come as close as anyone to understanding about the horse. It was Burroughs and his father's fault this had happened, because they had insisted on traveling when night was coming on. Your fault . . . *your* fault . . . *all your fault,* he wanted to shout at both of them.

His father would know what was right. In the midst of everything his father would remain calm and sensible, with his imperturbable Buttes practicality. He squatted down by the roaring fire. "We got to carry him back, Pa."

His father, nodding, looked thoughtfully into the firelight. "It ain't gonna be easy, but we'll make it, one way or the other." His father sounded just awful, all tore apart. Guthrie looked at him—really looked at him—for the first time since the accident. "You hurt bad, ain't you?"

"Nuthin' to speak of, a little pullin' is all. I'll make out all

173

right. Don't do a man no good either to know he's done somethin' like this to a friend." He looked at Guthrie. "I couldn't make no other choice," he said, rising. "Let's git him where it's warm. He never was one to like the cold." He bent over his old friend. "Jesus," he said softly. "Jesus, jest look at him."

Burroughs was conscious, making small sounds from inside his wounded chest and the flaps of his mouth. If Burroughs had been an animal dying in the woods bear-mauled like that, and if Guthrie had seen in the animal's eyes what he saw in Burroughs' eyes, he would not have hesitated a moment; he would have destroyed the poor suffering thing. An act of mercy his conscience demanded, yet here he was doing everything in his power to keep the maimed man alive. He did not understand: it went beyond understanding. He just kept talking to Burroughs, that was all, telling him to hold on, with the absurd but stubborn idea his talking would give Burroughs a lifeline to which he could cling. "You're gonna be all right," Guthrie insisted over and over in the face of all evidence to the contrary. "You're gonna be all right, jest don't give up."

The cutting went well, the washing up badly. The moment Guthrie applied the cooled, boiled inner shirt he had stripped from himself and cut in pieces to Burroughs' head, the red-haired man gave a shriek; and, impossible as it seemed, raised himself up, his eyes a curse and a plea. Kill me, my God, kill me, Boy, they screamed into Guthrie's face.

The wounds had to be cleansed. "You'll have to hold him down, Pa," he said. "Hold him down while I git his head cleaned up."

His father knelt down. "You're sure a sight, Clyde," he said. There was pity and wonder in his father's voice, and a terrible tenderness. They had been very close, these two men, two men in the wilderness without their rightful women.

He understood, too, that no matter how much strength there was in his determination and energy in trying to save Burroughs, he would never have been able to give Burroughs what his father did: the ability to accept the truth of what had happened. He, Guthrie, had said over and over, "You're gonna be all right," and that was a lie; he knew it was a lie, Burroughs knew it; but Guthrie's father had spoken the truth, and now that it was out in the open, they could all start to live with it. From that moment Guthrie realized later, things were better: there was no need to waste energy

174

in lying and trying to cover up, in the awful exhaustion of pretense. He found again, as his father held Burroughs and he brought the cloth to Burroughs' head, Burroughs screeching and thrashing and at last lying still, that his heart was beating wildly for both these men whom he loved, the red-haired one who was suffering so much without any seeming meaning to it, and his gray-haired father who understood and gave, with his unquestioning acceptance of the fact, this was how life was, some soundness to the suffering, as if, Guthrie thought, his father were trying to say to Burroughs, Now, Clyde, you and me have seen it time and again, and it don't make no sense, none of it, you and me know that, so . . . so jest hang on, git through the best you can, and then we can think what's to be done, but it ain't ever gonna be the same again, you and I know that, but Clyde, we're old enough to face it, and go on anyway.

Inert under Guthrie's hands, Burroughs lay like a rotting log left to disintegrate among the healthy wood of the forest. He breathed, gently, a dying man's breath; quiet, unprotesting, the tortured body and mangled face permitted ministration: Guthrie took the thin strips of deerhide and wound under them as best he could one section of flesh to another, anchoring the flap of scalp to the skull, the cheek to the face, the chin and mouth and ear onto the head. There was nothing he could do for the hole where the nose had been. He left it. But having conquered, or at least met, the prime problem, he was now faced with the knowledge he must go on and solve others. Burroughs would weaken and die without food; yet obviously nothing could go down that mouth, into that chest.

He went to the fire and sat down, his head leaden with fatigue. He was tired and sick and at his wits' ends and he had to make Burroughs eat. An insoluble problem, like why two such experienced woodsmen as Burroughs and his father had pushed on relentlessly in darkness. They just had: he had to accept that.

In the morning Burroughs was still alive, breathing in thin, shallow gasps, the flickering fire of life banked.

Guthrie was filled with a sullen resentment against the two men that he could not suppress, a feeling that they had let him down by their insistence on pressing on when they ought to have stopped, and this more than anything else angered and upset him. He had wanted his father, he supposed, to be

175

the strongest, wisest man he knew; and next to his father, he had expected Burroughs, a second father to him, to be both steady and resolute. That the two men on whom he had depended should turn out to be so foolish was a bitter blow to him. He was discovering there is no more disillusioning experience in the world than to discover you have put your confidence and love in weak, human imperfection.

He ate his hard cornmeal cake, gnawed at some dried meat, helped his father make a pot of strong tea. When he had eaten, he felt better, more capable of coping, as if after all there were some hope. He thought perhaps his optimism was only early-morning energy, but he had, after some warmth in his stomach, sense enough to seize on it and use it while it held. If they could just get some tea through that mangled mouth—

And then, suddenly, he thought he had an answer. He jumped up, looking at the dark heavy foliage all around. "Pa, what we need is some kind of reed—you know, some kind of hollow stem—" His father's face was blank. "We could pour tea through it," he explained, "and—"

"Through a little reed?"

"All right, then, some kind of funnel. That would work, wouldn't it?"

His father thought, pursing his lips, giving the suggestion serious consideration. "Might jest," he said at last.

"Birch," Guthrie cried, seeing in his mind's eye Kateri working with the pliable bark, fashioning buckets for sap season. "We'll cut some birch and make us a funnel and git somethin' in him that way."

They cooled the tea until it was lukewarm and then tried to rouse the wounded man. He lay unconscious, his small, almost extinguished breaths coming in shorter, swifter gasps. Guthrie was of two minds whether they should raise him or not; finally he hit upon the solution of elevating the head slightly.

Burroughs did not waken. Finally they gave up trying to get him to regain consciousness; the only thing to do was keep the tea close enough to the fire to remain warm but not get hot and when—if—he opened his eyes, try to pour it down him. Guthrie went to cut sticks to splint the nose. He had a plan and he spent all morning whittling at small green sticks, waiting for Burroughs to regain consciousness, but the stricken man slept on, only his hands moving convulsively now and then, a thin flutter as if the wind had raised them, sending them up, open, closed, trembling, falling, faintly spastic, then quite dead on his deer-skin-bandaged chest.

About noon Guthrie went to work on the nose. He took one long, widish stick and ran it from Burroughs' forehead down to his chin. This he bound to the head and used as a central support; he used two smaller sticks as side supports. He felt a curious sense of satisfaction, as if he had done something difficult and enviable; and yet when he looked at his work, he saw it was crude at best. But he had tried and that was what counted: to try.

He and his father ate a little at midday. His father's face was gray. He looked loose and unstrung, as if something vital had come free inside and the whole of his frame had come unhinged and did not hang right. Guthrie remembered his father saying, "Somethin's pulled," and he thought, No, he can't go bad on me, I can't manage the two of them; but his father had the look of a sick man, he moved like one, too, slow and unsure. Maybe it was the knowledge he had sent the bear toward Burroughs that was crippling him. Guthrie tried to understand. Instead he lost his temper. "You hurt?" he demanded, as if, should his father say *yes,* he would use his fists to punish such behavior.

Blind, instinctive rage burned in him, a fever to punish, to get rid of these old, hurt, needy men. He rose and faced his father with clenched fists. "Why the hell did you keep us goin' when it was gettin' dark? That's what I want to know —*why?* It's all your damned fault—yours and his—" He sat down, shaking. "You both got jest what you deserved," he said bitterly. "Jest what you deserved, jest exactly what you both deserved."

He left it at that, silent, staring at the fire, waiting for Burroughs to do something, open his eyes, or die.

Toward nightfall Burroughs began to make sounds again and Guthrie and his father went with the birch funnel and the tea to try to force a little sustenance into him. His eyes were open. He looked at them with that terrible, pleading petition, but he made no great fight against their helping him keep alive; he had given up. In the night he cried out and tried to raise himself. They listened to the screams, they tried to hold him down, they took turns forcing tea into the hole where his mouth should have been. In the morning he was quiet and still, with the bound chest barely moving. At noon they thought he was dead, but it took all that afternoon and part of the night for the red-haired man to part with what little life was still there, and even then he would not give it

177

all up, he held on, and held on; and on the second morning, though he was the color of the poplars of the forest, a strange dry brittle green, he lived on, the chest still slightly convulsive with air coming in, going out, coming in again, sustaining the faintest movements of life still hanging on. They poured tea down him and changed him as if he were a baby; they kept the fire at a roar now because the weather was growing colder and they waited, wishing at one moment he would die and get it over with and at the next that he would somehow manage to live and reaffirm their faith that impossible battles can be won; and, finally, exhausted, they stopped even watching and lay down for a time and slept as if they themselves were dead.

Nothing had changed when they woke. Burroughs was still faintly bringing in and expelling air, a man on the verge of death but not quite dead, a hideously maimed, horribly suffering man who still wanted, somehow, to live, and managed, somewhere, impossibly, to hang onto life.

Guthrie knew that remaining here, waiting for Burroughs to get better, was useless. Tea wasn't the substance of strength and although he began to grind the corn cakes down and mix a little with the tea, he felt no confidence in that either, for the main consideration was the cold and the inevitable snow. He and his father—his father faltering, stumbling, but uncomplaining—had put up a shelter of sorts; but the fact remained Burroughs belonged back at the New House with Kateri looking after him. He thought of the magic Iroquois medicine to bring back the dead, the dead hunter whom the birds and animals had restored to life because they loved him. Burroughs had loved the animals of the earth and the birds of the air; could not the hawk offer to restore his scalp to his head as it had done the old Iroquois hunter? Could not the birds bring herbs to restore him back to life?

He looked at the wounded man. Burroughs was a proud man who would never be able to stand the pity his scarring would inevitably bring. Yet surely a man was more than the features of his face.

The best plan, of course, was to go back alone and get help. Traveling on his own he would make much faster time than hauling one half-conscious and one faltering man through the forest. But he had to reckon, too, on the return trip. And if he did leave them, might not Burroughs die while he was gone, or his father get worse, be unable to help

Burroughs or perhaps even himself? There was really no choice. He had to take them both back.

It was in fact only half a day's travel back—for a normal man. But he would have to support Burroughs (*how?*) and he couldn't count on his father for much help; his father might not even be able to take the strain himself. He was stumbling; whatever had given inside him might be more serious than either of them suspected. It seemed quite likely to Guthrie his father was suffering badly and saying nothing about it; once on the trail, forced to keep pace, no matter how slow, compelled by his own system of values to help haul Burroughs, his father was bound to collapse. He would then have two helpless men on his hands. Anyway he looked at it, it was bound to be a formidable journey.

He squatted beside his father. They had not spoken much since Guthrie's outbreak of anger. Guthrie was pretty sure his father, who was honest on all levels, even that of himself, was answering to the charges of negligence and responsibility (as well he should, but squatting there beside him Guthrie was still moved to pity by his predicament, that compulsion for honest evaluation); he touched his father lightly on the arm and his father, looking at him with weary eyes, seemed to understand; his look softened, he made a tentative grimace that was close to a smile.

"We gotta try to git him back, Pa," Guthrie began. "Kateri—" and he saw a small light shine far back in his father's eyes—"she'd know a lot about what should be done, and anyway we can't stay out here, the weather's gitting bad, it's gonna git worse—" His father nodded, in agreement; so far nothing Guthrie had said was disputable, but they had not come to the heart of the matter. Guthrie took a deep swallow, forcing himself to keep his eyes on his father's, and went on. "We gotta move him, and normally—" He faltered, took a deep breath, and plunged on, "normally you and me, we'd make some kind of contraption to carry him in and we'd make it back without too much trouble, but—" His father's eyes brightened, aware, watching; Guthrie wondered if he knew what was coming— "But you're hurt, too, Pa—" It was a statement; Guthrie wasn't asking him, he was telling him his strength wasn't there, he was not sufficient for the responsibilities ahead—"You know that—" he said to mitigate the sting, a kind of plea for his father to be gentle in his resignation to what was— "And so I'm gonna ask you how bad it is, and I want you to tell me the truth, so that when I make my plans—" It was out in the open now, tactful as

Guthrie had tried to put it— "I can take that into account and know jest what to expect."

Was it a sigh his father gave or a grunt? He had taken out his tobacco pipe; he pressed his thumb down fiercely and firmly as Guthrie finished, and now, lifting the pipe between his teeth, he bent forward, using a stick touched to the fire for a light. He was giving himself, Guthrie saw, time to think, to be fair. He was a very just man; even amidst the apprehension he felt waiting for his father's reply to this challenge to his absolute authority, Guthrie could not suppress his pride in his father's rationality. It came to Guthrie his father was what might truly be called a good man. He wanted to ask forgiveness for what he had just demanded; he would have liked to beg his father to forget his words and what they meant; he would have liked to hand authority back, without any excuses, without—Guthrie hardened toward that weakness in himself that was pity and which might mean all their undoing.

"It's tight some, here," his father indicated, pointing to his groin. "But I still can pull my own weight—and more," he said. But what Guthrie noted was that he had not disputed who was in command. He knows, too, Guthrie thought. It was the worst of the whole bad business, that his father realized only too clearly what was involved. This trip, in its way, had been as much his father's undoing as it had been Burroughs', all because two impatient men had insisted on going against their own better judgments.

"Can you walk back? I mean, make it on your own all the way?" Guthrie asked anxiously of his father, who was accustomed to getting up at three o'clock many mornings and going ten miles to do a day's work on his farm and ten miles back before breakfast. "Because if you think you can't, Pa, it's best to say so now; you can stay here and wait for help. There's the fire, you got plenty of food, there's no *need* for you to come—"

"Jest how you aim to git him back alone?"

"I can maybe manage one," Guthrie said.

"Then I'll do my own managing, don't you worry none."

"You sure?"

"I'm sure."

"It ain't that I figure to rile you, Pa, I jest gotta know is all. You can see that."

"What I can't figure is how you aim to move Clyde there all by yourself." But what his father was saying really was, I can make it myself, but don't count on me for any extra

180

help. I can't help carry. I'm sorry, his eyes said, though his face remained expressionless, but I jest can't. And you can't move a man like that on your own. You'll kill him if you do. And of course his father's point was well taken: how was he going to transport Burroughs over all that rough ground (Guthrie thought particularly of the shale); he couldn't carry him saddle-back, not, as his father said, with a chest wound like that. He could not pull him all that distance.

Some decisions, while inevitable, ought never to have to be made, but circumstances force them; leaving it at that, which Guthrie felt would assuage his conscience in the future when he had time to think, and if the trip should cost Burroughs his life, he set about getting ready. He had two choices: to pull Burroughs some way or to carry him. Pulling a wounded man single-handed over rough ground seemed a certain sentence of death; no choice but to carry him. Moreover, forced to slow his own pace, he would be giving his father a chance to go slowly, without his feeling he was holding them up. Three days for the trip, carrying dead weight like that across rough terrain, but there was nothing else to do.

He went over and took a look at Burroughs. He was sleeping with a rattling sound going in and out in his chest; he woke regularly, every three or four hours, for a few minutes, and they were able to funnel a little tea with corn meal down him. He didn't seem better or worse, still just dying, but it was taking him an awful long time to do it; maybe that ought to be encouraging.

Guthrie began to break camp. He separated provisions for three days into the smallest amounts possible so that one pack, loaded with all they would need, was quite light. He figured to get his father to carry that and his own blanket; it wasn't much, but the way he saw it anything at all might be too much for a man with his insides all pulled out of shape.

His father observed, offering neither advice nor help; he was using the occasion, the first major one of decision, to let Guthrie understand that he had willingly abdicated authority as head of this expedition. Without looking up, but with warmth in his voice, showing his father his appreciation, Guthrie said, "You reckon you ken carry this? I'm goin' to leave the other stuff. If we travel light, we gotta a good chance. If you can tote this, I can take him."

"You're gonna *carry* Clyde all the way back?"

181

"It's the only way. You know any better?" Guthrie was gruff, he knew he was taking an awful chance.

"No," his father said shortly. "But you'll kill him sure as God made bad days like this."

"There ain't no other way, Pa. We wait around, the snows'll come, you know that. We'll never git out."

"But he'd be stronger—"

"I can't carry him through snow."

"Can you carry him all the way without it, though, that's the question."

"I ken try."

"Yes, I guess so. A man's always gotta try."

For this moment, before they began, they were in harmony; later, when the hardships came, there might be disputes, anger, bitterness, quarrels; but for the moment they were united, respectful of one another. It was one of those rare good moments.

The large fire had to be extinguished completely. When they had pulled it apart and broken down the larger logs, Guthrie got his axe and began chopping, digging, covering. They spent half an hour burying the coals; then Guthrie took another quarter of an hour getting ready to lift Burroughs. He had worked out a plan whereby he would use a blanket as a compress between Burroughs and himself. The blanket, folded, would be wedged between his own body and up against Burroughs' chest, a large compress, tight, to keep Burroughs' chest in place. First, he wrapped Burroughs in one blanket to keep him warm. Then he folded his compress-blanket very carefully so that it made a neat pad. Guthrie figured if the pad held as a wedge, it would both keep Burroughs steady and also act as an additional compress against the wounded man's chest. He told his father to hold off hoisting his own share of the equipment until he, Guthrie, was ready to go. He needed a hand getting Burroughs up and the compress-blanket in place. He explained his idea for wedging the pad in great detail, realizing he was being too explicative, but his father didn't get insulted or hurt; he listened carefully, nodding, licking his lips, nodding. "It's a good idea," he said when Guthrie was finished and Guthrie was immensely grateful to him for his patience, his sense of justice.

Burroughs was not a big man, but he was heavy the way woodsmen are, with a thick, strong, solid, muscular body; there was no spring to him as Guthrie got him up on his back: he lay against Guthrie like a solid stone, the injured head hanging to one side, swinging against Guthrie's shoulder. As Guthrie's father painstakingly put the compression blanket in place, Burroughs gave a groan; then he subsided back into unconsciousness. "It works good," Guthrie's father said. Guthrie could tell by the feel of it that the blanket was going to do its job. "You go first, Pa," he said. He wanted to keep an eye on his father, but in order to put a good face on the request, he said, "To break trail."

They set off slowly. Burroughs was heavier than Guthrie had anticipated, and awkward; this part of the forest, with its narrow, trampled trail was fairly easy to maneuver, however, and so long as they were on level ground, the going would not be too bad. What Guthrie dreaded was the descent through thick brush, that part of the trail around the enormous granite boulders and over the shale, but he was grateful for all the cutting they had done at the onset of the journey, hacking out the worst of the brush. Also he had a foreboding of rain—why not? It was that time of the year and that kind of trip—

They were not even on the trail an hour when Guthrie had to call the first rest stop. He would have had no trouble keeping going himself another hour or two, slow, steady, bent to the weight, his mind a blank, his body directing the necessary push and pull, the proper shifting for the stresses and strains; but ahead of him his father was floundering; he had tripped twice and Guthrie could tell by the sharp, stunted angle of his body that fatigue had already set in. They stopped, his father stripping the pack and remaining blanket from his back, and lying down, his head resting against the roll. He was panting and his face was ashen. He looked at Guthrie, who was squatted beside him with Burroughs still on his back. He's not going to make it, Guthrie thought. "You all right, Pa?" he asked aloud.

"Awful thirsty," was all the trembling voice answered.

"There's the creek up ahead," Guthrie said encouragingly. "Not too far."

"It's a good two miles," his father, who knew every inch of this land, said testily. Two miles had once been nothing to him; now Guthrie saw that in his present state even a mile, half a mile was too much. Painfully his father rose, however, and bent, faltering, over the packed roll, forced it up and onto his shoulders, then stumbled forward, not looking back, swaying from side to side. Guthrie didn't quite know what to do. On his own he would have been able to make twice the distance in the same time, but he couldn't expect to do more

183

than go slower and slower and a man who is fighting against his natural pace will tire more than one pushing himself. They would creep along, straining the strength out of themselves with such slowness.

He stopped, not because he was tired, but to allow his father to get ahead so that he might find his rightful pace and keep it until he came up on his father again, but he soon saw that this stop-start system would work well for him but against his father; Guthrie was able to rest frequently but his father had to plod on, never quite outdistancing Guthrie far enough so that he had to be called to wait and could then rest himself, although Guthrie relieved the monotony of the march by allowing his father to get a little farther ahead each time he set off to catch up with him.

"When we get to the creek, Pa, why don't we make camp and rest? Tomorrow I'll go on by myself and you can wait."

"You're goin' to leave him with me?"

"No—when I said myself, I meant, you know, him and me. He's not that heavy, I could make it maybe in a day, pushing some; at the most, a day and a half. But now—you know yourself you're in no condition to keep on. You know that, don't you, Pa?"

The truth again: how would his father take it this time? After a pause he said, "All right. How far's the creek?" Then he laughed: he knew very well. "Plumb tuckered out," he said. "Too tired even to rest. Let's jest git there," he said, pitching forward but keeping somehow on his feet. "Seems an awful long way for a man to go," he said, "for a drink of *water*."

It had taken them well past noon to make two, possibly three, miles; at the creek—actually an upper shoot of the Indian River—a sullen rain, more like a drizzle, began to fall. A small cold mist rose from the pebbled surface of the water; the rain looked as if it would keep up that way all day, slow and steady, sure of itself. Guthrie cursed the waste of time necessary to build a shelter, but he saw instantly that his father was incapable of going on or of even getting together his own lean-to. He eased Burroughs from his back gently and laid him under a big pine, a small protection against the shower, covering the unconscious man with the blanket he had used as the wedge; then he turned his attention to getting a fire going. He chose a spot near a large rock, cleaned out a space with the butt of his axe, patted it down with his feet, stomping out unevennesses, stopping every now and then to remove rocks. The rain was not a downpour, but steady, soaking everything.

He used the axe to cut some good-sized heavy pine limbs, set them up with poles he cut from small birches, laced the limbs overhead one on top of the other, crude and unreliable in a strong wind, but usable until he had the fire built, his father and Burroughs settled, and could take the time and attention needed for lacing. He was beginning to worry as much about his father as he was about Burroughs.

He made the lean-to fairly quickly, got the fire going with a minimum of trouble, took the folded birch pail from his father's pack, filled it with water, set it up on poles over the fire. His father had come, as soon as the fire caught, and settled, hunched over, as near it as he could, his head hanging down exhausted on his chest, the rain beaded on the back of his buckskin shirt. Burroughs was conscious now, his eyes open in the hideously swollen, scarred face. The eyes, Guthrie was surprised to note, were quite calm and there was lucidity in them. It was the first good sign he had had.

He bent down and began talking, reassuringly, as he got ready to make the move, explaining, placating, promising. Burroughs did not answer, but in his eyes there was a flicker of expression, of commendation, Guthrie felt. When he lay Burroughs near the fire and got him rewrapped in the blanket, the eyes were glazed and dim again. It was the pain from moving him, Guthrie guessed. He made tea, roused Burroughs and got a little into the injured mouth; then Burroughs slept, heavily, undisturbable. Guthrie had given Burroughs the blanket compress, unfolded, to lie on; Burroughs was wrapped in his own blanket; that meant there was only one blanket to leave for his father, cold and wet as he was, but apparently his father did not mind; he was sound asleep rolled into the cocoon of his blanket, stretched lengthwise along the warmth of the big burning logs. Guthrie went to do the lacing; he could not have slept if he had wanted to; his head—and heart—were full of too many things.

He worked carefully, securing each bough separately; three or four days would probably pass before he came back—this time with Narko, taking the long way around to avoid the shale—but in the meantime a bad storm might strike. He wanted to protect his father from any bad weather that might come; he laced the top, then commenced enclosing two sides, the lean-to open onto the fire; in that way his father was protected from bad weather and from animals.

185

Guthrie figured he would get Burroughs down, leave him with Kateri, take Narko and come back immediately; three, four days at the most. He was not uneasy about leaving his father; Odder Buttes was more at home in the forest than he was in his own home, but he was a sick man who shouldn't get too far from the protective fire. He had water near, and Guthrie planned to leave most of the food; he would only take some dried meat to suck, that way he would be traveling light—he almost laughed, traveling light except of course for Burroughs on his back.

He was not hesitant about going out without much sustenance; Indians went for weeks on the trail with only some hard maple sugar and ground corn meal; he himself had often gone off for the day with only the smallest of rations, testing, training himself, seeing how long his body could work at maximum efficiency with a minimum amount of sustenance, the Indian way.

An Indian would no doubt have found a better way to close and seal Burroughs' wounds, but Guthrie was white. Even the few trappers and renegades from civilization who went with the Indians and lived like them, discarding all their former ways, their former language, even at times it seemed their former thinking, were imprisoned in their pretense, their delusion, by the color of their eyes, by an expression caught there in a moment of savage cruelty or in the midst of some strange custom no white man would ever comprehend, no matter how hard he tried. A man was three-quarters defined at the instant he emerged from the womb; one-quarter was up to him, but even so it seemed to Guthrie he was short-changed. Too much of the future had already been laid out in the past. There were things inside a man could never strike out, no matter how much he tried. Better to come to some sort of reconciliation and live in what unanimity he could with what he couldn't change.

He was not an Indian and would never be. But nor was he "all" white. He had a foot in both worlds. It seemed to him that that ambiguity was so much a part of him that he was like someone who belonged to no world, the stranger standing outside the closed circle who longed to step over the imaginary line that walled him off from a world where he felt he might, perhaps, fit in. Every man needed a world to fit in. Hate was being outside. Hate was being unlike everyone else. And hell, he often thought, was just that: hate.

The worst of the trip Guthrie counted behind him; on his own he would be able to move much faster, not have to worry and strain wondering if his father was going to hold up. He felt a certain satisfaction, finishing the final side of the shelter, as if for a fact the trip were over and he was relieved of his responsibility.

He started at sunup. Mist hung heavy in the great limbs of the pines, the spruces and larch; a fine rain fell. On every surface, no matter how small, moisture had collected in thick iridescent beads; the earth was slick and colored with wet. His father slept. Guthrie did not try to shake him awake to say good-bye. A man did his duty best without the formalities; then he did not need praise or pardon. Dignity, Guthrie was beginning to believe, came from a certain slope of silence. Perhaps it originated in the reticence of nature, but it seemed to him a man gained in stature in proportion to the unmentioned hardships he set out to conquer. Evidence always existed: it merely took perceptive eyes to evaluate. He honored his father enough to believe his father had the eyes of understanding. It was a gift to covet one day for his own. But a man had to earn everything that counted in his favor, eyes that truly saw, hands able to touch and identify, ears sensitive enough to separate sounds, an understanding heart. If you chose, as the Butteses had, a life that relied on yourself, then you had to develop that sense of self, you had to be willing to risk it in defeat. He felt that of all the people he had ever known his father would understand best how he could get up and go away without even saying good-bye.

Guthrie filled one small pouch with pemmican, left the rest of the food for his father. He wrestled with the compress he made of the folded blanket, securing it this time against Burroughs' chest while the sick man lay on the ground. He took deer laces from the neck of his shirt and leggings inside his pants. The pants were open to the knees, but the outside of his legs was protected by wrapping the loose parts of his pants into his boots. Then he crouched down, bent back as far as he could, straining, seized Burroughs unseeing by bending his arms over his shoulders, and hoisted him onto his back. He shifted his weight, adjusted Burroughs as best he could; resting a moment, he bent forward, picking up his gun and his axe, hitching them into the strap across his chest that held the pouch for powder for his gun—they were awkward but he had to have them—and then struggled to his feet, letting Burroughs' weight fall onto his shoulders; balanced himself, caught his breath, rose with one full but slow swing,

187

and started off, looking (but not pausing) at his father, still sleeping by the fire.

He followed the stream. Half a mile it narrowed and there was a natural stepping-stone bridge which he could cross. The brush was bad—it always was along water where, with so much moisture, everything grew profusely—but he went with the fine first strength of the morning. Later in the day when he was tired a passage such as this would have caused him great discouragement, but buoyed by the feeling of getting away on his own, he swung his body against the brush, using it as a tool to clear away obstructions. Had there been sun he might even have been happy, it was that kind of anticipatory feeling he had. But the rain was a nuisance and definitely slowed him, fogging his vision, running down his face into the flapping neckline of his shirt where the laces were missing. Soon his chest was wet, he began to feel cold, just a chill, nothing serious, but he knew that later on, if the weather did not break and the sun did not come out and dry him, he would be frozen to the bone, so stiff with cold that his timing would be all off. He put the idea away. There was no use in borrowing trouble, he had enough right now; anyway the sun *might* break through and all his worrying would have been a waste. He couldn't afford to waste *any*thing.

His pace was steady, not fast, but faster than the day before; Burroughs' weight had not yet begun to bother him. Guthrie knew it was there—another nuisance like the rain— but it was not a threat yet. Later that too would be another matter. As the day progressed, Burroughs would get heavier and heavier until Guthrie would feel it was not a man he was carrying on his back, but the whole, wide, weighing world. Well, it was not the first time a man had carried a friend out of the forest. Nor would it be the last.

Guthrie's father had once (speaking, Guthrie now recalled, of Burroughs) used the word value. "He has a store set up of them," his father had said of Clyde Burroughs, "but there is not one of them can be bought. They're only for his own use and he helps himself frequently from the shelves." His father grinned. "You haven't any idea at all what I'm talkin' about, have you, Boy? Not that I blame you. What I mean," Guthrie's father said, serious, "is that Clyde Burroughs's got a lot of things he believes in. They're like a structure inside, something really, I suppose, around which he, Clyde Burroughs, is built, a good sound structure that holds him up, that can be counted on, no matter which way the winds blow. That structure is his values, the things he measures the way he acts against. It's a good structure Clyde's got, his beliefs are good ones; and he lives by them, he don't jest pay them lip service the way most people do. The important thing, Boy, is to have a good sound structure like that and never let nothing ruin it. Not many men can claim that."

Guthrie paused, resting, reconnoitering. On the opposite side of the stream the land sloped severely down toward Federation Lake. He was near the boulders; he could see them burst out of the earth, great granite protests. What would be a problem was going downhill with those big rocks to outskirt and then that shale to maneuver. He hitched Burroughs up a bit, heard a groan, and asked over his shoulder, "You awake?"

"I been awake for miles," Burroughs said. "I felt every step of the way. But you went gentle, Boy," he added quickly. "You done as well as anyone could." His words were rattley because they had to come through that torn orifice that had formerly been a mouth, but Guthrie marveled that he could speak at all.

He would have to cross the rocks carefully. If he were to slip—once more he put an unmanageable thought from his mind. He let himself go blank, emotionless, devoid of feeling and anticipation, of consideration of any possibility except the one of getting across the stream. He was using the Indian method of making himself passive in the midst of a hostile universe, of not wasting himself wondering about its malevolence or fighting back angrily against its injustice, but letting everything drain from him, except the knowledge that he was, and part of his being was the burden on his back, as much a part of him as an arm or a leg. Guthrie stood still for several moments, loosening one muscle after another, calming every instinct, relaxing his mind to the point almost of not knowing. The procedure took a long time; he was out of practice; but he could feel the gradual unwinding of the tensions in his body, the quiet flow of something so basic it had no name, though the name he gave it was "being." His "being" began at last to be part of that larger one around him, the giant boulders, the great trees, the greater sky; nothing existed in him save the calm sense that he was at one with them; but whereas they did not move, he and the clouds could: he put his foot on the first rock in the stream and started across.

The rain had raised the water; it swirled foamily, covering most of the rocks, washed back and forth over the others.

Where the rocks were wet, they were slippery, and Guthrie in his big boots and with Burroughs on his back tensed. He stopped, his feet on two separate rocks, his body swaying. He tried to let his mind go loose again, but Burroughs grabbed at him, frantic, and he began to lose his balance, throwing out his arms.

"Stop," he shouted, knowing at the same time Burroughs would never stop, he was caught in blind panic, unable to get hold of himself.

Guthrie lurched forward, almost running, racing across the rocks before his feet had a chance to slip off, driving himself by blind impulse.

They crashed onto the opposite bank. Guthrie went down, sprawling, Burroughs on top of him. The back of his axe slammed into his chest, terrible slices of pain knifing up and down his ribs. He knew immediately what was the matter: some bones were broken or, with luck, just cracked. But to go on now carrying a man of Burroughs' weight—he lay still and wept, tears of fury and recrimination against the unfairness of what had happened. If only that danged fool Burroughs hadn't—

He got to his knees, swallowing the spasms of anger and tears. Burroughs was hunched up on his back screaming, "I'm bleeding, I'm bleeding . . . oh my God, I'm bleeding terrible. . . ."

Burroughs lay on the ground, flat, with the chest which had opened up facing the sky. Guthrie left the old bandage—clotted with blood and impossible to pull away without opening the wound further—in place and took the blanket he had used as a compress and tore it into strips. The blanket was all he had and he was thankful for it, filthy as it was. He used the new strips to pull the old bandage back together. Burroughs was sobbing; all he wanted was to die and get it over with. Well, it isn't going to go that way, Guthrie thought angrily. You haven't put me through all of this just to go and give up and leave me with nothing to show for what I've been through, nothing but a corpse. If you'd just kept still, you dang fool, none of this never would have happened. Aloud he said, "You're gonna be all right. You hear?"

Burroughs wasn't listening. He was just blubbering and talking to himself, saying he wanted to die. Guthrie grabbed and held him. "You're gonna be all right, you hear!"

He felt like giving up himself. And he hated Burroughs with such an intensity he could have killed him, *put him out of his misery just the way he wants,* he thought. Blind with rage, he stomped off and sat on a small rock, knowing he had absolutely no other choice but to go back. He could not leave Burroughs. Furiously he commenced ripping up the rest of the blanket; he was going to have to strap up his own ribs to get any distance at all.

He hated Burroughs. He hated his father. He did. He didn't care what they'd done for him or how much he had admired them. They were nothing but dang fools, *dang fools, dang dang fools.* He'd like to see them both dead and gone, that was the long and short of it, both of them get what they had coming to them, leave him a little peace to rest in.

He remembered suddenly his fall from Arthur and how Burroughs had stayed at the house, helping to care for him; he thought of Burroughs going down to the pasture with him. "You aimin' to get back on that animal after all that's happened?" In Guthrie's head he could hear Burroughs, plain as the day he said it; in his head he saw Burroughs standing, shrugging (to deny any complicity at all with what went on in the world?), "Well, it's an old horse," he had said. He hadn't sounded even hopeful. Most of the lore Guthrie knew about horses, Burroughs had taught him.

> ONE white leg, *buy* him,
> TWO white legs, *try* him,
> THREE white legs, *send him far away,*
> FOUR white legs, *keep him not a day.*

But a good horse, Burroughs had said, was never a bad color. You should not hate a man because he was hurt and helpless; yet a voice inside of Guthrie argued stubbornly, It's his own fault and what's his own fault hurt him.

It was nearly noon, he calculated, and yet there was no sign of sun. The rain was falling as steadily as ever. Rain before seven, clear before eleven, he thought bitterly, another of the lies they tell you. Lies, all of it lies, he raged. You do your duty and everything will work out. Be strong and you'll get through. Face what is and accept it, act on it. Lies, all lies. The whole of his childhood seemed a tissue of lies that had been used to deceive him because if he had had any idea of what the world was really like he never would have bothered growing up. But he saw—oh, too clearly!—the insurmountable stones, the wild woods, the rushing river with its slippery dangerous stones, the sky that would pour rain or snow on him, and the humans, like Burroughs lying over there hysterical and frightened, without any of his values to hang onto now when he was so badly hurt and in mortal danger. Structures . . . values, he thought, raging at everything, nature, people, his father, the anger and bafflement of his own heart. It none of it means anything, he wanted to cry out. It's all just like this trip, painful and chock full of sacrifice and pitfalls, good intentions come to bad ends, carelessness that ends up in disaster, and underneath it all this goddam hard cruel land that won't let us get back and this blubbering idiot who brought all this on himself and *me* and now lies there crying and asking to die. Go ahead and die, Guthrie shouted at Burroughs from inside his heart. See if I care. See if any of it—he looked at the rainswept landscape —cares. Why *should* you want to live?

He flopped down on the ground and covered his eyes with crossed arms, blotting out the universe. There was such a pain inside he couldn't bear it, but it was not his ribs that hurt him so, it was the force of his disillusionment. He didn't want the world this way. He wanted order and endeavor, reward and punishment justly meted out; he raged for fairness and responsibility, some enormous, eternal code of ethics which would rule and regulate the working of nature and men; most of all he wanted to believe that he, Guthrie Buttes, was all part of some large ordered scheme, that he had his place in it, a place of value and importance that would give meaning to his life. He would be unique and the world would see that and give him his chance to show how he could live a good and meaningful life, how his efforts would mean something, would *move* the world on its way a little. He cursed Burroughs and his father and their white ways; he cursed Kateri and Ohguesse and their Indian ways. He cursed himself, somewhere between each; his heart cursed everything and nothing, having no name to call this absence of any meaning, any overall justice, and at last when he was too tired to think or care any more, he lay cursing the fact that he had to get up, get Burroughs back on his back, and start out again, because even if there wasn't any meaning he knew he had to pretend there was.

They were moving very slowly, more slowly even than when his father had held them up. There were many boulders to circumvent, which meant that a good deal of their effort took them no distance; also the pain in his chest was sharp, persistent, punishing; but worse was Burroughs' insane blabbing and weeping and thrashing. Pain and fright and despair had pushed him over the thin line of rationality; he was a wild, wounded man blindly trying to escape his pain and fear; and though he was more than half dead and almost certainly all the way out of his head, his panic had given him strength, he was fighting against Guthrie's efforts to help him. Half of Guthrie's energy was now expended in trying to keep him in place. But things could after all have been worse. For instance, it might have been the sharp blade of the axe instead of the blunt end that smashed into his chest. That would have killed him, and he might, in that lunatic jumping from rock to rock have lost his rifle in the water, so all in all something must be working on his side. That something might eventually knock Burroughs into unconsciousness, might even offer Guthrie an unexpected piece of luck. It didn't do to damn everything, he might turn off what small favors fate was willing to begrudge him.

He stopped, breathing hard, half out of his own mind with Burroughs' carrying on. They were nearly at the shale and it was getting dark. Best to camp and get some rest. If Burroughs could make it through the night, he would be at the house by noon the next day. Twenty hours: it seemed an impossibility, an eternity, to be gotten through.

At the next boulder, almost the last, he found a natural opening and decided this was a good place to lay up. The relief of getting Burroughs off his back was so intense that for a moment he couldn't comprehend his emotions. Then he knew what it was he felt, happiness, exaltation—from all this horror he was actually being permitted a few moments' respite. He must remember, he must always remember, this instant of elation. He must hold it in readiness against the moment when that terrible sense of desolation and aloneness and worthlessness overtook him as it had overtaken him after the fall at the river.

Without Burroughs on his back, he was able to breathe without too much pain. The opening in the rock was perfectly situated to keep them out of the wind. With a canopy of boughs, they would even be free from the rain. He was too tired to care about eating and twenty hours more or less wouldn't make much difference to Burroughs, but they absolutely had to have a fire. Exhausted as he was, Guthrie took his axe and began to chop. He gathered branches and laid out a fire. Burroughs was still conscious, but he had stopped that infernal racket; he lay with enormous dark terrified eyes, his twisted mouth making silent cries, but mercifully no sound escaped that torn flesh.

Rain and cold crept in around the fire. The wind had changed direction and a fine spray blew against the shelter. Burroughs had been seized by a chill and in order to give him warmth Guthrie had to lie right next to him to give him some of his own heat. They had no blanket; it was in strips around his ribs and holding the compress against Burroughs' chest. He lay rigid, paralyzed with fatigue, biting his lip until the blood came to keep awake, and when that no longer served to arouse him from falling down into his dreams he took his rifle and laid it on top of his chest and pressed it against his hurt ribs. The pain kept him alert. When his eyes closed and he could not get them to open again, he ground the rifle against himself until the intensity of the pain fought back sleep. Then he lay awake for fifteen or twenty minutes before his eyes closed again, his head nodded, and just as he felt release he forced his hand to bring pressure against the gun, pain snapped him to his senses again. He was afraid to fall asleep for fear of rolling over on the wounded man. Twice he got up and fed the fire, but some time toward morning in spite of all his determination he plunged into darkness, overcome with such an exhaustion that no device, not even the painful one of the rifle, could hold back the moment when he huddled down at last in a deep and warm sleep with a fatigue that went beyond anything he knew, his body far away from him in another remote, unknown place, resting, reassuring itself, his mind unable now to make it obey. Later, much later, his thoughts would return to that release and wonder at it. It seemed to him that that insistence of his body on sleep, regardless of all the effort his mind had made, was somehow like Burroughs' uncontrollable panic after the fall, as if Burroughs' body had perhaps obeyed some instinct his mind could not control, and Guthrie was able to feel that there were times men could not be judged for the moment of failing, but for the effort against it they put in.

He lay a long time listening to the wind and to the small doubtful echoes inside his heart; he had lost the need for sleep in the tightening of something inside, some instinct that held him listening; and then he realized what his ears were straining for: he believed in his heart that somewhere out there in the wilds was a panther whose call would come. It would be a sign of recognition, one equal to that Ohguesse had made after *their* painful journey when he had looked at Guthrie's father and made his statement: "He complained not once . . . not once did he say he was wet nor hungry nor tired nor afraid." Ohguesse had given him a piece of panther skin then to receive a portion of the medicine of life. But Guthrie knew now that the medicine of life was doled out begrudgingly bit by bit and you had to earn it two and three times over. What he was waiting for with the panther's cry was some sign of recognition that he had earned his way this trip. He waited all night, but the call never came. He got up, thinking you had to accept that there were very few times when you truly understood whether you had done well or whether you had only done what was expected of all men.

IV

He had taken two sick men out of the wilderness, one more
than half dead, one who would be dead now if it hadn't been
for him; and the other, sick enough; he was pretty confident
that both of them were going to be all right—he had more
faith in Kateri than in any doctor, not that there was one
for miles around, but if Burroughs or his father had needed
one he would have seen they got it. Hadn't he got them out of
the woods? What, then, was an overland trip down to the
Falls?

Guthrie stroked past the end of Algonquin Island. The
Landing lay ahead shining under the sky. The dusty streets,
the shabby little cabins, the rubbish and refuse left rotting
wherever it lay—all the ugliness and squalor—were camou-
flaged by distance. He saw only a sleepy little village occasionally shifting itself under the sun.

Burroughs' general store lay straight in front of his paddle.
He knew it almost as well as he knew his own house—the
pot-bellied stove which was a meeting place for the trappers
and furriers, the cheese knife in the big wheel of yellow
cheese, the spittoons, and the long log benches against the
wall. He thought of the smells—molasses, vinegar, kerosene,
oil—and he saw in his mind's eye the potato spout over the
oil to keep it from dripping on the other provisions. Whenever he and his father had come across by water, Burroughs
would be waiting for them to dock. He would have seen them
coming and have calculated almost exactly the moment they
would arrive. Two strokes from the dock, he would appear
grinning. It was odd now to think of both his father and
Burroughs laid up back at the house.

His eyes ran familiarly over the cows grazing near the
houses, in the fields in back of the improvised barns, browsing
under the gnarled limbs of orchards that gave fruit, drink,

and—in the spring—scent to the little village. There were small patches of gardens cut out—where pumpkins were stacked, bright and big, and to Guthrie beautiful, the old patches of beans, potatoes, onions, peas, turnips, squash, cabbage, a neat patch for flax. Guthrie remembered the purple flowers. In such sunlight as this morning it seemed to him wrong that there were no flowers, but all the flowers were over for the year. There had been hard frosts, and even the fall flowers, the asters, dahlias, and chrysanthemums, were gone.

Two or three years ago there was only an occasional wandering peddler with a pack on his back who came through with cloth and spices, indigo dye, needles and pins, combs and beads. Burroughs had run the only general store, his supplies running to traps and tools, animal equipment and the rough provisions woodsmen wanted. When he set up store, Burroughs had never considered women coming to the Landing, and he still thought the idea absurd, though there were families, real families, not just a trapper and his squaw in a sod shack, real families in houses all up and down the shore. The new store was what Burroughs contemptuously called a woman's cubbyhole; he had reported indignantly that it stocked ribbons and buttons, all kinds of tomfoolery crockery, pots and pans, candy, rice, even a bird cage. What was more astonishing was that it didn't take butter and eggs in exchange; that store ran on *real* money. Contemptuous as Burroughs might have been, he was wrong in not seeing that the Landing was growing and that it would soon be prosperous enough for a cobbler, a post office, a school, even a church.

There was also someone else at the old Guthrie mill, though people still called it Guthrie's place. It would be called that until a new owner came along with a personality strong enough to dislodge the powerful memories of Guthrie's grandfather.

Many changes were taking place. At the Landing now it would be Old Odder, Young Buttes. Guthrie thought of his father: sallow, gray, edging along the bench of the back porch toward the warmth of the sun. His father's life lay behind him. *His* life lay ahead. *Young* Buttes.

Pa got hurt some, he told himself, but it's not permanent. He gazed uplake into the wilderness. Someone came and bought them woods, he thought, and that was the start of it all. That property rightfully belongs to us, someone comes and takes it because they got money. We work hard for every single thing we got, some people jest born getting. If those Raymond people from down Albany way hadn't come up here and meddled, none of this would have happened. It's changin' things that leads to trouble.

Against the silent swoop of the paddle—low, strange, and insistent in the rhythm of Guthrie's strokes—came a sense of sadness. Ohguesse was dead. The word had come down from trapper to trapper all along the trail from Canada until at last it had reached the Buttes Place. He, Guthrie Buttes, had never been initiated into the Bear Clan, nor would he ever be, but he was nevertheless, in his heart, where it counted most, part Indian, the white son of the red warrior with partridge eyes.

Ohguesse's land and people had changed. Everything had to change; no way in the world for life to hang onto being what it was. He closed his eyes, envisioning his father a month before, his father now.

Why was it his father remained weak and listless, but Burroughs kept getting better? For a fact, he was almost ornery. He kept telling Kateri he was going to get her to go up to the reservation and get one of those masks the Indians made; he would wear that and nobody would know the difference when he took it off, his face would be no different from one of those grotesque masks the Iroquois wore. He had been patched and stitched as best Guthrie and Kateri could, but he was a dreadful thing to look upon, even to them, used to him; and his chest wound, which ought to have killed him, had sunk the whole front of him in, but he breathed on, defiant, getting better and better. He was already talking about going back to the Landing and letting them all see what a sight he was, but alive, damn it, he'd pulled through; not many men could say that after the kind of mauling he'd got. Red-headed people, Guthrie was deciding, were put together on some very peculiar principles. He doubted if people with run-of-the-mill heads of hair could understand them.

"Tell me, son, that new womany store runnin' me out of business?" Guthrie shook his head. A gleam of satisfaction leapt up in Burroughs' eyes. "I guess not," he agreed. "Not with lace and ribbons and the like. This is *man's* country."

"It's changin'," Guthrie said. "Lots of new people comin' in—they're talkin' about buildin' a church. You never had families before, it was always jest trappers, their women." He flushed.

Burroughs conceded the point with a rueful shrug of his

shoulders. "They was a different breed before, and that's the truth."

"The way Pa is I don't see he's gonna git no better and this place, I can't run it jest by myself, I can hold it together, but I can't really run it, not right, it'll jest be a patch and pound job; and this place—it's got *potential*. We clear some more land, git in an orchard the way we should, we could raise *cash* that way, not jest have to count on tradin'. With cash, with money in our hands, there's a lot of possibilities open. But, Pa, I cain't talk to him, he jest sours up. He's tired and wore out, but I'm not tired, I got more energy now than I know what to do with it, and I don't want to see it sucked up in a lot of worthless little chores jest to keep the place hobblin' along, I want to build it up, but I need help. I thought as how maybe I'd send up to the reservation—"

"I wouldn't do that, son—"

"Oh, I know what's been goin' on 'tween Pa and her all these years, if that's what you mean." He stopped abruptly, seeing something in the way Burroughs was watching him that made him ashamed. "And the other, too—my grandfather," he said, though he had never before openly confessed to such knowledge: it seemed somehow a betrayal of his grandfather's weaknesses, which ought to have gone in decency into the grave with him over behind Guthrie's mill. But in this case the weakness could not easily be buried; bloods would mix where oil and water would not. He felt a deep wound over his grandfather Guthrie's sins, that they could haunt the present so fully and still be put next to his name. Even in death sometimes there was no end to the guilt. My blood is up there on the reservation, but Pa's ain't, he thought. It's the whole difference in us. Neither my Ma nor my Pa—but mine. It goes back three generations, but the bloods mixed then.

He wanted to get away from this knowledge; it seemed to him that every new thing he acknowledged imposed a burden on his spirit. He knew that maturity did not come without resentment and hatred and sacrifice—in some tribes a boy came to manhood only after being turned loose in the wilderness with nothing but a knife and told to survive there six weeks to show that he had the powers necessary to preserve his family and his people—and Guthrie was sure that part of courage and endurance had to do with simply having a job to do and doing it. Without whining. He always remembered that to Ohguesse this was the most important part: to go through hardship without complaint. Now he felt there were hidden things to life that were better not known, evil secrets in every man's life for which shame was not large enough a word to cover their degradations; his grandfather had been one of those men they meant when they said, He likes bear grease, he likes bear meat. That was what they said about men who kept Indian women; you had to face the truth when it met you head on.

Likely as not they said that about his Pa.

If women had such a powerful way over men, he ought to know why. Couldn't expect to find out where and who he was, isolated over at this mountain farm—his Pa had his woman, he was going to find out what it was made a man break himself down over one. He had things to do at the Landing, no problem getting away this time of year with trading to be done, supplies to get in.

He'd get drunk—why not?—get a woman, yes he would.

He kept thinking about what Burroughs had said. His grandfather had had Indian children—maybe somehow he and Ohguesse were actually kin. No way of knowing, ever. That wasn't right. His Ma had had kin to her half Indian. Kateri? No way of ever knowing. He looked down into the secret depths of the water, right in the middle of the lake, at its deepest part. Men had dropped strings with weights attached a hundred and fifty, two hundred feet down and still not touched bottom. It was white way down there at the heart of the lake. A milky, mysterious whiteness when you looked into it that was strange and foreboding, as if it said, There are secrets you can never know and this is one of them, what it means when the dark waters turn white.

Guthrie stroked on, looking into the heart of that secret light. At the center of all life there was a secret; everything important was unknowable. And that seemed to him wrong, too. Why should the world be set up so that it was impossible to know the answers to the most basic questions? A man ought to be able to answer where he had come from and where he was going and why, and most important of all, who he was.

He stroked harder now. You could drive yourself crazy speculating on things there were no answers for. The universe had certain invisible walls that no man could go beyond. He imagined these white and translucent, like the heart of the lake, but made of a substance so hard that nothing in the entire world could penetrate it, made so that forever and ever a man was blocked off from the true image of himself on the other side.

200

Guthrie pulled the canoe ashore and hauled it up on its side. His ribs hardly bothered him at all. Well, why should they; at his age things healed fast. His father had a hard time getting the simplest things to mend. There was nothing broken or out of place they could find in his father, but his father was badly injured nevertheless—another secret evil, something that couldn't be seen. It came, Guthrie thought, when he fired the gun to hit the bear in the shoulder and topple him on top of Clyde.

He passed Burroughs' store with a twinge—it would never be the same again because Burroughs would never be the same. He had changed even in Guthrie's mind; Guthrie no longer pictured first the wonderful red mop of hair but instead the dreadful lacerated scalp, the flaps of skin hanging down from the face.

He passed into the tavern. Actually it was hardly a tavern, just a place to meet and buy hard drinks and tobacco and gunshot makings. Here, after a fashion, food could also be had and, if necessary, a place to bed down in the loft over the barn.

He ordered beer. He would have preferred harder stuff, but his funds were limited, and a woman cost. The question of how much kept coming back to tease and annoy him. He wanted to be fair, but he didn't want to git took. He asked for his beer in a low voice, holding his own counsel, waiting; coming across the lake, he had pictured this moment very clearly in his mind—his coming in and ordering the drink, the men clamoring around him, pounding him on the back, shouting out greetings, congratulating him on being The One Who Brought Burroughs Back. Old Odder, Young Buttes.

He put his mug down. To get drunk, he had anticipated, would be a thing of wildness and joy, not this heavy, guilt-filled feeling, this bad taste in his mouth, the painful presence of all these cold, accusing eyes; they hated him for his young body that was getting stronger and stronger while their own bodies were wearing out. Power attempts to entrench itself, but you cannot stop the body from breaking down, no matter how hard you try, he thought.

He left the drink, the men, the dingy room, plunging out into the open air and bright sun. He spat the last of the beer out, bent for a moment inspecting a nail that had been lost in the road, picked it up and pocketed it as a talisman. You found a good straight nail you were supposed to have good luck. He went toward the outskirts of town where the half-breeds, the old broken trappers, a few Indians lived. Poor

Town, it was called, a collection of shacks and huts that deserved the name. If liquor had failed him, there was still the woman.

He kicked back the brush, sent a stone singing off the end of his boot, thinking of the cold-eyed men back at the tavern. They don't understand no more, he thought, what it is to feel. That's the worst part about gettin' old, strong feelin's go.

He wanted to run and shout for the pure pleasure of being alive. He leapt over fallen stumps, small bushes, high rocks, the sheer joy of his hot blood bursting inside him. He ran along the old Indian trail that paralleled the lake, running and jumping, throwing his arms out, not caring a damn about anything except being free and away from the town. The town was bad. Living in towns was bad. When people got together in town, they got bad.

When he reached the end of the bay, he was panting, the blood pounding so hard in his head that he felt faint, but the gladness in his heart was stronger than anything he could remember in a long time. It's all ahead of me, he thought, my whole life is ahead of me.

He bounded into the air with a shout, sprinted over a fallen log, and came down with a thud on a small, childish collection of bones anchored onto a tumble of black hair; the girl gave a grunt as he hit her, then lay still. He could feel her jarred breath under him, a series of spasms. Her skin was light with the silver sheen of cream, but her hair was thick and black and coarse, Indian hair, and the face was an Indian face. She opened black Indian eyes. But when she spoke, it was without the sibilant Indian hiss; white-raised, he thought, like Kateri. "What you doin', jumpin' on people like that?"

"How was I supposed to know you was hidin' under this here log?"

"I wasn't hidin' under no log," she said indignantly. "I was restin' myself, jest restin' myself and you come along and jump right on top of me." She scrambled up, supple, slender, surprisingly tall for an Indian, looking him square in the eye with peculiar black eyes, the depths so bottomless that it was like looking down into the lake, the eyes white as that water way down deep.

They stood in front of one another at an impasse. There was the difference, the skin difference, the sex difference, that had drawn them into two hostile forces. He was white and a Buttes. Everyone knew the Butteses.

202

The Guthries, too, he thought, stubborn to his mother's heritage.

His breath was wedged sharply in his chest; his heart jerked about alarmingly. He was like someone who had just learned that all his possessions—his house and barns and land, even the clothes he wore—have been taken away, and he must start over, naked, new. It was as if his whole life were hanging, at that moment, in the space between breaths, in the open palm of possibility.

He was Kateri's and Ohguesse's as much as he was a white man and woman's. The wonder of it was that *he* saw the truth so clearly.

Polite people made things go. If you were at your own house, you offered refreshments. He felt around in his pocket for the maple sugar. It was wrapped in an old piece of cloth and when he brought it out, the tattered covering shamed him.

She was watching suspiciously, as if she expected him to jump her. He'd done that once; there was no advantage in the stunt a second time. He sat down to calm her, breaking the sugar in two, holding half out to her. The greed in her eyes reminded him of Arthur (poor dead devil) and the wariness of all women (dangerous, desirable). He watched those two impulses struggle. She took her half swiftly, moved back, keeping a good ten feet between them.

He had the feeling that you used the same rules with horses and women, it seemed logical—to try to instill confidence and to hope to work up a little enthusiasm on both their parts for him as a provider.

"Reckon we're in for another hard frost. You live at the Landin'?"

Some motion with her head he took to mean yes. "Out a spell."

"I don't remember seein' you around—but then we live across lake—" His head made a jerk back toward the opposite shore. She waited. Something more was apparently expected. "We don't git over much. You new 'round here?"

"Pretty new. You're Guthrie Buttes, ain't you, the one brought that man back?"

He had never seen anything like her eyes, never, not with all the Indians he had known. Indians had black expressionless eyes, hard like some finely polished stone, dead as stone, all except Ohguesse, whose eyes had been unnaturally bright; but these eyes had a depth and a tone that he associated with leaves and fur and the soft moss on the sunny side of the stone.

"We been farmin' back in the hills," she said, "but we give up farmin' awhile back and come up to the Landin'—we figured we could maybe do better here in town. It was hard workin' one of them back farms. Rocks, mostly. I'm helpin' out to Mr. Sawyer's store 'til my Pa finds somethin' of his own."

She made another movement with her head, finished chewing, wiped her mouth with her hand. He passed her his half of the maple sugar. He was hoping the dividing and then his going without would make more of an impression than if he'd given her the whole lump straight off.

"You don't want yourn?"

"You take it."

"I couldn't take yourn."

"I want you to have it. Take it."

"Why you want me to take yourn?" Suspicious again.

"Like it's—you know—a gift. You don't want it?"

Eyes white as water, never saw eyes like that before in his whole life. He handed her the rest of the sugar, watching her, but not too carefully, just friendly like, trying to smile, trying to show he had not one bad idea in his whole head. "You know me, but you ain't told me who you are."

"I should have been called Edra after my Pa's Ma; my Pa, he wanted me to have her name, but my Ma, she said I had one of his names, I should have one of hers, so she called me Osceola—Osceola Patterson."

Guthrie placed Patterson, a gnarled brown trapper who'd given up the woods and got himself a hardscrapple farm and brought his Indian woman and a passel of halfbreed children down from wherever he had them sod-hutted, and then sat around hoping they'd farm the place for him. It was a joke at the Landing. She wouldn't work, people said, 'til he married her; and then after he went and give her his name legal-like, she wouldn't work neither. Lost the place and are squattin' over to Poor Town eatin' 'coon and squirrel and what they can come by in the woods.

She didn't seem quite so tall to him now, and she maybe had the Indian smell—greased skin, sweated skin clothes, oiled hair—he couldn't tell, being ten feet away from her, but she looked too pretty to have come out of such a dungheap. Still, breedin' didn't always tell. His father had got an awful cull out of two first-class horses he'd bred. Couldn't it work the other way 'round, too?

He got up—slowly so as not to alarm her—and stood chewing a leaf thoughtfully; his heart was pounding painfully, he'd just seen the curve of her breasts, the fleshed full neck which ran into the V of her dress. She was breathing hard, her full breasts rising and falling. He couldn't think of another thing to say. He stood there breathing hard, too, much harder than she, and she looked at him with those translucent eyes and he felt sick, the air was quivering with his emotions, with the frantic silence opening up between them, and he heard himself breathe out (he could not speak, his voice was caught between the lock of his heartbeats), "What could I do—" and then the sounds dissolved, mostly because he didn't even know the end of that sentence himself. Was it "to make you like me?" or "kiss me?" or "come to me?" There was no way of knowing, standing there sick with sensation and longing while she looked white-eyed up at him and breathed back, faintly, "What'd you say?" and he trembled all over.

Night had pressed down its dark thumb; a gray smudge was imprinted on the sky. He had told her all he could think of that was important—about his mother dying and being buried under her own special tree; about growing up with Ohguesse and Kateri, going to the reservation for the medicine feast and the blizzard and coming home; about Arthur and how he'd failed there; about Burroughs and bringing Burroughs out of the woods; and, finally, his confidence growing, about coming to the Landing to get drunk and get a woman. He was afraid he might forget something important; he wanted her to know everything, not necessarily to approve, that wasn't necessary, no, just to see him as he was and accept him like that and maybe like him.

Plum-colored, the lake lay resting in front of them at the smudged end of the sky. They were lumped together in front of a slight clearing which allowed them a view downlake— at least twenty miles of water and shoreline opened before them. The Landing lay behind a cove and somehow Guthrie saw this as better; it was as if it didn't exist. If you refused to recognize something, did it go away?

No, only in your mind. Certain things had an objective existence of their own. Because he could not see the town, that did not mean its meannesses had dissolved.

The woods never slept. Animals lived at night as well as during the day; now they were busily getting ready to forage, to explore, to mate. Yet for a moment, because there were only the two of them, the two of them and the lake, the woods, he had a sense of order. A firm balance of terrors equalled peace. He felt a sense of soaring which said to him, *You are happy, you are happy and you know it.*

Under the violet light the water, peaceful, noiseless, scarcely moving, flowed toward the shore, a few rocks protruding their bony skulls above the gentle ripplets, a fringe of tall coarse grass bearding the willows; moss, tender, green, velvety, slipped over the bank stones under the pines and sneaked back into the woods where a scattering of insects were testing their hard, black wings. He wanted to touch her, but was afraid. His heart was beating painfully. He moved toward her, afraid to touch her, afraid not to. Her lips were moving, but when he bent forward to hear, there was no sound, just her lips stirring faintly back and forth, ready to speak or trying to speak and unable to do so; he bent closer, desperate to catch the whisper that fluttered there, her eyes huge now, his heart breaking up inside his chest, and he bent forward and touched her almost—not quite—open mouth; open-eyed, they pressed toward one another and then, breathing so heavily that her breathing was a part of his breathing, she wavered back, swaying; he put out his arms, and she must have put out hers, too, because their hands joined, he pulled her toward him; her eyelids fluttered and closed and then her mouth was on his. It was the first time he had ever kissed a woman and he didn't know how to handle the feeling. The sensation was beyond anything exhilarant he had ever experienced, even that moment when he had carried Clyde Burroughs out of the woods alive and into legend: already people said his name, hushed. It was impossible Burroughs had lived; yet he had. It was impossible Guthrie should feel like this; yet he did.

The wind chilled him, flat and full against his back, but it helped hurry the canoe. He felt, painfully, the disadvantage of his being on the other side of the lake, away from her. Distance would certainly not work for him; she would forget what they had felt there in the woods under the trees. And there were problems. Most certainly there were problems.

Having an Indian woman was one thing; being serious about one was another, especially in a place like the Landing where the boundaries of conduct were distinct; there was no indefinable area where black and white blended into gray. Small villages didn't understand shadings. But things were changing—that was the law of life, wasn't it, change. Nothing stayed still, not even this water when it was calmest. Time flowed through change. That was how history hounded men, by making them adapt or abandon the ideas they had grown comfortable with, had grown up being trained in and had accepted and then suddenly discovered no longer worked. The trouble with life was that it kept presenting situations for a man to solve that all his previous experience hadn't prepared him for. Like bringing home an Indian wife.

Would his father have an open enough mind to accept historical argument? No, he would mark it—rightly—down to evasion: The truth was it was feeling, desire, nothing else, that motivated Guthrie. And his father would know that. He was a wise and clear-headed man for all his aches and pains. How much, was the question, did his father value feelings? Not in the past, but now. Right now.

He dragged the canoe up on shore with numb fingers and stood for a moment looking up at the house, palely white, blotched by the brightly falling autumn leaves, beautiful. His father's house, erected at last, the house he had said he would have and had, after years of deterrents, finally brought into being. Wasn't this house the result of strong, determined feelings?

Not too long ago—before the woods, the woods had changed everything though, the woods were some kind of watershed between one kind of man his father had been and the kind of man he was now and the kind of boy Guthrie had been and the kind of youth he was now—but not too long before, the strong appetites of his father for life had begun to spring back, those two days of drinking and dancing and wrestling and singing and fighting and eating when they'd had the house raising. His father had proved something to himself and his neighbors when he'd got that house up. The lake took it once and his woman dying took the spunk out of him for a long time, but he'd said he was going to have a house, a real house, and he had one. He had not married his Indian woman and put her in the parlor, however. His Indian woman had stayed "in her place." And Guthrie resented this, though until this moment he had not realized this was so. Now, climbing the path to the house, he understood that buried deep inside him was the feeling his father should have done better by Kateri. She had raised Guthrie. She had come back when he went to get her at the reservation. Why hadn't he married her?

There was no other explanation except that she was Indian.

He would have married a white woman in the same position. And if he hadn't married his own Indian woman—

Guthrie went up the path and through the shed off the kitchen where they kept the firewood neatly stacked along the far corner. When he opened the kitchen door, he saw Kateri's back bent over the stove; when she straightened up and turned to look at him, he saw the face as testimony that people didn't even usually end up with second best. Even second best was too much to expect if you were an Indian. For her the move into his father's room after the completion of the house should have been some kind of vindication, but his father had been too old and too tired to be susceptible to blackmail of the flesh. By the time she lay there, his father was too done in for her to use it to her advantage. A good workbench but the artisan could no longer ply his trade.

Now, Indian-fashion, she greeted him with a slight indication of her head; she was waiting for him to speak first, he was the man.

He began to thaw out over the lifted grates at the stove. The red, crackling fire leapt out to meet his frozen fingers; he smelled from the oven something hot and spicy. "Pa okay? Clyde better?"

She made a kind of grunt which meant nothing had changed. At the same time she put her hand up and touched her lips, running a finger over them uncertainly. Something was the matter. He was tired and cold and weary from the long paddle, from his problems.

"Your Pa wants to move downstairs," she said. "He thinks it's warmer down here in winter."

"But Burroughs is down here—does he want him moved?"

"He thinks it's warmer down here," she repeated. "He says he's cold up there."

"He's got a stove in his room. Why should he be cold?"

"He says it's draftier upstairs. You get the salt? The sugar?"

"Tea, too. I made good trades on the butter and squash and pumpkins. A lot of them newcomers hadn't had time to put in their gardens this year and they was willing to give good money for wintering things."

She was pleased; a light glowed in her face.

"We'll be short next spring on furs, though," he reminded her, "with Pa laid up. We'll have to take it easy on everything, cut down. We got to look ahead." He wondered what provisions for the future Indians ordinarily made. Everything Indian had once again become interesting to him. "Kateri," he said. She stopped, alert; to her keen ears his voice must have betrayed the maneuvering he was trying to conceal. "I was jest wonderin'," he began, "you know—about next year. We're goin' to need help around the place." He stopped. Her face had closed up. "Help" meant outsiders. She wanted outsiders to stay away; safety meant sameness to her. Well, he supposed she would oppose him, but getting touchy and irritable would get him nowhere. He suppressed the desire simply to let everything slide. A weak man lived by what happened to him, a strong one by what he tried to force. "Man help," he said sharply. "For the clearin' and plantin', the hayin' and cuttin', the real hard work. We get a man, a couple of men, maybe even three—the place could support them—we'd make out real well. As it is—or as it's goin' to be—we're jest goin' to be scrapin' along, a pinch-penny place. This place—I got in my mind what this place could really be. We should have ourselves an orchard, for instance, there's plenty of room, it's jest a question of clearin'. Three men could clear the space in no time at all. But I can't do it by myself—and he ain't got it in him no more."

"What makes you think Swift Arrow and the others would want to come down here and clear this place?" She had read right through his mind. He wondered if she understood that with a lot of Indians around the place, one more or less wouldn't look so—well—conspicious. Of course, an Indian wife would be conspicious. "Maybe so, maybe not. No way of knowing. I was thinkin' of askin', was all. To find out."

"It's not like you think. You don't live the way they do up there—on nothing, a handout here and there, freezing and hunger those long winters, nothing to do summers, you got no idea."

"Why wouldn't they rather be here, then?"

"Ro-de—" It was such a long time since she'd called him that that she caught him off guard; somewhere, walking up the hill, he had uncovered the suppressed realization that his being white wasn't fair; it was too much of an advantage, one he had done nothing to earn, to be Indian was unfair, but what could he do about the accident of skin color and bone formation? Her calling him "Ro-de" made him recognize what could not be righted and his responsibility for a thing that had happened to Ohguesse, to Kateri, what would happen to Osceola, things over which he had no control, but from which, nevertheless, he benefited. Her face averted, Kateri said, "None of them would come back because after Ohguesse left this place he would never come back again—

209

not here," she said quickly, "but this country." She looked at him. "Much as he loved you—you *were* his son—he would not come back to this land. Because of the wrongs it had done him, and our people."

"I'd stay," Burroughs said, "if you was to ask me. I know I'm kind of broke up in bits and I won't never be as strong as I was, but there's still a lot there, if you was to ask it to come up. And you could trust me, I guess you know that. And that means a lot, more than maybe you can know, Boy. It turns out there ain't many men can be trusted. But what you done for me, I got a debt—"

"I don't want you to feel that—"

"Maybe not, but I do. Somethin' I can't discharge. And anyway I don't really want to go back over to the Landing, not looking like this. You say all these new people comin' in, I reckon I can sell the store, I won't take no loss on that. And I ain't got no one to go on to, it's more like you all was my family. Ever since my woman run off I ain't had no center to things, nuthin' I really cared about to push me to do much one way or other with my life except the store; and then you come lookin' like this into a place fillin' up with families—well, women and children, they don't want you around; you can't blame them, I ain't exactly a thing of beauty; they's interested in ribbons and lace and the like, they don't want no man looks like me with 'em when they's fingerin' pretty things. Over here," he said, shrugging, "you might say I was safe—safe from being seen," and he submitted for Guthrie's benefit that rueful, ironic smile that had become his answer to fate. "And your Pa, he'll straighten out, you'll see." The conviction in his voice surprised Guthrie. "It's jest gonna take a little time. Your Pa lost somethin' when you brung me in. He couldn't do it, he knows that, but it goes against the grain that you done it. When a man like your Pa has to face he ain't what he was, it goes hard with him. Pride—the loss of it—can make a man sick as anything else. Sicker. I can come to terms with this—" He lifted his face, showing it off again in his own perverse pride— "easier than your Pa can come to terms with the knowledge his son can do what he can't no more. You think on that a bit, Boy, and see if it don't make sense."

He pictured the scene with his father very clearly in his mind. *Not here, you don't bring her here, not with the Buttes name,* his father would say. *Not leastwise while I'm alive. I won't have no Indian carrying the name. Come to some ar-*

rangement with her, but not the name, no Indian's gonna have the Buttes name.

Inside Guthrie's head his father said *my land . . . I raised this house . . . my house . . . my land . . . mine . . . mine.*

Inside his head, belligerent, Guthrie answered his father. It ain't all yours, Pa, I don't care what you think. This land, this house is part my Ma's, too, and part some of those Indians you don't want no part of because they helped raise me and because part of my grandfather's blood is up there on the reservation.

I never asked to come into the world. That was your doin' and because you done it, you owed me somethin' and that somethin' was raisin'. I don't owe you nuthin' for what was your responsibility to do the same as anyone else. You jest done your duty and you don't git credit for doin' what you should, what everyone else does. You gotta give to git credit in this world.

Jest like I spit you out, his father said inside Guthrie's mind.

Sure of his father's opposition, Guthrie went, antagonistic, to have it out with him. He was sorry his father was sick, old, tired; but he was sorry about a lot of things he couldn't change, like the color of Osceola's skin, for instance; and anyway it wasn't his *fault* his father and Burroughs had made that basic error in the woods, though sometimes they seemed to think so, likely as not wanting him to take the blame for what was their own fault; but the fact was he had done the best he could and that was what he was trying to do now. He didn't want to "come to some arrangement" with his girl: he owed her in part the sacrifice he could never make for Ohguesse; he owed her most certainly the vindication for all Kateri's years of hard work and loyalty; he owed her most of all the honesty of being what he was, a man who wanted her one way or the other on one level—even to forcing her —but who, on another, saw that the better part of him could hold out for what was right because in the end that would make the getting better. And righter. It was *righter* that mattered terribly.

"Are you *serious* about this girl?" his father asked. "I mean, do you really care about her or is this one of them attractions that, you know, git you all worked up and then awhile later you can't understand what it was got into you? Don't look at me like that. I know a thing or two about feelins like that. Why wouldn't I? Your Ma wasn't the only woman I wanted or wanted me. But I was choosy, Guthrie. And I hope you'll be, too. I saw your Ma once and I knew. Or maybe it was she who knew. It would be hard to say now. I didn't know nuthin' about her. I didn't have to know nuthin'. It's your choice and your choice is good enough for me. If this is the girl you want, you only got to say so. If she ain't, if this is a young feller feelin' his oats, you tell me and I'll understand. You'll still go over but I won't—you know—think nuthin' serious of it. If it's serious," he said, "I'll be feelin' one way about it and if it ain't, I'll be feelin' another. It's jest that I'd like to know."

"It's serious," Guthrie said.

"In that case I'm tellin' you how I feel, how I've felt all these years. I think you got a right to know." He was frowning crookedly, painfully. "You know, it's funny. You hear all the time about how some man works all his life and builds up something—a farm or a business, somethin' he's real proud of—and he's got his son and the son's got no interest at all in what he's made. I been lucky, I know that. The work and belief that's gone in this place, you understand and appreciate.

"The Butteses been here two generations now and I hope they're here for more generations than I ken count. What I mean is, I'd hate to see the line of continuity broke by anythin'." He licked his upper lip, then bit down on it, as if he were trying to hold back words he didn't want to say. "The girl, Boy, does *she* understand?"

"You mean—" It was painful, too, for Guthrie to bring out his own question— "because she's Indian?"

"They don't think same as us, Boy. I wish they did, but they don't."

Guthrie wanted to go to the fire and throw some tobacco on it, the way Kateri used to, to clear his head. Everything was mixed up and confused inside, and it was so important that he get things straight. "I think part Indian myself," he said at last.

"No, you don't. You want to think that sometimes, I reckon, but you don't. You think like a Buttes."

"I don't think the same as you, I—"

"No two people think the same, but the strain is runnin' the same in you as it does in me."

"I got my Ma in me, and my Grandpa, too."

"Well, that's a fact." It was as if Odder Buttes was reconsidering, and while he turned these conflicting ideas over in his mind, Guthrie said, "He had an Indian woman, Pa, and you—you had Kateri—but I—I aim to marry this one and do

212

right by her because things ain't the same anymore. A man gets a son off a woman he cares about don't have no right not to do right by her."

Odder Buttes looked at his son. "People don't have to be alike to feel for one another," he admitted. "Sometimes there is that thin line of feelin' holds them together no matter how different they are. That's what's important, that thin, thin line. It's so easy to break and once it's broke, it don't heal back. It's one of those things, like eyes, once they're gone, you can never git them back. It's that way with this special kind of feelin' between people. When it's there, nuthin' can interfere with it, nuthin' can separate those people; and when it's gone, nuthin' can really ever be straightened out with them, nuthin' explained, they're jest strangers resent one another, git irritated with one another, don't understand one another one little bit."

He turned away from Guthrie and gazed out the window at the lake. A smoky velvet haze hung over it. "Your Ma and I had that feelin' right from the start and it lasted until the day she went. If you bring that girl here with the best intentions in the world, Guthrie, and if she come willin' to try her heart out, maybe it will work for a time, but what you got to be absolutely sure is that it's somethin' can last for a lifetime. If she was to leave you—even like your Ma left me—how would you feel about them children you're talkin' about?"

"You mean they'd be different—they wouldn't be like me?"

"You're my flesh and blood," his father said.

"Ain't they gonna be mine?"

"Then there ain't no more to be said, is they? You're my son, you got my fixed way of lookin' at things. It's finished then, ain't it. You're like me, once you make up your mind, nuthin' changes it."

Guthrie bent down and looked into his father's aging face. "You felt that all along, Pa, the whole time, or is it somethin' you got to feel lately, now that I'm almost growed and seem more like you?"

"The whole time. But we Butteses, we don't show things much. You know that."

The lake was open, but it was far too cold, with the end-of-November winds, to make the crossing by water any more. The only way to get to the Landing was to go the long way 'round on foot or horseback, a time-consuming trip that ought

213

only be made under absolutely necessary circumstances. Yet at the first opportunity after the hog had been butchered and the meat cut, salted, and put up to smoke, the mess cleaned up, he began talking about getting some trading done, putting in more winter supplies. He didn't fool anyone, he was sure, but they all went along with the idea that of course this was an absolutely necessary trip on account of what he could get for part of the hog.

There had never been a slow horse on the Buttes place; a lame one maybe, like his father's old Cobbie—that was one thing, when a good animal went unsound, one that had given faithful service, you didn't send it down, you turned it out to pasture and let it spend its last days in a way you thought right—but a slow animal, that was another thing, it meant that the animal wasn't willing or it had been born poor in the legs, some structural weakness in its conformation; and it cost as much to feed a bad horse as a good one, his father always said, git rid of the bad ones and spend on the good ones.

Narko had been bought for her disposition, which was admirable, but she still had the long good legs of a runner and she had a big heart; as they came at a full gallop down the hill—Guthrie not even letting himself think of the old edict, Never, never run downhill—he felt that she was putting out as she had never done before, as if the urgency in him communicated itself directly through to her and she was determined to get him over the miles at a speed even he didn't know she had in her. They came at full dash around the bend and set off down the road, the splatter of the horse's heels making a tattoo on the hard ground, Guthrie bent forward in the saddle to take the weight off his front legs, those legs that had to carry most of the impact of the run, leaning into the neck but keeping a three-point contact between crotch and both his legs so that he might steady her more easily, if she stumbled, or stay with the saddle more readily if she shied or spooked.

He estimated it would take a good two and a half or three hours more by horse. He would have to walk her out after a while and cool her off, then let her out again gradually, with the excitement she felt and which he found almost powerless to control, feeling so keyed up himself.

In the brilliant blue and white fall sky, in dark semaphores, in wide arcs, the hungry birds were prowling. In the field in front of him the full colors of a late autumn were running like a full cry downhill toward the warmly lit waters of the lake.

The horse carried him into the woods. There were still colors everywhere; one of those peculiar autumns when instead of the leaves coming into full force mid-October, they had been held up; red, brilliant yellows—they must be brighter because of the weather—and great globs of green and lavender looked like multicolored blankets spread out over the earth. The fallen skeletons of old leaves, ferns as fine as feathers—he stopped and broke off a limb that had grown across the old Indian path, almost overgrown and out of use. The trail, used for so many centuries by so many different nations, was at last going back to the woods. In another decade it might vanish entirely. Like the mutilated birch, which ought to be removed, the tangle of brush here ought also to be cleared out, the old trail widened to its original swath; he had made many resolutions to restore it, and acted on none.

A wall—stones tumbled down and in some places fallen away completely—lay directly in front of him. He could see it quite clearly, the far marker of the Buttes boundary, the legal designation on their deed that ended Buttes acreage and made the mountains and hills beyond another man's. Whose? That man down in Al-*ban*-nee no one had seen. Raymond, they said his name was, and he was rich, richer than anyone else maybe in the whole state.

Guthrie reined in Narko and stood quietly amid all the activity of the woods, the complaining birds, the fleeing small squirrels and chipmunks, the lulling hum of bugs. He had arrived at Indian River, now a dry pebbly creek instead of the usual racing frothy stream. It was a sad thing, dried out that way. He could see how far down the water had gone by the fact there were animal deposits all along the sides of the stream. The raccoons and skunks, the opossums, even the wood rats, normally squatted so that their deposits were washed away by the stream's high water after a rain, but there had been no high waters because there had been almost no rain in two months. Just this strange hot fall and this dry, dry weather as if somehow nature were acting out the strange dry and hot feelings Guthrie had inside himself. All along the creek animal remains were atrophying; there were brown burned-out patches in most of the fields.

The pain he felt—compounded of so many losses, the going of the old Indian trail, the falling apart of the old stone walls, the terrible drought that had wracked the land, was augmented by the knowledge that he himself had been the one who had killed the woman his father loved.

I been livin' with dyin' all my life, Guthrie thought. It started out the day I was born and it's gone on all the time I can remember. Not just people dyin', but good things, things gone away or gone into disrepair, that's a kind of dyin', too, jest like there's dyin' of the spirit, somethin' went out of Clyde and out of Pa in the woods and won't never come back; and somethin's died in me, too, the boy that was once so young and green and full of no sense at all and now it's more like I can't even remember what the boy was like, goin' down the hill to whistle to a horse he had his heart set on winnin' jest like now I'm goin' downhill to a woman I got my heart set on havin' and please God, if there is one, who knows, don't let it end up the same way.

The children, her brothers and sisters, were darting in and out and around the horse's legs, their voices raised in teasing. They made fun of him until the mother, all shouts and slaps, raised herself from her lethargy for a moment and drove them away. He stood in the wind, silent, staring at Osceola's mother, a thick squat woman who motioned him out back. Patterson was lying under a wagon, working on some loose underpinning, and Guthrie got off his horse and knelt down and peered under the wagon.

"Hello, Mister Patterson," he said uncomfortably.

The old woodsman shoved himself sideways and raised his head a little. "You the Buttes boy, is it?"

Patterson was sweating real bad. His eyes were screwed up and sweat was running off his forehead right into his eyes. He went back to fussing, paying no further attention to Guthrie.

"Osceola around?"

"They's up back, her and her sister, gettin' nuts." His voice carried a terrible grievance in it that said, Serve one master one time, another next. The luminous lesson of his pained words was of springs made many years before by another man which remained in his heart now. He could have told his own sons of swinging lamps in the old tents and the brackish lake slapping back and forth against some dark shore as if these were still a part of his own life.

Who goes among the crows must croak like them, who gets among goats must jump like them.

God and your children are all you got. Patterson would

216

have preached things like that, given half the chance.

Guthrie raised himself, dusted himself off, and looked up toward the hills that rose in back of a conglomeration of tumbled shacks. He went around a shed and past an enclosed pigpen, the little fenced area where the milking cow stood, tail ineffectually fighting flies. He heard a horse stamping in its stall inside a broken-down building.

Up back, sloping from the small trickle of stream that Patterson had dammed up for his ducks, there ran a long sloping series of hills, a tangle of brambles, the perfect place for blackberries, raspberries, hickory and filbert trees. Guthrie could see a strange girl in a bonnet and thick gloves downhill and way up, near the top, a blurred figure that must be Osceola. She was standing looking down; then suddenly she waved and began running.

He watched her become distinct, and he loved her with all his heart, and he could not have said in a million years why; she simply filled a place inside him that had been empty before, a void waiting for someone very necessary to enter and take possession; she was in some way he only vaguely understood his payment to two worlds, but she was more, too, running toward him, laughing, unmindful of the torn clothes, the bruise of dirt about her mouth, her eyes sparkling, her whole body alive with delight. He loved her because he had made her happy. She was the only person he could ever remember that he had been able to make this happy. And he didn't think he would ever love anyone ever again in the way he felt at this moment. It seemed to him there were two classes of women in the world, Osceola and all the rest. She came up to him, not smiling now, a little hesitant, hanging back because she was probably afraid of coming on too strong, of giving away her emotions, and hence of being in jeopardy, someone offering herself too cheaply and therefore not to be highly valued, while he thought, She owns me, and it can't be helped, it can't be helped, any part of it, it's all settled some way I didn't even have any say over.

He held out his hand, to take the pail she was bringing.

"It's all right," she said. "I can do it."

"No, no, it ain't. I'll take it."

She hesitated, her head bent with the long dark lashes sweeping over her cheeks, the mouth dark, the hard determination of her face, one of the ones who would stand up when others were failing.

He took the pail. They began to scrabble toward the house,

picking their way over broken boards, rusty nails, the debris of chickens and ducks, cow dung, horse manure; yet Guthrie felt as if he were floating over the earth, scarcely touching it. At the back door he set the pail down and looked at her, waiting to see what sign she would give him.

She took his arm and they walked on, slowly, together, talking some, but not much, with that mysterious pulse binding them together until at the turning, he said, standing right there in the middle of the road, "I know I shouldn't be talkin' to you like this, but this feelin' has come over me, it's the first time I ever had a feelin' like this, and I don't know what to do about it; I kept thinkin' I could make it go away, but I couldn't, and when I saw I couldn't, I didn't know what I should do—I kept thinkin' I *had* to git rid of it, but deep down I didn't want to, and so I said to myself, You got to tell her, you got to git it out. You know it's wrong, but you got to tell her how you feel. I've got this feelin' for you I know I can't do nuthin' about, but I can't help it. I jest want to be with you, talk to you, see you—I got this feelin' inside me and—oh God, I jest don't know what to do about it."

Her mouth was moving, sounds came from her throat, words he could not understand, only the murmur, the throaty lift of sound, everything deepened in him: he was happy, so happy, he might have made offerings in gratitude.

And then his name, out of her throat.

To love: had there ever been any other end from the beginning? If you come to the moment, he considered, of being fully in life, certain puzzles drop into place. You have been edging toward this understanding the first second you entered the world without ever knowing it and now certain principles become clear. What fundamental law did life recognize but the final one to love, to live in commitment? There was an astonishment in his head and hands, in every part of him, standing there, trembling, trembling as the shock of expectation went through him.

Give with the right, take with the left, a fragile balance which adapted itself to the inevitable: for defeat, loss, disappointment, failure, all the diminished dreams, a man gained in exchange the invincibility of caring. In the end, since all gifts were destined to be disparate, the gift of love might just be divisible with death. But where boys asked for love, men gave it, and got back their intuition of immortality.

Old Buttes, Young Buttes—the Butteses to come. He felt

invincible, looking into the heart of creation, suspended in the singing of his blood, drawn down into the white waters of her dark Indian eyes.

PART THREE

Cobus's Book

The principles of knowledge are always controlled by desire, by anticipation, and by hope.

—Malinowski, SEX, CULTURE AND MYTH

I

Two hundred years before, "the fire that never dies" had burned brightly, a symbol of the five tribes who ruled these woods. Two thousand-odd warriors of the Iroquois Federations—the Mohawks, Senecas, Oneidas, Onondagas, and Cayugas (later to be joined by a sixth, the Tuscaroras)—called themselves "the men surpassing all others." They lived off the game of the land, the fish in the waters, and when the rigorous winters came, they cut wood to shelter themselves from the winds and snows. The great massive forests were then as they had been when the first French explorers, the *coureurs de bois*, penetrated the wilderness and looked with awe on the cathedral-like columns of tree trunks stretching as far as the eye could see and so high overhead the mind could not distinguish their end. Other white men came, not for the interests of exploration, but for the land beneath the great forests, and the deer-horned confederation found itself being pressed first by British and French, then British and American, and finally by the Americans alone. The Indians said these wars were like the two edges of a pair of shears; the Indians were the cloth between that was cut to pieces.

Thrust from the forests, pushed north into reservations or migrating with Brant into Canada, the Iroquois left the great forests and remote lakes behind to those settlers who began timidly—long after most of the Eastern seaboard had been opened up—to press their way through brush and burdock, hack out farms, scrape the land flat and erect houses, painstakingly plant orchards, carve out roads, seeing always the dream of the new world, of vast unspoiled lands stretching out before them, a limitless challenge, an endless continent to be grasped, the new world where the pale hand of the aristocracy could turn no soil and hold no power, where the church could not manipulate God's and men's laws.

The New World was like a blank piece of paper on which men might write the outlines of a better world, a world in which the mistakes of the past were not to be repeated and perpetuated, where the minority did not break the majority to their wishes, where one man did not hold power over countless others. The red men did not fit into these plans. They were unfortunate intruders on the dream, and so they were pushed back, shunted outside the dream, and when occasionally they rebelled at being shoved out of the way, brutal wars broke out. Red and white flew at one another; it was difficult to distinguish the hunter and the hunted.

But the white man had guns. He had machines of war. He had pieces of paper which proved in his own courts of law that he now owned the land. The Indian gave way—he had no choice, and up through Albany poured hundreds of eager settlers, pressing into the last of the wilderness along the Northeast, opening up vast tracts of hostile lands where the winters were so bitter that the strongest shelters could not keep out the bitter winter cold and where the summers were so brief that the first fruits came only to be caught by the early frosts. But the land was free and it belonged to those who took and subdued it. Men were no longer serfs or peasants or bonded men; they owned land, thousands of acres of land. It was theirs to do with what they wished. And often what they wished—most often—was to make money, so they put the land up as it had been put up in the past, as a pawn for power, and the bright white paper began to be written on in the same words and phrases as before—*greed, graft, conniving, betrayal,* showed up oftener and oftener in bold print, a tale of conspiracies and sell-outs that linked the land from one person to another until it was time for new plunderers to come and rob the earth of the greatest of its treasures, the great forests which greened the hills and valleys as if, indeed, this were the New Beginning.

Lumbermen were making drives as early as 1813 down the Hudson to Wings—then changed to Glens-Falls, but no one was paying much attention, no one except old Mowatt Raymond down in Albany, who had an eye for the future if ever one had been put in the head of a man. In the 1840s he began buying the land adjoining the Butteses along with thousands of forest acres, big, wild unroaded areas, around Racquette, Tupper and Long Lakes. People tapped their heads and said, *loco,* and turned with one of those superior little smiles that meant. Of course I got a lot more sense, too bad I ain't got his money, I'd really put it to use.

What's he want to go and piss his good money away for on worthless land like that? they'd complain.

A fool and his money, someone would observe sagely.

But ten years later they said old Mowatt was "smart as a skunk and twice as crafty." They said he had "a genius for enterprise." Oh, old Mowatt was chockablock full of manifest destiny. A shining example (the Albany *Times*) of American enterprise.

"An upstart," Cobus's grandfather said. "Summer people . . ." The last was the worst insult he knew.

Cobus's father tried to be fair. "They bought the land, Pa . . . you know as well as I do that was anybody's right."

"If you mean I shoulda—"

"I don't mean nuthin' and you know it. I'm statin' what was. And he's not a bad sort, I hear. Raymond's fair, they say. Itchy-fingered maybe, his hands got the feel of money and can't let go, but ain't that true of most of us? He's within his rights if he wants to put up a loggin' camp—"

"A loggin' camp?"

"That's what he bought the land for, Pa, to timber it off."

"What do you mean 'timber it off'? Where they goin' to timber it off to, old Guthrie's mill? It ain't big enough to—"

"They been doin' it quite a spell already, Pa. Then they figure to float most of it in on the spring freshets over on the river down to the Falls."

"It'll never last," Old Odder Buttes said with certainty. "It's jest the kind of fool scheme summer people would get mixed up in."

But he was wrong, for it was timber men talked of now, lumber and board feet and how many logs could be hauled out in a season. The woods resounded with the sound of axes, the crash of felled trees, the footsteps of hard drinking, foolhardy, irresponsible, maniacal sons-of-bitches who were, Cobus's grandfather said, cutting all the wood in sight and killing themselves in river tie-ups or those deadly brawls in town along the spring river run when they got drunk and out of hand and stomped one another with cleated shoes, and he was glad of it. Odder Buttes predicted that when they were finished, those sons-of-bitches, only small pockets of forest here and there would be left, and that only because they had been overlooked in the excitement and rush to push on, and that first growth, virgin wood that had been here since the beginning would have vanished under the woodsman's axe.

"Terrible men," he said because he was unable to understand them. They had no interest in land. Owning land, farming it, were meaningless concepts to them. The traits that made them heroes in the woods were the very ones that branded them trash in town. Cobus found the idea that the same man could be entirely opposite things simply depending upon the place he was in bewildering. It was impossible for him to balance opposite notions at the same time and come out with any kind of proper picture. Were these men giants? That was what the woodsmen said. They claimed there were men back in the woods who could perform feats no other man in town or on a farm could even attempt. But the townspeople scoffed; fools, they said, reckless fools who ain't got no sense of responsibility, ain't got no sense of proportion—who cares if they can do some of them blame things they say they can. Do them things make any difference? Who will even remember them fool things in three, four years?

We will, the woodsmen said, angry, banging huge fists on the bar slab.

You'll move on, but we'll still be here, the townspeople thought smugly.

Everything was changed. Cobus's grandfather kept saying so, and it was true enough. "Fools runnin' around in Washington *and* fools in the forest," he said, "both of them ruinin' what God made to be set up right, the Landing fillin' up with thieves and Irish, the country gone to hell, and no place better to see it than right here with these land robbers, like the Raymonds, loggin' everythin' in sight."

Change meant the world Cobus's grandfather knew was being wiped out. The woods were going. His way of life was disappearing. Gone, all of it, and he was an old man in his son's house. Everything, it seemed, turned its back on him.

"They had better not tangle with Clyde, them woods cutters," his grandfather used to tell anyone who would listen. "Clyde'll give them more than they reckon on. Jest they git one look at him—"

For Burroughs was gone. He had gone into the woods to live by himself. He had tried to fit in at the New House, and for a while he had, or it seemed he had—he did his work and kept to himself—but when Cobus's mother got pregnant she got so frightened of having him around, afraid he would mark the child (the children, it turned out, twins, Cobus

225

and his brother Clyde, whom everyone called Tip); she couldn't control herself, she would have hysterics if he came anywhere near her, would fly out to the barn and hide as soon as she caught sight of him coming up to the house. Indian superstition he'd mark the unborn.

He had gone one day, without much of a leave-taking; he had said something, Cobus was told, to all of them, but it was only hearsay he had, he didn't remember Burroughs much really. At the beginning he had come back now and again, queerer than ever, with his mutilated face and his living out in a tent on the edge of their fields, like an Indian, refusing to come up to the house for meals, even though it was only old Kateri, Odder, Cobus's father and mother, and Cobus and Tip. Then Burroughs quit coming at all; they thought he was dead, but every once in a while someone brought news. No, he wasn't dead, just holed up on his own in the Cold River region, in a shack of logs chinked with sphagnum moss; he fished and trapped, had plenty of wood to keep him warm winters; he wouldn't even come to town for the basic things like flour, sugar, salt. He used bear grease and deer tallow for shortening, and what he couldn't get himself, he did without. Trappers and loggers who came on him always knew him of course—the face; but they said they only got a glimpse of it. He would hide behind a tree to talk or stoop down and crouch under a covering of brush. Those passing would leave some supplies by his cabin, but it was also said that when he did come on someone to have a "talk" with he always asked that word be sent back to the Butteses that he was all right, he'd try to make it down one of these days.

At first Old Odder had believed he would come; then even he began to realize the old scarred man felt more comfortable in the woods than he did around anyone, even the Butteses. Cobus had only vague recollections from when he was little of Burroughs coming and camping out at the edge of their property, events so far removed that they were more like myth than fact; then, when Burroughs went into the woods for good and lived up on the Cold River, he heard of him as the Hermit of Cold River Flat, that's what they called him, and a picture formed in his mind of a red-haired man running around in a covering of skins, kind of crazy, keepin' out of sight, duckin' in and out of bushes to avoid people, a real crank that people were afraid of because of his difference, a man the woods had taken and made one of its own.

Now it was assumed he was dead. Nothing had been heard from him for years. Thinking that he had just quit sending messages down, Cobus's father had gone up to look for him, had gone straight to the cabin, knowing where it was from other trappers, but there was no sign of life, just some old skins moldering on the sand bed at one side of the hut and the odds and ends of someone who had once squatted there. "He's dead," Cobus's father had said, and said it in such a way that the matter seemed settled, but then apparently he had got to thinking about it and one day months later he said, without any preliminary explanation, "I'm goin' back lookin' for Clyde again. I got to thinkin' and maybe he ain't dead at all. Maybe he jest moved. Maybe he jest went farther in."

"What gits into you, Guthrie, you want to go traipsin' up there all the time?" It bothered Cobus's mother that his father set so much store on Burroughs. Couldn't she see it was a tie he had with Burroughs because he brought him out of the woods? Now the woods had got him again.

His father took out a long braided snake of tobacco and pulled at it between his teeth; a plug broke way, he began to chew. More and more Cobus noticed that his father was giving into what he thought of as "Indian ways." The tobacco, for instance. He hung it the way the Indians did out on the summer porch and dried it there. Going in or out of the house you went under it, the smell of it fell down on you; and when Cobus's father sat, he sat with long leaves in his hand, braiding; those he stored in big crocks in the kitchen, and he smoked or chewed them as the notion hit him. Nobody but an Indian hung his tobacco or braided it that way, just as only Indians dried their meat any more and ate it jerked. But Cobus's father said he liked it that way. All summer he had long thin strips of meat drying in the sun.

"But supposin' you do find him," Cobus's mother said. "I mean, what you aim to do with him?" What she really meant was, You ain't goin' to bring him back here, are you?"

"I jest want to talk to him," Cobus's father said in his stubborn voice. "Jest talk to him. That's all right, ain't it? To talk?"

So Cobus's father had gone, taking the old spotted mare, Narko. He had stayed away a week, going over the territory slowly, thoroughly; but he had come across nothing, no traps that would indicate a man was in the area, no bones of animals killed for meat, no skins or the remains of animals from which they had come, which would show a man was living off the land. He came back disappointed but—oddly—convinced Burroughs wasn't dead, but hiding.

Cobus's mother couldn't understand it. "What makes you think he's still alive—an old man like that, why, he'd be over seventy now, he couldn't live out in the woods alone, not at that age, and you didn't find any sign of him, what makes you so sure he's still alive?"

"Jest somethin' inside me says so." Cobus's father didn't often argue with his wife; it was as if they had some kind of understanding worked out, he'd leave her be if she didn't take her tongue to him.

A week later his father began packing again. "Where you off to now?" his mother demanded.

"North," Guthrie said. "Up to the reservation. He's gone to the reservation."

Cobus's father went to the reservation—he was gone a week—and when he came back, he said yes, Burroughs had been up that way and it was rumored he had gone North, maybe into Canada to where Brant's people had settled. Kateri, who had left to go back to her own people the year after Burroughs had gone off for good, was maybe with him. Cobus could see it was a comfort to his father to think they were together.

Cobus's mother was good and vexed. Any mention of Kateri had that power over her. She said nothing, however, possibly, Cobus suspected, because she was ashamed; she and Kateri were the same, even though Cobus's mother had never admitted it—even when Kateri had decided to go back home. Because one married white and the other didn't made no real distinction in his eyes. Kateri said she wanted to go back home and nobody tried to stop her, not even his grandfather; she was old, how old nobody knew; it was hard to tell with Indians, the skin of their faces drew back against the bones instead of falling into folds and wrinkles the way old white faces did; old and silent, secret unto herself.

She went back up North about the time the Raymonds took to working the woods and the word came they were making money hand over fist and when they'd cut everything in sight around Federation Lake they were going North to take even more, they were going to be rich, richer than anyone in these parts, and what's more they were going to put up a fancy big house on the other side of the point and come up summers in carriages, with darkies up at the house to do all the work. That's what people said.

The Indians were no longer keepers of the fire that never

dies nor men surpassing all others; the settlers themselves were no longer first holders of the land, those original whites who had appropriated the forests and girdled the trees, letting in light, burning out patches, cutting and chopping and carting away until nothing remained of the great trunks and the primordial pattern: men and oxen moved over the meadows and put in corn, manipulating the environment to suit their needs.

If you had black Indian hair and black Indian eyes, if your skin was dark and your nose flat and the whole cast of your face looked more Indian than white, people not knowing the story would have said likely you were all Indian, but of course everyone over to the Landing knew the story; he could just imagine them saying every time he went past, What you suppose ever made Guthrie Buttes fool enough to marry? Pity on account of the boys. Wouldn't want no sons of mine hybrid. *Halfbreed,* the worst thing you could be called at the Landing, no one knew better than Cobus, who'd heard it at least once a day every day of his school years, an epithet burned shamefully into his heart so that the mere acknowledgement of the color of his skin when he looked at his hands was a humiliation, a testimony that he wasn't as good as other men. It was a recognition made doubly painful because his twin, Tip, was light and white looking and was almost never called that bitter name. Tip was going to be smooth and oiled and finished as a lovely tool; his mind was sharp and incisive, his methods cutting and precise; but he, Cobus Buttes, did not have a finely honed mind. Maybe in the pattern of things he was meant to find a way all his own, but he couldn't do that staying put. He knew what there was to know here and it wasn't enough.

That was something he desperately needed, a sense of security inside himself, never mind what other people said. People set store by the appearance of a thing, not by the thing itself. He looked Indian, Tip did not; therefore, he would have to be Indian, Tip could pass for white, and the double standard of blood which passed judgment between brothers, twin brothers at that, had to balance within his own heart, and the only way he felt he could rid himself of the shame he felt inside was to get away from the Landing and their evaluation—*halfbreed*—and go into the woods where there was nothing but the big trees and the wide sky, a place where men hadn't put their dirty thoughts and destroyed so many good things. But weren't they destroying the woods?

And if he went into the woods, the woods he loved, he would be helping them.

Everything was all mixed up inside him. He needed to go into the woods; yet he should stay on the farm. He hated the notion of the forests being cut and yet another part of him ached to help cut them down. Heroic deeds were done in that cutting and he needed to know them. He wanted to do some of them himself. Yet his grandfather, his father, despised the kind of men who would travel over an area and leave it nothing but a graveyard of gray stumps.

Cobus knew, too, how short money was, and if Tip went to the Academy in Glen Falls that would mean a lot of extra expense. It was not a good time to be talking about a hired hand. What he himself might make in the woods wouldn't cut an inch one way or the other. Logging wasn't the way to make money. But it wasn't money he was after, but being out on his own. Nevertheless, there were certain rights inside yourself you had to listen to as well as those that pressed from without. The difficulty was how to make his father see that.

His father and Tip were on the back porch calling to him; they were starting down the path to the brook. He had promised (and forgotten until this moment) that they were all going eeling. His father carried a lantern to lure the eels from the depths of the water up to the light where he and Tip would lance them with three-pronged spears, shattering for an instant the still water; in spattered spangled droplets the glistening body of the eel would flop through the air, flung back to the bank and into darkness.

He and Tip could fill a barrel in a night. Boiled in vinegar and water with spices, the eels were one of his mother's favorite dishes. Eels were still plentiful, but not like in the days when the Indians went after them. In a few years. . . .

They walked in single file. The moon lay so close to the horizon that Cobus felt he could reach out and grasp it. The white arms of death, people said. Yet he felt secure in the midst of all that had been built up, so impatient of illness, weakness, failure in others, feeling the strength of his own body and the promise of immortality.

His father put the lamp on the ground; Tip handed him a spear. He and Tip were waiting for the moment their father picked up the lantern and took his place on a rock in the center of the stream. There he would hold the lamp and let them spear, would occasionally, so deft was he, hold the light in one hand and spear with the other. Eeling was one of the times Cobus marveled at the strength and control of his father, so much more finely tempered than his own powers.

His father took up the lantern and moved to make the jump to reach the rock. It was not a long leap, but it presented problems because the rock was slippery with green slimy moss and because the waters about it were deeper than they looked. In this part of the stream there was a steep drop-off from either bank. When the boys were little his father had worried they might be tempted to come down and play about the banks, and this was one of the few places on the farm forbidden them unless he was along.

The waters were thick and black, coiled, it seemed to Cobus; a great rush of rapids was just a little way upstream under the bridge and the combination of white water and darkness had never before bothered him, but he felt a certain lightness of head, a kind of strange trembling of limb. The time to tell him I want to go away is tonight, he thought.

Somewhere a dog whelped; he could hear the wretched cries as the pups pushed their way out. Across the fields the sweet moist scent of growth came. The fields continued to push. His father's fields, his father's land, his father's house, his . . . it was all his: that's why Cobus wanted to go. He wanted to find something of his own. His father would say the farm was his—and it would be. But it was not his now.

Tip was a book boy; he would go to school, not just the local school, but maybe even as far away as Albany. Already his teachers were pushing for him to go to the Academy at the Falls next year. It was just about decided. So the farm would one day be Cobus's. He should stay on it, work it, cherish it the way his father did, not go running off into the woods on some fool's errand—moonstruck, no wonder he kept looking up at that white-lidded eye.

But going away—trying to lead his own life—also made him feel guilty, selfish. Nothing he could do, it seemed, would be right.

His father would never in the world say *no,* but he'd be cut right to the quick if he knew Cobus even wanted to go. His father was a quiet man—but, Cobus thought, but that don't mean his feelin's don't run deep. I'm a lot like him. I got a lot of things happenin' inside me, but they don't come out in the open where they show. He was conscious more and more that he and his father were alike, even though they didn't look alike.

His father gave his usual signal—"Ready, boys?"—and,

swinging the lantern, jumped the brook in one great stride; for a moment he tottered on the slippery rock on which he landed, but Cobus was not afraid. *His* father would never fall.

Dragging the barrel was hard, sweaty effort and Tip complained he had the worst of the deal, being out in front; Cobus changed with him and then Tip said Cobus wasn't pulling his share. Their father walked in front, the lantern making an arc of light as it moved with his swinging arm. He was a big powerful man—more muscle than bone—and when he was irritated, as he was now because of the bickering, the hunched valley of muscles in his back grew deep, and truculent, a warning which Tip, sensing his father would favor him to compensate for the fact that Cobus was his favorite, chose to ignore, belaboring the night quiet with querulous accusation. Having tried to mollify Tip by exchanging places, Cobus said to himself, To hell with it, and trudged along, rehearsing in his mind the arguments he would give his father. He had enjoyed the eeling; it was bad to spoil that by arguing. He just wished Tip would shut up, but he would never dare say so. What his father tolerated in Tip he looked on as bad form in Cobus. Since this double standard had operated from the beginning, Cobus did not find it unfair; it just was. Cobus, going over arguments and counter-arguments in his mind, shutting out deliberately the litany of complaint in back of him, was startled to find his father halted—he almost ran into him—and angrily turning around. "Stop it. Now just stop it once and for all," he said sharply.

Tip dropped his end of the barrel, probably as surprised as Cobus by the outburst. For a moment Cobus hung on, but the weight, all pushed forward, was too much for him. The barrel turned over, eels glistened under the lantern light.

It had been a long time since Cobus had seen his father so angry. Words poured volcanically from the open maw of his mouth, the very air around him seemed smoky with sulfurous speech. The two boys bent silently and guilty under his reproaches, stuffing slippery and slimy eels back into the barrel. Cobus felt the scene an ominous warning of defeat for his case. Yet a stubborn resolution to "get it over with" made him determined to go through with his plans, regardless of the omens. As the two boys righted the barrel and waited, their father commenced again down the rocky path, still muttering about switches and straps.

In the kitchen Cobus's mother had the brown crockery

eel jars laid out. After she washed and cleaned the fish, she would salt some of them down and put others into the enormous smoking pot on the stove. She was half turned to them, a woman burned dark by the outdoor chores, with black Indian brows and thick black hair, hair that never streaked or grayed but held its jet color; with high cheekbones, a handsome woman, a strong handsome woman with a mind of her own and dangerous volatile moods that you had to reckon with; but in his eyes she was beautiful, and no one could ever talk against her because he had a loyalty to her that came from her own unquestionable sense of self. At the Landing they might sneer with their voices when they called her "Mrs. Buttes," but that's what she was and she never forgot it. Dignity sat upon her as if she were a great lady. And possibly, Cobus believed, she was.

Cobus's father sat down with a grunt and began to complain to her about her sons' behavior (they were at such moments hers entirely). Her deft fingers were sorting and stripping; she was listening while she worked, commenting with a nod of her head or a soft clucking sound in the back of her throat. Cobus saw how hopeless she deemed defense. After a time his father ran out of energy and just sat, drumming his fingers against the table in disgust; finally he ceased even that, got up and took out a braid of tobacco, chomping down on it moodily. Cobus stood in the dim kitchen light watching his mother's quick thin fingers with the greasy-looking eels, his father's thick blunt ones working with the long, dry black strand of tobacco. Unaccountably he felt terribly moved, as if he were at the heart of his home; it was here in this dusky light, in these moving fingers, in the spit and groan of the stove, the flashing fire in the lamp, in (he noted) the absence of Tip from the room. It seemed impossible he could ever want to leave here and go away, and yet the wild pounding of his heart urged just that: to part from what was known and sweet and safe and go out into the dark and frightening unknown.

"Pa," he said. "Pa, I got to talk to you about the woods."

His father was more a listening man than a talking one; his earnest concentration centered on Cobus's working mouth. The hesitations and stumblings did not trouble him; inside his mind he was working his way toward the vortex of explanations, searching out the still calm center of all this anguish. His eyes were still fixed on the tobacco in his hands, but his mind was on his son's words, weighing, judging, and —at last, Cobus saw with an immense sense of relief—identifying, understanding. That understanding was a miracle Cobus had never dared anticipate. He loved his father profoundly for it; yet he wanted to go, wanted even more to be on his way because that act of empathy said to him the human heart was never closed no matter how old or bruised or bitter it became, and if this were true everything in the world that was bursting inside a boy's breast beat feebly still in an old man's—and they could discourse together and perhaps touch understanding inside each other.

His father's voice seemed to him ancient—faded, gravelly —but it was a voice also full of concern and sympathy. "Not this fall," his father said. "Next year, maybe, but not this year. There's too much here—"

"Guthrie, he's got his heart set on goin'." There was a high flush on his mother's face, the nervous gesture of pushing back her hair, the flame that flickered up and down in the pupils of her eyes while, calm and rocklike, his father sat determined to meet fire with stone. "But, Guthrie, I do understand and though I'd rather he was goin' with Tip down to the Falls—" Her breath caught, for she was talking about something about which she felt very strongly. She did not want her children to be farmers, halfbreed dirt workers, their lives confined to this small parcel of ground; but if she must make a sacrifice, she would always sacrifice Cobus for Tip. Tip was the one that struck the deep responsive chord inside her while Cobus and his father held a common bond. Cobus she would allow to be caught, chained, and claimed, but one of her children was going to fly free—the one who didn't look like her, who had no guilt because he wasn't constantly being called halfbreed.

"He can go next year," Cobus's father said. "If he's that set on going, one more year or less won't change it none. He's needed here. *He* knows that."

"He's fifteen, old enough to make his own decisions."

"Almost old enough."

"No, old enough. He's got rights, too."

"Winters, things ease up," his father said as if he were talking to a child. But he was talking to himself. "When the snows come, I can—"

It was the end of the argument. His father looked down, studying his gnarled hands. "Yes," he said, "I guess he does have some rights of his own." Then he got up and they heard him going upstairs to bed.

The Raymond house had been finished late in August.

Plans had called for it to be finished a month earlier so that the family could spend the summer at the lake, but like most building schemes this one had been way off in time and cost. Not until nearly the end of September had the mansion been completed, and now the Raymonds were installed—crazily so, the Landing said, with winter coming on.

Wagonloads of fine furniture had been carted up, though Old Man Raymond had laid out (he said) a "rustic" camp, a kind of blending of the old rude log cabin and a fancy Swiss chalet—Adirondack Swiss, he described it drily to the local residents. The wagons were followed by more carts of linen, china, glassware, a whole wagonful of wines, one with a great thick rug for the front room and imported marble columns for the back maze. The house was said (Cobus had not seen) to have a porch, which Raymond spoke of as a piazza, also a belvedere, or gazebo, as he called it, all magical names that people at the Landing repeated solemnly, as if they were reciting incantations.

It was the largest house anyone around had ever seen, the main part forty feet square, two and a half stories high, with brick walls a foot thick. A hundred thousand bricks were said to have gone into that house. Fireplaces kept its rooms warm and cozy, their four chimneys jutting up from the ends of the house. There was a huge barn with a cupola twelve feet square and the initials M M R on the barn roof, the letters standing for Raymond's full name, Mason Mowatt Raymond, but the local people said they stood for Much Money Raymond.

The Raymonds, it seemed, had much of everything everyone else had little of. Their horses, for instance. Cobus found details of the house and china and rugs and all dull, he envied their horses. They were said to have a stallion that cost five thousand dollars and mares that had come up from Virginia, real jumping animals that the trainer, who came up with the animals, could steer over high stone walls and big three-rung fences without any trouble at all. The Raymonds had matched carriage horses and high-spirited stallions that they hitched to their buggies. They had the most beautiful cart horses, the handsomest riding mounts; they even kept a matched pair of oxen, the finest and most closely matched pair anyone around the Landing had ever seen; they weighed well over two tons and were almost pure white, and it was said that over the backs of these oxen four bushels of wheat could be poured without rolling off.

The Raymond women never worked but were waited on by

men with white gloves or by grooms who handed them fine-gaited horses. Children were sent out to play with expensive carts and ponies instead of having to mend fences, water stock, gather in grain. The people at the Landing looked on the Raymonds as mortals set apart by the gods for special dispensation—rich, gifted, golden.

The fact his father had lent him Lady instead of having him take Narko or hitching up the work horses to the cart indicated to Cobus that his father wanted him to meet the Raymonds for the first time on some kind of equal footing, whatever reservations he still held about Cobus going into the woods. A man who had a fine animal could look any other man in the eye. A fifteen-year-old riding an animal like Lady to apply for a job was quite different from a farm boy coming down by cart to ask for work. On Lady or in a cart, he was the same boy and he wasn't. It was odd to see it like that. Going up to the Raymonds' beautiful mansion by cart would have made him hesitant, a petitioner.

A week before there had been three days of unexpectedly cold weather, killing off most of the garden (the sprouts would hang on till mid-December); then the weather had gone back to a kind of mild, almost hot spell, alternating with cold nights; the trees had suddenly begun turning, though the height of color, everyone locally agreed, usually came about the middle of October. He was going into the woods—he never for a moment doubted Old Man Raymond would put him on; come riding up on a fine horse like this, how could he turn him down? He urged Lady on. They were near the old Guthrie mill; he could hear the water, the whir of the wheelstone, from almost a quarter of a mile away. He would let Lady out a little, but now he kept her checked in; they would not go into a good canter until after the hill, there were too many unexpected things there that might spook her and it wouldn't do to come unseated and dust up his clothes on a day like this; nor did he want to lather her up. The weather was warm and her winter coat had a good start already; she would show any exertion at all, and to arrive with a sweating horse too hard run would show a foolhardy or careless boy. But a little run on such a day. . . .

There was a wagon at the mill, men on the stoop; he waved, and while he was still in sight of them he let the horse out to show what she could do. He felt her begin to collect under him and knew that her neck was arched, her tail high, her movements gathered in so that she showed all that good blood. Behind him he heard a cheer.

Lady sped down the road, her hooves pounding, mane flying, the wind soft and sweet on Cobus's face. His heart was singing, as if the whole world was opening up to him and he had only to reach the top of the next hill and there would be the whole wide wonderful view of what lay ahead.

He reined the horse in, letting her fall back into a fast canter, then a slower one, then a slow trot, and then stop. He sat in wonder looking down on the Raymond house for the first time, the huge Raymond barn with its initials, its cupola, the fenced-in field where a group of horses had caught their scent and were running toward them, whinnies filling the air.

Lady was heaving under him, and when he reached over and touched her flank, it was damp. Even that short run had excited her too much; he would have to walk her slow and rest her awhile before he went up to the house; but under him she had begun to tremble and strain at the bit. She wanted to go up to the fence to the other horses. Horses, he had found, were as gregarious as men. You leave a horse in a field all by itself for a long time, it got sullen and listless. Horses loved company but, again like men, they were timid in their overtures for friendship, nosing forward, drawing back, giving shrill little cries of alarm, sorting out animals until they came on one they singled out to be a special friend.

He wondered for a moment what the language was in such a world, and then he saw a magnificent animal, jet black body, jet black mane and tail, detach itself from the group, a scream coming from somewhere deep in his chest, a call as terrible and piercing as an ultimatum. The horse came thundering toward them and Cobus had time only to think, Good God, it's a stud and not penned up, before he dug his heels into Lady's side. With all the force he had, he brought his back forward to free her hind quarters and dug his heels into her side with the signal to *run*. She shot forward at a full gallop. An instant's survey of the fence had told him it would not hold if the stallion decided to try to clear it— as Cobus was sure he would decide—just as he was equally sure from the high-pitched screech Lady had given that she was probably in season and—

The *and* he never finished. Using his heels harder and harder to urge her on, he passed the stallion coming toward them, heard the peculiar and unmistakable trumpet call of a

237

rutting animal; though he could no longer see the animal he could identify its path by sound. The momentary silence, he knew, was the animal in midair taking the fence. The jar of earth signalled the horse had come down, probably right on the road behind him. Another cry, and hooves, hard, fast, determined hooves, sent the animal close behind. He thanked God Lady was the kind of animal she was; another mare would have fought him to get to the stallion. But under the urgent beating of his heels and the insistent push of his back driving her into the bit, she galloped straight on toward the house. If they could make it, he—

There was a flash to one side of him, then a flurry of dust, animals' screams as the stallion reeled round, skidded to a stop, reared, and plunged back toward them. Lady simply gave way under him. He was never sure whether she had stopped so suddenly that she went down or whether the abruptness of the halt threw him. The next thing he knew he lay, stunned, at the side of the road, his head a splinter of shocks, the two horses running away. Lady's saddle had slipped to one side, the reins were dangling, and he thought, *Oh God, she'll get caught in them, break a leg, what'll Pa say;* and then, forcing himself to his feet with the wild notion of running after, catching her, he saw the reins catch underfoot, snap, the saddle slip all the way under her, the two animals going down the road in a runaway gallop, gone beyond all hope of stopping, headed straight for the open fields ahead.

"You have to *book,*" Old Man Raymond kept saying to Cobus, dusty and stunned and bruised, but in the front hall —and what a front hall—of that enormous house. "Book months in advance. We only allow so many servicings a year, we have to protect our investment. Surely even *you* can understand that, a five-thousand-dollar horse, you don't waste that kind of animal on grade mares. People have to come recommended and I *personally* pass on their animals. If the blood lines aren't right, I won't take them, I don't care how much they offer to pay. And now my good five-thousand-dollar stud is off there servicing some trashy Indian's broken-down—" He was beyond reason; no use for Cobus to point out he was only half an Indian and his horse had been merely going down the road when that five-thousand-dollar wonder had broken out of the field and toppled down on top of them and as far as they were concerned, him and his Pa, Lady wasn't any old grade mare, she had blood lines good as

238

any, they just couldn't prove where they'd come in, but all you had to do was look at her for yourself.

The veins in Old Man Raymond's neck were bulging. He looked as if there were cords swelling up across one part of his forehead; his whole face was purple. "I know your kind," he was saying in absolute, final delineation. "One of those rock farms, nothing but notes at the bank, a house full of children—and now my five-thousand-dollar horse mounting your nag. Who in the hell are you anyway, boy?"

"I'm one of the Butteses, sir. It's my father's horse. I come down to—"

"Your father the one that brought that man out of the woods, that man that was mauled by the bear?"

"Yes, sir, but that was a long time ago. I don't think folks much remember anymore—you know, it was—"

"People always remember a thing like that." When he said anything, he seemed to say it with complete, irrefutable authority. "Well," he said after a pause, "if it had to be anybody's horse, I'm glad it was your father's. What's done's done. You can't take it out on her. *William,*" he shouted at the top of his lungs, and for the first time in his life Cobus laid eyes on a black man. He had heard about Negroes, but he had never in his life believed he would see one. Just as people at the Landing had tried to tell him and he had refused to believe, the man was black as the ace of spades. "William, tell them to quit haying and go look for Satan. Take some grain, you'll never get him otherwise—maybe you won't with that either—I don't care *how* you get him, but get him, understand?"

"Yessir, Mr. Raymond."

"And William—you tell Styles to come here—*after* he gets Satan back—and tell me what he was doing out."

William hesitated. "He can't go, sir—he can't come neither —Satan, he got out, sir, because, you see, sir, he jest bit through Mr. Styles's arm, sir, and ran over him, and that's how he got out, sir. He only been out a minute, sir. I mean, sir, we was getting Mr. Styles up to his place, and Jed'd gone for the doctor—he was going to get the horse, Mr. Raymond, but Mr. Styles, sir, he was bleeding bad, there's bones broke in his arm, sir, so we thought—Jed, he thought he ought to go for the doctor first. We was on our way to tell you, sir, but Satan, he got out and there wasn't no chance." William waited, at the end of his breath, but somehow patient. He had seen worse things and lived through them; obviously he thought he would probably weather this, but it was going to be a mighty stiff storm while it lasted.

"Well, send some of the others—Noah, Hawkins, Old Pete—"

"Old Pete, he won't go, sir. You know how he is about horses, and that horse—"

"All right, Artin can go in his place. But get a group and go. I want that horse back here and in a hurry."

"Yessir." There was a pause. "You want me to go, sir?"

"I don't care *who* goes just so long as they get going and get that horse."

"Yes*sir.*"

"And bring some brandy—since you won't be going."

"Yessir." Cobus thought for a moment William was going to smile. But he merely backed away, moving instinctively toward the door.

"After you get the rest of them going for the horse."

"Yes—sir."

"Just a moment—"

"Yessir."

"How old are you, boy?"

Cobus had presence enough of mind to lie. "Sixteen," he said with conviction.

"Your father consider that old enough for spirits?"

"Yessir." He focused his attention, or what he could muster of it, on the thick rug under his feet. Incredibly colored birds with enormous spread tails with *eyes* in them looked up at him.

Old Man Raymond was moving purposefully across the hall toward an entranceway framed by wide folding doors. In back of him Cobus caught a confused impression of red and silver, dark polished wood and thick folds of drapes, something heavy and glossy in the corners. In his dusty clothes he stayed where he was. But Raymond, striding on without looking back, apparently sensed his hesitation and called over his shoulder, "Come along, come along, you can sit on one of the stools if you don't want to dirty up the damask."

He stood, Raymond, at a handsome highboy, cutting with a small silver instrument the end from a cigar. He was not a tall man but he had an air of substantiality; the hands engaged in working with the cigar were small and puffy, white and very well cared for. He don't ride much with them hands, Cobus thought. More than likely he didn't ride at all. Raymond smiled at him and Cobus thought, If he's so rich, why don't he do something about his teeth.

He thought of his grandfather. How old was he? He didn't know. But he did know the shuffling gait, the halting, silence-studded speech, the way the hands were never quite able to cope with anything difficult: "He got hurt bad in the woods," Cobus's father had tried to explain. "He was never the same after. But before—before that, you ask anyone over at the Landing, he was the biggest man in these parts —not necessarily in size, but in stature."

Living up at the farm that way, so cut off, so self-sufficient, Cobus had never thought about "bigness" one way or the other, but here in this house, in this kind of world, he could see how little he really knew of the world and the way it ran. Raymond was obviously a "big" man, but not in the way Cobus's grandfather was.

Despairing, he stood for a moment in the middle of brilliant sunlight raking chinaware, linen, silver, polished wood, the nap of the rug: there was absolutely no place for a dusty man to sit. The rug already showed his footsteps as if outlining the final path to perdition.

Raymond voices and bright, interested, shining Raymond eyes kept flying out at him from various corners of the room; laughing, low silky laughs, they asked him a multitude of questions without waiting for (or even, it seemed, expecting) an answer; and—horror of horrors—one of the girls, one he reckoned about his age—had picked up a fluted dish with what looked like something jellied and congealed on it and was advancing toward him, the dish held in front of her, a lovely, innocent smile on her face. He picked up a piece, popped it heroically into his mouth, and something brown and hideously sweet clung to the roof of his mouth and would not let go while this brilliant, shining creature in front of him said something that sounded like "mare roans," and delivered a similar glob into her own mouth. "Mmm," she said with satisfaction. "Divine."

Everything was hopeless, hopeless; no place to sit, his mouth stopped up with slop, his father's horse gone, his clothes in rends, his pride in shreds. Bitterly he looked back on the hour before when he had passed the mill, lightened the reins and given Lady her head. He had been a king then.

Old Man Raymond, an older lady (not so old as Raymond, however) and the girls were all staring at him curiously. Probably the lump in his cheek showed. The woman was picking a small sliver of silver needle in and out of a hoop on which was stretched fine, thin cloth you could almost see through; the thread she was using was red, and it ran like a thin trickle of blood from the needle in her hand to the white cloth on which the tiny stitches looked like small drops from an open wound. Her gaze was disquieting because it was so intense; she was studying Cobus and she gave the impression of having seen a good deal that was not favorable to her view of what a young man should be.

William reentered, crossed the room with a silver tray. There was a big bottle—the brandy, Cobus presumed—and glasses on such slender stems that they looked ready to shatter at the insult of a touch. Old Man Raymond nodded. "A drink will make us all feel better," he said, straightening his vest.

Gagging, Cobus had a dim, misty vision of the smile of young Mrs. Raymond, sewing, thin and tinny as her voice. "Not to be trusted," she said reedily. "I've said so a thousand times. Dangerous and—vicious. He ought long ago to have been—altered."

"A little fruity," Raymond said. "It didn't travel well for some reason. The jolting, I suppose."

Two years before he supposed he would have cried; now, in desperation, he forced the muscles of his inner mouth to ingest what was left of that poisonous glob inside, he swallowed, he gave himself up for gone, and in a voice as thin and tinny as young Mrs. Raymond's, but sharpened by sickness whereas hers had been honed by the dictates of good society, he hung onto his manners. "Your very good health, sir," he said and took a swallow from the beautiful thin-stemmed vessel in his hand.

"Yours," Old Man Raymond replied. "Excellent cognac," he said, licking his lips. "First-rate . . . you have to get into it even if it is a little on the fruity side. One swallow doesn't entitle a man to an epithet if he hasn't truly tasted the grape."

Across from Cobus the girl who had given him the poisonous glob went on popping those brown things in her mouth. Her mother had taken up a new thread, blue. Old Man Raymond was pouring himself another drink; the younger girls were staring at Cobus, wide-eyed with wonder. They all had been named for flowers or stones, it seemed—Pansy, Opal, Iris, Violet, Amaryllis, Coral, and they all looked alike.

What if that five-thousand-dollar horse had tagged Lady? Think of it, a colt from that big beautiful black stallion. A colt out of that stallion—

He drank a little brandy and it lay in his chest, warm and reassuring, bespeaking a better future. Yet, unaccountably, at the moment he put himself at ease in such surroundings, he was conscious of a curious shift in the atmosphere, an uneasiness. They had stopped speaking, eating, sewing; they were now looking at him, waiting for him to speak.

"I got my mind made up I'd like to log, sir. I mean, I know I can't be a logger right off, but I'd like to get a start. *Learn*," he said earnestly. "I'd be willing to do anything—helpin' out to git the hang of it."

"So you want to go into the woods, do you? You know it's a hard life?"

"Yes, sir, I know that, but I'm strong, I work hard, you ask my Pa, he—"

"Doesn't your father need you up at the farm?"

"Well, yes, I guess he could use me, but he's willing I should go, if I got my heart set on it. And there's Tip—that's my brother, we're twins—he's there to help, at least until he goes down to the Falls to school. They feel they could make out."

"I'm short a berth here and there, but it's what they call harness work, the grubby rotten details in any camp that have to be done. William?"

"The men's back, sir. They got the horses. The mare—it's one of her back legs, sir. A bit lame," William said quickly.

His father would kill him if anything had happened to that horse.

"Come on, boy, we'll take a look for ourselves. Don't borrow trouble. There's enough around as it is." He and Cobus moved toward the door at the same time. "I've got a man who knows all about horses. Styles, he—" Then apparently Old Man Raymond remembered about Styles. "Well, we'll take a look for ourselves."

They passed over the rug filled with those strange puffed up birds with eyes in their tails and into a small outer room where a door stood open, a group of men waiting outside, caps in hands, shuffling back and forth, shifting their weight from one foot to the other; as Raymond came out, they parted, leaving a clear path for him. Raymond made for the big barn with his initials on top of it. The men shuffled behind, half following, half hanging back.

Cobus could hear the stallion banging back and forth inside the barn. A voice behind him said, "The mare's in back," and they kept going, past the stallion whose eyes gleamed out at them in rage, whose dilated nostrils widened as they passed, who crashed against the barred stall door, but Old Man Raymond didn't even give him a glance. Cobus liked that in him, that he respected the injury of another man's horse enough to look at it before he checked his own animal. Hard but *fair*, Cobus thought.

Lady was in a large cow pen at the very back of the barn. She was standing with her back to them, her left rear leg off the ground. Even from the back Cobus could see gashes. She had got caught in something. "If you don't mind, sir," he said respectfully but firmly, "I'd like to look at her myself."

Raymond said nothing but stepped aside.

"Lady," Cobus said, and she turned her head. All the pride and beauty were gone out of her; she was streaked with dust, burrs clung to and tangled her mane; she made no sign of recognition. Usually she lifted her head and tossed it when someone came close; invariably she whinnied and moved close to be stroked or have her ears scratched, her muzzle teased.

"Lady," Cobus said quietly and moved to her side, resting a hand on the haunch of the hurt leg. She quivered and moved to one side, as if to get away from touch.

He withdrew his hand and went up to her before he even examined the leg, patted her neck, ran his hand up and down her side. "It's all right, Lady," he said.

Then he bent down and looked at the leg.

He stood up and faced Raymond. "I got every right in the world to ride down a road. But you ain't got NO right to have an animal you can't control git out on me, ruin my horse—my father's horse. I don't know how they do things down to Albany, but around here if a man's got an animal that's an outlaw he gits rid of him or he pens him up so good he *can't* get out."

Raymond came forward and squatted down. He was an old man and something ground in his bones as they came together in the effort of getting him down, but he stayed squatting, looking. Then he rose. Cobus thought it was a sigh he heard come from that old man. "I know that, son, and I'm sorry—"

"Sorry won't help that leg—"

"No, it won't, but we still don't know—I don't like to move her, but I'd like to get her out in more light so we can get a better look. What do you think?"

The fairness extinguished his anger. Raymond *was* sorry, and now Cobus felt sorry, too, and ashamed. But, like his father, he had loved that horse. "I don't like to move her, like you say, but—" He went forward and put both his arms around Lady's neck, laid his head against her. Tears were burning in his throat and against his eyes, but he bit his lip and choked them back. "We gotta take you outside, Lady," he said to the horse. Gently he pushed his hand against her neck, bringing himself around in front of her. "Back," he said slowly. "Back, Lady."

Dragging, then raising and refusing to put weight on the leg, she tried to move back. Cobus let her take her time. Gradually, step by step, she moved into the open corridor of the barn, between the stalls on both sides. He took hold of a halter someone had put on her (he wondered for the first time what had happened to his bridle and saddle) and gradually coaxed her forward into a square of light. As they came abreast of Satan's stall, the stallion went wild, kicking and rearing and plunging, but Lady did not even look up. Limping, hop-scotching, she followed Cobus into the shaft of sun.

The leg at least was not broken, but it was impossible to tell just how bad the gashes were. They were deep and ragged and right across the hock, the worst place, but when Cobus tried to get close and run his hand over her leg anywhere near the wounds, she panicked and lurched away. He knew then how badly the leg hurt her. Always before she had been gentle and tractable, no matter what they did to her. Heartsick, he stood up and looked at Raymond. He didn't know what to say; there weren't words for it.

"There a decent vet down at the Falls?" Raymond asked. "Take time but—"

"I don't know. Mostly cow men, I suppose. Not many calls for horses around here."

"Styles, when he gets up—"

"Mr. Raymond, what am I goin' to tell my father? It's *his* horse."

"You aren't going to tell him anything. I am. I can't ride over and tell him myself, though I wish I could, boy. But I'll send one of the men over for him. In the meantime you and I will stay here and see what we can do. You can put up with us, son, so you can watch over your horse until she can make it back, if that's all right with you, all right with your father. My man can bring your things back. If there's any way we can, boy, we'll make your mare all right. I give you my word."

"Yes, sir," he said. "I know that, but—" He couldn't go on. If he put his fear in words, it might make it an actuality. Words, it seemed to him, had a way of bringing things into being. Finally, he felt there wasn't any way to avoid it. "I just hope it isn't a tendon, that's all I hope."

He was so tired that he had tracked mud right over the bird-rug, putting out all the eyes of those outrageous things, the ones in their heads as well as the ones in their tails, not even caring, then caring terribly, sinking down on the steps looking at his muddy boots with dismay. "I'm sorry," he said, and just sat, tuckered out. "And I guess I owe you an apology, sir, talking the way I did." The old man had stayed right alongside him all those long hours, and at his age. It was dark, but Cobus had no idea how late it was. The house was silent, no one about. "You was with me all that time—and after the way I talked. I'm plumb ashamed, sir, and that's the truth of it. No need for you to stay, but you did. And after the way I went on."

"It was you, boy, that did the work."

Cobus shook his head.

"You ought to eat something."

Cobus shook his head again.

"You have to eat. There'll be something in the kitchen we can share—and drink."

Cobus looked up. "Not that brandy," he said.

"Cider—beer—what you want. I'm for a whiskey, four full fingers, neat. You did a good job on that horse, son. Slow, careful, thorough. You're your father's son."

"It ain't work when you care," Cobus said, and began to pull a boot off. "I'm sorry about the mud."

"William will clean it up."

"Strange birds they put on that, ain't they? I can't get over them."

"They're peacocks."

Cobus looked at him. "You mean they're *real?*"

"An Asian pheasant, I believe. There are several different species. Beautiful, aren't they, but said to be bad-tempered—like many beautiful things. Let's go get some grub."

Cobus stood up in his stocking feet (he was glad he had put on "good" socks, that is, the darned ones, that morning). He picked up his boots.

"Give me those," Raymond said, indicating the boots. "I'll have them cleaned for you. William will do it in the morning."

"He don't have to do that. I can clean my own boots."

"That's what he's here for, that's his job."

"I don't like to make another man clean my boots."

Raymond looked surprised. "Your people Abolitionists?"

"No, not leastwise that I know of. We don't have none

246

of them niggers around here, so I don't know what we are. The problem ain't never come up. But my Pa don't believe one man ought to wait on another, he don't think that's right."

"I don't *own* William."

"He's black, ain't he, he—"

"Well, all black men aren't slaves, boy. Most of them are, here in this country leastwise, but William's what you call a Freeman. He works for me, he gets paid like any of my other men, he can leave whenever he wants if he doesn't like the way things are."

"Well, in that case, I guess he can clean my boots, if he wants to."

"That's mighty nice of you."

"We kind of run stubborn in our family," Cobus said.

"So it would seem."

They went through a door on the right and into a long, low kitchen. There was a table in the middle with benches; copper pots and pans were hanging from a huge iron contraption overhead; bundles of dried herbs festooned the far wall; cannisters, barrels, baskets were all around overflowing with the autumn harvest—apples, corns, squash, pumpkins, pears. A smell of drying sage, of basil and fennel smothered the feel of free air. Graters, choppers, slicers, corers, presses lined the near wall. There were shelves of tankards, plates, serving dishes, mixing bowls, sieves and strainers.

Raymond went over and took down two plates and two tankards. "See what's out back in the summer kitchen and bring in what grabs your fancy. Bring in a lot, I'm hungry. I'll get the bread and butter."

Cobus found some boiled beef, half a roasted hen, a bowl of leftover boiled potatoes. Raymond was cutting bread on a board with a long wicked-looking knife when he came back. A mound of butter as big as a big man's clenched fist glowed on a plate beside the bread. "There's cider in a keg out back, but it's new, hasn't had a chance to work much. The beer's—I'll be damned if I remember where they keep the beer."

"The cider'll do fine," Cobus said.

"I don't think it was a tendon," Raymond said, slicing, not looking up. "But some of those cuts were pretty deep."

"Yes, sir, they were." Cobus figured he might as well tell the truth. "I think at least one tendon's gone—sir."

"Well, you ought to know. You were working close. I

247

couldn't see that well. You don't think she'll come back?"

"She might and then again she might not. But she won't be any use for a long time whichever way it is."

"Your father sets a lot of store by that horse, doesn't he?"

"Yes, sir, he does."

"Well, let's eat. We'll have another look in the morning. Like I said before, I'm awful sorry, son."

Cobus was up before anyone else. He was used to getting up early, and even though he had very little sleep, because this was an unfamiliar house, a strange bed, an unknown atmosphere, the worry about the horse, he woke just before daylight. Habit was so strong in him that sometime before daybreak he gave up trying to settle himself, put back on his shirt and pants (he had slept in his underwear) and, without his boots, sat by the window waiting for a little light so that he could go down to the barn again.

He just couldn't figure out what he would say to his father. He could tell the story of course, but when he went over it in his mind he always got to a place where he couldn't go on, it seemed to him he should have done more—predicted what might have happened when he first sighted the stallion, stayed on instead of being thrown, *something*. No matter how he went over it in his mind, he came out feeling responsible.

He felt bad about the mare, but he felt worse about his father. Like Raymond had said, his father set an awful store by that horse.

A gentle tapping woke him. He had fallen asleep in the chair; outside, the world lay gray and miserable under rain. There hadn't been enough light to wake him when it came. "Yes, sir," he said quickly, getting up and going toward the door.

"It's me—Ardis," a girlish voice said.

When he opened the door, the girl who had eaten all that gluey mess was standing in the hall. She had on a fancy dress, the kind he'd seen his mother wear maybe three, four times in his life, funerals and weddings, the rest of the time she kept it packed and put away. He wondered if it was Sunday and maybe they were all going churchway, but then the scheme of the week came back to him: it was Wednesday. He thought for a moment maybe Lady was dead, that was why she was dressed up; then he said to himself, Don't be a damned fool, it's the way with these folks.

"Here's your boots." She handed them, cleaned, to him. "Grandpa said to tell you your mare ate. He thought you'd want to know that. It's a good sign," she said encouragingly. "You ought to eat, too." She was trying to put him at ease, though he saw she was nervous herself. Her hands were fidgeting with one corner of her dress, just didn't seem to be able to let it alone. "Your Pa's here," she said.

"Pa's here?"

"Grandpa said to tell you he came over this morning. He's down in the barn now with Grandpa. Your Pa said you did as good a job of cleaning out those cuts as a doctor could've done. You know we *all* feel bad about—about what happened."

"I know you do," Cobus said at last. "And that almost makes it worse. But I can't come down without putting on my shoes." He was holding his boots in his hands helplessly.

"Well, why don't you put them on?"

"Seems like I should, don't it, but—well—I never put my boots on in front of a—in public, before."

"I'll wait in the hall," she said, smiling. She had lovely teeth. For some reason he was enormously glad; teeth like Old Raymond's running in a family of girls would have been a pitiful thing.

His father was in the kitchen, drinking coffee, Raymond something stronger. The first thing Cobus said was, "It's a tendon, ain't it, Pa?"

His father nodded. "But we maybe can pull her out of it, lots of rest, graining, kept in a stall where she can't put too much weight on it, run."

"I'm sorry, Pa, I—"

"Things happen sometimes you can't control."

Cobus remembered a saying of his father's: there aren't any accidents, only errors. He wondered if his father was thinking of it, too. And of course his father knew as well as he did that the chances of a horse with a tendon gone ever being sound again was like asking God to move the earth over a little.

"Can't count all the wrongs," his father said, as if he were reading Cobus's mind. "Maybe get us a colt out of it anyway."

"No maybe about it," Raymond said.

They both looked at him.

"They're bringing her around now. She *looks* good, but of course there's no way of really knowing with a yearling, but the blood's there, shows up in the conformation, it's the disposition you can't count on, not 'til you break them. But

249

she's good at halter—" He broke off. "Now, Mr. Buttes, don't look like that and don't say what I know you're going to say. It's my horse and my horse did the damage and it's my *right* to make up for it."

"I understand, Mr. Raymond, and don't think I don't appreciate—"

"I *want* you to have her. Givers got some rights, too, Mr. Buttes. You got your obligation to me to receive what I want to give in the spirit I give it. You grant me that much, don't you?"

"There's a good chance Lady—"

"It's not you I'm giving the filly to—it's the boy."

Cobus couldn't believe his ears.

"A boy cares for animals the way he does ought to have a good horse of his own to work with. You got a good animal, Mr. Buttes. I just hope she won't be a lame one. But this mare is for your son."

Cobus's father looked at him; he opened his mouth to speak, then shut it. Cobus knew he was waiting for his son to say what had to be said. Cobus chose his words carefully out of respect for both his father and Old Man Raymond— and, in a matter of speaking, for himself as well. "I'd like to have her, sir," he said. "But I'd like to feel I worked for her as well. The horses you got around here, I know I couldn't never afford to buy but, well, sir, if you'd let me go into the woods and just work, would you consider that part payment? And the rest—"

"You're lucky, Mr. Buttes, to have a boy like that. My own son—he's been sick, a lot. He's down in a place now, down South, for his health." Raymond tried to smile. "We throw girls," he said. "My boy, he's never been able to ride. I always loved animals, good horses, you know, and then my son, he had the leg sickness when he was small. We were lucky to save him at all, but his legs were never right. He's never really ridden in his whole life," Old Man Raymond said. "I used to hold him on sometimes when he was small, and someone would lead the animal around. But he's never been on all alone, to ride by himself. Imagine it—he's never ridden a horse alone in his whole life." The notion seemed beyond him, as, Cobus realized, it was beyond him. A man who didn't have a horse of his own, a horse he cared about, it didn't seem to Cobus he *was* a man.

II

William, holding onto the reins, pulled the buggy up and looked at Cobus. "Here's where you git off," he said.

Cobus picked up his knapsacks and got down. Standing in the road, looking at nothing but a giant forest of trees and a slender little road cut roughly between them, not a sign of civilization around, he felt a joyous lift of his heart. "I'm mighty obliged to you for bringing me this far." He held out his hand. William looked at it a moment, then took it. They shook. "And I'm obliged, too, you're goin' to look after my filly this winter while I'm in the woods. Pa don't have time, farmin' alone the way he is."

"It'll be a pleasure, Mr. Cobus. That's one pretty filly. Never seen one that color before. Pure yeller-like."

Cobus never had had any terminal facilities. He knew he ought to be on his way, but he couldn't think of any way to part. "Well—" he said.

"Good luck, Mr. Cobus, sir." And William flapped the reins, the horse started, and then began its turn to go home.

Cobus started walking. William had said it would be two or three miles in. The air was clear and crisp, the sky a bright blue; he felt ebullient, filled with a future in which anything at all was possible. More than anything else he was marveling at the way the Raymonds had accepted the situation. They didn't seem at all put out by the fact his mother was an Indian, he a halfbreed. He had wanted to say something about how grateful he was to be accepted for himself, but that was the sort of thing you didn't talk about. Still, something ought to have been said, and he hadn't said it. The Old Man had given him a filly and made him feel at home. The Old Man had got on with his father right off. But of course nothing had been said about young Mrs. Raymond meeting his mother. The men might meet as equals, but women, they had a different way of judging things. Being accepted wouldn't really mean anything unless his mother was able to walk across that blue rug with those wonderful birds and sit down in one of them fancy chairs and have William hand her a cup of tea. He almost laughed. The whole picture was absurd: a darkie handing an Indian a cup of tea. But he didn't care, that was the only way the situation *would* be right, and he could never in a million years picture it. For the rich Raymonds it would be all right for a halfbreed Buttes to muck around in the barn and maybe eat in the kitchen, but no Indian was going to come calling in their fancy drawing room.

All right, he would put all that out of his mind. Wasn't that exactly why he had come into the woods, to put all that out of his mind?

As Cobus came out into a small clearing, he heard a voice, happy and jaunty, raised over even the raucous cries of the crows.

> *"Oh, a soldier told me just before he died,*
> *His wife was never satisfied,*
> *Until he invented a prick of steel*
> *Driven by a great big wheel. . . .*
>
> *Two balls of brass delivered the cream,"*

the voice sang happily,

> *"And the whole fucking works was run by steam."*

He could see no one, but someone could most certainly see him, for that voice rumbled from somewhere behind the mammoth balsam and cedar, pine and hemlock, *"Who* sent *you?"*

"Mr. Raymond," Cobus said.

A figure stepped from the woods, enormous, angry, barefooted. "You're not the *man* he was gonna send up?"

"I'm Cob Buttes—" It was the first time Cobus or anyone else had ever shortened his name, but he figured: a new life, a new name.

"And just what might that be?"

"Be?"

"What do you *do?"*

"I'm supposed to learn, Mr. Raymond said."

252

"Holy happy Christ, a cookee." The man spat. "Christ on crutches, a cookee. That your gear?"

"Yes, sir."

"Come on, I'll see to it you find your way to the bunk-house. Send these greenhorns out in the woods, lose 'em on the way to get water, git under trees and get theirselves kilt, can't even—farm boy, ain't you? The shoulders—plowbent, not axe-broad. You know anything about lumberin' at all?"

"Damned little," Cobus heard himself say.

Surprisingly, the big man laughed. "You learn or git kilt. That's the way it goes out here. Those that don't—the woods are full of them. Left behind. Don't chew, don't liquor, don't womanize, can't cut trees and they send them out to me. Ken you fight? Woods-fight—bite, gouge, stamp, use caulks, hold your own with a man twice your size?"

"I don't believe so," Cobus said miserably.

"Then you best stick by me—you'll learn plenty around me. Try some of this," he said, holding out a snake of tobacco.

"I don't reckon I will. I don't have the taste for it."

"You do what anyone tell you, *that's* the job of a cookee: to take orders. From everyone."

"And I aim to do it," Cobus said. "So long as it's loggin' and not somethin' private that ain't got nuthin' to do with loggin'. The woods is one thing, something personal another."

"You willin' to back that up with somethin' besides your big mouth?"

"I guess I got no choice."

"Son, I could kill you."

"I reckon so, but if it's gonna come to that, it might as well be sooner as later. As you say, them that don't last find it out right off."

The big man was incredulous. "You mean you're *willin'* to fight?"

"Well, I'm not willin' to chew so I guess it adds up to the same thing, don't it?" He was tired to the bone. The last months nothing had gone right on the farm, they were in hock up to their ears, his father had got one of his spells where he wouldn't talk about what was troubling him and that was always more frightening than when he ranted and railed because it meant the trouble went so deep that Guthrie Buttes was afraid even to name it. Then he had got this job to help out and there had been those long, back-breaking hours to help finish up the haying and get the farm ready for winter before he took off for the woods. To say nothing of the long walk after William let him off at the logging road and the feeling luck was running against him and was going to keep on that way, that somehow he had quit being young this summer, and him only fifteen, it was all just too much: he wouldn't much mind being put out of his misery.

"Danged if you ain't jest like Amos, all piss and vinegar and nuthin' more. No muscles, but he thinks he's a man."

"I never *said* I was a man."

"No, that's a fact. But you sure try to act like one."

"You gotta begin somewhere."

"Well, that too's a fact," the big man conceded as they went toward the bunkhouse. "Leave the door open and air this stink-hole out. Pete can't abide air, he's smoked straight through, jest like some hog that's been butchered and hung. It runs with cooks. Never been within a mile of one didn't stink like salt pork."

The logs of the walls had been stuffed with moss; there was an exposed beam roof made of rough bark; at one end of the long rectangular open room stood a long slab table, at the other, bunks three tiers high along which lines had been strung and clothing hung haphazardly; running around three walls of the room was a bench, the split half of a log, flat side up, supported by thick wooden legs. Smoke came from a sunken fire in the center of the room. Overhead a hole in the roof presumably was to dispose of the smoke, but it hung low, refusing an escape. There were cranes swinging out over the fire, and on these pots, and at one side a man, blackened by soot, smoke, and dirt, holding a long, thick spoon. "Pete, here's your new boy."

A small blackened man turned, looked, and spat. "Ain't no good," he said. "Won't have him."

"He's what Raymond sent."

"Orville?"

"No, Old Mister Mowatt. Go on over and let him have a look at you."

Cobus moved toward the fire.

"Fifteen at the most," Pete said. "Where does the Old Man *find* them?"

"Farmin'. Hayin's done, they scatter to the woods."

"Every goldarn year. They don't even know how to boil tea let alone bake bread."

"It's a challenge. One the Old Man sends out to you every year. Well, you could at least say he don't pull no surprises."

"He can start drawin' water—if he knows how to carry."

"I guess he can do that, can't you, son?"

"If the pail ain't too big," Cobus said. "Otherwise you best git out the ox."

"You got yourself a snappy one this haul," the big man said to the cook and ambled over to a bunk, rummaged around, found what he was looking for, uncorked it, hoisted it to his mouth, took a long slug, wiped his mouth, and said to Cobus, "A little of the eagle's sweat? Turns up his nose at B & L, don't like the grain. You got yourself a fancy one all right." But he said it with a perverse sound of satisfaction.

It was the beginning of Cobus's initiation, which lasted all that year. He never got really into the woods, but he knew he was being tested, and he cultivated what patience he had, trying to learn the lessons of the logger's life. It was a hard life, much harder and tougher than he had expected, beginning, as the loggers said with their strange sense of humor, anywhere after midnight—that was a new *day*, weren't it? As cookee, Cobus had to be up even before they were to sound the gong and get the bunkhouse up and going. "Daaylight in the swamp!" he hollered.

It was pitch black outside and often the first streak of dawn was hours off, but the cook was up, the fire going, teamsters were stirring, for the oxen had to be watered, grained, and ready. Cobus banged on the gong and bellowed; the men, grumbling, tumbled from their bunks, put on what little clothing they hadn't slept in, some went out and washed, but most just went to the table and ate.

They ate in silence. It was a rule of all the camps; nobody talked at meals. The foreman or bull (here Big John) ruled outside in the woods, but inside was the cook's domain. The cook wanted silence, he got it.

When they had eaten, they filed out into the darkness. Most had a mile or more to walk in the black woods before they came to the place where they were cutting. The cutting was supposed to be finished by the time the snows came; then the men would load, skid, and stand. But while the good weather held, they spent ten to twelve hours a day in the woods, their axes felling the huge white pine; for when they talked timber, they meant white pine, though some cedar was cut to be used for shingles and some hemlock bark was sent to the tanneries.

The men worked right up to midday without a stop. At noon Cobus and the cook piled loaves of bread, beans laced with slab pork, and tea onto sleds and sent them out to be eaten where the men were cutting; at night the crews stumbled back into camp for more bread, beans, pork, tea.

Sometimes a deer or bear was killed and for a few days there was meat, but the mainstay of the meals, all of them, was bread and beans. The beans were cooked in a hole while the bread was baked against the open fire; both were either burned or half cooked, but nobody ever complained. Poor food was something the loggers seemed proud of.

They were the strangest breed of men Cobus had ever encountered, but he felt comfortable with them: they were dark as dirt; many of them had mixed blood like himself; they did not question a man's heritage, they were only interested in how many board feet he could cut, how boldly he could fight, how many good stories he could tell about the women he'd had, and how hard a drinker he proved himself.

He had been in camp a month when the weather began closing in and the first snow came. It was thin and patchy, nothing to stop the cutting, but it worried the men because if the big snows came early, the cutting would not be done on time; the camp started working a fifteen-hour day—longer for Cobus who had to be up before the loggers and went to bed long after them. Sometimes he was so tired that everything became fuzzy, days lost their demarcations; he got up, rang the gong, helped with breakfast, cleaned, swept, brought in wood, got the food for nooning on the sleds, got more beans ready to go in the cooking hole, served supper, cleaned, fell into bed, an endless unvarying routine that left no time for all his problems; he had walked out on them, it seemed, when he went into the woods. He had the bark dark skin of the Indian, the black bottomless eyes that could go white with feeling; high cheekbones, the thin Indian mouth. But his father was in his body, tall and slender and full of sinew. Both bloods were in him and his mind was like an ambiguous ledger on which each had hastily scribbled, trying to make an impression that would carry him through the rest of his life. He was stranded somewhere inside himself that he did not understand. He had no idea who he was outside of the fact he was a Buttes, and he was an Indian, but that was to do with his parents, not himself.

It was a terrible thing to be so dissatisfied with yourself, but he couldn't help it. He didn't want to look like an Indian; he wanted to be an invisible part of his world, so much like everyone else that he faded into nonidentity. But everything about him—he was getting too tall, tall like some white ancestor, too tall for an Indian, too tall really for an ordinary white—his height and looks set him aside as someone who was different. He was difficult NOT to distinguish.

So people noticed him. Not in the way they noticed Tip, approvingly, there goes a boy with a great future, but uneasily, there goes a strange one, no way of knowing whether you can trust him or not. Most likely not.

The men in the woods didn't give a tinker's damn who his mother had been or what his brother was like or even, in the end, what went on inside himself. So long as he kept his mouth shut when he should and did his share of the work and went nowhere out of his way to get into theirs, he fit in. If he went under, they could even cut his initials in a tree. Then forget him.

His brother was at the Falls filling his head with all kinds of knowledge while all Cobus was doing was refilling the bean hole, sweeping, carrying in wood, fetching grain for the animals. Yet Cobus would not have changed places with him. He had made his choice and, he felt, he had learned much from it, much maybe books couldn't teach.

All through the end of March and early into April Cobus and the others waited fidgetingly for the thaws to set in, the big rains to start. Big John took to wandering around in his red underwear (the warm weather, he said, brought out the germs that had been froze into a man's clothes all winter long), barefoot, irritable, singing,

> *"Oh, take it in your hand, Mrs. Murphy,*
> *It only weighs a quarter of a pound,*
> *It's got hair all over like a turkey,*
> *And it squirts when you shake it up and down."*

Cobus had heard when the first logs started downstream, Mrs. Murphy—Old Connecticuty—knew. At the first small town where the loggers piled in for the night, they always found her tent set up and the old girl ready for business. Outside the tent a man helped himself to a dipper chained to a barrel—Old Connecticuty's rum, it was three cents the dipperful, a man's owings on his honor—and inside fifty cents for five minutes, or a full hour, a full five. Big John was thirsting for real unwatered rum, for Old Connecticuty knew her customers; what she sold they bought knowing they were getting the honest stuff and thus she preserved her trade without real competition, though many a younger, prettier hooker had come and then been run out of town and scores of bartenders had seen their businesses smashed over watered-down drinks.

The mounting sense of tension was reflected not only in Big

John's restlessness, but also in Pete's increasing irritability, Cobus's own feelings of doing nothing but wait, wait, wait, and in the entire crew's edginess. Fights were more frequent, the men were short and curt with one another; men who had been friends all winter suddenly and unaccountably had a scuffle over some minor incident and ceased speaking; men who had grated on one another and who had taken pains to avoid each other now went out of their way to provoke a quarrel. There was the sense of suppressed violence in the air, something unseen but menacing that hung over the whole camp. Day after day Cobus rose to ring the gong with a feeling of dread that that morning would bring the cataclysm, until one morning he stumbled into rain, real rain, the steady kind that falls in early spring and goes on and on making the heavy snow vanish with miraculous rapidity, swelling the little creeks and sluggish backstreams into roaring torrents, turning "dry" beds all over the countryside into roaring rivers, opening up the frost in the earth and bringing what was known as Mud Week, when anything with weight sank and mired, and culminating, Cobus knew, in that wild time when the logs went out and the whole crew threw itself into the fury and madness of The Drive, work that went on from the first glimmer of dawn until absolute and total darkness descended, day in and day out, seven days a week, work that soaked men to the skin, kept them jumping and running and rolling the logs to keep from shivering in the icy spring winds; injury and death were old hands of the drive, the pace cruel, a jam-up inevitable, disaster never far away. At bad bends and curves in the river men lost their hold and were found miles downstream, crushed by thousands upon thousands of logs that had swept over them. Men were caught in jams between logs and smashed to jelly. They were toppled unexpectedly off what looked like an easy run and drowned before anyone could get to them. They slipped, skidded, tripped, stumbled, lost their balance, were swept up on rocks or knocked under by collisions—there was no end to what might happen in a moment, in the flickering of an eye, that would put an end forever to a man's time in the woods—and this went on, this threat of death, this pressure to keep going, get the logs in, until a logger no longer knew where the logs ended and the land began, until the entire world seemed nothing but one long onrush of water covered with logs and small men with long sticks trying to control them.

Cobus would not go downriver on water. He was a cookee. The cookee went with the cook and was responsible in part for the four big meals a day that had to be provided to keep the men going. At first he had been a bit resentful, feeling he wouldn't get a chance to see anything, but early the morning of the initial run, he understood he was in perhaps the best of all positions to watch the drive. After breakfast, when the men went down to open the loadings and let the logs go, he and Pete were working like whirlwinds to get away and down-stream to be ready for the first and second lunch, both of which would be served to the men where they were poling logs—there was no time for them to stop and fuss, but they had to have food, and plenty of it. At supper they sat, if they could, if they weren't too dead beat tired even to eat; but during the day cold beans, cold slabs of salt pork, plenty of bread, hot tea, was what kept coming to them, what kept them going.

Pete and Cobus had a huge wagon pulled by oxen with which to dispense chow, though Cobus had watched enviously when Big John left in a special rig pulled by two fast black horses. It had been sent up a week before especially for the drive. The horses had to be fast because the bull boss, the boss of the drive, was the most important man of the whole crew, the one who raced in his rig back and forth trying to keep account of all that was happening, trying to free jams and also directing operations to break up one that had begun. Big John had gone out, standing up, waving his hat, his cheek bulged with B & L, at his side a big crock of special Eagle Sweat that he claimed made a man breathe twice as fast and thus enabled him to work twice as hard. The men cheered—Cobus cheered until he was hoarse, even Big John himself cheered—and then the driver gave one last crack of the whip across the horses' backs and the rig ran off and the curve swallowed it from sight.

Cobus and Pete were not long behind. They left the camp a mess, but what did it matter? There would be plenty of time later, after the logs were down at the Falls and the men had drunk up their winter wages, for a couple to sign on and come back to clean up. "To hell with it," Pete said. "We got more important things on our mind. You're gonna see, boy, oh, you're gonna see. There ain't nuthin' like a drive."

And there wasn't.

The last part of the morning and the early part of the afternoon they had kept abreast of the logs; but as Pete urged the oxen on, they passed the logs and came to clear water, not a log in sight, just the rushing, tumbling spring floods cascading south toward the Falls.

259

The passing patches of "white water"—foam-crusted roils of raging water that flowed frantically in, out, and around boulders and bends, places the loggers dreaded, for here jams easily occurred and an incautious man, trying to ride the logs downstream to keep them apart, was in especial danger—made Cobus realize for the first time what lay beneath the seeming placid stretch of wood he had been viewing all morning. On the shores near the white water small groups of men were spreading out, ready to pole logs away from the big rocks so that they wouldn't stack up, keeping the masses moving so that none of the timber sidetracked along the edges or into the eddies to begin a pile-up. Darkness was falling and the men waved and hollered to the food wagon as it went by. In a little while they would come into camp and get some rest.

When the wagon pulled up at the site of the initial camp, the first thing Cobus noticed was a tent, one big barrel with a tin dipper attached to a chain at its side: Old Connecticuty.

He saw her come out every quarter of an hour; she was watching, as he was, for the first signs of the drive and the men who would come with it. She had an indistinct face in the twilight, but her body was recognizable enough. She was one of those large women whose legs look like melted wax. Her arms were thin, however; embracing takes a lot out of you, he thought, and shook his head.

He heard a distant rumble, at first almost indistinct; then growing louder and louder until it sounded like a continuous thunder. Upriver the logs were drumming their way downstream, over rocks and against banks, crowding and crashing against one another, a drumming sound Cobus found repeated in the beating of his heart, which seemed to pound faster and faster, as the booming came closer; then almost stopped as he saw the first logs, the leaders, come flying into sight; these were the "advances," timber that had shot free from the great wedged flow of the main drive, and was now pushing freely, almost gaily, downstream, bobbing and dancing over the water, a mile or two ahead of the great mass of logs. The village boys stopped their gaping and ran excitedly to the bank to watch, their faces alive with interest where for the past hour Cobus had seen nothing but the sluggish kind of sullenness which strangers and strangeness often produce in people enclosed in the narrow world of the back woods.

Logs were coming in greater and greater groupings, beginning to choke up, crowding together until it was moving logs you saw, not water, the great rushing expanse of Hudson completely hidden by thousands of logs rolling over its surface. The noise never stopped, a grating, a grumbling, crashes and collisions, great pile-ups flying up in the air with screams, falling with thuds, turning, tumbling, rolling on, caught and whirling round slower and slower, while Cobus held his breath and thought, *a jam,* then slowly, sluggishly breaking free, moving once again, mile after mile of millions of board feet, downstream to the mills.

The men came last, wet, chilled, so tired they stumbled; the logs would go on moving though, and what they were praying—at least what other men would have said passed for prayer—was that there was no jam-up during those dark hours, that the morning would find the mass of wood still free, still southward bound. They fell on the food, still observing the rule of silence, even in the midst of the run, wolfishly hungry but too tired to care that they were eating soaked to the skin, that the temperature was falling, that it probably would go below freezing before the night was through, though a few found the strength somehow to tumble toward the tent and the dipper of rum, Big John in the vanguard, shouting and singing, no stumbler he, unbuckling as he strode, while those left behind raised for a moment their weary heads, shook them in disbelief, and floundered for the bunk tents, dropped down in chilled exhaustion, the sound of Big John's singing in their ears,

> "Oh, take it in your hand, Mrs. Murphy,
> It only weighs a quarter of a pound . . ."

In the misty darkness of predawn, a halo of moisture hung over the Hudson, but the sound of the logs, now downstream, was still in their ears. The sound had been with them all night, loud and persistent at first, then gradually growing lower, no more than a groaning, until at the moment Cobus had risen, cold to the bone, and groped his way to the gong, what he heard was a kind of eerie whisper of wood gone downstream but still calling to the men to come, it was only a matter of time till a jam-up.

Jam-up came midmorning while Pete and Cobus were passing out the last of lunch. Suddenly, unexpectedly, they came on a great pile of logs, stacked up solid, with ends jutting out every which way, pointing up in unlikely places, a massive, solid mound of logs piled high like jackstraws. As the wagon pulled up and Pete involuntarily stopped, an oath on his lips, Cobus felt his heart turn over, sickening inside his stomach, involuntary; for ahead of him, racing frantically back and forth over the unmoving mass where more and more logs were piling up every minute, were small figures, the loggers feverishly searching for the key log, what the men called the King, that one log that when moved would dislodge all the others, and the jam would suddenly shift, give an awful roar, and race free again. If at that moment a man was not quick enough to run. . . .

The small figures, running, prying, jumping, pulling with their swing dogs, pushing, poking, prying, leapt from log pile to log pile, and all the time the logs that were coming downstream were backing up, piling up on the stopped logs, the jam was growing and growing . . . and then Cobus heard a cry—men were running and scattering, a great grinding sound came from somewhere deep down within the pile-up, then a crunching, a sudden whirling, a flight free, the logs went with a whoosh downstream again.

"God's grace," Pete said, and slapped at the oxen.

Cobus was surprised. The cook's tone had been reverent. Pete said over the creaking of the cart, "Never a year goes by we don't lost one or two in one of those things. It's like a law, you can't have a drive without losing men—but it's always almost sure in a jam-up, a bad jam-up. That weren't nuthin', jest a little piling. Wait 'til you see a *real* jam-up."

The scene had scared Cobus. Those little running figures had looked so small, so powerless. "I seen enough."

"You'll see more, count on it. You know how I come to be a cook? Well, I went into the woods my first year and seen my brother go under—at Moulton Bar, it was. We was almost at the end of the run, near Warrensburg, ain't no distance from there to the Falls, but it's a bad point on the run, men always go under at the Bar, one year or another. My brother, he had been in the woods five years, he was what they called a big woods man, didn't seem *nuthin'* he couldn't do—and then here at this Moulton Bar, there was this jam-up and he went, jest like that. He was on top of the pile one minute, the next you jest didn't see him. I mean, nobody saw him go, he was jest kind of sucked in. He was wearing this red scarf —he always wore it—you could spot him anywhere in the woods or on the river with that great big red scarf flying out from him. We never found him that spring at all. Not till fall —and then twenty miles downstream. Some kids saw this red sticking up through some weeds near shore. It was his scarf, still on him. I said I'd never go near another camp, but it's funny, it gets you. Once you been in camp, it's like it's in the blood. Don't matter what happens you keep comin' back —one way or the other. But I don't cut, I don't ride the river, that I don't do. You take Big John—he lost a brother, too. He went at the stretch past Deer Den. John hisself got him out, but it was too late. He was crushed like you crush an egg, take it in your hand and ain't nuthin' left of the shell but bits if you close your hand hard. He was jest like that, Amos, not a bone left in him whole. They buried him there, hung his caulked boots up on the tree, carved his name in the trunk—always do, when a man goes under, put his name on a tree where men can see, show it's a bad spot, warn others. Sometimes you see two, three, four names on a tree. Chow," Pete cried, "And *hot* tea." The little figures got larger, life-like, as they came running toward the wagon. One of them was even waving, as if breaking up a jam was nothing at all.

There were two more jams on the way down, but none of them bad, the men said; regular, was the way they put it. And, miraculously, they lost none of the crew; there was a broken leg, but what was that, just an inconvenience, really, it would be mended by fall, and come cutting time the logger would be back in camp with the others.

With such luck the spirit in camp each night grew more and more celebrative, the line to Mrs. Murphy's tent longer and longer. Men even began to get drunk, bad drunk, so that they got up bleary-eyed and unsteady for the day's run, a bad business when every reflex, every minute decision was needed; but there were no mishaps, just the bad luck with that leg, and the logs went past Deer Den and Moulton Bar— Cobus saw names cut in the tree; there were names cut in lots of trees along the way, some from years back so far that the bark had started to heal and close up; and every day was like the one before, deadening with fatigue, deafening with the noise of the logs, deadly with danger, and still their luck held—it held all the way to the Falls, where the run was finished, the boom in, and Old Man Raymond himself came out with a shay, William driving and the floor covered with jugs of rum and a big bag bulging with wages.

William was a sensation. A lot of the new men had never seen a black man before and they wanted to touch, then to rub to be sure none of the color came off; but they still didn't believe. William was like an apparition from another world that had no business existing at all; in one way their curiosity spilled over into a kind of inverse admiration; in another it was tinged with fear and superstition. Black for them had always been associated with evil. Though many of

263

them came out of the woods that color themselves from wind, sun, smoke, and the absence of baths, William's would not go away. It was as if they were saying to themselves in wonder, Imagine being that color ALL your life!

Old Mowatt Raymond got drunk right along with the rest of them, Cobus included, and they sang and fought and went down at last at dawn to look at the miles and miles of now stationary logs, quietly chained in. They would never move again, those millions of board feet that had roared and swirled down the river; they would be taken out and cut into wood that went into homes and businesses, into buildings everywhere growing up as the nation grew. They stood in the early morning sun and looked drunkenly at what they had cut down, a great path in the forest, and had carried over water miles from where it had grown since before the first of their forefathers had come to this land. They had cut down a forest and brought it to the biggest of the mill towns in the East and in a few months it would all be gone, sawed into smooth shapes and sent out all over the state, so that by the time they went into the woods next fall the water here would be empty of wood, empty but waiting for them to come down next spring, and stand again in the same kind of wonder that men could conquer the giant forests, that these logs lying still for miles and miles under that first morning light were proof that a man could come and conquer what seemed, as he stood in the forests, under those mammoth pines, unconquerable. They were conquerors—the forests would fall before the power of their hands. They stood unsteadily, drunkenly, but suddenly still and awed.

Mowatt Raymond invited Cobus to go back with him in the rig, though it would be crowded, three instead of the customary two in the single small seat. They would make do, he insisted. He was going into the Falls first, to see his "girl" —but he knew Cobus wouldn't object. Cobus was no doubt anxious to see his brother after all this time. "Seen a lot of your brother—we kept the girls, leastwise the oldest one, in the Academy all winter after all. Decided to stay put up here. Don't think we'll do it again. Winters get pretty rough this way. But we did get down a few times. Your father went with us once," he told Cobus. "Seemed to enjoy it. I know I did. Like to have a man I can talk horses with around. Your brother's done well—he and Ardis are kind of neck and neck to see who's head of the class."

William let the horse out a little. A slight mist, not quite a rain, stung the air. It was going to wet them through before they got very far. "And Grandpa?" Cobus asked.

There was a pause, a sigh. "No better," Old Man Raymond said regretfully. Then he cheered up. "Your filly's filling out, boy. You're going to have a real horse on your hands. And you did more than what was expected of you in camp—word of Big John himself and, believe me, he don't pass around compliments." He turned to examine Cobus. "How'd you find it—up to expectations?" And he gave a chuckle.

"I don't know yet—I mean, what it's really like, cuttin', runnin' the river. I was just a chore boy, sir, not—" He swallowed hard. "Did Big John say anythin' to you about next year?"

"You got no worry there. You have yourself a place, if you still want it in the fall."

"I'll still want it." The river drive had made up his mind.

"Don't count on what's ahead being what you want right now." Old Man Raymond turned his hands over meditatively. "The nation's growing, everything's changing," he said in a kind of wonderment. "And anybody who wants to get ahead has to do the same kind of changing. With the canals in this neck of the woods we stand pretty well to cut a slice of the pie. And wood's only the beginning of it—the wood'll be gone one day—" To Cobus this seemed an impossibility; he had seen the forests stretching farther than the eye could see. "But something else will take their place. And a man who . . . business interest you at all, Cobus?" It was the first time Cobus could remember Old Man Raymond calling him by his rightful name, not boy or son. It marked a turning point. "I'm nearly seventeen," Cobus said to himself, and the thought surprised him. Somehow there was an enormous difference between fifteen and sixteen. One was a no-man's land; the other marked a boundary across which the adult world beckoned. He stood on that line now and looked into this new world. It seemed to him no surer than the one he was on the point of leaving.

"I don't rightly know *what* interests me, Mr. Raymond," he answered, using the name instead of the more formal address of "sir," and thereby indicating he acknowledged the transition in their relationship. "Some people seem to be born knowing what they want to do—my Pa, for instance, he never wanted anything I know of except being on the land he's on, and his Pa before him, my grandfather, he knew exactly what he wanted, that mountain farm we got over there. It had to be a mountain farm, my grandfather didn't

265

have no respect for valley people—he thought they didn't put themselves out enough, I guess. My grandfather, he thought the point of a man's life was putting himself up against something hard and fighting it out. But my trouble —like a lot of other people's, I guess—is that I just don't have an idea in the world what is worth pitting all my strength against, what I want to spend my *whole* life wrapped up in." Hard as it was to explain, Cobus made a try. "It's like, you know, there isn't just one of me, but a whole lot of me's down there inside. I could be any one of them—if I stayed in the woods, that would be one me I could be; if I stayed up at the farm, another. If I decided to go West, a whole other me would start growing. Everything depends on how I choose, but there are all those—" He groped for the proper word— "—all those *potential* me's down there, all of them making demands, sometimes I can almost hear them calling out, and it's like, I don't know which one to listen to; they all got strong voices, good things to recommend them. But the point is, which one is the real me—which one in all those voices is the me I'm supposed to be, the best one? It's so danged hard to figure out," Cobus said hopelessly. "You just don't know how to tell it to someone else, leastwise I don't."

"I thought you did pretty well myself," and in back of those words rang real conviction. "You ever thought that all those me's might fight it out among themselves and the one that wins is you?" Cobus didn't believe it, but he didn't want to be impolite. It seemed to him the most important thing, just the thing Old Man Raymond had missed, was choice. Something in his face must have given him away: the old man was frowning. "Or maybe lots of men do make the wrong choice and try to get out of it by an argument like that."

"Tell me, Mr. Raymond, did you always know? I mean, what you wanted to be?"

"I always knew I wanted to make money, lots of money. I guess that's one way of knowing, though I wouldn't reckon it's the best. If you hold some ways of living are better than others, and I do—and it's that notion I suppose they're always preaching about, serving God instead of Mammon, and the like, can't get away from it lately, preachers are going and coming, it seems, all spring. You heard? No, I suppose not, where you were. Regular religious fever's sweeping the whole country." Old Man Raymond shook his head. "God knows where it'll end. These tent meetings and shouting and conversions and all always seem to me just to end up in an awful lot of unwanted babies. You get young girls and boys steamed up like that, they gotta let off their energy some way. And it ain't, as they say, always sound. Lots sounder though," he reflected, "to my way of thinking than telling people they're going to burn in hell, roasted every day for the rest of all eternity, though don't go repeating that. It's bad enough I've made money without my holding the Scriptures up to scrutinizing as well. People never forgive you making money, Cobus. They don't forgive you for not making it either— nothing people look down on more than the poor, but nothing that makes them madder than someone being rich. One way or the other they're always going to say something against you. Turn up here, William, this is the street. He *never* remembers," Old Man Raymond said to Cobus in disgust.

They were approaching the Academy, a brick building with shining windows like eyes and a balustrade running round like a piece of lace. William was sent ahead in what was now a full rainstorm, ringing the bell to the front door to make arrangements for their visit. Old Man Raymond and Cobus waited in the carriage, Cobus growing more and more uncomfortable. Though he had tried to clean up as best he could, he was still wearing camp clothes, and not too clean at that—a heavy red woolen shirt, thick pants, boots, a knitted cap. Finally he took the cap off, feeling that might lessen his backwoods appearance. He had no notion at all what to expect of Tip—their nearly eight months apart in such drastically different circumstances left Cobus with no picture of what his brother would be like now.

He began to fidget. It seemed to him it was taking an awfully long time for someone to do a simple thing like answer a door. An idea—which for a moment seemed to have no relation to the situation struck him: *sometimes the simplest things are the hardest;* then he saw the progressive process of his thinking had been triggered by the word *simple.* He was wondering how much words actually shaped thinking when the door opened and William, taking off his hat so that he stood bareheaded in the rain, began speaking. He was left on the doorstep, getting wet, as he made the explanation, an act that angered Cobus because he was sure that no white man would have been left to stand in the rain like that. But a nigger, an Indian—

He sprang from the coach, his cap still in his hands, and ran up the steps. It was the sharing of skins, the dark skins that set them apart, and different hair, different eyes, a whole different way of looking at life.

"She says you and Mr. Raymond can come right in, Mr. Cobus. I'll go tell Mr. Raymond," and William started back down the steps, thereby removing himself from the scene and hence any need to make a stand.

But nothing could now calm Cobus. His rage was like something searing his insides into a flame of hot unforgiving hate. He would have liked to hit the woman standing in front of him. It's the Indian blood in me, he thought, and the woods. Before I went into the woods, I wouldn't have been half so mad. It gets to you, all that fighting. Pete's words flashed through his mind. *It gets to you; once you been in camp, it's like it's in the blood.* But at the same time he knew his anger was larger than the incident at hand; he had suddenly, in the space of two days, come up against the total fact of what it meant to be different—black, Indian, half-breed, what did it matter—the curiosity, the stares, the demeanment, being treated like an object instead of an individual, as if being different meant being worse.

His blood set him apart from others, just as William's blood set him apart. No matter what they did people would look down on them. The country's changing, Old Man Raymond had said, but it was never going to change so much that the color of a man's skin wouldn't color the way people felt about him.

In place of the anger he was now flooded by a profound feeling of helplessness so that, standing on the stoop, the rain running down his face, he asked WHY? And there was no answer, he knew there would never be one because the answer lay outside somewhere in the plannings and workings of a universe he did not understand, would never understand, because it was so large and overwhelming and he was so small and insignificant there was no way to even out the proportions; he was like one of those toy figures running around frantically on top of the log jam, trying to find the king log, the key one, which would dislodge all the rest and make them run smoothly, the way they should, downstream again.

"You're standing getting all wet—what is it, son?" He was back to being "boy"—"son"—again.

"Nothing, I jest—" He couldn't go on. It seemed to Cobus that if the older and the wiser knew these things—and *hid* them as they had—they, too, increased the evil by concealing it, pretending it didn't exist, glossing it over with the concealment of words. Words, always words covering things up.

"You sick, Boy?"

Cobus shook his head. Old Man Raymond probably thought

268

that the matter with him was the aftermath of too much rum, the release of fatigue after those long, punishing days on the drive. He's saying to himself, Cobus thought, "It's" just caught up with him. He don't understand what "it" is.

Then Raymond—it seemed the craziest kind of statement for a man to make under the circumstances—"I did right when I gave you that filly. A man's right to trust his instincts —leastwise some of the time. But, lord, boy what a life you've got ahead." He said it with great sadness, while Cobus stood, shivering, and thought, I know.

They were ushered into a small room, more suited to young ladies in satin slippers than men with muddy boots. Mowatt Raymond remained standing, gazing at a print on the wall of a man in what looked like a metal suit leading a large white horse, both surrounded by an aureole of super-natural light, and there was a rainbow painted in vivid primary colors arching over the horse's back. "Unbelievable," Mowatt Raymond said, "simply unbelievable." Cobus said nothing, sitting on the edge of a hardwood captain's chair and looking at the other wall against which hung another illustration "Bonnie Prince Charlie Bids a Final Farewell to His Followers." A young man was standing up in a boat, his plumed hat clutched to his breast, mist rising all around him, and on shore a crowd of men and women were weeping, handkerchiefs knotted against their pale faces. The Prince was wearing, in Cobus's opinion, mighty fancy duds to put out to sea in a small open boat like that, but Cobus was in no mood to pick at particulars; he was wet, glum, and unhappy. He wished he were back in the woods: he thought of the smoky, steamy log camp with nostalgia; this "nice" room oppressed him with its horses with haloes and its princes in fancy clothes.

The door opened and a small, excited woman with eyes like skinned grapes called out happily, "They'll be down in a minute." She banged the door shut before they could answer.

"Miss Weed. Elocution—running your voice up and down the scales the right way."

Cobus raised his eyebrows.

The door burst open again and Cobus heard a girl's voice exclaim, "Grandpa!" and what seemed a somersault of skirts leapt over the space between the door and Old Mowatt Raymond; a figure flung itself on the old man with such force that Cobus was certain he would be toppled. In the doorway his twin brother stood grinning. "Hello, Cobus," he said.

Tip was dressed like a real gentleman, his hair carefully combed and parted, elegant shoes on his feet. Cobus wondered where his father had got the money. He was standing in an attitude that preempted admiration and his eyes were shining in anticipation of appreciation. He didn't look Indian at all. Anyone passing him on the street would never think, "halfbreed."

The atmosphere, Tip's fancy clothes, the girl's incessant chatter, his own dampness and feelings of inferiority were all working on him as a depressant. He did not belong here; he belonged out in the woods or up to the barn with the cows and horses.

"Like to look around?" Tip offered, while from the corner came a female squeal of protest. "Oh, Clyde, wait—let's have some talk first and then—"

"But your grandfather's been around," Clyde—Tip—protested. "I'm sure he doesn't want to go round again—do you, sir?" Tip asked, turning to Old Man Raymond for verification.

"Not if I can help it," the old man said.

"You stay and visit, I'll take Cobus round."

The girl—the one who'd given him that terrible thing to eat, the one who'd brought up his boots—she was pretty enough if you liked a lot of flashing of the eyes—the girl now turned those fiery eyes on Cobus and took him all in with one swift glance of appraisal. Then, confused, she looked down. Ardis, he remembered that was her name. In her confusion a soft blush of embarrassment lay on her cheeks; she was twisting her hands. He wanted to back away, edge out of the room, run down the hall and out the door. Be with William, he thought. In the grave atmosphere of this room the serious white-faced stone heads of famous men (at least Cobus assumed they were famous), larger than life, glared at him from atop wooden columns; when he bent forward in his confusion to receive a better view of those insolent eyes, they revealed the need of dusting.

Tip took his arm. When he looked up he saw the girl had her back to them, nattering away again with her grandfather. He plodded after his brother without saying anything. What is there to say, he wondered, in circumstances which cannot be altered. He would have liked, irrationally, to have shouted, The truth is I look like my Ma and Tip, he don't. *He* looks white. He thinks white maybe. But me, I don't.

They plodded on, Tip pointing out reverently "the Offices,"

270

passing "Elocution," "Geography," "Literature," "Natural, Moral and Mental Sciences," "Pencil Drawing," "Music with Use of the Piano." Finally Tip led them into a room whose walls were lined with books and where inspirational messages ran round the cornices. "An earnest heart never needs to be told to take a book," one said; another, "Open my pages, Gentle Reader, and learn about Life." The ones that bothered Cobus most were "Though his ears were deaf, his head made music to serve the stars," and "Though you are bound to love your enemy, you are not bound to put a sword in his hand."

He sat down at one of the long tables and stared at a stove in one corner glowing red hot to which Tip had gone to warm his hands. "That hall is like ice," Tip said, shivering. But Cobus had been comfortable in the cold clear air of the hall; here in the hot, stuffy room he felt as if he were going to be struck down by seizures. He was sure no windows had been opened in this room all winter, that the pupils had been breathing and rebreathing the same air over and over. Tip was examining his hands, looking at Cobus over the outspread palms, waiting from pride for Cobus to speak first, to tell him how marvelous all this was, how lucky Tip was to be a part of it. "Let's go back downstairs," Cobus said with an effort. "I don't want to keep Mr. Raymond waiting."

Tip bent over the stove to get a large surge of heat before they tackled the cold hall again. "You've changed," he said. He was waiting, Cobus felt, for Cobus to say the same thing. Dutifully, he did. Tip looked up, pleased. "You think so?"

"You're like someone from the city now." The compliment took a lot of effort; what he wanted to say was, You don't look Indian at all, no one'll be able to tell if you stay away from home. How would they get through a whole summer together, they were so different. There was a saying (he had heard someone say it—Raymond? Big John? Pete?), Blood is thicker than water. But he didn't think in this case it had any meaning at all. Who would want to be a halfbreed? What pride could you take in a mixture of blood? How could he blame Tip for one day turning his back on him? He couldn't. They were brothers, they weren't. Nobody was his brother. He couldn't imagine another human being in the world like himself.

Downstairs Ardis was sitting primly and prettily on the hard captain's chair. She rose when he came in. "I've just been telling Grandpa," she said, "that you've got to stay for

271

lunch. It's all right. Miss Weed said we could ask you."

Cobus shook his head. "You stay to lunch, sir. I'll wait outside with William."

Raymond started. "What do you mean you'll wait outside with William? It's raining."

"Yes, sir."

"William will get his vittles in the kitchen."

Cobus looked down, his mouth firm.

Raymond looked pained, cleared his throat, rustled in his chair. "Hmmm," he said. Finally he looked at Cobus. "You'd rather not have lunch?"

"Not dressed like this, sir."

There was a silence.

"Maybe some other time?" Cobus said to placate them.

Raymond rose. "Maybe it'd be better all around if we got on. I've got a lot of cleaning up to do to finish a drive, and I'm sure this boy wants to get home."

He was a man who understood without your having to draw a diagram for him, a rare thing in anyone, particularly the old, Cobus felt. For the first time he recognized that what he felt for Old Mowatt Raymond was more than respect or esteem. The feeling he had was closer to the one he had kept in his heart all these years for his father, a deep tie he couldn't define, but which was the strongest feeling he knew. A kind of lifeline.

It was a strange summer, cut up in compartments, in which he led different lives which seemed to have no relationship to each other. He worked hard on the farm and he tried to find time to work with his horse, and once every ten days or so, if his father could spare him a Sunday, he went with his colt on a long trip into the woods. Often he went as far as the Raymond house. He would stand and look on those great initials M M R, and then shyness would overcome him and he would turn around and go slowly home, often walking because he did not wish to push Tokay too much. A two-year-old, even a strong one, could only take so much; the bones were still forming.

Tip was working, too, but in a rebellious way, constantly pointing out changes his father ought to make, protesting against the really hard jobs, continually backing out of a chore to get back to the bunch of books the school had let him bring home for the summer recess, not exactly shirking, but holding back. He never offered, he always waited to be asked. A lot of the time he spent with his mother, telling her

272

stories about the Academy which she asked him eagerly to repeat again and again until Cobus knew them all by heart and hated each and every one of them. His mother seemed to have no time for anyone except Tip; she wasn't interested in logging (not that he blamed her; it was hardly the kind of thing to attract a woman's attention), but she was always pestering Cobus's father to let Tip go down to the Raymonds and do some "work" with Ardis. "They've school things to attend to, Guthrie," she would say.

Cobus felt himself growing more and more resentful. He tried to channel these feelings into his work, "work them out," but no matter how hard he punished his body, his mind was still there, angry, with a feeling of having somehow been injured. Nobody expected anything more of him than what he had already shown, but for Tip, they—even his grandfather —held high hopes. After the Academy he would go on to college—she really believed this, his mother, crazy as such a scheme was—or read with a lawyer; she had made up her mind on the law because it was the best way to get into politics and from there, who knew? Though as yet she hadn't brought herself to say so, Cobus knew her well enough to assume she had her sights on Washington. She had got to the point where she was willing to sacrifice anything and everything for Tip. Tip was going to be a Great Man. They were all going to glory on Tip's successes.

"Cobus," his father said in a voice it was absolutely impossible not to pay close attention to, "the thing you got to understand is a man either has a feelin' for some things or he don't, like the lake, like the land, like horses. Burroughs, Clyde Burroughs, the man Tip was named for, he had that feelin' for horses. Clyde Buttes, he don't. It's something you have to recognize, Cobus. Tip don't mean to keep you from workin' with your colt, it's jest thoughtlessness on his part. Some things can't be put in a man, they're born in him or left out, and that's the end of it. You was born one way and Tip another." But Cobus's father didn't say which was better; instead he raised an inscrutable face and then it seemed to lose some of its hardness. "He may come to be a Great Man, Tip, like your Ma says, but he'll never have the feelin' for animals the way you do." It was the closest his father could ever come to saying to him, I love you, son, for what you are, not what you ain't. But that still didn't settle which in his father's mind was more important, to be like Tip or to be like himself.

"So maybe what I'm tryin' to say is that I want for you to

273

carry the proper sense of proportion of—of seeing things for what they're really worth."

"I'm tryin' to do that, Pa."

"I know you are. And that's why I'm goin' to give you one day off a week the rest of the summer to work with your filly. I don't want you to keep her here," he said forcefully as Cobus tried to interrupt. "If you try to work her here they'll be too many interruptions, too much temptation on my part" —and he smiled—"to git you to come down to the fields for 'jest a little while.' Tip's had time off, now it's your turn."

"But Ma—"

"Your Ma and I've had our misunderstandings before and we'll have them again, I reckon. But on this I've got my mind made up. It's Tip's turn for the load awhile, whether he likes it or not. Tell me," he said as Cobus brought the tokay-colored mare out into the sunlight, "you ever seen such a summer as this for weather?" Then he was on his way down to work the fields, striding forcefully to his work. Cobus watched him go in a kind of wonderment. He had never really understood his father—he knew some of the bare outlines of his life, how he had been brought up a lot by Indians, the story of how his father had brought that terribly mutilated man out of the woods, that man for whom his twin brother had been named, and he remembered his father's concern all his life over Clyde Burroughs, his going way north to find out what had happened to the old hermit. A bond like that lasted all a man's life. The gift of life imposed an obligation on the donor. He thought of how desperately his father had been in love with his mother, had rowed week after week in winter weather across the lake to court her. His father had tried, really tried, to explain some of what went into his thinking to him. As if he were a man.

Wednesdays were to be his days at the Raymonds'. He would leave early in the morning and reach there well before noon. Smoke would be rising lazily from the kitchen chimney in back; the rest of the landscape lay drenched in honey-colored sunlight and stony silence, as if time itself had stopped in the midday heat and everything about this world were frozen forever (as it would be, later that winter, in his mind), obedient to Cobus's wish that this moment of emerging from the woods to the Raymond clear would never change.

That first morning he was tying his horse up when William hailed him from the barn, a reminder that there still existed

274

outside this static world a hostile one crowding against him with its hot breath of resentment, its angry and determined prejudices, its strong role of punisher for the wrongdoer. William had no more to do with his blackness than presumably the gods had to do with his own unhappiness; nevertheless, a relationship existed. William came out, carrying some kind of heavy tool and squinting into the bright light. "Your Pa's mare dropped her colt yet?"

Cobus shook his head.

"I got a bet on its bein' black, like that old debil. Stand to make myself a pretty little sum. Mr. Raymond, he figures it will go like its ma, a sorrel. That filly of yourn sure has filled out."

"She's had good pasturin' and plenty of grain, but she needs a lot of work. And up to the farm, well, I'm jest not gettin' it in. Pa said I could bring her down here and work her here, if it's all right by everyone. I want her trained correct," Cobus tried to explain. He knew he was asking a favor and he was embarrassed, but he cared more for the horse than his own pride.

"She sure got nice legs. No legs, no horse, Mr. Raymond always say. He ain't here right now. Gone down to the Falls. You reckon on stayin' over?"

Cobus was but he had to wait to be asked. "William," he said, hesitating, while William ran a practiced hand over the mare's withers, measuring. "Pa, he said he thought maybe I could take a turn comin' down here, workin' with Tokay for a spell—for a little while anyway," he ended lamely. It seemed to Cobus he hadn't made himself quite clear. "I mean if Mr. Raymond agreed, he thought—Pa thought—I'd maybe get what's left of the summer to work on my mare some. So long of course as Mr. Raymond agreed. I mean he might— I don't know—think it was an imposition."

"I doubt that, Mr. Cobus. You know this here mare was out of Satan, aren't many around here. Mr. Raymond, he'd want to know she was trained right. He likes a good horse well turned out, same as you and your Pa." There was a pause, William looking at the ground, ruminating, one hand resting on the mare's withers. "He's got good hands," he said at last, "and he sits a tight seat and he got—horse sense. For a fact, old as he is, he done better with the horses this year than any trainer we ever had, Mr. Styles included. The animals ain't so nerved up. And me, well, I been watchin' so long, it's almost like I know, so together we make do. Only," he admitted, "I haven't got Mr. Raymond's—like—confidence. They's days, I tell you, I plain scared of that black debil. Only people ain't afraid of him are Old Mr. Raymond and Miss Ardis, and he know that."

"*She* rides that stallion?"

"Yessir, she ain't afraid of nothing on four feet. She got her granddaddy's confidence. I jest hope it don't kill her."

The sounds of a carriage came clearly on the sleepy midday silence. "Reckon that Mr. Raymond now," William said. He looked at Cobus. "Maybe it'd be a bit easier if I did the askin' —you know, sort of save you the embarrassment," he said off-handedly while Cobus felt the first of a great many debts he would come to owe William over that summer.

They worked the little mare hard and she would be lathered up, panting, little spasms showing in the hindquarters back near the large joint of leg. William and he would walk her out until she quit heaving altogether, even the faintest trace; then Cobus would brush her down, clean her hooves again, give her water and take her back to the stall, hay her, and just before he left he would give her grain. The rule was water, hay, grain, in that order.

Let Tip stay with the kind of clean-hand things he liked, he'd take this life and the life in the woods any time—except for one thing, Ardis. He liked the way she came out and stood beside him and chatted easily of horses and lumbering, but still it wasn't the same kind of talk that she had with Tip. Her talk with him was brief and to the point; but when Tip came, she put things aside and devoted herself to what he wanted to talk about, books and music and what he would be when he graduated and started a career.

Cobus would lie awake at night and try to think of things to say to her that would keep her around him longer. "Look," he'd say to her desperately, "look at how well her chest is fillin' out," and Ardis, dutifully, would look at the horse's big V-ed chest and agree with him, then turn away, getting ready to go to the house, while Cobus, ready to run any risk, put out his hand; she turned about abruptly and gazed at him with those big gray eyes, and he said, swallowing all pride, "I'd take it as a favor if you'd stand by the fence tomorrow and watch me work her out. I can't see how she's doin', you know, myself, but you could tell me—you know what she should be doin'."

The next afternoon she hung over the fence watching him put the horse through her paces, frowning, sometimes calling out a compliment, mostly just silent, speculating. When he brought the lathered horse in, she told him he was doing well, but she said it in such a way that she made him uneasy. He knew there was something else she wanted to say and didn't. He took his courage from where it had dropped, defeated, at the tone of her voice and raised it, ready to hear the worst. "There's somethin' you ain't sayin' though, ain't there, Ardis?"

She looked away from him, reddening.

"Isn't there?" he insisted.

"Well, it's just that I—I don't know, Cobus—it's just that I can't see why you don't want to do more with yourself than just work with horses and go out in the woods."

"I'm different than Tip."

"Of course you are, nobody's the same, only—only, I don't know, just watching you out there—you've done wonders with that horse, you really have, only—only I mean, you could make so much more of yourself."

"I don't take to schoolin'."

She looked at him, exasperated, and for the first time it occurred to him that if she wanted to remake him she must care for him. Women don't go to any trouble over a man they aren't interested in. He was so elated he didn't know what to do. He had forgotten that she didn't like him the way he was, he only thought of her liking him at all. A terrible shyness came over him. He had to take this new knowledge apart and look at it and see how much he could bank on it, and to do that he had to be away from her because when he was near her, he didn't think straight. He wasn't sure he could think at all, he was so filled with emotion.

He analyzed those few sentences all the way home. He thought that if he could make her see that there were other things in the world beside stone busts that long ago had written something down that she had to study now in a musty old library, that there were men who found themselves in relation to the earth and the way they worked with it, she might understand him better and just like him for what he was instead of trying to make him over into another Tip. He could never be like Tip, even if he tried, but he didn't even want to try: that was the crux of the matter. What *she* didn't see was that a strong man could protect her, and what she didn't see was that in his own way he was maybe stronger than Tip. There were all kinds of strengths, that was what she missed seeing.

Her disembodied voice trembling on the still summer air echoed inside his mind, fused with the whole summer sensation of the land, a vast rolling memory of low hills whispering with wheat and low flat fields stabbed by stalks of corn; a glow, not more than a smudge, of purple mountains, and the molten sky—love had come to him that summer not only in the form of a name but also in the recognition of how much of himself he defined in terms of his work and his land; he had made a frightening discovery, and his new knowledge was this: he often lost himself in every sense of being "himself" when he was with other people; the only times he could depend upon his responses not making him uncomfortable, or astonished, or ashamed, the only times he was at ease with himself, and hence happy, were those hours he spent away from people—working in the fields, working with his horse, alone under the sloping ceiling of his room with his dreams and his hopes and his fears, and his imaginings of Ardis; sick with sensation, the sick sensation of love because he had that rare feeling that if he only dared and if only the moment were right, he could tell her anything—the truth was he wanted to tell her *every*thing—and it was this realization, this recognition that there was really no one else in the world to whom he wanted to reveal ALL of himself, that made him at last define the second kind of love a man could have, one that went beyond his work and himself.

"Ardis—*Ardis*—"

"I'm coming, Ma."

"*Ardis*—"

Her name and the summer fields, the flashing stars and summer skies: he lived almost totally in loneliness, but his heart said to him that if he were patient and worked hard and deserved her, he might one day be rewarded with her love. Since he cared so much, how was it possible she could not care at all?

He looked at her (his whole dedication chalked out in his eyes) and she gazed back with those clear, untroubled, beautiful gray eyes, somber, weighing the declaration, not answering, not (yet) offering anything of promise in return, but not looking away from him either, returning his gaze as steadily as he gave her his—was that not in itself a promise to him that he could *try?* And then, too, there were those moments when his arm brushed against hers and he felt the current run swift and unpredictable, sweet and dangerous, between them. A man didn't make that up on his own in his mind; it must take two to set vibrations going.

Turning away, his heart pounding so violently that it seemed to him it threatened to leap right out of his breast and into her hands, he was stopped by the force of his feeling; he turned back and gazed at her, and she was looking after him with those grave beautiful eyes that made words choke in his throat; he wanted only to reach out and take hold of her, draw her closer to him, not yet into an embrace—he could not bear not to see her eyes, that beautiful somber look that held him speechless in its spell—but close enough so that their flesh grazed; that sharp, painful current ran back and forth between them, he was engulfed with longing and sickness and desire—and then, very very gently he would draw her closer until their bodies locked, he lay his cheek against hers and turned his head slowly side to side against her cheek, a wordless declaration of his undying love, and she, slowly, wondrously, turned her cheek against his, saying silently, *I, too;* he was not sure where he left off and she began in this embrace that filled his mind, but gradually, so slowly he would not even be aware of it, his mouth would move toward hers and hers toward his, their faces would melt together, their mouths would melt together, their eyes, closed, would be inside each others' eyes; kissing her with closed lids he would be drowning inside her eyes, her beautiful, still, grave eyes, saying her name again and again. . . .

"Ardis—*Ardis*—"

"I'm coming, Ma."

"*Ardis.*"

Her name and the summer night, her name and the summer stars, her name and the pounding of his heart, her name and the formless embrace which was more real to him than any real embrace any man had ever known, he went on his journey into the woods, a man who in one long walk in the dark woods leaves behind the bad side of himself, perhaps in the echo of a name, believing as he walks this isolated track through the vast silent forest that there might be certain journeys in which a man made peace with himself and said to himself, there is this voiceless cry inside that says, alone . . . alone . . . and I fight back, refuting it with another kind of knowledge; were she in my arms, this chasm of otherness in which we all seem enlocked might be dissolved and instead of shouting across the distance of great space, our words lost in the distance and in the wind, we would be whispering into one another's ears, My love . . . my only love . . . my only love that will last all my life.

"Ardis—*Ardis*—"

"I'm coming, Ma."

"*Ardis—*"

His happinesses remained inside his mind. He could never bring himself to say anything to her about how he felt, to translate his dreams into some kind of action that would make them real.

Tip went off to his final year at the Academy the first Monday in September. William came and got Cobus the following Friday. The marrow autumn lay dark and fluid under the threatening wrist of winter; cold and rain had fallen on them at the end of August, as if there would be no autumn, only that terrible summer heat, then the early sleet of winter. Old Odder Buttes, bent and lame, showed how mean the spell was. He had taken on one of his stubborn spells.

Cobus's grandfather was maybe the oldest man in the Adirondacks; his hair was white, his eyebrows were white, his skin was so white you could look right through it and see the blood beating, bluish, behind the thin parchment-like covering. Even his laugh was white, like the lapse of light the lake made when it frothed and foamed under a glittery July night when the wind sent up a storm from the south bay. Only his eyes refused to follow the pattern. They were black and menacing and when Odder Buttes, angry (the way he was angry now) leaned forward it was like he was all flashed out in light and dark, some evil old angry ogre come out of the roar of the mountains to teach man how puny he was, how little he knew about the workings of the world: he belonged back, to another era, when (he said now, his pale white shrunken fists bruising themselves against the tabletop in fisted rage) a man didn't *ask*, he did. "You want to go back in the woods again, go. Don't ask. You're a man now, Cobus. Men don't *ask*."

A rheumy cough rose, angrily, from his grandfather's interior. He was riled and would commence on one of his coughing fits; Cobus would be blamed. In the valley they said Old Odder talked with owls and put spells on the crops, a by no means impossible assumption from the look and sound of him, a fearful old man whom everyone deferred to because he had lived (he said and who could dispute it?) more than a hundred years, every one of which, Cobus was sure, he had reminded everyone of how he had walked over the mountains to find his farm and now the whole damn mountain was being picked apart by *city* people.

The Raymonds, he meant. He hated them—the presumption of their money, naturally, but he was uncharitable to their reserves of strength, too. *Weak*, he said spitefully, they're *weak* people, I don't care how rich they are.

It was not true, but the force of his grandfather's authority made it seem so. For a time Cobus had believed them inferior because they set up so poorly in his grandfather's sight.

"You know what you want to do," he said now in disgust. "Do it. Jest 'cause it's *Raymond* land—"

"He don't want to take nuthin', Pa," Cobus's father said defensively. "They asked him to come back at that pay. He's goin' to apprentice now. That's how come it's more money."

"Maybe so, maybe not. The Raymonds, they always did buy their way. If he wants to go into the woods again, let him go. It's his business. He knows we need him here."

Cobus's father had his own stubborn streak. "Not so much winters—"

"One of them should stand by. Tip's goin' to the Falls, Cobus should—but if he don't see that, he don't see that."

Cobus took up his coffee mug and buried his face in the strong ersatz smell of chickory. Bitter fumes rose from the cup, bitterer ones assailed him from his heart. It is terrible to love those who do not love back.

His grandfather bent forward and peered myopically into his face, searching out weakness, cowardice, all the boyish faults the old have no patience with, especially this longing for love. Cobus, looking at him, associated him with an age of iron. And Cobus feared him: in the hold and threat and astonishment of love.

Some people, it seemed, were easier to love than others—better looking, easier dispositioned, and of course happier (because they were loved); some people seemed born second-best and all the efforts in the world couldn't make them the kind of people others admired and envied. Cobus had tried and tried to make his grandfather love him, and admire him; but there was always an element of blank in his grandfather's feelings for him, as if he associated Cobus with pain and disappointment and Tip with pleasure and accomplishment. All the offerings of his heart that Cobus had brought him over the years were empty admonitions; his grandfather was walled from him by some solid resentment whose foundation Cobus would never understand, never break through. He could look at his grandfather all his life and ask, *Why don't you love me like you do Tip?* and never get an answer. There wasn't any answer.

He rose, resting his weight against the table, looking at this study in age and decay, the white light of evanescence, in front of him. Ever since he could remember Cobus had been looking for an outstretched hand from his grandfather, some sign the gulf was gone; it was Tip the old man had

281

taken by the hand and led over to the cove to look at the female fish lying, bright-eyed and frightened, over her nest of eggs; Tip he had turned to when the pain in which he was enclosed ever since that accident in the woods took over and annihilated him so that he seemed nothing but eyes and agony—"Bring me a cold cloth, boy, that's a boy. My eyes—" It was Tip of whom he boasted, Tip in whom the swelling joy of an old man's pride resided, Tip on whom the gnarled hand fell and rested for reassurance.

"It's all right for Tip to do what he wants, but me—I gotta do what's best. That's the way it's always been, the way it's always gonna be. Tip's the one who's best. Because he's smart—and because he don't take after Ma." It was said.

Cobus's father made a noise like a horse snorting through his nose. He rose, large and threatening in his anger; but a fierce flame of righteousness burned in Cobus, he would not keep quiet just because they did not want to hear the truth.

For a moment a sick kind of silence regimented the room. A dumb, dull knocking beat at Cobus's heart. "I'm goin'," he said leadenly, "because I want to and because—because it's no good bein' here."

"A willful one," his grandfather decided, as if that evaluation was at last the symbolic equivalent of washing his hands of Cobus.

But Cobus's father had lived all his life by the rigid rule of *Grant what is right*. He looked at his son not in anger but resignation, and a kind of pity Cobus couldn't identify. "None of it *his* fault," he said. "Hit's jest the way things is—because of a lot of foolishness way back. Don't pay it no mind, son, you go and forget what was said."

"Don't you *dare* forget," his grandfather said. "This land is Buttes land. You owe it all you got. Don't you never forget that."

Why, then, didn't the same law hold true of Tip?

When, at the end of the lane, Cobus turned back to catch sight of his grandfather, of the figure of his father high on a ridge, stilled by the oxen he had been leading out to pasture, he felt he was a part of all this—and the picture settled in his mind to remain there for winter reference, a memory against which he might call forth the strange ambivalence of what was home. Was it perhaps also true that all things of depth were shaded in ambiguity?

Seeing Big John, barefoot, his cheek swollen with a large plug of B & L, a jug of Eagle Sweat in one hand, come out of the woods hooting a greeting, it seemed for a moment he could say, There's a simple happy man nothin' bothers. But this, too, was untrue. Big John carried always inside the death of that younger brother, Amos, and often he became moody and morose. "It weren't fair, he wasn't doin' nuthin' to git it," Big John would say sullenly.

Now he looked Cobus over. "You growed," he said.

"Some," Cobus admitted. He had let down the stirrups on his saddle twice that summer. But everything was growing, changing.

"Didn't take on much weight to go with it, though. Need some beans in you. Still turnin' yourself against such abominations as chawin'? Drink though, as I remember it." He gave the great roar that with him passed for laughter. "I sure do recollect that last night of the drive down to the Falls, like to kill a boy to put away rum like you did." He held out the jug.

"Too early," Cobus said.

"Never too early. Gonna learn to cut this season, is you? Well, come in and put your Kennebeck on the bunk next to mine. Since you're early, you got somethin' of a choice, though bein' young, there may be some disputes develop." Big John said it with satisfaction, looking forward to the first fight.

"I aim to do my own protectin' this year."

"Not without trainin'—it's all part of your program. Cob—" The nickname gave Cobus an ache of anticipation for the long winter months ahead; it had been such a long time since he'd heard anyone call him Cob. He was back in the woods, safe. "Don't want to take on more than you're ready for. One of the things I aim to do this year is train you—"

"Gougin', kickin', bitin' off ears?"

"You better believe it. You don't git nowhere in this world without the best pair of fists in the crowd and a couple of good strong legs for stompin'."

Yes, he was in the woods and would have to obey its laws or leave. In town Tip would be learning an entirely different set of rules. And in between was Ardis—no, she was at the Academy, too, with Tip. In his world. One of the strongest reasons he had wanted to get back to the woods was the discovery of how hopeless his love for her was. What puzzled him was that he didn't even know how he had come to give his heart, the relinquishing had been so gradual. All that summer he had been building toward this knowledge and

283

trying to run away from it; he had known and rebelled against his feeling and pressed it deep down inside, put other things over it, trying to bury it, trying to prevent its ever getting away from him. But it had a mind and power of its own.

Big John began with notching. Notching, it turned out, was an art, at least it seemed so to Cobus, who watched Big John's mastery with the kind of awe he had experienced previously only in the presence of a man who could tame a wild horse. Concentration, precision, accuracy of calculation, care, practice—and a touch of genius—these were all necessary to notch. Notching was done so that the tree had a fulcrum from which to fall and did not splinter several feet up-trunk as it came down, thereby ruining good timber. "The barber-chair stump,"—a long, disfiguring splinter rising from the stump of a fallen tree—it was called in derision.

A tree had to be carefully calculated for a clean fall. It must not be notched too much nor too little, not too high nor too low; generally, the notch went about waist high at a forty-five-degree angle, twelve inches off the ground. The notch was made in the direction in which the tree was to fall. This fall was determined by the trees and spaces in the area. A fall must be clean so that the tree's upper limbs did not catch or splinter on other trees.

Big John swung his axe into a big white pine and the chips flew on either side of him. "Have to have the chips fall right," he said, without pausing. "Only bury part of your axe when you're chopping—with the heel or nose of the blade, and then that's got to be exposed for them chips to fly right. You work the near side first, then the far side, you won't have no trouble gettin' the chips to go right." His chips went right, but Cobus had no such optimism about the ones that would come off his axe. "Now is the time when you lay her out for falling." Big John rested his axe on the bottom part of the V-shaped notch. The axe head lay flat on the notch with the helve pointing where the tree was to fall. This method worked fine, Big John said, for "straight-up-and-down trees," but a slanting tree required all kinds of modifications. "Say the tree leans north," Big John explained, pulling from his pocket a plug of tobacco and anchoring it between his teeth, tearing off an end. "Well, then you got a choice. It can fall east, it can fall west, but it can never on God's green earth fall south. Suppose you want it to fall west: then you notch it on the *western* side of the trunk. Then you kinda chop away at the eastern edge, see, but slightly toward the north, so you keep the back part—the south part—of the tree as a counterbalance to the slant. You got *that* drawin' it to fall west. See?"

Cobus did not. He just stood, stubborn and bewildered, watching all day and hearing the same kind of unintelligible instructions, understanding nothing, absorbing nothing, trundling along in Big John's wake grimly telling himself he *would* learn, it couldn't be that hard; he thought with envy of Tip at the Academy having nothing more strenuous to master than a few Latin verbs, some pronouncements on Natural, Moral and Mental Philosophy, a little Pencil Drawing.

All that first week he did nothing but watch Big John notch. Big John did *only* that. He would not stop to finish the trees; another lumberman trailed behind making the back cuts and "bucking" (cutting) the thirteen-foot logs. Notching was what Big John had set himself to teach Cobus, and that was all at the start. "You mess about at the beginnin' and don't do the first thing right," Big John said, "the whole thing ends up a mess." Big John went from tree to tree, pointing, explaining, showing, unbelievably patient for a man with such a bad temper.

Cobus plodded after, watching, listening, learning nothing. A week went by and then a second; it seemed to Cobus Big John must have made notches in every white pine for miles around.

Finally at the end of the second week they came to a terrible looking tree; it was huge and it leaned crazily to one side, its top foliage all lopsided so that it would be thrown off in the fall. All around it were other pines hemming it in so that there seemed no place for it to fall free. It was this tree, Big John said, Cobus should start notching on.

Cobus looked at him as if he were crazy. Big John stood chewing complacently, looking right back at him happily. Nothing could have pleased him more than to have given Cobus a real son-of-a-bitch on which to start.

"Well, I guess the undercut's got to be deeper than usual, the tree bein' so big and kind of leanin' like." Though Cobus looked at him for verification, none came. So far as Big John was concerned, this was Cobus's problem all the way, let him solve it. "Maybe better to make two notches instead of one on a tree this big," Cobus contemplated, "then join 'em up." Big John was looking a little pleased. "And we'll have to hold a corner,' on account of the lean," by which he meant he aimed to leave a little more wood on the opposite side from the lean. "There's a wind blowin' in the direction we

285

want her to fall, so I guess that'll help topple her over."

"You figured her real good, boy, now chop."

Cobus went about the notching carefully. He made the first undercut quite a bit lower than the usual foot height and he made it small; then he made a second triangle above this and, satisfied that the two were lined up carefully, made from the two small V-notches one large one. Holding his breath, he laid his axe on the notch to check, making compensation for the wind and "holding the corner." It looked all right to him, but who was he to know? When he looked up questioningly, Big John was grinning.

For another week Cobus notched while Big John watched. It was an expensive, time-consuming way to train and one hardly ever done, Cobus later learned, but Big John had apparently made up his mind Cobus was going to be a real woodsman down to the last detail, damn what Mr. Orville Raymond, down South with his baths and interesting diets might say. Occasionally, though not often, Big John stopped to point out some small technical flaw in what Cobus was doing, but for the most part he just watched Cobus cut.

After that, they went to the back cut, which came quickly and easily to Cobus. All the time and care Big John had put into the first part of the operation was beginning to pay off; Cobus was looking at trees not with an outsider's eyes but with the practiced, calculating, measuring glance of the woodsman. The back cut was not so intricate an operation, not so exacting a decision. The tree, V-notched on one side, stood waiting for the cut from the opposite side that would send it toppling; that opposite cut, the back cut, was made about two inches up from where the undercut of the V was and parallel to the undercut until only a couple of inches of uncut wood remained. The back cut *never* went all the way through; those two inches of holding wood were needed as a hinge for guiding the tree as it fell. The tree went—using the axe to push from the opposite side of the fall—with a cry, "Tim—be—r-rr!" to warn men to get out of the way. Big John cautioned Cobus not to stay too near the stump; there was always the danger the butt might kick back, occasionally sideways.

Cobus was working the real logger's day now and he looked with pity and condescension on the new cookee who was doing all the menial jobs he had done the year before; he got up with the cry "Day-li——ght in the swamp!" instead of making it; he went into the woods for a back-breaking day of ten and twelve hours of cutting the great white pines, nstead of staying back in camp putting down beans and weeping up.

Most of the pines went 150 feet and it was not surprising o be cutting one well over two hundred feet. He and the crew were still cutting and skidding at Christmas, waiting for enough snow so that there would be a base for the sleds when the loading, bobbing, and drawing would begin. The year had been extraordinarily moderate—Cobus could never remember a November like it, warm and wet, like April; even into December there was the deceptive feeling of spring. On Christmas day the temperature went up almost to sixty. He knew the exact reading—58°—because he had been sent for by Mowatt Raymond; when the runner came in to give Cobus the message that if it was over fifty he should come out for the holidays, the crew couldn't believe it was that hot; t had never been so warm in December.

William came to the end of the logging road to meet him. They were so glad to see each other that they embraced and for a moment Cobus thought he might break down and cry. He had not realized how much he had missed William and the Old Man. He saw how completely split his life was, one part of him belonging to the life at the Landing and the other, so different, here in the woods, the rough world of lumbermen.

All the way to the Raymond house near the Landing, nearly a four-hour trip, Cobus kept asking William one question after another—about the horses, the house, the family, the Academy, his brother, and finally about Ardis.

"She been sick," William said. "Mr. Raymond, he went down and took her out of that school and brought her home a couple of weeks back. She got this cough, it don't go away, and that worried them. But she better now, Mr. Cobus, she almost herself, ridin' every day in this good weather—you ever seen anythin' like it?—your mare mostly. Keepin' her in shape for you."

Cobus felt a surge of happiness at the idea of Ardis using something of his.

"But her Grandaddy, he don't want her to go back to school for a while, maybe not at all this year, not until she completely well. Says one year won't make no difference, she can drop out this one and finish next, it's about the same; but your brother, course, he miss her fierce and he keep tryin' to persuade Mr. Mowatt to let her come back."

Cobus was home only three days. It was an extraordinary dispensation Mr. Raymond had made him, letting him come

287

out for Christmas, and he never forgot the old man's kindness because he always remembered that Christmas; those three days were some of the best and worst of his life. He spent a good deal of time at the Raymonds'; Ardis had got his mare quite collected and going well in the extended trot, and those times working with her, when they were so close and so intensely interested in the same thing, stayed with him all the rest of that winter; he would take out these memories and relive them slowly again and again, lying in his bunk after the long day's work, trying to recreate each and every moment—and failing because he could never remember exactly what she had said or what he had answered; but that failure to remember was a pleasure, too, for it permitted him to embroider on a particular moment, savoring what he could recall and imagining those moments he could not, so that with improvisation scenes that had in reality lasted four or five minutes took as long as an hour to go through in his mind.

He had almost persuaded his mind to give up the image of her turned back; almost, but not quite, for there was always an abrupt end to the pleasure of reminiscence when in the midst of remembering how she had been out in the training field alone with him, he would recall how she always managed to bring the conversation around to Tip so that they always ended up talking about the one thing she was really interested in, his brother. She waited for Tip eagerly, was terribly dejected if he didn't come with Cobus, if instead he stayed back to study for his examinations, coming up after the first of the year; she seemed to have an obsessive need to be with Tip or, if he weren't with her, to bring his name into every conversation. She was always saying it with a special kind of emphasis, as if there were magic in the name itself and by the mere act of uttering it she was somehow able to render Tip under her power. She liked Cobus and enjoyed being with him, but it was Clyde Buttes she loved, even when he made her unhappy.

The two families shared Christmas dinner at the Raymond house, William waiting on table in formal attire. Cobus's grandfather never got over the fact the man wore white gloves as he passed the plates around. There was a small exchange of gifts—Cobus gave Ardis a handsomely worked pair of leather reins which he had decorated himself in camp with a red-hot poker; and she gave him a new saddle pad, store-bought, which he badly needed. She had had a "miniature" done for Tip to take back to school, and Cobus would have given anything in the world to have been able to take that likeness of her back into camp with him.

On the surface, the party seemed a success, but it had its bad moments. His mother was not at ease, and his grandfather got to talking and couldn't stop, monopolizing the conversation for over a quarter of an hour. His topic was also unfortunate: the deterioration in the "new" people coming into the Landing.

Cobus's mother had fussed and fussed about her dress. She had taken out her good one and aired it and it looked all right until she put on her hat. It was all wrong, the hat. It made the dress look all wrong, too. The dress was very pretty, but it had been conceived for a small, feminine woman and on Cobus's mother it obviously had no idea how it should behave. The hat was, however, the great mistake; while waiting for the others his mother could not stop fanning herself feverishly with it, the ribbons flapping this way and that. She was not a stupid woman, and she knew right off she had done something wrong, but she couldn't put her finger on what it was.

The dress was wrong, the hat a total disaster, but her mouth and eyes—Cobus's father bent forward just as they left their house and seized her with both his arms, hugging her. "You're a good-looking woman," he said, "and that dress don't take away from it none."

"It's the dress," she had cried, a kind of question to them, but mostly put to Tip who should know.

"Leave the hat home," he said.

"But I have to wear a hat, it's so cold. And besides it wouldn't look right, coming there bare-headed. It's the hat that's wrong, Tip, is that it?"

"Make it plainer," he said, as if grasping at any straw. "Strip it down to nothing—"

"I could—" Her voice rose on a hopeful note. "I could take the ribbon and roses off." All during the drive she had been unraveling and plucking out. When they arrived, the hat was near nothing. It looked as if it had hung in the barn all winter, but no one said anything.

Old Man Raymond met them at the door, jovial and hearty. Tip was hanging back, as if he were a separate guest who had just happened to arrive at the same time. He's ashamed of Ma, Cobus thought, and his own life-long burning shame answered that accusation, even as he saw that this was unworthy of her. Standing there in the front hall on the blue peacock rug, she looked like a strong and resilient woman, one who wouldn't break under strain. Old Man Raymond held out his hand and she took it firmly, as if it were her right. Young Mrs. Raymond and the flowers and jewels that were her girls pressed forward and awkwardly they made the social conventions cover the next few minutes until they went into the dining room.

Like his mother's hat, the meal was too fancy, it needed stripping down. There was a chilled and mayonnaised lobster course first, all kinds of game birds cooked in all kinds of ways, a large brown, brightly glazed turkey, a standing roast of rib, salads with scarlet curlicues of pimentos and bright green bands of peppers; breads, cheese, cakes, punches, coffee, urns of tea; and William passing in his white gloves.

Cobus was terribly conscious of his calloused hands, his cracked nails, the lumpy way his suit hung haphazardly on his body, his awkward feet in the store shoes that weren't quite the right fit, his thick, tongue-tied speech, the bumbling way he ate his food. In contrast, Tip sat elegant and at ease, eating slowly, leaving a silver knife lying lazily on his plate, talking quietly but animatedly with first one, then another of the Raymonds. He looked as if he belonged in this elegant dining room, more like one of the Raymonds than one of the Butteses.

His grandfather *was* right. The world didn't need hunters or trappers, woodsmen any more; it needed people like Tip who were clever with their heads, not their hands, who could manipulate and make fancy talk with suave, smooth voices. Rough voices, rough ways were of no use now.

His mother marveled all the way home. "That table," she recalled happily. "I never seen such things in my whole life. And the silver, it was so heavy you could hardly lift it to eat. They had those thin plates you could see through, Guthrie, painted with *real* gold.

"I only knew one other day like this," she said. She turned and looked at her husband. "You remember the day you jumped over that log on top of me, Guthrie? You were so handsome, I never saw a man stand so straight and tall in my life. You come jumpin' over that log and landed on me and knocked the wind right out of me, took my breath away. I can still see that field of flowers we walked through. You don't know what it was like, either of you," she said to her sons.

He had to leave early because it started to snow and there was something in the air everyone recognized as the end of that long, false springlike weather and the beginning of the hard winter. William didn't use the horses to take him back; they went with the oxen, and it was blowing so hard, the snow swirling so badly, that they had trouble keeping to the road. William was genuinely worried Cobus wouldn't be able to see his way back down the skidway to camp, but Cobus pooh-poohed such a notion; he felt it would be easy to follow the path because it would be the only real open clearing in the woods. Even so, the weather was so bad by the time they got near camp that he had some doubts himself. He knew if he blundered into the woods and out of easy hollering distance of the road, he could hold very little hope of coming out alive, but he didn't let on to William, who was openly and loudly troubled, saying he didn't think it was right for him to go off by himself alone in weather like this, something might happen to him.

When they reached the skidding road, Cobus saw a familiar bull of a figure standing shouting, drunk as a lord, weaving about, bellowing, "I knowed they'd bring you in today. Snow's gonna sock us in for the rest of the winter, so you either git back today or you don't git back at all. Brung me down the cart with the ox and a couple of jugs of Sweat, been waitin' over an hour."

Cobus had pocketed a couple of the fancy cigars Mr. Raymond had passed around after Christmas dinner and he had begged a bottle of that good brandy Mr. Raymond was always raving about for Big John. He climbed down, William handing him the knapsack with the brandy, the cigars, and some other fancy provisions he wasn't quite sure how Big John would take to. "Maybe it'd be better if you waited it out at North Creek, William. This is a pretty bad storm."

"Don't you worry none. I'll get through. And I'll see to it your horse is looked after—and Miss Ardis, too, Mr. Cobus. Don't you eat your heart out worrying over her, you hear?"

The face was a mask of pleasant sociability; Cobus put his hand up and the two men shook. "You take care of both of them, but don't say I said nuthin' except about the horse."

"I don't say nuthin' about nuthin', Mr. Cobus, you know that."

Cobus took his Kennebeck; he wished he had had something better to give William for Christmas besides the lumpy figure he had whittled at camp that fall. He had tried to make it a likeness of a horse's head and it was better than he had talent for but not as good as he had seen in his mind. But William had his friendship, his real friendship, Cobus had given him that, but did he know? It seemed important to Cobus that he should. It was as if, standing in the midst of that terrible blizzard, he had at that moment a premonition of the growth that was going to kill William that spring, those rapidly multiplying cells no one could see but which were even at that moment busily preparing for the end four months away, eating away at William's insides and destroying him day by day without anyone seeing or knowing. "You been a good friend," he began, but it was William who was master of the situation. "You, too, Mr. Cobus, a good good friend. Ain't many men got a friend like you been to me, a real friend."

Cobus shook his head. "I—good-bye, William, I'll see you at the end of the drive in May."

But he never did. William was buried the end of April while Cobus was out getting the logs ready for the run down to the Falls.

The next summer Clyde—who no longer tolerated anyone using a nickname he said sounded childish—had graduated from the Academy and was down in Albany reading law. He liked everything about city life and he was always gay and exuberant when he was home; they all looked forward to his visits, to their breath of the great world that lay beyond the boundaries of the Buttes property, but Cobus's father seemed literally to live for them. While Clyde was in the house, he was full of laughter; as soon as he left, he became morose and silent, subject to nervous, irritable outbursts that cut Cobus off from him completely. They were two men who worked hard side by side all summer with nothing in common and much that put them in opposition. When he looks at me, Cobus thought, he sees my Ma, but when he looks at Tip, he sees himself. It's as simple as that. But nothing is simple, especially the answers a man tries on himself to justify his feelings of inadequacy.

Cobus's life remained deeply divided: the summer part on the farm he was at odds with himself, the rest of the year strangely at peace in the woods away from the world. As a lumberjack he did not make much—lumbermen seemed to work for love and not much else, or perhaps for the chance to get away from it all with an excuse that was acceptable —but Cobus was putting what little he did earn away. He wasn't quite sure for what, but he wanted something set

292

aside in case. He was tall and rawboned and gruff—lonely, too, he would have said if he thought of it. He knew at the Landing it was said he had the strong streak of bitter pride that ran in rambunctious Indians, whereas Tip Buttes was "more like his Pa." Cobus ought to have been considered a catch—he was obviously the one who would run the farm and he was thrifty and hardworking—but the girls shied away from him for the obvious reason of his mixed blood as well as the fact that he was standoffish and quick to take offense. It was said of him—with a shake of the head—cold water takes a long time to melt ice.

So much was happening. Even coming out each spring from his brief sojourns in the woods, Cobus found an altered world. The whole nation was in the throes of change, even the sleepy backwater village of Buttes Landing. There were nearly four hundred inhabitants of the Landing now. There were three general stores, a school, a post office—the mail, though there was still no real winter mail service, came in by horse or packed on the back of a man on snowshoes when the weather permitted; there was an inn of sorts besides the usual tavern that put up people in the big overhead loft, the usual small busy private premises with a blacksmith shop, a saddler, a wood-working shop, the local doctor and the local undertaker, who made the caskets himself and kept the carriage hearse down the street in the building next to the grist mill; there were harness, wagon and sleigh repair shops and while no lawyer, a pettifogger whose knowledge of the courts was sufficient for most of the routine business of the Landing—drawing up deeds and wills, and the exchange of simple legal summonses. The town was energetic; a constant air of activity hummed over it, men going with pace and purpose about the daily details of their lives, wanting to do better than just get along. Cobus used to think there was something in the joint mixture of mountain and lake air that urged them on, infused in them extra vitality; outsiders said of the Landing that it was "small but snappy," an apt judgment; for besides pursuing their trades vigorously, most of the townspeople were also deeply involved with the issues of the day, the tide sweeping West, the nation growing and bursting, spilling out all over the new continent, floundering always Westward. Cobus had seen Tip's copy of *The Democratic Review*, in which John L. O'Sullivan had written his famous phrase "manifest destiny." "To overspread the continent," he had written, "allotted by Providence for the free development of our yearly multiplying millions."

Much, much was happening, but all the changes seemed to be occurring in other people's lives. This was no longer a country of self-sufficient small farmers making up a seaboard rural agricultural society. While Cobus himself might stay on the farm, thousands of others fled; they could find work easily—not always pleasant or well-paid, but work, and in the city where they wanted to be—because every day new inventions were turning the country away from tilling to trade. Steam pushed transportation across land and sea, made the machines hum in the shops; the press, the telegraph, the railroad, the steamship were altering forever the old way of life. His father had a new filly, black with white socks, Tip had Ardis, Mr. Raymond was buying and selling and preaching "manifest destiny," but Cobus went on with farming, with the woods; summers fanned into sections of plowing, planting, weeding, reaping, threshing, laying down larder against winter; autumns he met Big John to set things up in the woods, coming out the following May with the drive, the years so much alike they seemed to fuse into a wash of time in which Cobus could not sort out which year what had happened. Which year was it, for instance, Orville Raymond came home and acted so terrible that it was decided once and for all to post him South permanently? Which year was it Old Man Raymond quit riding, the rheumatiz too bad for him even to try to sit a saddle? Which year was it they had the bad drought and which one too much rain? Two years, however, stood out. First there was the spring of 1850 when he met his father on the porch at the house after his winter in the woods, and his father had such a look on his face. Odder Buttes was gone.

"He musta went into the woods. He took his gun off the wall and he musta jest walked into the woods." Cobus's father looked down at the pale pearly object he held in his hands, an old battered watch. "And he don't plan to come back. He came here out of nowhere and he aims to go back the same way he came, walkin'. Like there was no beginnin' nor end, come and gone, out of the woods the same way. Maybe," he said after a moment, "it's the only way." To Cobus's astonishment, he bent his head. "Lord," he prayed, "make it a fittin' end."

Then there was the next summer, when Tip told them he wanted to marry Ardis. There was no surprise to the announcement, but there were problems. How would the Raymonds take to having a halfbreed son, even one that didn't look Indian? The Old Man accepted the laws of love as natural, regardless of the kinds of blood involved, or so it seemed, because he never showed anything but pleasure in the disclosure. Yet there was an uncomfortable moment when young Mrs. Raymond wept and left the room, and for days after when she saw Tip she put a handkerchief to her eyes and shook her head, never coming right out and saying anything. She wasn't Raymond blood really, and the old man must have spoken to her because, after all, in terms of dollars and cents she was living in his house. But she was not happy over the match and neither, in a strange paradox, was his mother. "He'll go off and leave us for good now," she predicted. "He's outgrown us. When he comes up, he'll be down *there.*"

She saw very clearly he was severing his ties with them, moving on to something grander, something more in line with his vision of being Well Thought Of. It was as if he had given up being a Buttes and started thinking of himself as a Raymond.

Ardis and Tip were married the next year, on June 21, her birthday, and then she went out of Cobus's life, but not out of his thoughts. He felt she would never leave his mind, never, no matter what happened or how many years passed. He scarcely saw her now that Tip stayed on in Albany practicing law and making a big name for himself; and even summers she only came for a week or two, some of the holidays. She was his sister-in-law, it was a distant kind of friendship and even that got somehow distorted because they couldn't ride that summer she came up after being married, she was big and awkward and withdrawn, with that "going-insideness" Cobus had learned to associate with pregnant women. The child was stillborn, and then she became even more distant and detached, as if she could not bear to share the loss with anyone. The child had been a boy, perfectly formed, but strangled during birth by the umbilical cord; he was buried up back, in the Buttes cemetery on the hill, near the big tamarack tree, Emily's tree, it was called, under a stone marked

BRED ON EARTH TO BLOOM IN HEAVEN
INFANT SON OF CLYDE & ARDIS BUTTES

and Old Man Raymond had made them add

FIRST GRANDSON OF MASON MOWATT RAYMOND

He wanted to be buried up there, too, he said—if the Butteses would let him; the families were bound together now, weren't they? Going down into the earth at a place with such a view wouldn't bother him half as much as being stuck in that ugly little cemetery over at the Landing and he'd be damned if he'd be buried in a big impersonal place like Albany. Cobus remembered him standing at the graveside of the unnamed grandson—very old and rheumatic now, so badly crippled in the fingers he could no longer hold the reins in his hands. Yet he kept the horses—and his hope—alive: there *would* be a male, a perfect male with small, strong, sturdy legs, that would be lifted up on a horse and given reins for the first time before his fading eyes. He held on, bent, in dreadful pain, using a cane, crippled and twisted and indomitable. He buried Orville one of those winters Cobus was in the woods, not in the Buttes cemetery up on the hill, but down South; tainted blood could apparently go into the roots of the magnolia, not the northern, stronger pine. He lost Pearl—one of the bright clutter of gems and flowers that had made the house always a clatter of female voices, females scurrying in and out.

HOPE LOOKS BEYOND THE BOUNDS OF TIME
WHEN WHAT WE NOW DEPLORE
SHALL RISE IN FULL IMMORTAL PRIME
AND BLOOM TO FADE NO MORE

PEARL
daughter of Orville and Belva Raymond
aged 18 yrs and 5 mts & 24 days

When Cobus thought back to that first year he went into the woods in 1843, when he was fifteen, to the final year, twelve later, when he determined never to go back again, the only clear true pictures of those years were the first and last, and one spring and one summer and all the rest was a haze through which events floated up to him with the peculiar unreal quality of an object discerned through fog or in a dream. He knew, yes, things had happened, but when precisely or how in the feral flow of all that had happened he did not know; summers behind the harness of the plow and winters behind the axe in the woods blended into one continuous action, pierced here and there with an unexpected occurrence, the drowning, the hunting accident, the Mexican War, all the commotion over the Compromise of 1850; but these seemed not to have touched him, they were unreal, like a distant hill one sees all one's life but never climbs: it is there, but it has no real meaning because it has not been touched. Everything, everyone, the whole country, was changing: but not Cobus Buttes.

Yes, even him a little.

Now when he and Big John went into the woods to work side by side, equals, if anything Cobus was the stronger, tougher, and even more determined and unprincipled fighter than the man from whom he had learned. He did not drink hard, but he could drink almost any man down when he set his mind to it; he had Big John's contempt for women (leaving Ardis aside, for whom after all these years an emotion removed from any other remained), creatures to be used as an antidote against appetites, and—when a man got ready —to be sized up for the kind of sons they might be expected to produce and, passing the proper measurement tests, married, bred and kept, as the saying went, barefoot and in the family way; otherwise, women were to be avoided; they were dangerous because they were capable of removing a man from the rough, raw world of men where he belonged and hitching him to a yoke from which he would never yank free. That kind of woman—the women like Ardis—were the ones to worry about, to stay away from; the others—well, they might give a man a spot of "trouble" now and then, but that was one of the hazards of the night so to speak. What sons a man might have sired under such circumstances were really not sons of his own but aftermaths of the long winter in the woods, nothing to do with wanting or planning or willing. Cobus seldom even wondered if somewhere in one of those little river towns there might be wandering a child with Buttes blood. He thought a good deal about Ardis's own son, however, born the year of 1854, the Old Man at last with his dream made real, a strong sturdy boy who carried his name. God willing, after the drive at the end of the year, Cobus would help hoist the boy on the back of Tokay and put the reins in his hands, prop the child up while the crippled old man looked on. Life was vindictive, of course; it ought to be William setting the boy up.

Cobus had never felt stronger; he was looking forward to one of those competitions when a man pushed himself to cut 110, 120 trees a day. A few side bets, he might make a tidy little sum. Big John, too. They worked close enough to be brothers, though Big John, only into his thirties, was already beginning to suffer from the logger's complaint—crippling arthritis. All those winters of cold and wet had taken their toll, he no longer much went barefoot, for instance. Mornings his bones creaked and made strange grinding sounds finding their way into their sockets; both shoulders troubled him, he was never entirely free from the piercing pains of bursitis. He drank more and sang less and sometimes it seemed to Cobus he went away into a world of his own no one could penetrate, where he stayed hours on end, being visited by what Cobus had no idea (the lost real brother Amos?), but what or whoever's presence clouded his eyes with sadness, made him almost gentle during these spells, he was so quiet, so removed from the men around him.

When the time came and Big John no longer could take one of those camp winters, he would quit too, go look for that woman whose wide hips would provide good sound sons, marry her, and set up at the farm for good. In the meantime, he felt with Big John that peculiar and particular pleasure of two men who share the same life together over a number of years, who respect and admire each other; and with the long years cementing their friendship, the two were like two parts of the same tool, the twin sides of pliers, opening and closing in unison in order to accomplish the same job.

They went into camp with a new cook—Pete having gone, grumbling, West with the new movement of loggers pushing manifest destiny into Michigan. Push, shove, push. People frenetically kept going on, always on, and no end in sight until the ocean backed up against them, floods of men and women washing Westward to the sea.

Only he seemed to remain calm and unconcerned, land-locked in the woods. Even his own tribes had disbanded or disappeared, his mother's people forgotten.

Most of the area they were cutting was mountainous, uneven at best, at worst, with steep, difficult grades over which the logs had to be hauled. The sleds took the logs to banking grounds where they were branded and awaited the spring thaws and the final phase of the logging operation, the run downstream to the mill. The sleds always had trouble with their loads. This year was no exception, it had just been worse than most. Hills were scraped of ice and snow to keep the logs from running away and crashing down on the men. On the steepest hills a snubber was used, a heavy rope fastened round a stump which, when attached to the sled and slowly let out, prevented the sled from going too fast and overrunning the team. Chains were also used on the

298

sled runners for braking, but these were not very reliable and a nuisance as well because of breakage, catching, friction-heating.

There was always trouble in the woods and Big John had accepted that as a part of the job, even managing wryly to laugh at what could go wrong, the possibilities were endless. But this year Cobus noticed almost from the start that Big John was short on humor and long on worry. He hounded the men—constantly anticipating dangers and disasters they all knew and took for granted but which now, with Big John's endless repeated warnings and admonitions, began to occupy more of their thinking than was wise. A part of their brains should be alert to what *might* happen, but too much pre-occupation with an impending accident might bring it on. There were always accident-inducers in camp, men who talked so much about the varying possibilities of disaster so frequently and vividly that they unnerved the other men, threw off the delicate balance of their brains and bodies, made them suddenly awkward in their old easy routines.

Now it seemed to Cobus that Big John, who had gone so assuredly about the most perilous work, who had always volunteered as one of the first men to sort out a jam, who instantly was alerted to others' dangers and went to their aid, had become a kind of Weepin' Anna himself. His mind seemed suddenly to have added up all the times he and other men should have been hurt or killed and hadn't, a tally which had impressed on him for the first time how really hazardous the work was and how staggering were the odds against a man finishing a season in one piece. For the first time Big John talked about his brother Amos's death, the death of Pete's brother, the deaths of all the other men he had known; he told morbidly over and over stories of mutilations, of men struck down by freak accidents or destroyed by a seemingly safe routine operation; he harped back time and again to all the stories he had ever heard about bad luck, ill-timed and strange coincidences, unhappy turnings of chance.

The men began to respond. One was caught by a "widow-maker," the falling tree shearing a branch from another tree as it came down, the logger was pinned under, the bones in his ribs and legs crushed; another miscalculated a fall, an almost unheard-of occurrence in as seasoned a woodsman as this man was, and did not get out of the way in time and was hit by a flying bit of stump, not seriously, but bad enough to put him off logging the rest of the winter. From all sides Cobus heard uneasy mutterings.

"You figure," Cobus began one night when he hoped Big John was drunk enough not to take offense, "maybe you're ridin' the men a little hard on what *might* happen? You know—"

"Cob," Big John interrupted, "you're only a kid in this game, don't matter how *you* look at it, but I been in the woods more than twenty years, I *know*. Oh God, I know it all, each and every bit of how one thing and another can git you, don't matter how careful nor cautious you be. Takes the best men as well as the green and no good," he said with passion. "Goddam son-of-a-bitch no-good fuckin' woods."

The mishaps and accidents continued—a bad slide, when a stand of logs unaccountably gave way and went tumbling downhill; a long thaw late in January that went on almost to the middle of February and held up hauling, bogged operations down in mud and slime; and finally the fight Big John got into with the new cook, who walked out of camp without a word the next day. There was not a man who wouldn't cheerfully have killed his bunkmate simply for a feeling of relief from the suppressed sense of impending disaster which underlay every day's operations; yet, oddly, there were few fights, as if the men were deliberately holding themselves in check acknowledging that murderous impulse eating away at the whole camp. Every winter stories came of camps that exploded into one of those murderous contests, one of those orgies of blood which were all traceable directly to this kind of pressure.

By March Cobus woke every morning with dread. Now that the cook was gone, Cobus, with the cookee, was doing the best he could to keep things going, but he was disappointed not to be out in the woods skidding. The sudden advent of good weather deepened his resentment. He had not signed on as cook. But there had to be a cook, so—

A sense of loyalty had made him volunteer for the job, a sense that friendship demanded moments of blind allegiance, when to question would have been to judge, and to judge would have been to condemn.

The camp rounded March and went into April with the barest nerve threads of the men holding things together. The weather—wonderful, warm, with such sun as Cobus had never known before this time of year, a summer sun that poured a lyrical warmth down on them—meant that the drive would come early. He was thankful for that. He had made his mind up: this would definitely be his last winter in the woods; yet he said nothing to Big John, who was already beginning to make plans for next year, talking as if they would both be back early in September to set things up again. Cobus believed many of the men, like himself, would never work in a camp with Big John again.

The weather made a sudden reversal just as the freshets sent the logs on their way; now there was a plunge in the temperature and brutal winds that day after day knifed straight to a man's bones and left them sharp with pain. Big John had gone ahead in the carriage, lashing the horses on, as much motivated by the terrible pain in his shoulders, Cobus knew, as by the frantic fear something would go wrong now at the very last when the winter's work was nearly finished.

Cobus arrived early at the camp grounds they always used the first night of the drive. There was the usual assortment of small, excited boys and curious men who had in previous years made friends with some of the loggers and were now waiting for them to come in. Cobus went ahead with his preparations as best he could; yet he had the nagging sense something was missing. In all the pieces of river life he had known so many years one was missing; and his not being able to place the missing component upset him. He kept stopping to look around, trying to locate the source of his uneasiness. And then it came to him. Old Connecticuty's tent. He felt a knot of apprehension as he made a quick inspection of the grounds, hoping that somehow in the confusion he had missed Mrs. Murphy's ragged tarpaulin stretched on its flimsy poles, the tacky piece of canvas that flapped as a front door, the rusty dipper, the keg of rum. The atmosphere of the run was already bad enough without adding something as seemingly significant as this. Though loggers liked to boast they weren't much superstitious, they were like all other men in seeing omens and portents in the natural flow of life and its disruptions. Old Connecticuty's not coming would only be open to one interpretation. When Big John strode into camp —when the other men rode in on the logs—and discovered the tent was missing, the barrel of rum with the tin dipper was not waiting for them—not one of them would interpret it as anything but a bad sign.

He went about worriedly getting the great vats of tea steeping. The first of the logs had been going by singly, then in ones and twos, for some minutes before it occurred to Cobus that Big John and his carriage ought already to be in camp. He watched the logs a little worriedly because they did not seem to be thickening; they still sailed down in ones and

301

twos, with an occasional small bunching. It was queer, but it actually seemed to Cobus the logs were getting further apart, thinning instead of thickening, instead of jamming—and at the word *jamming* a cold seizure took hold of him, he felt as if his heart actually stopped beating.

He ran across camp shouting—he had no idea what—then frantically began trying to get the oxen hitched to the wagon again. He was shaking so badly that he could not manage the thick straps and buckles. Finally, desperate, he turned to the waiting men and said, "Has any of you got a horse I could borrow—Big John should have been in by now and—" Afterward he was sure it was the expression on his face, not the urgency of his words, that prompted one of them to fetch a big cob, an awkward lumpy animal, but Cobus was so overwhelmed with gratitude that he found himself babbling the most exaggerated thanks while he hoisted himself into the saddle and felt the horse settling heavily under him. Even if the animal could scarcely be prodded into a trot, it would still be faster than the oxen. It was big and heavy, but it was willing, and that was all Cobus cared about. Shouting encouragements, bending over to pat it in praise, he got the animal into a canter. The terrain was dangerous because of the mud; the horse had a better than even chance of taking a bad spill at this pace, but Cobus pressed it on. Light was failing fast; the first evening-feeding birds were already circling in the sky.

He had not gone more than a mile before he found the river clogged with logs. Far downstream in the dimming light he could see masses of timber, stratum after stratum of piled logs, crisscrossed crazily, jutting out at odd angles, upended, dripping, like thousands of wet pointing fingers. All up and down the line in descending darkness frantic figures darted, poking, prying, spearing at a log here, there, scampering up and down, trying to find the key log to dislodge; but even from here Cobus could see the men were working too close to shore to do any real good. Not that he blamed them; to venture out midstream in such a jam-up was to invite death. Near shore there was a chance—a man could always scurry to safety when he felt the mass moving under him—but out in the middle, for all the swiftness fear put into a man's feet, he had too far to run over too difficult a course to have much chance of making it.

The jam-up had occurred in an especially wide bend of the river, one in which he remembered from other years bubbling white water churning over glistening brown rocks, and he was pretty sure what had happened—a log had stuck on one of these rocks and caught; another caught against it and then another and another and another until quite quickly masses of logs were jammed together, piling up. To get the logs going again someone—more likely two or three men—would have to volunteer to go out in the middle and—

He beat the horse forward. He knew that honor made it imperative for Big John to be the first to volunteer, and he wanted to be beside him, no matter what the odds, scrambling over those logs, looking for the one that would break the jam-up. It seemed to Cobus that if he could keep beside Big John somehow his presence alone would be protection. He felt that so long as he was with the big man luck could not break against him.

He pushed the cob on desperately; it was now nearly totally dark and the scene had a black wash of disaster flowing over it. Ahead of Cobus a small figure was scampering from pile to pile, the long pole in his hand balancing him as he jumped from stack to stack of enormous jackstraws. As he reined the horse in, knowing he was too late, he heard someone shout, "Watch it, Big John," but the figure apparently had not heard, for it ran from mound to mound, up and down the great hills and valleys of piled-up logs.

Cobus heard a shout. The logs trembled. A great groan. A roar. They broke free.

He saw that one small figure dance high, run wildly, leap, skip, bounce like a puppet on a string, jerked up in the air, then rattled down, jerked up again, while the logs "hauled" all in a wild rush to run free. The figure stopped fleeing. Cobus could see it had made the only decision left, to try to ride one of the logs downstream; for in the massive shifting of the break-up there was not time, as he knew, for anyone, not even Big John, to scramble to safety.

The logs plunged headlong dizzily downstream, as if in the moment of that great loosening all the power they had accumulated in the jam had suddenly exploded and cascaded them furiously free. Big John passed Cobus, his feet moving in time with the vibrations of the log he was riding, balancing himself as the water turned the stick of wood under him, as another log bounced or jostled his log; Big John went by in a rush before Cobus could even give a cry of encouragement. He turned the cob watching, wondering how in the darkening night Big John could make his way.

All about Cobus the rush and roar of thousands upon thousands of logs making their way downstream shook the earth; even the blackening sky seemed to vibrate with that ceaseless moving; and in the darkness one lone man twirling and keeping time on one lone log, moving downstream in a great burst of fury, that single log twisting and turning and Big John dancing in time to its rhythm, moving over the waters of the Hudson at a dizzying speed downstream to Glens Falls and the end of the run.

It was the last Cobus ever saw of him. He never knew whether the waters claimed him, the logs dumped him, or some pile-up farther downstream sucked him under and ended forever the tobacco chewing, the monumental drunks, the barefoot saunters out into the autumn frost, and a friendship so deep that to say it had lasted ten years gave no inkling at all of the depth and intensity with which, at that final bend in the river, he watched Big John go and knew somehow that it was impossible he should ever make it safely to shore. But in a man's heart there was always hope. That was the essence, to have hope.

III

Having a local boy like Clyde Buttes so prominent down in Albany with the Big Men, and talk of his running for high state office, Attorney General maybe next time round, had put the little village in the limelight for the first time, not on any national scale of course—Clyde Buttes wasn't that important, not yet leastwise, but he was young, give him time, a lot of people said—but so far as the Empire State was concerned he was big apples. Every time Cobus went across to town, he was buttonholed and asked what his brother thought about the coming election, as if Tip's ideas were somehow sacrosanct, and though Cobus repeated time and again how Clyde thought Lincoln would win but the South wouldn't split—there was more talk in the air than action, in Clyde's opinion—the Landing people shook their heads half in affirmative and half in disbelief. There were an awful lot of men at the Landing who were sure war was going to come if the Rail Splitter got in.

Controversy might greet his words, but Tip—Clyde—was never mistaken for anything but a Great Man. He impressed the townspeople with his fancy clothes and his air of utter assurance; though he only came for a few scattered holidays during the whole year, he made such a figure that people talked about him the rest of the time. He was "theirs," the one small-town man who had made good in the wider world and his success was also in a way theirs, a proof that they *could* get out and make a place for themselves if they so chose. Tip stayed down in Albany attending to his affairs, actively engaged in politics, a staunch supporter of Lincoln, but somewhat (surprisingly) hedging on the slavery question. To Cobus there remained no doubts or compromises: to own a man, to have the power of life and death over him, was of all the things he could think of the one he considered completely and absolutely wrong. He could understand some killing, or even murder when it was a matter of life and death; he could even see how people, helpless, found themselves unfaithful (he never saw Ardis without understanding this); lying and cheating, deceit and disloyalty, he had seen so often they no longer much disturbed him; he understood (too well) the mechanics of bad faith and irresponsibility and the lack of principles of the man who did not honor his word; greed, graft, dishonesty, dishonor were all occurrences too frequent to be commented on or be upset by.

But not slavery.

Tip argued slavery was economically profitable for the South but not so for the North; it was a question of practicality—"live and let live" was his attitude, but whenever the issue of slavery came up, Cobus had a picture of millions of Williams in bondage, unable to exert any control at all over their lives, and the idea so sickened him that he turned away, shaking his head, as if the whole thing were beyond argument.

He wondered if one day, telling his grandchildren about his friendship with William, how he and the black man had spent hour after hour patiently training a great golden horse, of how close they had been, the bond of brothers, really, Cobus wondered if his sons would look at him in disbelief, thinking to themselves, Of course he's not telling the truth, it's just a *story*.

Like his own mother, their grandmother, being half-Indian. They wouldn't believe that either because she was dead and gone, no one decent was descended from an Indian; therefore, they weren't. Cobus thought of his mother sitting stony-faced in her chair braiding the long strands of tobacco, unable to move her legs, no one knew why, just wasting away with something inside that was eating up her muscles. The soreness had started in her legs; she was not a complainer and the first they all knew something was wrong was when she began limping. Still, she pushed their help away. She didn't want sympathy; all she wanted was to be left alone. Even talking about pain was not a part of how she saw you ought to act. Be silent and endure, it was the Indian code Cobus had witnessed in his father; now he was seeing it first-hand in his mother.

She started sitting a lot. She would sit, impassive, for hours staring ahead, her hands busy, busy, but the rest of her set in a flat stillness. He often had the feeling that if she turned sideways she would go out of existence; it was as if she were two-dimensional.

Then, in only a matter of time, Cobus noticed that her hands were not so busy; she was pushing them to keep them going, something was happening to her hands. At the end she had been only eyes, lying wasted in the upstairs room, never complaining, looking up at them with expressionless eyes in which, occasionally, it seemed to Cobus he trapped an expression of resentment—against those, he thought, who were well, who were up walking. She had been sick a long, long time. It was terrible how long it could take to die. The thought made him reexamine a lot of feelings he had. He had resented Big John's going so suddenly, so unexpectedly; but now he saw that perhaps this was better than the long slow deterioration of the body, with nothing left inside but the wondering mind. His mother had had months and months to ask herself again and again, Why is this happening to me? What have I done to deserve this? Why doesn't it *end?*

The last two days of her life she lay without opening her eyes. She looked quite dead, rigid under the blankets, with her face like a stone idol, engraved, it seemed, on bone; anyone looking at her would have said she was dead, but a faint whisper of breath went in and out the wasted, non-functioning body. When it stopped no one was ever quite sure. One hour she had been almost dead, the next quite gone. They buried her up back. The graveyard was growing. And somehow that thought comforted Cobus. It was as if the Butteses had put an unremovable mark on the land with all their graves, that their bodies had given back what they had taken from the strong soil, and that in the shadow of the mountains where they rested, they set a seal upon the place. *Theirs.*

Cobus looked at his children. Their Indian blood hardly showed; no one, looking at him, then looking at them, would make a direct blood connection. His children did not look Indian; they looked like everyone else, American—so that he felt a sense of estrangement even with his own children, he couldn't help it, no way to change it ever, it seemed, even marrying hadn't done it.

Cobus was thirty-two years old, substantially settled at the New House, with his wife and children, respected (he supposed, God knew he worked hard enough) but held apart. Half-Indian. If it hadn't been for Katherine, he supposed the aloofness would have been even more pronounced. People would overlook anything for Katherine.

Only man or woman I ever was really close to, really thought like, he considered, was Big John. Big John, he was another who would appear unreal to Cobus's grandchildren. In a few years lumbermen like Big John would be another vanished breed (like the Indians), figures of the fancy in a fairylike tale. He thought often, for instance, of how he had finally gone downstream to recover Big John's body several days after he had been swept away, how they had buried Big John in bark, hung his caulked boots from a branch of the tree under which he had been laid, the traditional marker of the dead lumberman. He remembered how, after the drive was all over, he had gone back and carefully carved Big John's name in the tree near the spot where Cobus thought the body had probably been flung high in the air, then sucked under, just around that bend where he had last laid eyes on him. The exact spot he would never know, but that didn't really matter. What mattered was carving a man's name in a tree, even if that didn't seem nearly enough of a tribute for a man like Big John. The tree would grow back together and obliterate the letters. He supposed that was why he insisted on naming his first son John.

The only person that summer after Big John's death who had been able to wrest him out of himself had been Ardis, and then she had only been able to do so briefly, for she was never up at the Buttes place much and he restrained his desire to go down to the Raymond house often because he understood too well what it was founded on. If Big John was the only man he would be close to, she was the only woman he would ever care about, he was certain, and she belonged to his brother. . . .

Yet now and again emotion overrode reason and he went. He took Tokay early of a morning, a fine ride in the cool hours, arriving in time for the late Raymond breakfast, at eight, not at the summer farmer's hour of four-thirty or five. While Cobus ate, his horse was walked, cooled, grained, rested; later in the morning Ardis would emerge in her riding clothes and work Tokay carefully over the old training course. It was never used now and weeds and brush were crowding it out; it looked unkempt and neglected, but she put Tokay properly through her paces as if the place were as fastidiously kept as when the house had been the center of a life that revolved around horses. Big John's death had been as destructive to the old man as it had to Cobus; he scarcely left his upstairs room anymore, getting up only to sit at the window and stare out at the lake. "Your father told me once his

308

father said the lake gets everything in the end. Maybe it's fitting it rounds off the end of so many lives. I got nobody close to me anymore—except you and Ardis. You more than her, boy. But forget I said it. An old man gets sentimental. I'm sorry she didn't take you. Yes, I've known all along. Didn't think I did, did you? Well, life's not fair to anyone— and that's that." He gazed out the window, silent for a second. "She's got a beautiful seat for a woman," he said. It was some kind of benediction.

"She's beautiful," Ardis would say admiringly when at last she reluctantly got down. "I wish I had something as fine— but it takes so much training, unless it's naturally there, you know, bred in the bone, as they say it is with Morgans. I've been thinking of getting one, Cobus—a Morgan—what do you think? People say they're gentle and you know Clyde won't let me have anything with a spit of spirit in it. Gentle but *very* beautiful," she said wistfully. "I do miss a decent horse so. Clyde doesn't understand. To him a horse is—well —just a horse."

"They've got thick necks. They're square-built. They're *work* horses."

She said nothing, looking down at her hands. He felt ashamed. "You hear tell what wonders they are," he said in a conciliatory tone, "I'd like to see one for myself."

"So would I. And you know, they're not really very far away. I mean, half a day's trip, we should come on some, and even if we didn't see what we wanted, to buy, I mean, well, we'd have seen, we'd know if they were all people say."

When she had begun saying *we* in that confidential, special voice that seemed to signify this was a part of their lives only she and Cobus could share with each other, he felt a lightness, a dizziness descend—the early rising, the long ride, and then he was never able to eat much breakfast, too nervous and excited, wrought up; now in the hot midmorning sun she was standing so close that he might have reached out and enclosed her in his arms, saying quite naturally *we* and planning out a trip for both of them, a trip that would take at least two days and would mean the close contact of a carriage, for she was not up to such a long, hard saddle ride.

Was it possible? No, of course not. Yes, yes, of course it was. Anything was possible just as anything could be unjust.

Scrubbed, soaped, slicked, he was down at the Raymond barn by seven the morning they were to start, a clear summer day, cool now with the dew still dazzling the eye where the sun struck the trees and arms of shrubbery leaves. He put Tokay in an empty stall, wondering how Ardis would hold up in bad heat; she was game, but there were no two ways about it, she was also delicate. He went with the stable boy, whom he did not like—no one could ever take William's place, but this raw boy was slipshod where he thought it didn't show and he could be sassy, too. Cobus was curt with him when he saw that the two carriage horses hadn't been curried down; he himself was so impatient to be off, and had already put in a good ride this morning, that he listened with something close to disbelief as the sullen excuse was given that down here work didn't start until eight, and the boy hadn't had his breakfast yet.

"Damn your breakfast. You rub these animals down within an inch of their lives and then you get your breakfast. It won't hurt you to do a little work before you eat one morning of your life. You knew Miss Ardis wanted to get an early start. What did you mean to do, keep her waiting?"

The boy made no answer as he began to brush the horse farthest away from Cobus, but there was a terrible look of rage on his face. "I'll do one myself if the carriage is in order," Cobus said. He went back and began inspecting it minutely; he didn't want any mishap because some small worn place had been overlooked. He felt his humor returning as he went over each section carefully and saw all was greased and well cared for, the coach itself neatly brushed out, the struts dusted, the whole thing in quite good order. "Well, that looks all right," he said to the boy. "I'll do the roan. Be sure to clean the feet, I don't want no stones makin' one of them lame."

He received no answer and mentally made a note to speak to Ardis about getting someone else. If she bought herself a decent horse, as apparently she had it in her head to do so, she ought to have a good man to look after it. This boy was impossible; it was all work to him, there was none of the love that was so necessary when you were working with animals. A sulker also communicated his bad temper to the animals; they picked up his moodiness. He was rather surprised Ardis hadn't sacked him before, but Cobus supposed it was because there weren't really any good animals in the stable anymore and her own interest had lapsed. Once a thing started to go, it went fast. Cobus remembered vividly the day he had set little Mason Raymond on Tokay and put the reins in his small hands. He thought of the look on the Old Man's face. Yes, he thought, we must find a really good horse and get that boy started. He and Ardis: they would do it, it would be a bond between them. To plan for such a thing was wrong, Cobus knew, in the worst sense of the word, but he couldn't help himself. She would be the only woman he ever wanted.

She came out and he took her hand—she had held it out with a smile, pleased with the day, with his early arrival, with the coming expedition. He held for a moment that warm soft thing and then, having to release it, looked at the pink lips telling him to come in and have some breakfast, it was all ready; she was so eager to eat and get away that he thought, Before this is over—but could not bring himself to finish the thought because maybe there wasn't any end, just wishing.

They made the first leg of the journey through the beginning opening of early morning: it was not a hard trip and the constant shifting of scenery from the high Adirondack foothills to the long low sliver of lake into the valley where the farms ran flat and safe over toward the canal and the beautiful Mettawee—whose name, Ardis said, always struck her as wrong for an American river, it ought to have been English from its sound—gave them an ever-present source of pleasant small talk. The horses jogged along, the hired girl who was chaperoning hung out gawking; the sun was warm and soothing, they were pressed together so that it seemed to Cobus there was no need to talk, their touching flesh communicated. They stopped on the banks of the Mettawee and ate a little lunch and the maid ran up and down the bank like a child, washing out the plates and splashing water on herself purposely. The lunch had come in a basket held between the maid's feet, some cold meat and buttered bread, pickles, fruit, a cider punch, and nothing had ever tasted quite as delicious to Cobus in his whole life. He hated to leave the rushes and the sound of the water and the look of Ardis with the sun on her semi-leaf-shaded face, her hands lying still and—the word was sweet—in her lap and a fly buzzing around her heat-haloed head.

They crossed over into Vermont by early afternoon. Cobus climbed down at the first farm feeling that luck was with him, as it seemed to have been from the start, Ardis holding up quite well in the heat, and now this man, slow in speech, with a strange, edgy accent, but as keen, Cobus saw right off, about horses as he himself was. Yeah-ess, said the man, he knew whair they wair Morgans, and as he went on, wearing down speech as if his words went across a great field in which

311

there were boulders and the words had to elongate and stretch themselves sideways to make it round those rocks, the voice hard and flinty, that of a man used to fields a plow had trouble getting over, Cobus felt an affinity for him, for all these Vermont farmers who struggled against terrain as hard as his was to get a little living out of the soil. They were made hard and tough by the life; he liked that.

Northways, a crooked finger pointed, up thair, he said, too-oard Mid-dle-burry, that's whair they kept thair best hoareasses, and he smiled, sharing with Cobus the secret of caring about the shape of back, shank, flank. Cobus thanked him and asked him if Middlebury was far. A good pee-ass, the man said, but stay-eight a-head-ed. You'll not missass the place, he said, hoarseasses as far as the ey-ey cane see.

They drove on into the afternoon, with short stops for the horses to rest. Cobus unhitched them and gave them water at the big log troughs along the road where spring water was piped down from the Green Mountain foothills. That Ardis had had enough traveling was apparent; she drooped beside him, eyes encircled by dark shadows, face worn white with fatigue. Yet she smiled back at him gamely, trying to hide how tired she was. He was on the lookout for an inn when they came to the top of a rise and suddenly, in front of them, as far as the eye could see, just as the man had said, there lay one field of horses after another, stretching from either side of the small dusty road.

He brought the carriage to a halt. She stood up, shading her eyes. A few of the horses raised their heads, curious over the disturbance the carriage had made. Forever after there would be imprisoned inside Cobus's mind this scene, every detail etched in order of its importance, the beautiful day, the beautiful animals, the beautiful girl standing beside him. What he was feeling, he knew, was not the feeling Ardis had, though she said the word *beautiful* with a catch in her voice. It was not, he saw, the scene that made so much difference, as an idea that made him feel queer, as if there were no real worlds at all, but only many many millions of individual ones, each cast in the eyes of its perceiver, as if "the world" did not exist at all, but only bits and pieces, parcels and snatches seen and sieved through endless eyes and minds. And hearts. His heart was what illuminated the scene; it was so full of love and gratitude.

She sat down and Cobus raised the reins lightly; the horses started up, briskly now they sensed the end of their day's work. Below, in the hollow of the hills, a farm waited, low, white, rambling, with big red barns and a long stretch of white board fence with corrals.

"You're all dust," Ardis said. "I must be, too. Give me the picnic basket, Mary Emma, so I can wipe a little off. We don't want to look like a couple of gypsies come thieving."

A man was coming up from the barn, wiping his hands on the sides of his coveralls, looking at them not maybe curiously but at least questioningly. "We was directed here from over near Fair Haven," Cobus told him. "Man down there said you had Morgans."

"You lookin' for a horse?"

"My sister-in-law is," Cobus said quickly, wanting to get the situation straight from the start.

"Morgan's the name, we come right down the line from the first one had that little bay." He pronounced it bay-ay. "Katherine Ann," he yelled up toward the house, "we got visitors want to see a horse." He turned to Cobus. "You get down and get the kinks outta your bones and have something cold to drink and then we'll look the horses over. You best stay the night. There's 'comadations up the road a piece, but ain't worth the drive to see 'em, and don't think sleepin' in my house," Martin Morgan said quickly, "obligates you none because it don't and what's more I don't sell a horse to a man—or a woman—I don't size up as right. You and the lady will have to ride before you buy. If I can't match a man— or a woman—to a horse, I don't sell," Martin said flatly, "in which case I charge for the victuals you et and the bed you slept in, and I ain't out nuthin' and you don't need to feel you might be under some kind of obligation."

His grandfather and Old Man Raymond—Lord, how at home they would have been. "This is Mrs. Buttes, my brother's wife. This is Mr. Morgan, Ardis. He's goin' to put us up—"

"Yes, I heard," she said, smiling. "It's awfully nice of you—I liked the way you put it. Cobus—" She bent her head in his direction— "he rides well, real well—you'll see. He has the touch, my grandfather used to say, and I like to ride, but I've been—sick." She paused. "I want something good, but not *too* good, if you know what I mean. I want spirit but I don't want to spend my time fighting every inch of the way. You don't want a battle when you're older," she said, smiling a little, looking, Cobus thought, sort of sad. What did she mean "older"? She wasn't old. *He* wasn't old.

"You get in your duds and let me try the horses out on you. I know my animals better than you." He was smiling, a small smile, but it was he, not Ardis, who was going to run this show. She gave in graciously, with a little laugh. Cobus could see in her face, though, how tired she was. "She ought to rest before she rides," he said, turning to Morgan and addressing him as if it were man to man, almost as if Ardis weren't right between them.

"Too hot to ride now anyway. Wait 'til after supper, when it cools down. My daughter'll show you to your room, you lie down—"

"Mary Emma," Ardis called, and the girl got out awkwardly and came toward them, a flat-chested green country girl nothing would ever turn out properly. "She's sort of to look after my things," Ardis tried to explain. "She's good in the kitchen, too. Since we're putting you to the extra trouble of three more people to feed, I hope your wife will let her do what needs to be."

"T'ain't my wife. She's passed on, twelve years ago. The sugar. Buried her on her birthday. Rained. My daughter manages now, with a girl we got from down to town. I reckon they'll make out all right. Nothin' fancy, but what we give is usually fillin'. I like meat," he said with conviction. "After a good day's work a man needs meat."

The girl in the kitchen, her sleeves rolled back to expose strong brown arms, was working with dough. At a table behind her a small, dwarfed creature—Cobus at first took her for an overlarge child—was peeling potatoes. He was a little stunned: the girl with the dough was so big and strapping and beautiful, so full of health; the one with the curls of potato skins dropping from the bright blade of her knife was so small and misshapen and ugly. He had always felt the maimed and misfortunate ought to have special dispensation; yet it worked out just the opposite, more often than not, they seemed punished for afflictions instead of pitied.

"I can't leave go of the kneadin' for jest a minute, Pa. You want to show them up—the man and his wife can use Ma's old room—"

"It's his sister-in-law, Kate."

"Oh," she said, slapping the dough down and looking disconcerted. "Well, in that case put her in Ma's room and give him the one at the end of the hall. There's no sheets, but won't take no time to put some on."

"We don't want to put you to any trouble," Ardis began.

"No trouble at all," the girl said emphatically. "Pa and me look on guests as treats. Your girl there—" Apparently Mary Emma's presence had also been taken in—"she can do the sheets, Pa'll show her where the linen's kept. There," she said, banging the dough down, quickly dividing it into four equal portions without even glancing down. "Let me jest wash my hands, cover this, and I'll show you."

Cobus judged she was maybe twenty-two or -three, not thin and wiry like her father, but filled out with flesh round and full and the color of an apricot. She wiped her hands, stomped smiling across the kitchen toward Ardis; she seemed full of the whole pleasure of life for being able to move around on earth. Next to her Ardis looked small and thin and weak. The trip was hard on her, Cobus thought, harder than she let on.

Martin Morgan had a big brown dusty bottle in his hand. "We'll be wanting mugs," he said to his daughter.

"There's cooled tea, too," she said in the direction of Ardis, "if you'd rather." She slapped four big mugs down, went back and returned with two more. "Been berryin' this morning," she remarked. "Lucky, wasn't it, almost as if I'd knowed company was comin'. There's *two* pies. And a *good* roast, Pa," she said, laughing. "Now, what's it to be," she asked herself, "beer or tea? Guess I best stay with the tea. I drink any of that beer this time of afternoon, Pa, there's no tellin' when supper'd ever appear. My, it's nice to have *folks*," she said, her face shining with delight, as if the extra work they would make for her was one of the nicest things that could happen. "I've a mind," she said to her father, "to drink the beer after all." But she poured two beers for Cobus and her father, then poured out four tumblers of tea, giving the first to Ardis, the next to Mary Emma, the third to the dwarf, taking the last herself. "Martha can't speak," she explained, "or I'd have introduced you. She was born— bad in the ears." She bent down and took the knife from the strange fat pudgy hand, moved the mug of tea toward it, smiling. The dwarf looked up at her. Whether she spoke or not, Cobus saw, she and Katherine Morgan communicated. He felt strangely ashamed: an act of tenderness often did that to him.

What was left of the large roast lay like a small wizened fist on the plate. They had gone through most of the fresh bread, too, and two large platters of snap beans laced with bits of brown crisp bacon, two bowls of potatoes, and most of the two pies. Now they were ready to ride.

Ardis had changed to plain everyday horse clothes. They were worn, a testimony to the fact she was serious, not some

315

fancy society woman on a whim. She still looked tired and strained. She had eaten little but been very complimentary— too complimentary, Cobus had thought at one point. The Morgan girl had flushed more in irritation, Cobus decided, than appreciation at Ardis's repeated praises. "It's just plain fare," she had insisted. "We didn't know company was coming," and she looked at Ardis's half-finished plate as if to say, If it's so good, why don't you *eat?*

She too had changed. Her outfit startled Cobus. She was wearing—well—what looked like men's clothes. Pants, a shirt, vest, long scuffed black boots. Apparently she was going to show the horses.

Mary Emma and the dwarf were left to clean up. The air was still, hot, heavy; it seemed to fall down on them like Vermont marble, but neither the girl nor her father took notice. They were gathering up halters and lines, making rapid comments to one another, calling horses' names back and forth, agreeing on some, disputing others, arguing over one in particular, Bay Boy. "He's not broke proper," the girl kept saying stubbornly. "He's not ready, not a woman's horse, never mind he's been altered."

"I didn't say we was goin' to sell him, I jest said we should show him."

By the angry line of Katherine Ann Morgan's mouth, Cobus saw she was dead set against the idea. "Showin' him puts the others to disadvantage," she said.

"All right, bring down Bonnie and Princess. We'll start easy and work up," he explained to Ardis. "Bonnie—she's a good trustworthy one. You can walk under her legs and she won't move—though I wouldn't recommend doing it," he said, sort of smiling. The prospect of showing off his animals had brought a flush to his face, that and the beer, no doubt. He'd drunk through dinner and he was standing at the fence now with a mug in his hand, drinking and sweating.

The girl opened the gate and walked out into the pasture. "Wind's agin' me," she said. "But I'll try callin' 'em down." She raised her voice and began to shout. "Bon--nie, Prin*cess.* Bon—*nie, Princess!*" Cobus watched her walking around hollering, big and sure of herself, loud-voiced, going through all that heavy heat on top of that heavy meal as if none of it bothered her. Cobus began to feel tired himself; he sympathized with Ardis, leaning against the fence as if even the effort of breathing were a burden to her.

"Bonnie, Prin*cess,*" that strong voice came back to them. "Bonnie, Prin*cess,*" and Cobus felt the animals, once they heard her, would have no choice but to be drawn in. What could hold out against such a will? Katherine Ann Morgan had stopped pacing, stood waiting, but her voice went on in its incessant summons. "Bonnie, Prin*cess*, Bonnie, Prin*cess*. . . ."

Two horses stepped into a high quick trot—and Cobus felt something tighten in his chest as the two picked up speed and he saw for the first time the famous, short, swift Morgan gait, low to the ground, exceedingly compact, very fast, those short strides covering an immense amount of ground, however.

She had finally and mercifully left off calling, was simply standing, waiting, not patiently like any other human being would, but shifting her weight back and forth restlessly, as if even that small amount of having to wait were too much for all the animating energy burning inside; she had to keep moving, if only in place.

She patted one, put the halter and line on the other, and came back toward them, first at a jog, then a run, one horse trotting rapidly behind her, the other, the untethered one, breaking into a canter and passing her. Cobus wondered why in the furnace of this early evening oven and at that pace she didn't drop dead. He didn't believe a human heart existed that could stand such punishment, but when she came up to them, running full speed, she was laughing with happiness, her hair flying, her eyes full of delight. He had heard Morgans went small, but the girl's exuberance seemed to diminish that nearly thousand pounds of flesh beside her until it seemed like some plaything, a pony perhaps for a child, but no horse a man would sit astride.

"Open the gate," Katherine Morgan cried. "I'll saddle her out there."

Cobus fumbled with the latch while she fidgeted impatiently, smoothing down the horse, making sure the hairs lay flat so that they would not bunch up under the saddle and cause a rubbing, a sore. When she came through the gate, she bounded, the horse almost on top of her. She bent over as she passed him and grasped a brush that lay by the fence and was stroking the horse rapidly over the back even as she ran along. She took the horse full circle, then dropped the brush again, reached over and grasped a saddle off the fence and swung it expertly on the animal's back. "You hold rein," she said (incorrectly since the horse was still haltered and lined), "and I'll saddle. She blows up," Katherine Ann Morgan complained, tugging at the cinch with all her strength, "but I know a trick or two myself. Haul her around," she shouted at Cobus while she was still hanging onto the girth, running beside the horse, tightening it as Cobus turned the animal around. "Whoa—there you are, done to the right notch without any to-do at all. Pa, give me the bit, will you?" She grabbed the halter and unfastened it, slipped it around the horse's neck, holding the halter like a line, and without looking, took the bridle and slipped it all in a single movement into the horse's mouth and up over the head. "Good girl," she cried, slapping the animal on the neck. "Good Bonnie." Then, before Cobus really saw it happen, the girl was on the animal's back, snapping, "All right, let her loose," and Katherine Ann Morgan was away, giving the mare only a brief moment to walk out the kinks and adjust to the rider on her back, then urging her faster and faster until the hooves, stepping more and more briskly, pounded the hard summer earth; the horse swung downfield and began to do figure eights, half halts, change of lead, flying shifts, dead stops, walks in slow, even, then fast step, a regular canter, an extended one, and finally a full gallop, whirling at frightening speed away from them and into the glare of the heat.

"She'll kill that horse," Cobus heard himself saying.

The father took his time answering. "Won't hardly be winded," he answered at last. "Morgans got stamin-nah."

They certainly do, Cobus thought, half in admiration, half in exasperation, both at the horses and the people. A flying flash downfield told him the girl was heading back; they arrived, girl and horse, hardly winded. Katherine Morgan sprang down. "Jest warming her up," she said to Ardis.

Ardis came forward slowly. She had been trained by her grandfather to move precisely and carefully. Never get on a horse, Cobus remembered the Old Man saying, until you check *all* the equipment's in order. Cobus was proud that despite the impatient girl beside her Ardis looked at the way the bit was set, running her hand between the horse's cheek and where the bar was attached to be sure it wasn't too tight, testing the throat latch to see that it was all right, checking the girth to see the hairs under weren't matted; then quietly, composedly, she said, "I'd rather ride sidesaddle, if you don't mind. It's what I'm used to." In all the haste and excitement, this was the first time Cobus realized the girl had been riding astride, like a man. It was absolutely the last straw.

Then suddenly he saw Ardis's exaggerated praising of the dinner and her almost full plate returned to the sink in a new light; he thought also he understood the girl's deliberately coming down in that man's get-up and flying 'round the field like a wild woman as calculated affronts. But why? What reason was there for this animosity between them? He was as certain of it as he was certain of his own perplexity in the face of it, even though outwardly they were being as polite and nice as could be to one another.

"Reckon Ma's old saddle up to the barn would serve, Pa?"

"Needs oilin'—"

"No, I kept it oiled along with everything else. No use lettin' good leather go dry even if we never use it." With a toss of her head and a stretch of her long legs, the girl ran toward the barn. "You unsaddle, Pa," she called back to them. Behind her, on the back porch, Cobus saw Mary Emma and the dwarf watching. He didn't blame them because at that instant he was absolutely sure the whole evening was going to turn into quite a performance.

Katherine Ann ran (what else? Cobus thought, she's not going to walk this whole day, nor tomorrow neither if any of us lasts) and swung the sidesaddle up on Bonnie's back. It was in perfect condition, cleanly oiled; she had kept it that way—there had not been time even at the rate of speed with which she was moving to run over it and give it a swift polishing in the barn. He had then and there his first indication of who actually ran the farm, looked after and trained the horses, kept the equipment in order, mucked out the stalls, did all the disagreeable, time-consuming work of the stable, things Ardis had never even dreamed a woman could do. He knew, too, that unless Ardis understood this she hadn't a chance in the world of holding her own.

Cobus turned to Morgan. "Your daughter do most of the work with the horses?" he asked in a slow, careful, precise voice that was meant to be a warning to Ardis.

"AY-eeh," Morgan said with pride. "I dassn't pitch a fork of manure."

But Ardis was too busy settling into her seat to pay attention, moving her body slightly but perfectly to adjust to the strange saddle. On her face was the absorbed look of someone intent on one thing and one thing alone; she had not heard or, if she had heard, gave no significance to the remarks.

Cobus stepped up to her, a terrible need to protect her in his heart. She was up against something she didn't understand —he wasn't even sure *he* understood—but if this girl bested her, she would never be the same in his eyes again; and

319

he was a man desperately determined to protect his image. "Ardis?"

She looked down. His voice had been quite sharp. "Ardis, Miss Morgan works *in the stable* with their horses, so of course she—well, she *knows* them." What he was trying to tell her was not to expect too much from herself at first, to work slowly at putting the horses through the same paces Katherine Ann had, something honor and whatever female pride the hell was at stake she was bound to have to do, to equal, but better to excel.

Her face closed him out; like a shut and locked door, it seemed to say, Stay out, you have no business in this. She lifted her hands lightly, scarcely moving the reins; but the horse would have felt that small signal, the light touch of good hands that can direct an animal without others even observing; the mare moved forward, but somewhat hesitantly, recognizing there was a strange rider on her back and going, Cobus knew with a flash of certainty from his long years around horses, to give her trouble right off, to test her and see if that strange rider couldn't be unseated or at least unsettled. At that first moment of rebellion—which a less experienced rider wouldn't even have recognized but which Ardis sensed and interpreted correctly in an instant—Ardis stiffened her back, using the force of her muscles to propel the animal forward. The mare tossed her head.

A horse ridden by a good rider, a horse properly put to the aids—obedient and willing to answer the pressure of legs, hands, back, and voice of the rider—did not give this sign of defiance, did not disturb the tranquil picture of horse and rider moving as one entity. But Ardis looked completely unperturbed; she was holding herself more erect, however, in readiness; she knew what was on the animal's mind, though she gave no sign she did. At that camouflage, Cobus felt a tremendous pride in her; she might just beat this audacious, impossible girl at her own game, on her own horse. Or horses, he thought with a sinking heart. For even if Ardis mastered Bonnie, there would yet be another—and another—whole fields full of horses. And Ardis would have to compete on them all; she could not settle for the first horse she tried. No real horse person *ever* did that.

The endlessness of a nightmare that went on forever stretched before Cobus's imagination.

Suddenly the horse balked, began backing, crow-footing from side to side, shaking her head, as if to say, This rider won't manage *me*.

Ardis had two choices—to react immediately, sternly, try to force her will on the animal or to wait a moment, let the animal begin almost to make itself foolish with all these shenanigans and then try to take it in hand. Cobus would have elected the first, brute force, but he was a man; in a contest between a stubborn thousand-pound animal who had been loitering in the fields all day and a hundred-and-ten pound woman worn out by a long ride on rutted roads, the outcome was not even doubtful. All the advantages were with the animal. Sensibly Ardis simply sat quietly in her seat, the horse's prancing and backing seeming not to ruffle her at all. The mare paused in puzzlement, trying to decide what new devilment she could spring; Ardis said in a firm, absolutely-sure-of-itself voice, "Are you ready to settle down, now?" and gave the mare a good crack across the flanks with her riding crop to show she meant business.

The animal shot out in surprise and indignation into a full furious gallop. She seemed to go from nothing to everything in one instant. With his breath stopped and his heart in his throat—for Ardis was used to her obedient Albany plodder—he watched the mare carry her straight out in the open, where presumably the horse could get the bit between her teeth and —but Ardis was already reining Bonnie around in a wide circle; he understood in immense relief the tactics she was using, letting the horse run in an ever-diminishing circle until she could no longer run away from her; at the end of that time the mare would be spent, ready for the work she would be put to—and put to it well, if Cobus judged Ardis's mood accurately at all. Old Man Raymond had been a thorough and inspired teacher.

In back of him he heard the Morgan girl say somewhere between contempt and admiration, "Well, there's one thing you can say for her, she ain't just along as a passenger," and he understood the contest on this horse had ended in a draw.

Cobus thanked God for darkness; it brought an end of sorts to the whole ghastly affair. They had each ridden three horses: Katherine Ann had been thrown once and Ardis unseated twice (those words, Cobus felt, suited the actions of what had happened as well as the personality of the combatants involved), but Ardis had held her own, better than her own since she was dealing with strange animals.

Still it was a sorry business at best. Ardis was worn to a frazzle (and there was still the morning and more horses—endless horses—to be faced). Katherine had also apparently gotten a bad jolt on her grounding. She wasn't running around any more. She was walking, carefully and painfully, one of those walks that said her spine was killing her. Cobus himself was a wreck; he had begun to believe one of them would be killed before admitting defeat. The only one enjoying the whole spectacle was Morgan himself, ladled over the fence drinking mug after mug of beer—he had gone back to the house and brought four big bottles out when he saw the way things were going—and he went on burping and swilling contentedly into twilight, quite drunk by darkness. Cobus had to half-haul all three of them up to the house, the two "helpers" having disappeared shrieking the first time one of the horses reared and dumped Ardis backasswards over its hind quarters and under its hooves. Why she wasn't ground to broken-bone bits, Cobus never understood; but the horse, once having disposed of the nuisance of her being on its back, had daintily picked its way over Ardis, leaving her humped over, a brown blotch on the ground. The wind had been completely knocked out of her, but she pushed herself up on all fours, gasping, and managed to keep consciousness, an act of pure will that left Cobus breathless with admiration.

He was torn by the twin impulses of running to her rescue and leaving her huddled up, sucking for air, afraid if he went to help she would turn on him. In that moment of hesitation she managed somehow to get herself up to a crouching position and his decision was made for him by the look on her face. She was absolutely determined to go on. Katherine Morgan had hold of the horse, and eager for her coming triumph (this was before *she* had come to grief), she had stood dancing impatiently by, waiting for Ardis to admit she had had enough; yet, after what seemed several years of silence, Ardis struggled to her feet, shook herself, dislodging dust, and got back on. Then she gave the animal the worst wallop Cobus had ever seen her administer any animal, she who always counseled loving patience and understanding tender care. She had lost her crop somewhere in the spill; she took both reins and brought them simultaneously down across the right side of the horse's neck; the horse reared but Ardis hung on, and then one of those wild gallops and ever-enclosing circles to gain control commenced for what seemed to Cobus the thousandth time. It was this same horse—Spider—who was smarting from the object lesson Ardis had given it, who wrought its revenge on the Morgan girl.

She had changed saddles (she had given Ardis the "honor"

of riding first) and leapt confidently up, all smiles and seeming carelessness, when, before she had properly adjusted the double reins (it was a horse that obviously needed curb and snaffle) the horse bolted, bucking at the same time, and sent her flying up in the air, a tangle of reins, hands clutching for the mane, feet entangled in stirrups and the saddle blanket, which had come loose, and sent her a good fifteen feet through the air to land flat-backed on that hard earth, every bone in her body banged or bruised. She lay as inert as Ardis had a few minutes before, but her father, drinking beer under the whirling birds overhead sucking in their evening meal of insects, stayed propped against the fence, interested, but unmoved, like some spectator at a brutal and bloody event who luckily knows none of the participants. When his daughter finally got to her feet, Ardis was holding the horse; but she had the decency, Cobus saw, to keep her face absolutely expressionless. Not a word passed between the two women as Katherine limped back to the saddle. By this time Cobus was perfectly prepared for the animal to start rolling on the ground in order to pulverize any rider who was foolhardy enough to get on. Instead it settled down. So much for ever knowing what went on in the mind of a horse, Cobus thought. Or a woman. Because although night was approaching and this was only the second of the two horses to be "tried," they went on, glassy-eyed, to a third. Some semblance of sense must have communicated itself from Katherine Ann's aching bones to her stubborn brain because the third, again a gelding, was relatively tractable. Still he succeeded in getting Ardis off balance; she was too tired to right herself, having lost all power of control over her body; she slipped slowly, like something poured, from the saddle and slid down, landing on her feet, but obviously done in, there was no strength in her to get back on. Yet she did. She hung on through *ten* more minutes of monkeyshines and then called it quits. It was so dark that all Cobus could really see were the small shadowy shapes of the three people and the larger one of the horse, and overhead a "dry" moon, a quarter of a circle glowing pearly light laid in a sky so that if water were poured in it it would spill out. Two half-dead women and a drunken man: *some night,* Cobus told himself, as he shepherded them, limping and lurching, up to the house.

Old Man Morgan, the only person Cobus might possibly have envied, whom drink should have put into the lovely oblivion of sleep, proved not so unmoved as he had pretended out by the rail; instead of the sweet death of sleep, he went on about fifteen minutes after they had all disappeared into their bedrooms, lurching down the hall, and Cobus listened to him sock his way through the downstairs where, grinding out the door, he bumbled beneath Cobus's window and proceeded to retch up his insides. It was a dry moon, indeed. More went on here than met the eye. As Cobus lay on his bed in blank, numb despair, Martin Morgan throwing up in the bushes was proof enough he had not been totally immune to the dangers of that day. It seemed unlikely he had a weak stomach for spirits. A Vermonter like Morgan would know his capacities and pride himself on holding himself within them; pacing, it was called; but when a man's emotions got mixed up with his drinking, the whole syndrome was thrown off. He didn't just get sick and stop; he went right on pouring the stuff out of him until it was all gone. Cobus had to endure the agony of hearing under his window the dry heaves of the desperately ill drunk for ten or fifteen minutes more.

Some time in the night he must have dozed off—still with the groans of Morgan's misery in his ears—for when he was next conscious of sound, it was of a sharp, insistent rapping on his door. "Breakfast in twenty minutes," the Morgan girl shouted through the closed door and then he heard the uneven gait of one lamed going down the hall. She was not up rested, recovered, and running; that at least was to the good.

He went downstairs in dread. Everyone else was at the kitchen table. He sat down, nodding, not knowing what to say except "Good morning," in return for which he received a smile from Ardis, cheerful enough considering the conditions; an agonized nod from Morgan, who seemed to be hung this morning over the steaming edge of a coffee cup; no acknowledgement whatsoever from the distaff side of the Morgans, busily directing between stove and table the two serving girls in the passage of one of those country breakfasts that can kill even the well—great slabs of ham, platters of eggs, stacks of flapjacks, the leftover pie, bread, butter, and big pitchers of milk and coffee. The notion that anyone who had puked up his insides as poor Morgan had the night before trying to put down pancakes with syrup and pieces of pie wrung Cobus's heart. But he sank down on the long solid bench with best wishes for them all; he just couldn't see how all the good will in the world would do any of them any good or help him get down his own ham and eggs. "Well," Katherine Ann Morgan said, slamming down on a chair at the end of the table, spearing a slab of ham, "Pa," he looked up with dry, dead eyes, "I think we found ourselves someone to show Bay Boy." She turned to Ardis, magnanimously conceding defeat. "He's the only *real* horse on the place, and I always said I'd keep him myself, but there's a new colt—" Katherine Ann Morgan's eyes grew misty—"may even beat him, and if anybody should have Bay Boy, you should. I want to tell you, I never in my life saw such a little frailly woman ride the way you did. I mean, you take someone like me, big, with the weight, that's one thing; but the small ones, they can't really bring the pressure to bear. It was a pleasure to watch you with those horses," Katherine Ann Morgan said and she meant it. Her whole face shone with appreciation. She was *glad* Ardis had beat her. Apparently sometime during the night, with a clarity, rationality, and a disinterested objectivity Cobus wouldn't have believed possible in a woman, and with a generosity and unselfishness he would almost never discover in a man, the Morgan girl had weighed both performances and found hers wanting; the terrible directness and honesty of her nature, that awful vitality that sent her running and burning through life, compelled her now to confess she was second best; but that same straightness allowed this to be done without envy or malice. She was happy for Ardis—her face showed that only too plainly—she admired her and this girl looked on her stronger body, her larger fund of vitality, as unfair in a competition with someone who was as knowledgeable but whose body was weaker. Justice—it was the only word Cobus could think of, he had no real word to cover the thing that had prompted Katherine Morgan to take on defeat voluntarily and graciously—justice had left her no choice but to tell Ardis she *should* be the winner even if further struggle might show she wasn't; therefore, there would be no further struggles, she would abdicate from the contest, the crown would automatically be Ardis's.

It was a terrible thing to have done to *him*. He had wanted the romance of being in love, not the responsibility of loving. In the face of the ham, the eggs, the flapjacks, he might just as well, for all he had contributed thus far in his life to the course of human feeling, have never existed. These women were real; the old man was real. Everyone in the room— even the dwarf, even Ardis's snivelling little maid—seemed real, but he seemed no more than a figment of his own mind. As a person he was nothing, he thought, nothing, stumbling to his feet, mumbling something in the way of an apology, thinking only that he had to get out of this room with its two women whose very presence amounted to his having to continue to confront himself. He was empty enough at the moment not to want to make any more discoveries.

But women *never* let a man alone. With anxious eyes, Katherine Morgan took his escape as an aversion to her cookery. "Don't you *like* it?" she asked, painfully unhappy at the sight of his unfinished plate.

Cobus plopped down, sentenced to suffer more maple syrup, another heaping of ham piled up on his plate. What whim was it with women that assumed that if a man ate well all went well with his life? The dwarf, however, eyeing him from across the room with that strange dazed look of the dumb, seemed to comprehend despair. Unable to speak but compelled, he saw with a sort of horrified fascination, to identify with the suffering of others, she began to wave her small misshapen arms in the air; her eyes were wide with decision. The Morgan girl turned her attention to the pantomime. The dwarf was acting out Cobus's dilemma; yes, he liked the food, but no, he couldn't eat it. He was somehow sick.

"I'm so sorry," she was saying in genuine compassion, "I didn't know you weren't feeling well—you were ·sick last night, weren't you? I thought I heard you—"

Nobly, Cobus protected her father.

"Why don't you go out on the porch and we'll bring you some tea. It's a beautiful morning and fresh air—fresh air and hot tea," she said with complete belief, "can work wonders. I'm sorry I didn't notice, but I guess I was just too excited about Bay Boy—" Concern made her almost cluck over him as she shepherded him out to the back porch where true to her promise a glorious summer morning was plundering the earth of ugliness. This woman, all that furious energy: beside her Ardis no longer seemed so desirable. For the first time in—how long, ten, fifteen years?—he saw Ardis with the eyes of the outsider, a pleasant pretty girl already worn away by wifehood, the compromises, the miscarriages, the concealment of her husband's weaknesses from her own eyes, the eyes of others. *Nice,* that was the word people would always use to describe Ardis, and it was right, she was nice. But Cobus didn't want a nice wife; he wanted a strong, fighting woman who would give him as good as she would get, someone who could stand up to him and even best him when he needed being bested. Ardis probably was fitted for the role of the wife of a Great Man, but up on a farm—*impossible*. How was it he had never seen this before?

He looked at the perplexed girl in front of him. What a creature to give to the mountains; she would give them a punishing—and love every minute of it. Her love of life would be the salvation of him yet; she would not tolerate self-pity for the "wasted years" nor listen with any sympathy at all to his complaints about the past and being born with double blood. What was ahead was important; the past was over and done with. He wondered if she would even bother to try to redeem it. God knew *what* she would do, for at that very moment she was looking at him—for the first time sizing him up, he saw, as possible suitable husband material, so evidently his own thinking had communicated itself to her and he was no longer just the man who had tagged along with the woman who wanted to buy a horse, but a person in his own right, someone she must reckon with.

"Buttes," she said, as if taking the name out and turning it over for flaws. "Seems to me it has a familiar sound after all."

"It's probably my brother you heard of," Cobus said. "He's one of the big-wigs down to Albany. I'm the one stayed on the farm. We got a farm 'cross from the Landing. Up on Federation Lake."

"That's hard land to work, mountain pasture and all."

"Well, it ain't like this," he said, looking down the rolling fields.

"You farm, that all?"

"We keep a couple of horses, some cows, pigs in the fall." She looked disgusted. "*Good* horses," he said. "When I ride over for Ardis's horse, you can see for yourself." Her eyes widened. "I'd like it," Cobus said, "if maybe you'd ride Ardis's horse back with me, see for yourself—that is, if you had a mind to come, of course." She said nothing, but he could see she was turning it over. There were a lot of possibilities if you had imagination and one thing he felt he could say with absolute assurance was that she was a woman who knew how to take a thing apart and really look at it. A born examiner, if ever he saw one. All the troublemakers and doers were, like the kind who stayed up late baking that extra loaf of bread with which to get ahead of their neighbors. He could see the reflection of the candlelight by which she did her dreaming at night reflected behind the daylight eyes turned on him now, warm and brown and full of female investigation. He was sure his cause would have been helped a good deal more if only he'd been born better looking. But maybe not. Maybe the Indian part of it would present a challenge to her, and clearly any challenge she saw in him would weigh in his favor. She was the kind who liked to win over insurmountable odds. If people said it would be an impossible match, no marriage at all for a girl like her to make, then she'd gallop right to the altar to prove them all wrong. Everything everyone else would count against him she would total in his favor. A very remarkable girl: but how could you say such a thing without sounding like a fool?

The beautiful bay trotted toward them, shaking its small but perfectly balanced head, its little foxlike ears alert, thrust forward, listening; the tail arched proudly, sweeping back long, full, and glossy. The small size of the animal contrasted doubly with its broad breast, the extreme muscularity, the powerful sloping shoulders, the short, sure-footed trot: a perfect Morgan. If horses were in her blood, how could she bring herself to part with such an animal? Then he remembered her remark about the new colt. She was a creature who lived for the future; the past—this animal with it—had fulfilled its function; now she was ready to go on to other, newer adventures.

She was dancing up and down impatiently beside him, shouting the horse's name into the still air, disturbing again the lazy leaden mood of the larkspur and honeysuckle and goldfinches hovering over the high grass. Energy burned in her so fiercely that he felt the flame. She had forgotten him, forgotten the mellowed mood of the morning, pushed aside everything but her excitement at that strong, sinewy creature bearing down on her with its breathtaking beauty. Nowhere else in the world would you find an animal come out of plow stock like this and in no other land in the world would the peasant stock produce a girl like this. For the first time in his life Cobus understood how a man could love his own country fiercely, protectively, with something so strong in him that it lifted his heart to heights his mind could not conceive. He was able, too, in that instant to identify at last with the fierce thrust of energy and determination that had forced his grandfather through that long terrible trail he had cut through the dense mountain land to find his place on earth, his farm, his mountain, his lake, his particular piece of this country; to understand too the restlessness, that same spirit of push that had sent his countrymen further and further West, in the first wagon trains cross-country to find their part of the new land; and he saw with such finality that it would never be forgotten, the love of the lake and farm his own father had, so that nothing else was really important in his life; and he began, Cobus, in that moment, to seek inside himself a kindred feeling to the world in which, until that moment, he had moved as something of a stranger, a man who had borrowed the longings of others. His grandfather, his father, Old Man Raymond, Clyde Burroughs, William, Big John, the men in the woods—they had been figures to father the uncertain child who had yet to sort out his own needs; but he was a man now—or rather, he wished to be a man now, to stand on his own, with his own structure to sustain him, knowing beyond all possibility of doubt that this girl laughing and stroking the bay horse in front of them, leaning across the fence and presenting its beautiful head to them for affection and approbation, was the beginning of the building: the girl and the horse. Where they would go and what they would do, he did not know; they who were so different and who, because of this curious feeling between them, must destroy what had held them in some sort of security and strike out for a new life.

Cobus reached up and stroked the horse, calming it. The girl's nervousness, her uncertainty and excitement had communicated itself to the animal; Cobus had now to soothe both. As a man it was his obligation to put her to rights inside herself, to calm the hesitancies, the uncertainties, the doubts.

He moved slowly so that he was alongside her, barely touching her. He stroked the horse and he willed with every pore in his body that the girl be calm, too. But it was not calmness that communicated itself to her but a terrible thrust of longing which he could not submerge, as if, as he touched her, his flesh moved on its own, in spite of his mind, blindly groping for its own satisfactions.

His hands were on her, hers on him; then they were running, leaving the horse behind, through meadows, over a fence, until under the thick trees, in shadow, they lay on the ground unfastening the stiff, resisting garments that cut them off from one another, until, naked, on the flooring of green, he was able to drive inside her the seed that cried out to bring forth a son that would link their futures forever on this earth in the passing on of flesh to flesh.

Your eyes, she said. Your eyes are white as water.

Now there were two sons, John and Lyman, and a third on

the way, and the horses—Tokay and that lovely colt Katherine Ann had brought over and trained and her filly; even Ardis's breathtaking Bay Boy was often left up at the Buttes place—"He likes it up here with his relatives," Ardis would say laughing, "And even though my intentions are good, the truth is I'm kind of lazy, he doesn't get the workout he should. Run him a little, will you, Katherine?" She never called her Kam and "running" meant working; even when Kam was pregnant Ardis thought nothing of the request. Ardis took for granted she was delicate and Kam strong: were the strong not put on the earth to serve the weak?

Life for Cobus had changed so radically that it seemed impossible he had ever lived half of each year of his life solely among men, that he had ever been complete or of any value at all, alone, on his own, without this woman who was his wife, who was his *life*, without the two small wild creatures who were his sons, without the whole of his life like an implement driven mainly by desire, for in the three years they had lived together he had never stopped wanting her, he had never got over the shock of excitement his body felt lying down beside her at night, he had never grown so familiar that his eyes stopped seeing the miracle of vitality that was in her; its unwinding was what made the world turn for him, and he was properly in awe of it, and her, but not so much that his feelings for her frightened him into submission. Worship makes for bad bedding. He loved her but it was an earthy idolatry made up of two tangled bodies fused into one groping for pleasure. When he looked at Ardis, pale, courageous but somehow helpless, he simply could not understand how he had ever once believed the whole world of love—the whole world of women—resided in her. It was not his love he had given in trust to her during those years, but some kind of outrageous romanticism that was the shape itself of youth; so long as he had been held in its grip, he had remained a boy; but when he had learned what the care and responsibility, the respect, of love meant he had begun growing into a man.

"Clyde says there isn't going to be a war—"

"But jest suppose there is, Ardis—would he join up?"

She was plainly perplexed. "I don't know," she said after a time. "I mean, you know he might better serve where he is than off fighting somewhere. Lots of men can fight, but Clyde, well, not many men can do what he can."

"That's true, but there's just one trouble with that line of reasoning."

"What's that, Cobus?" she asked suspiciously. Something in his tone had no doubt alerted her that Tip's having the dispensation of being a Great Man didn't quite sit right with him.

"Well, Tip's not likely to die doing his duty down in Albany, is he? But all those others, those ordinary men who weren't given that something special Tip's got, the ones who couldn't stay put at home or acting up in the capital and had to go join up, they could get killed, couldn't they?"

"I don't think that's a very charitable way to put it, Cobus."

Something in him wouldn't let go. "But do you think that it's true, Ardis?"

She turned away, her back in its long graceful gown arched in consternation, as if that arch were itself his answer; she bent over the cherry table and rearranged some silver and china. "You've always been jealous of Clyde, haven't you? Ever since the beginning."

If she wouldn't answer him fair and square, that was up to her; he was going to play the game according to the rules he believed in, not the ones she wanted. "Yes, I was, Ardis, or at least I used to be; but I'm not any more, I haven't been in a long time, not since we went over to Vermont and I brought Kam back."

She whirled around, her cheeks flaming. "Is that an aspersion against me, Cobus, because I can't have any more children, Is that what you meant? Because if it is—no, don't try to explain, I want this out—because if that is what you meant, I think it's a wicked thing to say, especially after how close we've always been—" She faltered, tears standing in her eyes.

"No, *that* isn't what I meant. And you know it," he said slowly, wonderingly. "You knew all along I was in love with you and you just used me when you needed me—made a convenience of me—and that was what was at the bottom of that business between you and Kam fighting it out on those horses that first day we were over at their farm, wasn't it?" he said, seeing it clearly for the first time. "You were jealous you might lose me the way you had me."

"How dare you, Cobus? How dare you talk to me like that! Jealous? Me *jealous* of a vulgar, coarse creature like that?" She was trembling in anger and outrage and with, he saw, envy; for Tip had told him a few months back they were no longer really man and wife, the doctor had told him Ardis must never, never have another miscarriage, and so that

331

meant. . . . "I've made other arrangements," Tip had said. "A man has to. We talked it out and she understands, but—well—to tell you the truth, it's going to be hard, especially," Tip grinned, "if something nice comes along. I'm fond of Ardis and of course I love Mason Raymond, but—" That *but* hung in Cobus's mind now; he felt a tremendous desire to be done with this scene, wished he had prevented its inception, but the woman in front of him in all her righteous indignation was determined, he saw, to pursue it to its bitter end. They were going to say things that would never be forgotten or forgiven, but maybe, he thought after a second, that would be right, to have the air cleared once and for all; for he admitted to himself a fact he had refused all along to acknowledge, that from the first Ardis had patronized Kam, politeness hardly covering condescension, and Kam had been smarting under the sting of that attitude all along and yet had said nothing because—it hit him with a flash of intuition and appalled him with its ramifications—Kam had understood he had been in love with Ardis and still wasn't sure some of that feeling wasn't in him; perhaps she was even afraid that he would always love Ardis. And maybe he was afraid of that, too, and didn't want to admit it to himself.

He looked at the enraged woman in front of him; she had called his wife vulgar and coarse and that was an affront to any man; she was a woman and had the advantage; he could not viciously hand her the truth, but he'd come damn close to the bone, he thought. "It isn't coarseness or commonness, Ardis," he said slowly and matter-of-factly, unemotionally. "And you know it. It's vitality—the kind of raw energy that makes the world run. You are a beautiful and graceful and accomplished creature, Ardis, and you know it and make others know it, too; I admire your looks and the way you act, but God help you if the money were ever taken away and you had to muck out a barn yourself or get down on your hands and knees and scrub a floor. My wife," he said with slow, steady emphasis, "would survive *anything*—and help others get through it, too, but your kind," he said, finishing with her finally, "your kind are just ornamental, Ardis, they're never going to pull anyone through anything, they're not even going to get themselves through unless they have help. And Tip's a lot like you—only tougher, because he's had to scrape up in the world to make himself recognized, he wasn't born with the silver spoon in his mouth; but basically he's the same, always looking out for Number One. You're right, his kind wouldn't join up. He wouldn't feel under any obligation to take his chance same as an ordinary man. He'll stay in Albany or wrangle somethin' down in Washington—"

"You've said quite enough, Cobus. I don't imagine that after this—"

"I won't be welcome in this house? That's all right with me, Ardis; it never was the same after William and the Old Man went—the life went out of it. But you're still welcome up on the hill. I wouldn't want you to feel funny about coming over, even if you don't want to come in the house. Feel free to go up to the graves; suit yourself, Ardis, one way or the other, because *I* don't care."

His words had crumpled her. He heard her, in a kind of pleading voice, one that was part confessional, part supplication, some hysteria, saying, "But I don't have anyone, Cobus. You know how it is with Tip, I don't even see him most of the time, he just leaves us up here; and when we're down home, it's no better, he's hardly ever home. It's like he's not a husband at all, as if he weren't really married to me anymore. I'm—I'm alone," she sobbed, "most of the time. I don't want to be shut out of life like this—and now—please, Cobus, don't—don't leave me, too." She threw her arms about his neck frantically, turning her tear-stained face up to his. "I can't help it," she said with an awful wrenching sincerity he could not turn his back on, "that the doctor said—"

Gently he disengaged the arms that were locked about his neck; holding her hands in front of him and gazing at her desperation, he felt like some kind of judge—perhaps he had even wanted that when he had spoken so bluntly—but now nothing of censure or blame was left, only a kind of strangled pity in the face of such desolation. Why should Ardis have to suffer like this? Because something inside her was slightly off balance and expelled her children before they were formed enough to survive by themselves—but how was *she* responsible for that? The proud, beautiful creature of ten, fifteen years before was now someone he scarcely recognized with her splotched face and supplicating eyes, the body that kept almost involuntarily thrusting itself toward his, as if by the mere touch of her flesh Ardis believed she could still keep control of him.

He bent and kissed her gently on the forehead, trying to show her how changed their relationship was, that pity, not passion, moved him. "We've said some things we shouldn't," he said. "But we'll always be close, Ardis. You know that."

She shook her head in denial. No, now she didn't know, that was just the point.

"Well, we will be. I'm sorry—about—you know, Tip. But I didn't mean what I said, that you couldn't—count on me. I was just excited and angry, but I'd rather—I don't know *what*—than know you were in need."

"Need," Ardis said. "I'm not in what they usually mean when they say 'need,' but I want lots of things, Cobus. Like love," she said, looking away. "Everybody wants it. People just shrivel up and die without it. And I haven't had any real —caring—for so long from Clyde, I've forgotten what it's like to have a man really love you, trail after you talking away half the night because he wants you to share something with him. I've forgotten," she said through clenched teeth, "what it's like to share a life with anyone. He's so cold to me—so cold and uncaring, Cobus—" She swung around to face him again, her eyes full of the furious greed to live, "Tell me what to do."

Living with Kam had taught Cobus a lot of things about the commitment made between a man and a woman, between a man and his land, his animals, his particular part of the world—to live out of sight of the lake would have been an impossibility for him now. She had taught him directness of expression, directness of affection, the need for reciprocation immediately, in anything where he was involved with someone or something he cared about—but nothing he had learned from her, even trusting to deeper instincts occasionally over the dictates of better judgment, had prepared him for this. For a fleeting second he wondered if a man was ever prepared for all the unexpected emergencies in his life.

"Stay up here, with us," he found himself saying. "Don't keep closing this house—your real home—and running back to Albany. Stay here, because we are family, Ardis—more maybe now than Tip—Tip, I don't know, he's—well, his place is in Albany, but yours isn't, not anymore. Let him be where he belongs, and you stay here where you belong. Don't tear yourself in two. Put yourself in one place, the place you feel you belong, and stay there. Give it a chance, Ardis, at least this winter." He looked around despairingly at the changes she had made in the house—those flowery things at the window, the heavy folded drapes hanging disconsolately around windows filled with pewter that was never used, and the pictures on the wall of people no one knew, it was all so ornamental, like what she had become, but then wasn't the place you lived an expression of what you were? "Tip belongs in Albany, but you belong here, in Buttes Landing. The Butteses and the Raymonds," he said with finality, *"are the*

334

Landing. You know that, Ardis. And Mason Raymond's both, a Raymond *and* a Buttes. So you belong here. He belongs here. Let the rest of it work out as it will—I think it will work out all right. Maybe not the way you might have wanted—but being useful is part of being happy, of feeling loved. A place can sometimes love you back as well as a person—if you let it."

He chanced touching her, wanting the warmth of his real affection for her to communicate itself but afraid, even after what he had said and tried to show, of being misunderstood; yet she caught the impact of the gesture as it was meant, managing somehow in her misery a smile for him, crooked, reluctant, and ungainly, but genuine—Lord, how an expression like that could make a man weak with gratitude for the fundamental courage that was in women. He took her hand without hesitation, holding it firmly in his. He might, he felt, have been her father—no, her grandfather—comforting the distraught child (and the image of her own father, weak, mad Orville Raymond, rose accusingly in his mind; deserted by her father, rejected by her husband, no wonder she clung to him in such desperation, the only man she had ever known who had not let her down had been that old, crippled man who was now dead and no earthly help to her in her adult life, but he could not replace Old Mowatt Raymond, he was made another way), but he wanted Ardis to know he still did care, he would not desert her, it was just a different kind of caring than she had expected, yet the kind that in the end might carry her a lot further than his old, unrealistic one.

"Stay here where you belong and begin to build again." The truth he believed in: he told it to her. "It's over with Tip. There's no use tryin' there and if you give your heart and energy to somethin' that can come to nuthin', nuthin' is what you will get back in the end. But here, there's somethin' that matters. I don't think I can put it into words, Ardis, but I think you've always felt it, the way I have."

He waited.

"Yes," she said into the silence, quite softly, "it's the only place I've ever thought of as home. But—" she hesitated— "but I don't think Clyde would let me stay, Cobus. It wouldn't, you know, look right."

He let out a hoot, half derision, half honest amusement. "You mean it might hurt his career? It might interfere with the image of his being a Great Man?" She didn't answer, letting her silence be as much of an assent as she could give and yet remain loyal. A wife was supposed to be loyal, wasn't

335

she, that was the first requisite. She's still faithful to old, outworn ideals, he thought. What will destroy anyone in the end is hanging onto wanting what you can't have. It's all right to see the world as it should be so long as you contract to live in it as it really is. That compromise was after all at the center of meaningful survival. "Well, I wouldn't let that worry you," he said without any feeling of disloyalty to his brother—they had ceased being *brothers* years ago, maybe they had never been, right from the moment of birth when one looked white and one Indian, one had the makings and mind of a Big Man and the other let himself be sucked into the vortex of the everyday life of the small-time farmer— "If it came to a showdown and you wanted to stay, I'd see to it you could—and without any unpleasantness. And that's a promise, Ardis."

"You know," she said wonderingly, "it might be something to hang onto after all—living here, not just coming up summers," and suddenly to his surprise she gave her old healthy, hearty laugh. "It'd just kill your brother," she said, "just kill him, having me come back here, leaving him down in Albany, all the talk."

"Let him stay in Albany. Don't worry about him. Think of yourself. He'll make out no matter what happens. Stop thinking about what your duties are and do what you think *you* want for a change."

Ardis gave him a look of astonishment. "You know," she said in puzzlement, "I always used to think Clyde was the one who was, you know, *smart;* but you have a lot of things figured out, haven't you, Cobus, a lot of things he never even thought about."

"Livin' in the mountains makes a man go inside himself and do a lot of thinkin' on his own—livin' in the mountains and lookin' like an Indian." She turned her head away. He let it go. Part of the truth you always had to keep from women like her. He knew that, why try to change it? Hadn't he just a moment before been telling her to be willing to accept what was, not try to make it what she wanted it to be, and here he was trying to turn the same trick. "We'll have to get you some decent help, Ardis," he said briskly, changing the subject as well as the tone, "if you're goin' to settle in. These people you've got now—"

"I know, I know, Cobus," she said with a sigh. "They've been like everything else in my life lately, just makeshift. I know better than you they're worthless, but somehow I just didn't have the energy to care. Now—" she said with a toss

336

of her head—"now there are lots of changes that need to be made. Cobus, you know, it would be kind of, well, divine justice to let Clyde try and handle the house down in Albany all by himself—if he ever bothers to come home that much."

"You must buy a new mare, Ardis, and start thinking of breeding in the spring. It's too bad they ever cut Bay Boy, but there's no use in not getting a good mare and having it bred, that is, if you're serious about getting this place goin' again. And—"

"—And I've got to take down these pictures and repaint and pull out the old furniture again, is that what you were going to say? You're right, of course. It always was a masculine house, never mind all the girls Grandpa had to put up with— it had a male air, it was him, I guess, and I tried to do it over frilly and fluffy and feminine and it didn't work at all. I tried to make it into something it wasn't—a woman's summer place —and it fought back. For which, I guess, we can be glad. It would have near killed Grandpa to see what Mason Raymond's become. You've got a lot of work cut out for you, Cobus, there. He's got a lot of his father—and my father— in him, God help him," she said, but in a tone that also announced she was finished once and for all with pitying herself for the past. To end something is sometimes to begin again, Cobus knew. He was confident that one more boy to cuff, comfort, and have curl up with him, like a kitten, as his sons did, would not impose any handicap on him.

He wondered if somewhere none of them knew anything about the Old Man was smiling and slapping William on the back—it was a nice thought—a man had them once in a while, even when he knew damn well they were nothing but womanish longings. He *liked* to think of William, Old Man Raymond, Big John somewhere in the silent spaces of the spheres able to stop and listen when his mind ran out to them with something he wanted to say to them or to point out something he wanted them to notice. Still it seemed to Cobus odd that death, which was probably necessary if only to give a man's life form, to impose on it the necessity of purpose and direction by the narrowness of its span (for what would urge a man on to accomplishment who had an in- finity of time, all eternity, to get anything done?), that the need for death was one thing, but that it was odd, too, how there was a need to believe in something beyond death. It was too hard, he thought, to consign those you loved to cold earth and speedy decay and nothing else. A man ad- mitted the necessity of death and he saw how it gave form

337

to a man's life and how it molded it into some shape, but *eternal* death, no, he couldn't accept that, no matter how realistic he felt it might be. A man wanted death on his own terms (like everything else); one kind of living for life, another for after life was over and this business on earth was assigned its successes and failures. To believe those he loved were dead forever, could not in any way see some of the things that came after their deaths to justify parts of their lives: that seemed to Cobus too unjust. Before Kam he might have been able to force it down and make it stick, but it was absolutely impossible for him to accept the fact that one day that miraculous creative burst of vitality that was his wife would suddenly stop forever in some sickness or accident. He loved her more than anything in the world and yet he was absolutely powerless to protect her from death.

He, she, they were all mortal: that was the knowledge that they carried and that perhaps Cobus, like the rest of them, tried to run away from. And he ran away from it not because of himself but because of the woman he loved. Had he been granted one wish above all others, he knew that it would have been,

Death, take her a long time hence, and while she sleeps.

IV

"When you aimin' to go down to the Falls and sign up?"

Cobus had had it all planned out. He was going to take time off from the chores, come up to the house and "sweeten her up," but as soon as he came in and sat down and started to dawdle over his coffee, she had seen through him. Characteristically, she had known all along that he was trying to manipulate her. It was a little frightening—and reassuring—to see how transparent he was to her. Now he realized she had been prepared for his enlistment ever since the election, that she more than he had understood that when Lincoln took office the South would make some gesture of defiance. The issue to him had seemed cut and dry, clear and unemotional: Lincoln had been morally right when he had announced in December, "Let there be no compromise on the question of extending slavery." *Extending* was the key word; the South could keep what slaves they had. So what was there to get so all-fired excited over?"

"If you were a Southerner," Kam said, "you'd see the insult. You'd think Mr. Lincoln was anything but sensible and reasonable, you'd think he was a self-righteous, priggish martinet, and if you had any feelings of honor and respect, you'd be damned sure"—he winced—"he ate some of those 'sensible reasonable' words of his. They'll fight, Cob," she said flatly. "What Lincoln told them was 'This is a bad thing you have, but we'll let you keep it since so much of your life seems to depend on it, but we will not let it spread. On that you'll have no say.'

"A man's pride won't let him stand up to that. You wait and see," she had said back in early December, "the minute Lincoln's sworn in—if he lives that long—trouble will start."

She was right, of course. She was always right. Why did he ever bother trying to argue with her? The secession of South

Carolina just before Christmas had been followed by those of Mississippi, Texas, Arkansas, Louisiana, Alabama, Florida, creating what to Cobus seemed a ridiculous kind of charade, The Confederate States of America; but that 'charade' had led, too, to the firing on Fort Sumter and Anderson's surrender, a few days before, only a little over a month after Lincoln had taken office. It was insurrection; from insult to insurrection, Cobus had thought disbelievingly as the news had spread from village to village. Now the President was calling for volunteers, and a group in Glens Falls was passing out handbills, holding meetings, and getting together soldiers for the Union.

He was going to go—there was no choice, really, not with William buried on his own land and the way he felt about things, that idiotic idea that William and the Old Man could see inside his mind and were watching and waiting intently for him to commit himself. Yet he knew he was being what most people, even he himself at times, would call a fool. He was thirty-three years old with what could be called, with obvious disapproval, "heavy responsibilities"—and yet there was no choice.

And she had known it, too, and expected him to go. His decision was *his* to make. A man most often had one set of values, one way of acting, and his wife another. Cobus knew now he had that rare thing for a wife, a woman who thought on issues such as this not in personal terms of gain or loss but in the larger framework of right and wrong. That he was leaving her with three small children on an isolated farm that would require, by his absence, an enormous amount of extra work did not seem to dismay her at all. Kam's decision —her support—came from a belief that a person must always do what was right, regardless of personal consequences.

She would tackle what came matter-of-factly, and somehow she would manage. Failing was repugnant to her; even her mistakes and what errors she did make she did not consider as such. "Learners" she called the things that had gone wrong on her. She lived in the present, looking forward to a future in which all sorts of unlimited possibilities abided; the world to Kam was always opening up, whereas to most people Cobus knew it was constantly closing.

"I don't want you to go, Cobus. Don't go," Ardis pleaded. "Don't leave us all alone here. You're all we've got."

"You've got yourself," he told her, while she shook her head, it wasn't enough. He had gone down to tell her he was going and—to be honest—to have one long last look at

340

the Landing. He wanted to commit each detail of it to memory so that later on, in camp, he would be able to go over it in his mind.

Buttes Landing had grown—a regular metropolis, his father would comment drily—but in a sense what his father said ironically in jest was partially true. The small compact village had spread, creeping closer and closer to becoming a town: it had overrun the mill, which was now surrounded by small, self-containing farms; it was moving slowly but surely toward the Raymond estate so that now when people spoke of Ardis's place, they said it was "on the edge of town." Standing at the window, watching Bay Boy running down in the meadow, he thought that in a few years this once remote and secretive place would be surrounded with peepers and spiers. Progress, they called it, but he wasn't sure.

He was leaving it all—wife, children, farm, town, even this woman beside him whom he had once loved and who was at this moment remonstrating with him to forget his "ideals," as she insisted on calling them, "and look at things practically."

He ceased after a time arguing with her; the afternoon was slipping away from him and he wanted to hold it fast in his hand, but it was scurrying with the figures below and in the sad, sweet plaint of her voice.

"You want to go away."

"No, I have to go."

She pushed back a loose strand of hair and gazed at him, as if she were accusing him of lying to her.

"Pa will come down and see you're all right."

"I don't want your father." She put her hand on his arm and drew him back into the parlor where Mary Emma, still with her, had laid the tea things. There were buttered toast and a pyramid of buttered scones on one plate, little iced cakes on another. A pot of red preserves shone in the late afternoon sun that was flooding the room, lighting up the faded peacock carpet in the hall. He felt smothered by a sense of the past, of all that was gone that had meant so much to him. So much had happened since he had first stood gazing down on those birds.

She was pouring, measuring precisely without having to be told the amount of sugar and milk he liked. She was a Buttes and he was a Buttes, Tip and Kam were Butteses; yet how far apart they all seemed. "I'm not goin' to get killed, Ardis. I'm too mean to get kilt."

"I don't want you to go, Cobus," his father had said

obstinately over and over. He was just like Ardis, you couldn't make him see. No matter how many times Cobus had tried to explain, his father turned explanation aside and hung onto that one idea, he mustn't go. Pressed for a reason, he shook his head and said gruffly, "Your place is here on the land." He never mentioned Kam or the children or himself; it was always *the land*. Finally, when he saw Cobus putting together the few things he would need to go down to the Falls, realizing the actual moment of parting had come, he did try to explain. "It's only you who's left," he said angrily, "who really cares about the place."

"There's Tip."

"No, he don't care."

"He'll grow into it one of these days."

"No, Cobus, he won't."

"How can you say that, Pa?" He didn't feel his father was being just to his brother. "I used to go off to the woods, but Tip—"

"Your going wasn't the same as his going."

"*What* wasn't the same?"

"He don't have the feelin'."

"Now, Pa, you know that's a lot of nonsense—"

"It ain't nonsense and you know it. Clyde's a good son, a loyal and dutiful one. It ain't his fault he ain't got the feelin', but he ain't and that's that, there's nothing to be done about it. He knows it himself."

Cobus was beginning to get exasperated, the way people always did when the truth they didn't want to acknowledge was being wielded against them.

"We been on this land three generations now—and we been in this country since the start. It ain't right that—"

"But that's just the point, Pa. The Butteses have been here since the beginning; they got their start on this soil, and done well. They got obligations for that."

Cobus took hold of his arm, but his father shook loose. "Jest don't get yourself busted up," he said angrily, and Cobus knew his father had given in, that he acknowledged the one fact that superimposed all the others: that Cobus was not going to give in.

Guthrie Buttes was down plowing when Cobus set out. Kam stood at the door, a child dragging off each arm; the baby was back in the bedroom in his crib. "Don't you sign up with no company ain't got horses with it," she said.

"Don't worry, honey, they'll all have horses one way or the other, I expect."

342

"Well, you try and see if you can't get in one of them regiments where they use horses fighting, not just for parading about."

"More 'n likely I'll have to take what is. In the Army there ain't a lot of choice. Keep well," he said, his throat tightening.

"You, too," his wife said in a hoarse voice. "Write," she said. "Write real soon, Cobus," and that was all she could say.

He went down the road without looking back. He waved, though. It was strange, going off like that, without turning around to look back, but waving over his head to give her some sign.

As he passed the end of the meadow, his father reined the oxen in and stood watching. When he was almost out of sight, his father came out from behind the plow and waved slowly, once, twice, then quickly, as if he would never stop.

"I know I can't stop you—" She held out blindly the plate of cakes. "But you know if anything happens—listen to me, Cobus, you've got to come back."

"I'll come back, Ardis. I got no choice. Too many people dependin' on me." He tried to say it lightly, dredging up a grim smile, but a smile. "It's goin' to be a short war. Ninety days and no more, they say. Nuthin' more than a rest away from the plow, some time, first time in years, to idle myself and do a little restin' and a little thinkin'. That's a beautiful dress you got on."

"I bought it for today." She put the platter of cakes down on the table. "Cobus—"

"Don't, Ardis, things are hard enough."

"Oh, Cobus, why didn't I *see*? Why was it Clyde I—"

He couldn't help himself, he took her in his arms. It was his wife he loved, but—

But it was like the preacher had said, He was in the hand of the living God, He who is under no obligation to any promise, so that men are held over the Pit of Hell, and ready to be swallowed up in Everlasting Destruction.

Two units were to form the New York Twenty-Second Volunteers, thirty-eight regiments made up of enlistments from Essex, Warren, and Washington counties. The officers were Col. Phelps, Jr., from Glens Falls (Warren County), Lt. Col. Gordon Thomas (Essex County), and Major John McKie (Washington County)—a democratic arrangement of which all the recruits approved, although once the excitement of enlisting and moving into barracks was over, the majority

343

of men were bewildered by what was expected of them. The oath of muster which they had all taken, which had been so stirringly patriotic, had not, however, offered any concrete advice on what was ahead:

I, Cobus Buttes,

he had sworn,

> *do solemnly swear that I will bear true allegiance to the United States of America, and that I will serve them honestly and faithfully against all their enemies and oppressors whatsoever, and obey the orders of the President of the United States, and the orders of the officers appointed over me according to the rules and articles for the government of the armies of the United States.*

Overnight that oath changed him from a man on his own to one who must muster, march, make way for any order anyone wanted to give him. It was a life completely devoid of privacy, personal respect, individual initiative—one that constitutionally Cobus was unsuited for, but he gritted his teeth and tried to accept the inevitable.

There was much to learn, beginning with that basic lesson that there was no glory in getting cold, muddy, and wet. There were many other illusions that had, also, to be dispersed. There was hardly a man in the regiment who did not believe he would see action against the enemy within the week. Few realized they would have to learn *how* to fight, a whole new way of handling Enfields and Springfields that felt awkward to hands used to muzzle loaders; a whole new way of learning to live in barracks and tents, of pacing a march with a reluctant body through miserable weather, of putting up with unreasonable officers and uneatable food.

Drill was monotonous and never-ending. Many of the new recruits could not understand the difference between right and left, no matter how many times it was explained to them. Finally, in desperation, the drill sergeants dropped the terms "right" and left," they had the men tie wads of straw to their right feet, and they drilled them by calling out "straw foot," "left foot," "straw foot," *"left* foot—" Age cut Cobus off from most of the men. He was nearly thirty-four, an old man in the eyes of the recruits; over two-thirds of them were in their early twenties or younger. There were many sixteen- and seventeen-year-olds, boys who had said they were eighteen so that they might have the right to kill.

The days passed so much alike that they blended into a kind of composite picture that Cobus labelled Army Life. This picture began with the first bugle of the day, the Assembly call at five o'clock in the morning during the summer and six during the winter, the signal to the men to get out of their blankets and prepare for roll call fifteen minutes later. Almost no one got up. Instead they huddled inside their blankets prying loose those last few moments of stolen sweet sleep. When the assembly bugle blew, the men leapt up, frantic, trying to do what dressing had to be done and run to the parade grounds at the same time. The majority slept in their clothes to save time so that the assembly line presented a picture of ragged, sleepy, irritable men trying to right themselves, rubbing their eyes, pulling at a boot, shoving a fellow soldier who got too close, elbowing and cursing their way into line. Cobus would think back to the booming of the gong in the forest, the cry "Day-light in the swa——mp!" as he looked around at the sleep-swollen faces.

He went, a little later, to breakfast call, feeling that if he had been able, like the drivers in the company, to work with the horses, give them their canvas nose bags of feed, he would have felt better about starting another day. He had asked to be assigned to the drivers' unit, but like everything else the Army did, it made a mess of this request. He never heard anything more about it, though men who came from the city and knew nothing about animals were sweating fear every time they went near the stable and begged Cobus to trade places with them, even if that swap meant they had to take their place in the front lines and be shot at.

On the march the men lived on salt pork, hard bread, an occasional piece of real meat, coffee with sugar (when they could get it). The issue of hardtack formed the basis of almost all their meals when they were marching. Most men learned to eat maggoty hardtack; they usually soaked it in coffee but they sometimes made up a weak soup over their campfires and soaked the hard biscuits in that.

Coffee beans were rationed out by portions into small piles. The men lined up and waited beside the large oatmeal sack from which the distribution was to be made. They grumbled and complained, they joked and shoved; but all their eyes were on the measuring out. For this a large rubber blanket was spread out on the ground and as many piles of coffee as there were men lined up. To prevent any fights, the sergeant turned his back and took out the roll call of the company. Then one of the soldiers would come forward and point at one of the piles. "Who gets this?" he would ask the sergeant and the sergeant, still with his back turned so that he couldn't see, would call out a name.

New recruits used paper in which they poured the coffee and then shoved it into their haversacks. Within a very short time the coffee absorbed the oil of the salt pork, the weevils of the hardtack, it got mixed with flour and salt and was useless. A recruit of a little more experience would try wrapping his coffee in a piece of his rubber blanket or poncho, which he cut off where it didn't much matter. This worked quite well at the start, but after a few days the rubber would begin to peel off or the paint of the poncho would rub off and the greasy salt pork and the coffee and the rubber would become one greasy mess. The seasoned veteran took an old plain cloth bag and put not only his coffee but also a ration of his sugar together and stirred them thoroughly before he wrapped them together. He had learned the hard way that his sugar was better mixed immediately with his coffee than kept separated and possibly used, in a moment of impulse, in other ways. If the coffee and sugar were mixed together, there was no need to ration sugar out cup by cup or to worry about it being lost or spoiled by contact with other provisions.

At home a man would have thrown a fit to be served the kind of food that in the Army he took for granted. The meat was mostly boiled and it was often spoiled. The cooks kept the best pieces for themselves and only threw into the pot what was fit for dogs, and any decent dog would have turned up his nose at that.

The day began and ended with bugle calls; the bugle calls went on endlessly all day, day after day, until they provided a background of sound that a man didn't even hear. To Cobus they were the heart of Army Life, more even than the marching and drilling; and whenever, years later, he thought of the time he spent in the Army, there came in his head the sound of taps, when, as the men sat smoking or telling stories, playing some strange instrument like the bone player, with the music of an occasional fiddle thrown in, when they were hunched over (as Cobus often was) writing letters, or moving draughts about the board, immersed in cribbage or euchre, or reading, some getting up and wandering down to the sutler's for molasses cookies at six to the quarter, or one of the sutler's pies, flat above and below, with unknown goo in between, where there arose over the fires the shadows of

346

night, the hum of voices, the silhouettes of men playing checkers or bent over writing boards, a momentary lull in Army Life, and then from out of the blue smoke and gathering shadows the roll of drums, the sound of the bugle would drift down on the air, and more and more sounds emerge until almost a thousand bugles were shearing the night air and nearly a hundred thousand men were rising and making ready to turn in, stopping for an imperceptible moment to listen, then turning, shrugging, drifting down through the campfires to the places where they would lie down and dream out the darkness.

On June 21 the New York Twenty-second left for Baltimore, under the escort of Captain Ainsworth's Albany Zouaves. There was a good deal of tension among the ranks as they paraded down the city's main streets to the steamers waiting to take them to New York. There wasn't a man marching who didn't know all about the trouble there had been in Maryland with Southern sympathizers a few weeks before, in April. A Baltimore mob had attacked Union troops from Massachusetts, and now as the bands played, the flags waved, and the Albany populace cheered, the men marched to the tremors of their own fears. Yet they looked very military and formidable in their dark blue jackets, light blue pants, blue fatigue caps and cowhide brogans. The Adjutant rode at the front of the column, followed by the regimental band; the sun caught the glint of thousands of muskets as the men tramped past a sea of waving white handkerchiefs and made their way through the center of the New York capital to the barges and steamers that would take them down the Hudson to Manhattan.

The stay in New York was brief. That night they were transferred to New Jersey and given for the first time uncooked meat and hardtack. Although the men had complained the Albany food was terrible—"the boiled beef tougher than an owl, potatoes not fit for hogs to eat," Cobus wrote home —they had good bread, even if there was no butter. Now the men were shocked to find that although supplies were handed out to them, they were responsible for the cooking. It was their first indication their bread would not be baked for them, baked as it had been baked in Albany in those huge ovens that had turned out twenty-five to thirty thousand loaves a day; that they would not bed down in barracks but in tents or bedrolls, that the whole Army organization itself might break down and desert them and leave each man to fend for himself.

Lice also began to make their appearance for the first time; from now on not a man would ever be exempt from them. Lice preyed on them all, from foot soldier to general. The only way—and it was only temporary—to rout them was by boiling a man's clothes in a cauldron into which a good handful of salt had been thrown. For the most part the men accepted, swatted, swore, and suffered.

They were learning to do a lot of swearing. After solving the cooking problem as best they could—most of them banding together to boil the raw, tough meat—they settled down to a fitful sleep, only to be roused around midnight to line up, march to railroad cars, and embark for Baltimore. The grumbling was deep and persistent, an undercurrent that threatened to drown out the steady tramp, tramp of marching feet.

The trip consisted of one long jolt. No sooner would Cobus try to get comfortable than the train would hit a stretch of rough track and he would be jerked awake again. At eight o'clock in the evening the train finally pulled in. The tired, tense men tumbled out to draw up in lines. Under the bright moon the band struck up a bold, defiant air, but the music—bright and brittle—seemed to Cobus to pose a challenge.

The ranks marched first through almost-empty streets, then into the heart of town where they were met by a few half-hearted cheers. The anxiety that had been real—almost bearing weight and shape—back in the railroad yard was gone; a man no longer felt the men all around him keyed up in anxious expectation. They were all march, march, marching through Baltimore on a serene evening with a band playing and as they passed from the center of the city toward the outskirts, there seemed little reason for alarm: Cobus heard only a few scattered cries for the Confederacy.

"By the right flank, by the file left, *march*."

It was a welcome order because it meant the column had reached the depot where they would camp. The band was playing loudly and enthusiastically as the head file entered and took its place in front of the building. Two of the companies, B and G, were to remain outside while the others filed in, but the critical moments when the columns had been openly exposed in the heart of the city were over, Cobus felt, as he passed with hundreds of others into the depot.

He had been expecting—he wasn't quite sure what. Trouble of some kind. Soon the doors of the depot would close over them all, food would be distributed; they would eat, take a pipe, gossip a bit, bed.

He was never sure later at just what instant the trouble began. All Cobus heard was the explosion, a cry; then there was a sudden barrage of firing. Snipers—apparently concealed on the roof of the building—began firing. Shots were also coming from the crowd pushing toward companies B and G outside.

Most of the Twenty-second was inside. Cobus had a moment of disbelief when under the glare of gaslight, he saw smoke, the faces of the panicked men outside and in; he looked around anxiously for those few men with whom he had made friends, Steve and Will and Old Molasses Joe, he was so slow the men said that he would freeze in January, but all he took in were the pressing crowds moving like a great tidal wave into the depot. Then the building plunged into darkness.

In the darkness he could see the flashes from the firing outside were increasing; round after round was being fired into the two companies stranded there. Inside the men lost their heads. They were trying to escape being hit by one of the flying bullets, some crouching on the floor, others trying, hopelessly, to hide behind buttressing, the majority milling frantically about as if they believed that a moving target was never hit.

Then, miraculously, with a hiss, the lights came back on. "Lines, to your *lines,*" Colonel Phelps called forcefully.

"It's Burge. He's dead."

Outside the steady firing had dwindled to a shot now and then. The panic had passed, possibly in the moment death had made its presence known.

It was games they had thought to play, and postures they had wanted to assume, heroics they had had in their hearts, not the vision of the still figure being lifted, its arms dangling, and trundled out like any of the pieces of equipment they had used all day, an object, a lumpy sack, no longer needed, that was Burge, who a moment before had been someone's comrade, a trial (no doubt) to his sergeant, an object of jest with his friends, someone's boy far away, now a lump whose heart beat no more.

In the clear early morning light of July the regiment moved two and a half miles out of Washington to the northeast to grounds that had been vacated by the Fourteenth New York Militia. They were in Virginia—enemy territory.

Then the regiment was moved to Upton Heights, where as a part of the First Brigade and the First Division, it became a part of the First Army Corps under McDowell. McDowell they had yet to see, but they were now called McDowell's men. It was strangely unreal: to belong to a man you had never laid eyes on, who had the power to order you into a line that might be the battle that killed you.

Many of the three-month militia who had enlisted were nearing the completion of their ninety-day service, and everyone kept saying that if there wasn't a fight soon, these men would go home without ever having seen a Reb.

On July twenty-first Cobus and the rest of the men from the Twenty-second had just formed lines for Sunday service when a courier dashed up. To run an animal like that, it was inhuman; the horse was all lathered up, its sides were heaving as if its lungs were ready to burst. Then suddenly Cobus thought, But that's how you *have* to use a horse in war.

He had a moment's knowledge—scarcely more than the change of heartbeat within his breast—when he said to himself, *I don't want any part of this,* and then the gathering realization came: I got no choice. He looked at the courier, he looked at the horse, he looked down at his own heavily booted feet. I never understood, not at all, he thought, a man my age, he don't know the difference between an idea and a living breathing body, how is that?

The defeated Union Army began straggling back from Bull Run that afternoon. Every street in Washington was filled with stragglers, the wet, the wounded, some still in a state of shock. That night men slept on the ground on their rifles. Once the drums gave warning, but it was false; the men, roused and ready, soon fell back sleepily on their packs.

Each day for the next two months Cobus expected a pitched battle for the capital. But the danger passed, the immediacy of defeat faded, the men settled back into the familiar notion that it would be a short war. They had had only a momentary setback. When the next battle came. . . .

It was a winter of activity, a camp of eternal preparations, endless marching, endless practice firing the new guns. Back at Buttes Landing nothing seemed to have changed from Kam's letters except that the children were growing so fast that Cobus, she said, wouldn't know them. Little John was a boy now, not a little boy, and even "The Baby," as she always wrote of him, was trying to walk. Cobus pictured her harassed, running after his smallest son who would, once on his feet, be into everything. "Mason Raymond is so quiet," she wrote once, but whether in envy or disgust Cobus couldn't tell. He was surprised to hear, however, that Tip had come and spent a week at the lake. He remembered with both pain and pleasure Ardis in his arms. He loved Kam, he loved Ardis, he didn't understand what was going on inside him at all.

The fine weather where the days burned with beauty passed. The rains came, the mud. Washington breathed more easily. With the roads a wash of mud, there would be no Confederate attack.

The rains brought a damp, rotting cold. General McClellan —they were no longer McDowell's men, McDowell was out —did not approve of barracks so the men stuck to their tents. Most of them banded together and bought small iron stoves to fight off the cold and mildew. Will and Molasses Joe and Steve and Cobus stuck together; they were older and from the same part of the woods. Steve had even been lumbering up near Brandt Lake. They were a taciturn foursome, but they were loyal to one another in a way the younger men wouldn't have understood; age always makes you protective, Cobus came to believe, because you've found out how vulnerable you are, how weak the dreams and how strong the adversities. He knew the places where his friends would fail and tried to protect them from their own deficiencies; he looked to them to do the same for him. He had become absent-minded since joining the Army. Too much thinking: he kept seeing his wife on the steps of the New House saying, Write, Write real soon, and he kept remembering how small and soft Ardis had felt in his arms. He would close his eyes and the two women would be right there with him, both making him shudder with want. Desire was like some sickness inside him now, desire not for one woman, but for two: how could a man hang himself up in such a situation, a man who had once prided himself on being in control? The Army he was grateful to for keeping him away from a place where he was dead sure he would make a mess of his life and others'. But the brooding had made him forgetful and one or another of his friends had always to be watchful that that remoteness didn't get him in trouble. The Army didn't want you thoughtful.

Christmas came and went, brightened by a box from home. All Kam's ingenuity had gone into making every inch count. She had tucked onions and peanuts, an apple or wrapped hard candy, into all the crevices and corners. There was not a bit of wasted space. She had remembered all the things he had requested—needles, thread, hatchet, nails, shoe preservative —and she had added many things on her own: pickles, preserves, coffee, tea, sugar, a wrapped round of butter salted down to keep, two pairs of thick but soft socks she had knitted, a cheese, and a lovely white thick fruit cake. Each thing was wrapped and, though small, was an offering from one of those he loved. Ardis had contributed the hatchet for cutting kindling, his father the round-headed nails for the heels of his boots, his sons' names were on the jars of preserve and the special rum-soaked ham.

Sitting alone Christmas night turning every item over in his hand, Cobus had held longest to the socks. Much as he fought against the pictures, he saw his wife undressing, letting down her long hair, and slipping into bed, blowing out the candles, and nestling next to him for warmth. Her bare feet were always icy from their final journey across that bitterly cold floor. She put them against his legs to warm them and then curled her arm around his chest, her hand, warm, lying on his stomach. Often—very often—he turned over at that touch and took her in his arms.

He put the socks down and took up the cake, carefully wrapped to keep it from drying out, soaked in hard cider to preserve the moistness, to give it that added flavor it needed. She had baked that cake before Thanksgiving, put it down in the cellar, gone down twice a week to pour cider carefully over the cheesecloth so that the cakes would be moist but not soggy.

On Christmas Eve he and Kam always trimmed the tree after the children were in bed. They had few gifts for the little ones, but the tree itself was the real surprise. Cobus went up in the woods and carefully selected a good round full one, just about the height of the parlor ceiling. He hid this in back of the barn and when the children were asleep, he slipped out and brought it in, he and Kam put the bulbs on, the colored paper chains, the candles.

The boys' stockings would have, at the toe, an orange—Ardis always saw that these were sent up from the Falls along with some Christmas chocolates. Kam made boiled sweets in the evenings, when the children couldn't see. There would be a toy for each, one that Cobus had spent long hours the weeks before carefully constructing, a wagon or a small stool; and he marveled that his father understood, Kam wrote, and had taken that duty to himself this year, constructing small sleds for the two older boys and a small pullcart for Sarton. Kam had managed with all else she had to do to knit him socks and "a good strong muffler for Father," she had written. He pictured her late at night knitting, her eyes half closed in fatigue, her head nodding, and that invincible determination of hers waking her up and forcing her on. The same spirit in everything she did: it would be done, and well, as it should be, no matter what the personal sacrifice.

He reached down and took out from his box the turkey, carefully wrapped, with its precious hidden cargo of applejack. It was illegal to send liquor to the men, but all of them had hankered for it and wives had tried various ruses to get it by the inspectors. Kam was one of the few who had succeeded. Cobus would share it with Mill, Steve and Joe, but for the moment he wanted to be off by himself; his friends had respected that and left him the tent to himself.

January and the first part of February were mild, almost like spring, but mud mired everything, even the men who trod on it, the whole camp was a quagmire; the unseasonable warmth brought out bugs as well as buds, sickness as well as spring sports. Measles and flies hit the camp hard; the men all felt "off" in one way or another. The air was a threat, warm, wet, spongy.

Cobus heard from Kam that nearly two feet of snow had fallen in the Adirondacks; trains were embedded, carts and carriages unable to get over the roads. She and his father had spent a whole day digging out to the barn. She wrote bitterly that the Landing prices were going up, up, up. Overnight the price of potatoes had doubled, coffee was sky high, sugar and pork and beef and matches were all climbing. Apples, always before six cents a peck, were now going for fifteen. She wrote of Ardis, "Tip is doing very well—coming up more often, too, Cobus. He was here for Christmas." Between the lines, Cobus read, "You weren't."

March, like a lamb, came to them to eat out of their hands. There never was such weather, the farmer-soldiers said. "Weather like this, it's good for the earth," they kept repeating over and over. "It opens it up."

At ten o'clock on the tenth of March—as if in the coupling of those two tens there was some kind of omen—the Twenty-second was notified that it was going to pull out the next morning. A trifle past noon on the eleventh Cobus' company began marching, about three miles from Centerville to a place called Fairfax Court. Two days later the men entered Centerville, and two days after that they marched to Alexandra, over twenty miles away, through driving rains, in seas of mud, with the wind and wet sickening every man in the company. The next day orders, inexplicable orders, recalled them to Upton's Hill.

On the fourth of April the regiment marched back to Fairfax again. The next day, grumbling, the troops went over the old familiar ground they had covered less than a month before, marching back to Centerville, then about four miles beyond. The following day found them beyond Manassas Junction, near the defeat of the previous year, bivouacked in a downpour of rain, sleet, and snow, getting soaked, Cobus was sure, just so that they could march back again to Upton's Hill.

He was miserable, all the men were—the weather was indescribable. Rain was worse than cold. In the cold at least a man's clothes and shoes remained dry. Even though he tried to protect himself by using his rubber blanket as a poncho, the rain seeped through. Making camp on muddy ground was a nightmare, for the fence rails—the ones that were left, mighty scant pickings after all the marches that had been made over this same ground—would not burn, the woolen blankets they had all tried to protect were nevertheless soaked through, even the hardtack was wet and soggy. Wet wood, wet food, wet blankets, wet clothes, wet guns, wet ground to sleep on . . .

The mud was so deep that the horses and mules foundered, men sank to their knees, cursing, trying vainly to pull them out. The caissons and artillery equipment mired and could not be moved. It occurred to Cobus the whole Army would sink from sight in that mud and leave the South free by default. No wonder the men sang sardonically,

> Now I lay me down to sleep
> In mud that's many fathoms deep;
> If I'm not here when you awake,
> Jest hunt me up with an oyster rake.

It was all a far cry from the days the men had deliberately courted discomfort to prove they were soldiers.

Nevertheless, they marched on and on, from place to place, without any apparent end in sight. His anger, the anger of the whole Army, made no difference: they kept on marching, rain and snow smothering their movements now. Ice formed on them as they walked, melted, dripped down onto their clothes. The sick call became an occasion not of jesting but of congratulations; if a man had a fever and chills and a racking

354

cough he might escape that endless meaningless maneuvering. But a man could not fake easily now the things doctors were looking for. A man had nearly to be spitting blood to be taken off the road.

Cobus looked across the broken bridge at the city stretched out on the horizon; he sat down and stared at his tired feet; he hung his head and said silently to himself, The whole goddam Army's run by a parcel of fools, we'll never lick the Rebs. They had gone through all these grueling weeks, that long, two-day terrible march, for what? To stand and stare at a broken bridge, that was what.

These thousands of men had been called up for the explicit purpose of fighting. They had as yet, after a year, to see one battle. All they had done was march up and down uselessly. Some tension which had previously held them in balance had, in the past month or so, given way. All around him Cobus witnessed senseless acts of violence when men suddenly lost control and flew into unreasonable rages. Vicious fights, stompings as brutal as any he had witnessed in the lumber camps, knifings as lethal as any of those encountered in the river runs.

Cobus was sure that "Little Mac" meant well—the God's honest truth was that he *looked* the part of a commander, sashaying around on that black horse—but something was missing in his make-up.

McClellan wasn't going to do more than move a lot of men about. He would shake up the Army and get rid of the dead wood that didn't know its hay foot from its right foot; McClellan could organize and delineate and get ready, but he was just no good at getting at the business itself. He was simply a man who was going to spend the rest of his life preparing. Any real accomplishment was beyond him. There were lots of men like this, but during a war a commander who was one of them was a dangerous and reckless thing to put in over men; he would kill uselessly a lot of his troops with his everlasting tinkering; he would insure a lot of landscape being needlessly chewed up in the war machines while he fussed and fretted; he would delay and delay until the people lost heart and said to themselves, Is this war worth the killing and heartaches, the sacrifices and losses? And more and more of them would begin to say, No, no, it ain't worth it. Let's settle this and live in peace again.

It was what Cobus would have thought, save for that single pocket in his heart that reminded him again and again: William, William, William.

The regiment remained on the banks of the Rappahannock. On the twenty-third the lines were in great excitement; Lincoln had come to review his men. He was a strange figure, too tall for the horse they had given him, his legs hanging down, almost touching the ground; he had a comic aspect bobbing in the saddle, that long skinny figure dwarfing the horse, the big black stovepipe hat bouncing up and down on his head, his hands all wrists and wrong movements trying to get the horse to keep in procession.

When Cobus caught momentarily the glimpse of that beaten face, he thought, He looks like a farmer, a mountain farmer. There was none of the softness of the valley people: the face that Lincoln held in rigid control, only the eyes escaping his vigilance, was one of sober contemplation. But the eyes grieved endlessly. That awful look made Cobus uneasy; it was as if those eyes had the ability to see things that other men couldn't, to know all that terrifying hidden knowledge held in the palm of the future; those eyes said, Just hold on, don't say nothing, it won't work out that way. Lincoln's eyes told Cobus it was going to be a long and brutal war.

The men moved out on the twenty-fifth, finally crossing the river and marching the six miles to Fredericksburg. They set up their field shelter tents—the big Sibley and A-tents having given way to the less unwieldy dog tents. The dog tent was a two-man tent, each man packing half. The tent could be hastily erected, and though it was confining, it served quite well as a shelter. The only furnishings were those the men carried on their backs—candles for lights, a tin dipper and plate, knife and fork and spoon with which to eat. When the men ran out of candles, they made "slush lamps," sardine tins filled with cookhouse grease, a rag at one end for a wick.

He learned, like the rest, to curl up and use his own body warmth to dry his wet clothes when he lay down in his sopping rubber poncho and blanket; he found out how to hunt supplements to his supplies when they ran out—keeping an especial eye out for beehives. There was nothing like honey to sweeten the bleak food that was the mainstay of Army Life.

There was little he could beg or borrow in the way of supplies from the people of the countryside. The route had so often been traveled by both armies that the people along the way despaired of keeping anything for themselves. Their fences had been pulled down, their livestock butchered and

356

eaten, their crops stolen or destroyed; they had given up working the land simply to supply one or the other of the armies; they lived, those who remained, in a state of hopeless sullen rage, hating both sides, watching with open hostilities the armies go back and forth. It was not unusual to come upon a corpse, its throat slit, lying in an abandoned field.

Army routine was so ingrained in him now, he had fired the Springfield so often that the action was now automatic, he had drilled and marched and executed flank movements so many times that these were a part of his reflexes, like breathing, walking, eating.

Cobus gave in to utter despair when on the thirty-first of May the men retraced their steps to within sight of Fredericksburg and embarked on the train for Fort Royal. Again it was impossible to cross the Rappahannock because the bridge was out, so—Cobus couldn't believe it—they *returned* to Haymarket on the sixth of June.

McClellan went, replaced by Pope. On August 20 the Twenty-second marched to the Cedar Mountain battlefield and camped. Naturally, they did not fight. But they nearly died of the heat and dust, an August so stifling men could not remember another to compare with it. The roads around their encampment were clogged with soldiers sick with heat prostration, thirst, exhaustion.

Then they were ordered to march back to the Rappahannock. The men made the trip back in a kind of delirium of disbelief, dust, dehydration. Cobus, hot and feverish, tramping under that furnace of sun and in the vortex of that dust, felt as if he could not go on. Yet he kept moving, his throat closed with dust, his eyes red and swollen with grit, his teeth and tongue coated with dirt, his ears stopped up by the noise of marching men, creaking guns, groaning equipment, braying mules.

The sand in his shoes rubbed the skin off his feet. Dust seeped through his clothes and mingled with his sweat and rubbed his neck, wrists and waist raw. The men reached the Rappahannock and got across on a makeshift bridge. On the other side they stumbled along in whirls of dust, foundering through knots of exhausted men fallen by the side of the road, pushing on and on, God knew or cared where.

He stumbled and fell, rose and marched on. On all sides of him men cried out to stop, give it up, it was no use, but he kept moving, as if the movements of life were life itself. Then it came to him he could not stop; his marching was as automatic as his firing the Springfield, his belief in the endless hardtack and boiled coffee, the inevitable sense that life would never be anything but moving on and on, going no place, arriving never at a scene of action, unable ever to find a concrete event in which he could shape the events of his training, but only this endless endless marching, marching on —and on—and—

Suddenly he found himself in the midst of firing.

One minute the men were moving in orderly formation along the line to the battlefield, the next shells were falling among them; there came the incessant thud-thud of large guns, the ground shaking under them. The rattle and din of muskets cracked and snapped all about them, smoke and dust and cries rose on all sides.

Overhead shells whined and screamed. Explosions rocked the earth under Cobus's feet. He stood absolutely still, too stunned to move, absorbed in his own inability to act.

"All right, goddammit," he heard a voice cry. "You wanted to fight, now get in there and fight. The first man who stops will get this—" The Colonel waved his sword. "Move," the Colonel screamed in a paroxysm of rage. "Move!"

In front of them rose a wall of smoke. It hid everything from sight: the enemy, the landscape, even most of the sky. Through this a thousand thin rapiers of fire pierced, rifle fire that found its mark in men all up and down the lines. Bodies fell with grunts, groans, screams, or—worse—silent and humped like stones.

"Get on, get on," the commander was screaming when a shell went through his horse. He tumbled off and went down and they heard him no more.

The line slowed; the men stopped, turned and looked at one another. They were still standing uncertainly when another regiment ran up in back of them, cutting off retreat. Now they were trapped between the enemy in front and rein-forcements from behind.

The firing kept up; all around Cobus the wounded and dead were piling up. Then he was being nudged from in back, men coming up thrusting at him to keep going or get out of the way, they weren't going to stand like dumb oxen in this open field and let the guns mow them down.

Cobus began to jog tiredly along with them. He had no real notion why he was going—to shoot seemed out of the question, he didn't think his arm would be able to lift a gun, it felt so tired—but a kind of dreamlike bafflement brought him along. He saw the regimental flag going down, saw a soldier he did not recognize spring forward and seize the

358

standard, then go down, too. Someone else took up the flag. It was torn and riddled. He couldn't seem to get it straight what he was aiming for. A flag couldn't do anything for them, it was just—

A shell burst near him, knocking him to the ground. He lay stunned, dirt pouring from overhead down on him, a man to the left of him with his head buried in his arm sobbing, "My eyes, my eyes. . . ." The enemy's big guns were trained right on this field; they seemed determined to blow every inch of it sky high. It was better, he perceived, to keep going and take his chances on getting shot from the Reb line than to lie in the midst of all that overhead heavy firing.

The thing that confused him most was that he had no real idea what was going on. His vision encompassed only a small portion of the Bull Run battlefield, and he couldn't determine what was happening here, how could he expect his brain to assemble information to tell him what was going on all over the area? And if he didn't know what the general pattern of the battle was, how could he know how he was supposed to behave? There was no point, for instance, in going in for an attack in the small area he was in if all along the front elsewhere the Army was retreating.

He had never thought of the war in terms of a few yards in front and at both sides of him; previously he had imagined a large battle plan where he was the central figure, the decisive point of fighting.

He ran and fired and dropped and fired, withdrew, firing, waited, firing, ran ahead again firing, withdrew again, resting, was ordered ahead again, ran with the rest against the grading, trying to fire, men falling all around him, the rattle and screech unbearable to his ears, the ground upending under him, dust and smoke and animals' frightened whinnies and screams from the wounded mingling with the terrible pounding inside his own head.

The air was filled with the racketing noise of weaponry, the screams of the wounded and dying, the noise of frightened animals being urged on toward the front. Overhead the cannons fired and somewhere the rat-a-tat of drums and the ping-ping of muskets mingled. It was impossible to dislodge the enemy from behind the protection of their grading. But he was on his feet again, shells bursting, voices screaming out orders, other soldiers crowding against him: they were being sent against the railroad grade again.

He was not quite sure just when the Army around him began coming apart. One minute it seemed the men were being mobilized to make yet another attack and were going, willingly, on their way through that murderous fire; the next, the will went out of them, possibly at the moment Longstreet's artillery began to rain down on them in a murderous firing that dropped men all about Cobus like grain cut down with a sharp scythe. He kept going until he found himself almost totally alone; then he dropped as if he too had been struck by the sharp blade of death, lying on the ground watching the attack splinter into bits and pieces falling this way and that. He had ceased firing—ceased caring, lying in dust and smoke watching Lee and Longstreet's men smash against the Union line.

Terrified horses, without riders, plunged all about the deserted battlefield. When they ran toward either line, they were beaten back by equally terrified men. The horses dashed first in one direction, then another, saddles slipping, in some cases hanging sidewise or under their bellies, reins dragging, slapping, tripping them. The air was a confusion of smoke, dust, whining bullets, cries of warning, of admonition, curses. The carts and wagons of war, the two- and four-wheel ambulance carriages, cannons and artillery pieces blocked the general flight, but only briefly. Terrified men pawed their way over whatever lay in their paths, pushing aside the wounded, crawling over abandoned equipment, breaking apart or overturning what they could, trampling on the fallen, the whole pandemonium illuminated by the sun, just disappearing, as red as the blood of the slain and fallen.

The roads were clogged again with the retreating forces of the Federal Army, with abandoned equipment and dead animals and overturned wagons and the remains of the stores that had been brought to the front to service a great attack. The stench of dead men and horses and mules filled the air; the smell of battle sweat and fear hung over everything, heavy, with substance, like a strange vibrating wave of despair. Here and there a dead Rebel lay in the road, stripped of his outer clothing, his blackened features and glassy eyes identical to those of the Union dead. Some lay in the beaten track of the train of wagons and caissons; they had been run over.

Any damn fool could have taken one look at that embankment and seen it was hopeless to send men against it. What was the matter with that son-of-a-bitching staff that they ordered all these men to try to take it?

Bull Run and the grading, his first battle, the one Mill went in: Antietam, his second, the church, the cornfield, the grape and cannister shot, the thundering barrage of rifle fire, the major part of the men in his division cut down in the first fire, the rest standing for a moment trying to rally as the Confederates rammed ahead, screaming that awful yell of theirs and brandishing bayonets, firing and refiring, cannons roaring: all his nights were filled with reliving those two battles; the firing, the dying, the screams and shouts and muskets and shattered animals went on charging and being cut down inside his head.

A man can never prepare for the bad things that are going to happen to him. He tries, he thinks he can; but when the blow comes, it is far beyond any anticipation of the imagination.

He was squatting, panting, too tired to move as he saw the next Antietam advance grouping to go back into that murderous range of fire. As he squatted there waiting for his courage to come back, men in blue, gray, brown uniforms met, mingled, fought, fell back. There were men running back and forth, back and forth, and nothing was being accomplished except an appalling number of casualties. Cobus was not even sure who held the cornfield.

A new attack was ordered, but first the men had to be counted. It was a slow business, getting them to assemble and line up under the trees. The officers went along the ravine trying to count how many men were able to go into battle. There were not many. How many had been merely wounded and how many had been killed, no one knew. Anyway, most of the men were too tired to talk.

The wounded that had made it this far and could go no farther were left. It was hoped that they would be helped back, but if the line gave away again. . . .

Here and there a man hobbled slowly, trying to make his own way to the rear. Sometimes one of the whole men would help bind up a wound or get the fallen on their feet and moving. Out of all the chaos and confusion and panic a few men were beginning once again to try to organize some help for the hurt.

The officers—by necessity—were impatient with this. They needed to get their troops organized and ready for the new attack. Cobus had been in battle now a little less than three hours and yet fatigue was crushing him. He could have slept quite soundly, he was sure, right under the roar of the cannons; but what he was going to do was go back into that awful cornfield and attack all over again.

The Third moved forward, Cobus borne with it, John Sedgwick leading the division, Sumner at his side. The worst part of the charge was getting over the fallen—some still pleading for help, for water, for a bullet to end their pain. Cobus fired. His gun felt so heavy now that he could hardly carry it. Yet he kept firing. The whole thing seemed ridiculous. He was repeating the same actions he had gone through at Bull Run with the same result: none.

He heard a shouting. Word spread that the church had fallen to their side—then that it had not, then that it had but the men had not been able to hold it. More than a third of the men who had begun the attack lay dead or captured or cut off.

All around Cobus men were falling or turning back. A series of tremendous explosions came just ahead. McClellan had turned the big Federal guns on the Harper's Ferry reinforcements and was blowing them out of the field. Men were scattering in all directions. The cornfield, for the moment, was held by neither side. It was a wasteland of dead and dying with fifty huge guns pounding it to bits.

For a short period there was a lull in the fighting while the generals seemed to be deciding what to do next. The wounded who could struggled in, dazed and bloody. Those who couldn't lay in the rain. Stretcher-bearers tried to get through to them and failed, the barrage was too great; they came back with wounded of their own, some of the men unable to speak after what they had seen. Cobus threw himself down on the ground and closed his eyes. He awoke with someone prodding him. A man he only vaguely recognized and could not place at all was bent over him saying something he could not understand. He heard through the noise and smoke and screen of his fatigue Molasses Joe's name.

He didn't even remember who Molasses Joe was. He didn't care. All he wanted was sleep. But his conscience—sharp, scalding, insistent—burned him back from sleep; a sick sensation spread over him, duty; rubbing his eyes, he struggled up from sleep, hoisted himself halfway to his knees and, crouching, he humbled himself, half squatting, before God.

Two- and four-wheel horse-drawn ambulances passing down the road to one side of him marked a straight path to the field hospital. Surgeons and doctors were working frantically trying to repair what they could, hacking when they knew no way to heal: the pile of amputated limbs near the tent rose breast high. Nor was there time to remove the rotting corpses or to bind up the men who were bleeding to death. But it was odd. For all those rotting limbs and all that gangrenous flesh, not a buzzard or carrion appeared over the battlefield. In Virginia no vultures fed on the fallen.

"It's your arm," Cobus said.

Joe nodded faintly. He was trying to speak.

Cobus put his head close to those straining lips. "Get them to cut it off, Cob—get them, to get it off, Cob—"

Cobus looked at the torn muscle and tissue, the shattered bone, the shoulder that had been blown away. "Joe," he said. "Joe—" No one would bother with Joe; there were others who had a chance. He held Joe's hand for perhaps an hour; then even that small grace was not necessary.

South of the cornfield there was a ditch that followed the slope of a ravine. Here the fighting had picked up after both sides had abandoned the cornfield below the Dunker church. French's men had made two assaults, had gained the ditch, then had been driven back, had come on again and were now fighting hand to hand when Cobus was rounded up to go in as one of the reserves.

Companies were so badly cut up that only a few survivors remained. All along the battlefront there were broken clumps of men fighting as best they could with no real idea of what was going on, for it was not in McClellan's power, it seemed, for all his fanaticism about organization, to put together one large, concerted drive. All along the line companies were being destroyed in bits and pieces because Little Mac could not get his men together to make one big overall push.

At the ditch the Union troops could not move forward and they had not for some reason fallen back. They lay huddled upon the ground burrowing for cover, firing when they got a chance, waiting for something to decide the course of the fight.

Israel Richardson, one of the officers, was pounding about with an unsheathed sword trying to drive the men into battle. He was purple with rage, flushing skulkers from hiding places behind trees and hayricks and even Army outhouses. Cobus watched without interest. When the order came to move forward, he would go. Before then nothing could move him. He picked up his musket and loped forward where the line was forming just outside the thick veil of smoke that rose from guns, burning buildings, and the dust of the ditch.

Then the wrathful Richardson was dead. It was noon and no one seemed to know what to do. They sat down beside the ditch, their backs to it, and waited to hear what McClellan wanted next.

The armies lay down that night scarcely out of sight of one another, and off and on throughout that long September night the heavy thud thud of guns shook the earth and stopped for a time the endless cries of the wounded. But there was no way to relieve the stench of the dead.

The following day the two armies faced each other in sullen defiance, the sun burning the living, rotting the dead. The wounded could not be picked up because the negotiations for sending the stretcher-bearers out had broken down in bickering, so the wounded lay out there in the sun and died. Smoke and dust still hung over everything; the stench of putrid flesh was now so strong that the men could not eat or sleep or even rest, though the picket firings back and forth were only sporadic and there were no real skirmishes. An uneasy quiet held the men tenser than the fighting the day before; in the let-up of the attacks, the full impact of what had happened in that cornfield began to be felt by every man. Suddenly a soldier going about his duties would be seized with a fit of trembling and would collapse. A great many men broke down that day. The rest sat and waited, waited and watched and said as little as they could.

The two armies lay within firing range of one another with the dying and dead in a no-man's alley in between for three days, and then Lee pulled back. Cobus's regiment was moved back, he was raised in rank—first to sergeant, which he held only a few days, then to a lieutenant. Cushing of Glens Falls had fallen in the cornfield at Antietam and it made Cobus uneasy to feel he was stepping into his shoes. Cushing had been well liked; the men felt his loss keenly and Cobus knew they considered him a poor second. Even Steve seemed to look on him not as a friend but an officer. He had even more time to himself, for he knew few of the ranked men, and by dint of his bars, he could no longer keep company with the enlisted ones. He had fewer onerous chores, better accommodations, he even had a horse. He had always envied Cushing his fine chestnut. But it was not this horse that Cobus got— Cushing's horse lay with its master dead under the shadow of the Dunker church—but a compact little bay; he would not have been surprised to find it had Morgan blood in it, but too much had happened now to make having a horse meaningful.

At the beginning of his enlistment the horse would have meant much to him, but when he went to get the animal, he was past caring about much of anything, let alone a horse.

He wanted rest, he wanted no more responsibilities, he wanted nothing at all except to be left utterly alone without one single solitary claim to his attention, but the horse was his, it was another responsibility, another chore, another thing in his life to be looked after. He looked at it sometimes resentfully; he felt no affection for it at all, though it was a good-natured and obedient animal.

He was weighed down by everything. Previously he had been a soldier who went into battle on orders; now, in a small way, he was a part of that hand that sent men marching out to death. But he was also curiously indifferent to his part in helping men die. Death was a statistic for him—so-and-so many men wounded, so-and-so many men missing, this many dead and accounted for. All that November as the company marched south to Bakersville, Birketville, Petersville, the notion of another day like the one at Manassas or Sharpsville engendered no fear in him at all. What would come, would come. There was no way to stop it, no way to alter it, no way to make his life have any meaning in relation to it.

He could scarcely recall what his wife looked like and the cheap tintypes, hideously tinted, that she sent of herself and the children were reproductions of strange faces he found it hard to believe he had to love. The notion that one day he would return to such unreal people seemed to him absurd. He had come to believe he would be part of the Army for the rest of what life remained to him.

He crossed with the regimental colors into Virginia and camped with the Army at Harper's Ferry. Once this scene of the attack by John Brown on the arsenal and Lee's recapture of it would have been of keen interest to him; he did not even bother to go round and look at it. John Brown was dead, the slaves were still slaves, in spite of what it said on paper; he was just a soldier fighting another politicians' war. He waited in camp to hear where he would be sent next, hardly caring, just as he had received the news of Lincoln's proclamation freeing the slaves without any feeling. What had once motivated his joining this Army he had long ago ceased to care about.

On the thirteenth the company found itself at Fredericksburg, fought well, were unable to do anything at all against the entrenched heights of that city—it was the old story of men being sent in assault against an impossibly entrenched position, like the grading at Manassas, the cornfield and ditch and fence at Antietam, and now the heights at Fredericksburg.

He was too weary to care about even identifying the faces that came in on the stretchers. The sergeants could do that. His job was to push the men forward into the bullets, to go forward himself. To keep firing, to keep advancing against impossible objectives: that was the main thing he had to do. Anything else was peripheral and unimportant.

He felt nothing at all when he learned he was in the contingent that was to be mustered out and sent to Fort Edward by train. He had broken hold with wanting to understand or face life; he sat sullenly by the train window watching the landscape being scooped up by the humming wheels. Outwardly the countryside looked the same—but everything was changed. The time of the small, seemingly self-sufficient farm was over. He saw that the nation's life was unalterably changed; he and everyone else who farmed these little parcels of land, believing themselves independent of the large outside world, would have to face the fact that the notion of anyone being self-sufficient was illusionary at best. Even the privilege of that deception would be denied them now—to feel self-sufficient on a little postage stamp of acreage belonged to a world that the war had put in the past. The whole current of life in this country was changed: small rural places with people working with their hands and horses to make the land love them, no, not any more, not any more so that it mattered; the towns mattered now—not the little villages so like the Landing that were flying past his train window, but real towns with mills and machinery, the hum of motors and creak of belts as the society turned away from its fields and locked itself into sweatshops where motors ran day and night, an industrial economy it was now, the war had made that necessary—guns and carts, ammunition and equipment, millions used, wasted, what did it matter so long as it was turned out and gobbled up. America hummed and whined on its belts and pulleys, inside its engines and on its conveyors, glowered at him as the train slid on its silver wheels into the big, black smoking cities which were now the heart and beat and pulse of the country—changed, all of it, changed, just as he himself was changed, a man who could never go back to being happy just to work with a horse, push a plow, turn over in a warm bed and enclose his wife in his arms.

Some things that break cannot be put back together. Maybe mended—he wasn't sure; the only thing he knew for certain was that nothing was ever going to be the way it had been, not with him nor with the country in which he had been born and for which he had fought.

At the Fort Edward station a band was playing, flags flying, handkerchiefs waving as the locomotive pulled in. They were heroes, and the buggies and wagons from miles around that had come to take the men over to Glens Falls for a gigantic celebration were testimony to that evaluation, but the men did not smile as they stepped down and looked at the happy civilian faces thrust out at them; they did not return the waves that were signaling their hero's return; they refused to ride over to the Falls; they had marched the whole war, they would march now. What was ten miles?

Somewhere a cannon boomed, and boomed again. In the clear June air the peal of churchbells rang. All along the road people stood cheering. The men marched under arches of evergreens and flags. The scent of spruce and pine was everywhere; it seeped from the sap of the freshly cut boughs and permeated the air with the fresh sharp smell of balsam, the bitter odor of pine, the sweet smell of spruce. If he closed his eyes and blotted out the major part of his mind's memories, he would be back in the woods.

An ache of acknowledgement opened up inside him. On the battlefield a man forgot the land under him and the big forests that had been here since the start of the continent; all he could think of was the clear transparent air and the vessels of death which were singing their way through it toward him.

They marched. He had walked the whole war. He would walk a little now into the aftermath of war, whatever that would be; it did not seem to him to have much to do with the singing and shouting, the terrible, endless cheering and all those people pushing and shoving to get a glimpse of the marching troops. No, somewhere else was what was to come, but for the life of him he could not identify where or what. A man was maybe always like that, asking the unanswerable questions.

The hour set for the regimental standards to be brought forward had arrived. The audience—silenced at last from their speeches, their cheers—stared at the bullet-shredded cloth and looked now, Cobus felt, with understanding eyes at the men in front of them, veterans of the Wilderness Campaign, of Bull Run, of Antietam, of Fredericksburg, of Chancellorsville. Surely, he thought, they must at last recognize in the weathered and aged faces in front of them only small traces of the men they had sent away; surely they must be wondering where all the others, those missing, were. Surely

367

now, at last, they must see what the war had meant in terms of human sacrifice.

But, no, they had begun to sing—joyously, triumphantly, with clear consciences: *Onward Christian soldiers marching as to war . . . with the cross of Jesus going on before. . . .*

". . . a crime, a crime," his father said, enraged, "the cost of things nowadays is criminal, the country's run by hooligans, that's what's happened to this great land of ours. People are hangin' onto their good gold and that no-good paper money is what they're trying to pass off on you. Some buzzards jest add a zero after a five and turn their fives into fifties. Nothing but privateers.

"The young men don't want to do their part no more," his father said, "not even with a bounty they give them, which you never got. Don't want to farm, neither. Run off to town, work at them mills, livin' amongst folks they don't know, don't know them, it's a strange thing's happenin' to this country."

Cobus had no business here. His business was with men roughened by the roughness of men; hard, brutal fighters who talked, if they talked at all, of hardtack and salt pork and gun supplies. Under this peaceful sky, the clear air on which no stench of blood or smoke or gun intruded, he was out of place. Nothing on this whole earth ought to have escaped; yet here all had gone free.

The presence of all this peacefulness was like an affront to all those he had left behind. Flesh had no meaning to him any more; yet he was alive, unlike the men still at Manassas, at Antietam, at Chancellorsville and Fredericksburg. But his father gabbed on happily, as if his coming home reverted the world to three years before, and his wife, leaning across and looking into his eyes, had the same mindless, sightless emotion reflected upon her face. He hated them. They were whole.

Silent, he hunched over, jogging with the wagon as it took him up the road home.

Every man is outsider to everyone, even himself, except his very own young. They trust. His children's eyes were full of wonder and bewilderment, yes, and curiosity, some, and a little hesitation, but on no one of their three small faces could Cobus trap the slightest trace of doubt. He was their father come home from the war. Their world was made right, just as the hot, voracious touch of his wife when she turned and let her hand fall on his arm signaled that her world was right, just as his father forever gabbing on about crops and prices and profiteers, turning now, as he did, and smiling happily on Cobus, his son home from the war, was proud and happy.

He wanted to protect this unreasonable faith of theirs that the world could go back to the past and relive again some moment, suspended, from which everything had been wrested and altered. He wanted to believe the message in his wife's eyes, the belief those fingers sent imploring him to put away despair and death and come back to them, come back to life, and life was love, those fingers said, she would show him. . . .

You don't know what it's all about, he wanted to say to them.

Light they said always went with seeing, but what he had seen had to do with darkness—darkness and death.

Old men like his father took it in and said, Well, yes, that's true, and then went on plowing, able to bear the un-bearable because it came to them gradually and amidst a world that dealt with them fairly. The crops came and went with different success and failure, drought, a bountiful year, one fair-to-middling, but over the long run, things evened themselves out, a man could keep up one way or another, the seasons running together and renewing, the harvest of the fields like the planting and sowing and borning and gathering of a man's life; but war had cut short that rhythm, had forced Cobus into a world where all that mattered was chance, the possibility perhaps of surviving, a world which stripped a man of his easy belief in tomorrow, a world whose only possibility was the opportunity to endure and thereby a world which made endurance itself meaningless.

"Don't jaw at me like that," he said suddenly.

Kam turned and looked at him. "I didn't mean to upset you, Cobus. I was jest tryin' to get your attention. It's like I been talkin' to you for ten minutes and you hain't heard a word I said."

"Don't pay me no mind. Take a little time, I guess, for me to git back in the saddle."

Once a horse had meant so much to him. Now, nothing. Yet the old terminology had come back to him just as with the scent of sap for an instant the old brave world of the woods had sprung up, uncut, in his mind.

She nodded. He knew suddenly that she understood his desolation, his apartness. He had never been able to hide anything from her and that at least had not changed. Though

369

he had tried to stay within himself and shut that self off from her by an act of will, she had somehow managed to reach through his defenses and see the truth. Her hands lay now quite still in her lap. It seemed to him that in their understanding they had quieted; the passionate voracity of their wanting was stilled. They were waiting, would send no more urgent messages until he was ready; and that in itself calmed him. He had been frightened by their intensity, the need of her demanding flesh. If she just let him be, he thought, he could maybe learn to like her again.

But not touch her. He felt he couldn't touch anyone. Ever again.

They turned into the old logging road that went straight to the Buttes land. They would have to pass the Raymond place first and the realization that Ardis would be out on the veranda waiting stirred in him feelings difficult to define, something close to gladness.

It was as if her weakness, her inability ever to face up to life, was the only appeal he could respond to now; he wanted someone like himself, in retreat from life. The weak didn't expect anything from you except failure, like the failures they had made of their own lives.

He raised his head and peered through the tall pines for the first white flash of the Raymond house, a handkerchief flag or a hand waving out of the dark verdant density; and he would be home then in a way that he was not home now.

A bird was flushed and leapt, in an arc of song, into the trees; a flash of sky suddenly broke through the pines, sun poured over him, blinding him; then the wagon jolted into thick shade and he heard insects massing to move in on them like—like an army getting ready to attack. Was it possible that even in the smallest section of the animal world there were the basic rudimentary rules of warfare?

And then, suddenly, in a tattoo of hooves, a figure on horseback fought through the forest, Ardis galloping toward him on Bay Boy, and he sat shocked still with astonishment. Ardis rode toward him the way he had never known another woman to ride—save of course his wife, who rode not like a woman, not even like most men, but like no one else at all he had ever known, you couldn't ever compare Kam with anyone else, it came to him—Ardis's wrists and elbows and hands so slight that they seemed insignificant in the schooling of that great muscled animal that flew toward him in a mad, unchecked gallop. Weak little Ardis whom he had left feeling that her life had ended long, long ago, one summer years and years before, when she had been a frail girl in a school parlor fluttering forward to meet her grandfather—and this same woman, whom he realized he had long ago written off as lost, was flying toward him at a pace that would put the fear of God in a strong man, and he was livid, absolutely livid with rage, he wanted to be the only one altered—why hadn't the rest stayed the way they should, stereotyped in life as they were in his mind, in a world that was rigid and because it was rigid and unchangeable was henceforth definable; he was far too tired to have to keep reevaluating people and places; and yet Ardis, plunging toward him on that galloping animal like some green thing breaking before his eyes, at one with spring rising with the mist right out of the ground around him, her skin pale and white, a breath, faint, hesitant, almost immortal, a whiff of white against the dark black brow of the far hill that told him nothing ever remained the same, that life had, every moment it was being lived, to be reexamined and reevaluated and lived in a new way.

His anger stemmed from this knowledge. If he was changed, so were they all and he would have to confront this in them and accept it and—worst of all—act on it when all he wanted was to be left alone, to be at peace, never to have to think too hard again.

"Don't make no difference to me, Cobus, whether you go or not—"

"What gits into you, Pa, you want to go traipsin' up there after all this time?"

"It ain't age, if that's what you're hintin', age and feeble-mindedness, no, it ain't that, though I supposed you'd like to put it down to that—" His father took out a long braided snake of tobacco and pulled at it between his teeth; a plug broke away, he began to chew. "I'm goin'."

"But you can't go by yourself all that way on foot, Pa. Whadda' people say, me lettin' you go off like that—"

"I don't care what people say. Never did, and I ain't gonna start now. I want to know what happened to him and the only sure way to find out is to go and find out for myself."

He sat down in the chair in such disgust it almost gave way under him. "You're all plumb crazy trying to redo me," he said. They might as well have notice served on them he was onto their game.

"Call it what you want, it still don't cut no ice with me, I'm goin'. I 'spect I shoulda gone a long time ago, but one thing or another always comes up. But I'm gettin' old and the rheumatiz is in my legs and next year may be too late and I got it in my heart to know what happened to Burroughs."

"You cain't go alone."

"Then it looks like you ain't got no choice."

"Not walkin'"—at least let's take the horses. It's more than a hundred miles—"

"You ken take your hoss if you want, but I'm goin' into the woods—I'm goin' into the woods the way a man should go, on his own two feet, and I'm walkin' where no hoss can go, sometimes hardly a man, and that's the way it's gonna be with me, Cobus, you do like you want, but you understand, I know these legs ain't gonna carry me much longer the way I want, they're gonna have trouble enough this year, bound to have give out by next, and so I'm goin' the way I want to go one last time."

Cobus—shaking his head—wanted to say to his father, You think when you get me in the woods I'll see something I haven't seen before, it's some kind of healin' you have in mind, but there ain't no more lessons for me to learn, I been through them all, including the biggest one they got, sending you off to learn how to kill.

"You don't put nuthin' lost back jest by walkin' in some woods," he said angrily to his chewing father.

"Eh?"

"I said, don't think you're gonna git me reshaped jest because I walk a hundred miles through some wood. I'm onto your game."

"If you're so firmed resolved on that, then why don't you show your real contempt by jest stayin' home?"

He had the last word, though.

"Ain't aimin' on runnin' into any bear this time, is you, Pa?"

They set off on Tuesday. Monday there were showers and a quarrel; his father wanted to go in spite of the rain, but Cobus was damned if he would start in that kind of weather. "I'm walkin'," he said. "You kin at least let me walk in a little comfort."

"You walked in the Army plenty in the rain," his father pointed out.

"That was about all I did in the Army. In civilian life I'd like to pick and choose a *little*."

"Git yourself all stewed up over a little drizzle. Afore you went there wasn't a man around for miles could even 'gin to touch you for strength, good raw strength, and now—"

"Now that don't matter no more. It's machines matter now, not men. It's machines do the work. You don't see things have changed—"

They set off in silence because there was this vein of anger running between them what with the arguing and rancor and the feeling each was trying to coerce the other into doing and being something he didn't want.

It was hot, too hot, but you might as well argue with those big boulders up ahead as tell his father they should wait till fall. The old got a notion, they acted on it right then, afraid there might not be time or energy enough later to git done what they had in mind. In the shade of the first big boulder, his father sat down and took out his bandana, wiped his forehead. "I always had a feelin' about this place," he said. "Somethin' to do with it bein' here before anythin' else. These big stones." He looked at Cobus. "You know, like they know."

Cobus shook his head. No, he didn't know.

"Well, it don't matter." His father pulled on the plug. "They do."

Going into the woods as if the past could somehow be summoned back at his beckoning. A whole way of life had passed since he first went into the woods, one his father would finally have to recognize when he came to the vast cemetery of tree stumps that spread like a graveyard hundreds of miles long over the alluvial land out into the horizon and on into eternity. His father would have to stand in incredulous revelation, see in one sweeping, disbelieving glance the vast endless wasteland of stumps, the dark tangled overgrowth, the screaming crows overhead. He would walk out of the primeval forest and into a no-man's land that had been made by man. Where man put his hand, there the earth lay wasted and disfigured, there men gathered together in servitude. What his father did not now know, nobody had known then; or if anyone had known, the knowledge had not bothered him. Cuttin' all those trees that were here right from the beginnin' and nobody even tried to put a stop to it. A band of men come and ruin the land—and he one of them—and not one of them really knew what he was doin', and when it was done, it was too late, no way of ever puttin' back what they had taken away. Sin and wickedness and graven images: The Lord Shall Smite and Crush and make an end to inequities.

Cobus would like to believe there would be a vengeance for all that ruin, but that kind of hope presumed order and reason and punishment and a working out of right and wrong. No. It wasn't anything you could chart, just blind unlucky chance. Somewhere Big John nodded. He understood.

His father started up the incline at a steady pace, Cobus tagging behind, both of them balancing their packs against the earth's slant. It was almost eleven o'clock, a punishing sun; sweat crowded Cobus's sight, dripped from his nose, ran down his neck. It was bad going; he wondered how his father, much troubled in his joints and short of wind, could keep up such a pace. But his father had what the Landing people were fond of describing as guts. That meant he belonged to an older, steadier time when not doing what was expected of you was the worst sin a man could commit.

And his father's pride—he always had to reckon with that. His father's pride made it mandatory for him to set a rhythm that most young men would find hard to accommodate. What his father didn't really take into account was that there was almost no rhythm Cobus couldn't adjust himself to; he had such good training in the war. He remembered running once at a full gallop a mile and a half, like to burst his lungs, but fear kept crowding his feet faster and faster. He looked ahead into the far distance where they would at last get out of shale and boulders and this steep incline that made traveling so hard; a line of trees like a stockade imprisoned the cool woods and old Indian path north. Here the trees were as they had always been, great monolithic giants whose branches sheltered a man from the sun and whose thick trunks made him understand how insignificant in the vast scale of things he was. His father had never been to the plundered part of the forest where every tree had been cut down and, walking through his own woods, he would never believe what lay ahead, no matter how Cobus tried to warn him. Racquette, Long, Tupper—all of them stripped. Men had come and laid the land bare; everywhere there was that change he had tried to point out to his father and which his father had resisted, trying to judge new ways with old ideas.

They rested, leaning against a rock. His father took out a long strand of braided tobacco and held it out. Though Cobus usually did not chew, he nodded gratefully and took a long pull. Here the feeling of tobacco in his mouth seemed right.

He could see almost completely downlake, twenty, twenty-five miles. Each island was clear and sharp in outline. Smoke hung over the Landing. It looked small from here, but it had grown in the past ten years. The war had brought its bustle even this far North. There was a little shirt mill, now turning out Army tunics, and even the smaller little places had government orders. The shopkeepers were speculating in commodities, the people hoarded and hung onto their gold. Meanness and suspicion were deep currents in the town life; people who didn't like you called you copperhead and traitor. A young schoolteacher had been run out of town for saying there were two sides to everything. The weekly paper was filled with wild accusations against the South and letters from its subscribers full of hate and the determination to get their own back on them Rebs. There was a casualty list posted on the bulletin board in the post office and Cobus had been shocked to see how many names had stars beside them. The first thing his eye had searched out was his own name, and he couldn't suppress a sense of satisfaction seeing the commendation beside it: RAISED TO LIEUTENANCY ON THE FIELD OF ACTION.

It was simply because I stayed alive they gave it to me, Cobus thought; longevity and nothing more; and yet there I stood like some young fool grinning and proud because it made me look good. He shook his head.

"What's the matter?" his father asked.

"Nuthin', jest thinkin'."

"We'll hole up early, camp by the stream. I'd like to catch me a couple of nice bull trout. Nuthin' like a mess of fresh-caught fish spitted over an open fire and a little warmin' liquor, night air, stars, jest bein' outside, free."

No one's free, Cobus wanted to say, but if his father didn't know that by this time, he was never going to know it.

The two-o'clock breeze had risen. Every afternoon about this time the wind came up. He was grateful for the cooling breath on his cheek. Sweat began to dry; his collar grew hard. He walked automatically, scarcely seeing, yet aware nevertheless of all that was about him—an animal's track here, a broken twig there, the sound of a bird high overhead, his father, hunched over, breathing more laboriously than he had in the morning; yet they kept the same pace they had set out with; if anything, it had picked up, they were making good time.

An hour later they startled a big buck in a highland marsh where great dead gray trees stuck up out of the black boggy swamp. The area covered maybe an acre, an acre and a half; it was the kind of place deer liked, deer and muskrats;

there was a muskrat den at the far end where they had come on the buck, big-antlered, standing with its nose buried in the mire, then looking up, startled; they had come on him downwind so that their scent had not warned him. Cobus's father stopped and turned, his face alight with pleasure. "Big as any I ever seen." Cobus nodded. He expected his father to move on, but he simply stood, staring after the buck. "And he never heerd us," his father marveled. "Jest because of the wind. Could have got himself kilt."

His father moved on slowly, with reluctance, the parable of the buck sticking in his mind, Cobus supposed, and rankling because his son had not got its meaning.

A few minutes later his father stopped again. He stood absolutely still and Cobus imitated that rigidity. He heard first one crash, then another: beaver. They went forward cautiously, but the beaver had heard them—they were difficult to steal up on—they had disappeared into their lodge. The lodge blocked up a stream; on both sides of the small dam there were gnawed tree trunks. Busily getting ready for winter, storing their food underwater in the lodge so that the green leaves would keep in the cool water, getting ready for new life, making their world secure against winter—but if we had a gun and were patient, we could trap them, Cobus thought. Jest like the buck—something the animals had no control over could sneak up on them and destroy the whole careful working of their lives.

His father had gone to the edge of the stream. He knelt and washed his face, scooped up water in his cupped hands. His pack slipped forward and Cobus went up to help straighten it. "Thanks," his father said gruffly, but Cobus could see he was pleased by the attention. "We'll work our way up a mite and then camp for the night. I don't look forward to doin' no walkin' in the heat of the day, leastwise not the first day out."

Four to five was the heat of the day. All day long the temperature would rise until around four-thirty the air would be like a furnace, the wind dry and dead. A man felt sick inside then, as if the whole of the world were somehow poisoned by an evil breath. Maybe it was. Maybe the law of the world wasn't good but evil. Think of the buck, of the beaver—only luck had saved them. This time. But there would always be a next time when their luck wouldn't hold.

They moved on. There was a bend about a mile upstream where the river widened, and there was a deep pool. It was a good place to fish because bull trout liked to rest in deep pools. There was also a natural cleared area among a big stand of pine that would keep them cool while they set up camp and would protect them if the weather turned sour. It was a fine place to stop and Cobus was glad his father took off his pack when they got there and began brushing aside pine needles. He didn't need to say they were going to stop here; his actions said that for him. He made a preliminary run over the ground, evening it off; then he took his knife and cut a long green branch, took some line from his pack and fastened that to the limb in a running rig, put a hook on the end. He took out a piece of lure he had made himself, a kind of spinner that he said the bulls liked because they wanted to show a man they weren't hungry, just angry and ornery, that they could match wits with him and win. "I got a new little catch on this," he said. "I jest want to see one of them sons-of-bitches try to get away from this." He went toward the water. "Make me a pit," he called over his shoulder, "so as to store what we don't eat up tonight. Put some cold wet ferns down, they'll keep good for mornin' and put somethin' solid in our stomachs before we hit that big patch of woods up over the river."

Cobus let him go on believing those woods were still there. He began digging the pit. A moment later he heard his father shouting and he knew he had got one and it must be big because if he was shouting he needed help. His father was still shouting as he got up close and he could see the pole bobbing up and down, being yanked this way and that, and his father fighting back; but he had only a green limb and it would give and the trout get away if they didn't do something. If that fish got away, Cobus knew part of the trip would be spoiled for his father—he had his heart set on bringing that big bull in with his new lure. Cobus plunged down into the shallow water near the bank, standing nearly waist-deep in water. It was biting cold, spring-fed, but it felt good after the initial shock left him. "Work him in, work him in," he shouted.

"What you think I'm tryin' to do?"

The fish was plunging this way and that, pulling the line and pole taut. "Yank up, Pa, for God's sake, yank up."

The trout spun out of the water and Cobus scrambled forward, slipping and going under. When he came up, his father was whooping so hard, he sounded like a madman. He was shouting and laughing and screaming with happiness, but he still had the pole in his hand and the trout was still jumping and Cobus thought, To hell with it, he was wet anyway. He swam and when his father made the next upward lunge with the line, he threw his coat over the trout and it made such an enraged leap, he went under again. But when he came up, he had the fish safely enfolded in the coat. Carrying it toward the bank was like trying to carry a large furious jumping stone. It must weigh ten, twelve pounds, he thought.

When he got to the bank, he was spent. He threw the coat up over the side and heaved himself up. His father was standing looking down at the fish with awe. It was the biggest trout Cobus had ever seen and it was still thrashing about, fighting for its life.

"Look at that son-of-a-bitch," his father said, marveling. "Will you jest look at the size of that son-of-a-bitch?"

"His size don't help him none now. His luck gave out."

He turned and went up to the camp and sat down on a fallen log. Nothing was fair, what was the use of talking about fairness when absolutely nothing in this world worked on the principle of fairness. It was then, in a sort of numbing instant of gazing at the last of the big woods, saved here from the axe because it was Buttes land and a Buttes wouldn't let loggers in, he had the first insight of what his father had meant when he saw the deer. The laws that govern life and death were unknowable. Even in the animal world where simple laws of survival should operate, there was no rational way to determine what was let live and what was made die. And in this mystery, for his father, a man could build his faith—because *he* was not responsible.

Cobus wanted to stand up and shout, You got no right, no right at all, if you was good and just the way you're supposed to be to make things that way. What kind of way was that to run the universe?

"Why, you ain't even got the fire goin'," his father said in disgust.

He shook his head.

"Well, I see you at least started the pit. Got me four of them. Big buggers but the first is the biggest of the lot. Reckon we'll sup all right tonight. Brung me some of the strong stuff, too. We'll have a little do, our first night in the woods."

It's his trip, let him git what he wants out of it; he don't need me ruinin' things. Things is ruined enough as they is. He commenced gathering wood for the fire, hearing his father prattling on happily about how them trout give him the battle of his life, that's what a man wanted out of a good fish, a fight, weren't no good to jest git a fish, one that don't put no obstacles in his way, what a man wanted was a kind

378

of goal in ketching his fish, he got his pleasure from the fight, from overcoming the obstacles, a fish that don't put up no fight wasn't worth ketching, didn't give a man no self-respect nor joy. A man got his pleasure from the fact he had to work for what he took in, like workin' to get that first fish, that was somethin' to bring home.

"Seems to me you're makin' an awful lot of pullin' in a fish."

"Maybe so, but if you look close at anythin'—I don't care how small it is—you ken git a lot out of it. It's how you look at a thing that makes the difference, not its size. Here's a little of that corn lightnin', that ought to take the spleen out of you."

"Eagle's sweat. You remember Big John, Pa? That's what he always used to call the greasing for your insides; anythin' strong was—eagle's sweat. First time I ever came into camp —he come out of the woods barefoot drinkin', singin'—Go under that way, no rime or reason to it—"

"His time had come."

"Oh my God."

"All right, so you'd like a better explanation. But I ain't got one, nobody has and your thinkin' you're goin' to come on one all on your own after all these thousands of years of nobody else comin' up with one, that's a kind of arrogance, ain't it?"

No use to talkin' to fools about what was most important to you, you'd only get a fool's answer.

He took the tin cup and drank, set it down and commenced building up the fire, encouraging it by feeding it piece by piece the little dry whittled slivers of wood he cut off the end of a piece of dead log. A small flame caught, died out, caught again; Cobus blew, it leapt up, with a hiss, then died in a whisper; he kept working with it, leaning down and using his mouth like a bellows until at last some of the large twigs began to catch, and he had a small glowing bed of embers.

His father spitted the big trout and turned it slowly over the fire, sitting on his haunches drinking his corn liquor and every once in a while basting the fish with a little of the liquor to keep it moist. Cobus knelt, flushed, the heat of the fire singeing his face, and poured another cup of alcohol, carried it over to his father, and stood beside him. There was no need to talk. Warmth was everywhere—the fire, the liquor heating their temples, inside, in the feeling that ran between them.

Finally his father said, "You think goin' up to the reservation's an old man's crazy notion, but it's more than that, boy. I'm gonna bring Burroughs home. Oh, don't look like that. He's dead and gone, I know that in my bones, known it for years. But I'm gonna bring him back where he belongs, up with the others up back. He belongs up back, with the rest." There was a look of dark, hard-won satisfaction on his face as he cast another stick of wood on the fire and poured his cup full of corn liquor again.

All of them, part of a pattern, a cycle of life and death, giving, taking, being wounded, having things taken from them, despairing, giving up for a while, some sinking in despair, but others—after a time—rising from the ashes of their hopelessness and beginning again, trying to live with life until the day they died: that was the quite basic assumption a man had to make every day of his life until he died, trying to live with life.

One thing at a time, step by step, day by day—first, you learned how to laugh, then you tried to learn how to love, and—finally, if there was enough time—you tried to learn to live with yourself; but above everything else, the laughing and the loving came first.

In the green woods, in the high light of the fire, he squatted, happy to chew on his tobacco, watching his father drinking and basting, linking for Cobus finally so that he could understand them the two opposing principles, pleasure and pain, in that one simple act of survival which men had practiced for thousands of years, and would go on practicing, even in sport, as his father was doing, because a man needed to feel his life was linked to the same rules that guided all living things, those mysterious principles which held them all in one careless hand; better to laugh than weep, and better to look ahead than back; to act, rather than be acted upon; to build, not let be; to head for life, not death. It seemed at this moment perfectly possible to him that in time he could work out a whole notion of happiness bound up in being tied to others, in making unrealistic plans for an unobtainable future, one that a man could dream of and savor during the long winter and run toward in the fiery furnace of summer.

He wasn't sure how all this was going to come about, but then, only a few hours before, he had never expected to encounter a day like this again: a day that went beyond all others because it had set in him a new kind of wonderment.

They were late getting to eating. They sat near the fire and ate the fish with their hands. Its meat was rich and sweet, with a pungent, almost spicy flavor from the corn liquor. It had been a long time since Cobus had tasted anything so good. His father had another fish going. He sat stuffing fish in his mouth, then picking up his cup and drinking. The fire shone off the grease around his mouth; his eyes were red-colored from the flame of the fire; he looked like some kind of wood devil, all blackened from smoke and dirt, shining with grease, those red eyes, and darkness brushing down on him, the stars bulging out of the black cup overhead, his father leaning forward, his red eyes shining, saying, "Nice, ain't it, out here in the woods, all by ourselves?"

Cobus looked around: alone? In these woods, he and his father? No, it didn't seem to him they were alone. It seemed to him that Kam and his children were with him, and his grandfather who had walked off into the woods to die by himself the way he wanted, away from people, alone—*that* was being alone—all by yourself, dying, in the midst of these dark woods, looking up at the sky and knowing that you were going back into the earth, not knowing if there was also going to be some kind of blending with the sky or not, but knowing that this was the final and last moment, the moment every man faced, all alone, standing face to face with death. He looked at his father, and in his mind he saw Kam and Old Man Raymond and William, his mother, fanning her hat as they set out for the Raymonds and that fancy dinner, all of them, held inside in the flash of an eye; his mother and Tip and Ardis, all of them crowded together, and he was not alone, he was with the living and the living aren't alone, not in the way the dying are because they are connected to one another by thin tenuous strands of love.

"Pa."

His father looked up, his mouth gleaming with grease. "Pa," he said, and he felt like breaking down and bawling, like some silly kid. But he felt relieved, too, as if something bad inside him had broken free and were leaving him for good.

"Pa?"

"It's going to be all right, boy," his father said. "Don't you worry none. It's goin' to be all right."

"Well," she said, reining in, letting Tokay catch up—hers was the swifter though shorter, stouter horse. Anyone looking at the two animals would instantly have picked Tokay as the faster, anyone, that is, that didn't know Morgans.

They had been running the horses across an open field, in

the full flush of the early spring day. It was their first time out together alone since his return. Cobus strained his eyes ahead toward Little Falls. He could hear water, but the woods that took over from the meadow only a few lengths beyond them shut out the sight of wild water.

"Well, *what?*"

"You know very well *what*," she said, smiling and yet serious at the same time.

He held both their horses while she dismounted. They would tie the animals while they walked up the rugged footpath through the woods to the smaller of the two falls. Cobus had recently done some cutting and the path was wider than usual. He and Kam began the sharp ascent side by side, almost—not quite—touching. They were silent; the thing that had to be said had been said and accepted on both sides; the tension was gone. He suddenly caught her hand, and she turned toward him, flushed, smiling. He moved toward her and closed his hand over hers. They went up the path with quickened steps, the birds shrilling in the trees, the wild sounds of the falls growing more and more distinct. He smelled pine and pitch and horse sweat.

He listened to the strange thundering sound of plummeting water, the voice of that wild shoot of rapids pouring over rock, the sound outside magnified by the wild pounding of his own heart: in the beating of his own muscle and blood, it was as if he were at one with the beatings of the universe.

The falls tumbled down the great granite boulders, leaving a thin line where it plunged downward, boiling around rocks, over boulders, flung up in the air, angry with white spray and a sick-looking yellow foam, a great plunge of power over a hundred feet of rock. There was another one, longer, nearly a hundred and fifty feet, farther up in the woods.

He had meant to make love to her beside the falls—under the trees. But the darkness, the great pines, the sound of the tumbling waters chilled him. He wanted warmth and light in which to touch her.

He took her hand and they walked upstream. They had for a moment to proceed single-file. It was very dark here; the trees let through little light. He wanted to touch her, to have that physical link, to make sure they were close.

The stream narrowed, a silver sliver of water passing through ferns that lined its banks, fine as feathers.

There were four finely fitted stones laid side by side across the water, and as she knelt down he saw himself as a small boy, earnest and excited, making things of the man's world—

a bridge to span things, that's what men made, wasn't it? And now he was a man, a man come home sick in the bone from war, and he didn't quite know how to get back to a world that didn't put killing first, but lived for other things; and so he had taken her back to those days long ago when he had been a builder. It was very well made, this small bridge, smooth, evenly fitted, strong. It had endured all these years and it would endure many more. Wisely, he had built in stone. Light green moss, dark green lichens, had fastened themselves to the bridge, but the stones were sturdy, they would last.

She crossed carefully and took the path down toward the cemetery. There was a small marble monument sunk into the earth. A black glade and the skeletons of old leaves—and everywhere the fine feathery ferns. Clutching her hand, silent, still, he looked down on the stone his father had made for his own mother, Cobus's grandmother, whom he had never known.

EMILY BUTTES
daughter of Guy Guthrie
died in childbirth
this stone erected by her only son
Guthrie Buttes
in the year of 1855

Here death made a rite of the righteousness of some lives. William, for instance. Democratic dreams flourished in very few areas of the earth—a dangerous philosophy that trusts small men, a radical notion that a man stood to be judged on his own merits alone. The weak—who could believe that the weak could sustain such a doctrine. But being called weak (and unworthy) did not make a man so; democracy could prove that.

The beating of his heart at this moment testified to the wonder of existence. All of Tip's highly prized honors weren't worth the glance his wife sent to him now as she stopped and looked into another kind of eye, the eye of a dark violet, bent dreamily under the weight of its dark green leaves.

In a moment he would press her down against those ferns to show her what he could not tell her, to explain what words would never say, but for the time being it was enough that their eyes held, that they were alive together in a world in which, it seemed to him, he now had some knowledge that good and evil did blend, and in which, in order to survive, and to make something of your life, you had to cling to the notion that even in the midst of pain and suffering and transgression, there would come—or perhaps be sent—something to renew your faith. It was a world in which he could believe, a world that promised life, even if it might not be the life he had imagined, nevertheless a life with much love in it, and though the love might be sacrificed or destroyed or misused, it was worth whatever price was paid for it, and as she turned to him, rising to meet him, holding out a hand, he saw in her eyes that she did understand. They would start again to work their way back to what love they had still kept intact. But in the meantime—in the meantime —they would lie down and make love—as one always does —over the dead.